# THE
# CHILDREN'S
# CRUSADE

**Also by Elliott Hall**

The First Stone
The Rapture

# THE CHILDREN'S CRUSADE

## ONLY ONE MAN STANDS IN THEIR WAY

ELLIOTT HALL

JOHN MURRAY

First published in Great Britain in 2011 by John Murray (Publishers)
An Hachette UK Company

1

© Elliott Hall 2011

A CIP catalogue record for this title is available from the British Library

ISBN 978-1-84854-075-0

Typeset in 11.5/16 Plantin Light by Servis Filmsetting Ltd, Stockport, Cheshire

Printed and bound by Clays Ltd, St Ives plc

John Murray policy is to use papers that are natural, renewable and recyclable products and made from wood grown in sustainable forests. The logging and manufacturing processes are expected to conform to the environmental regulations of the country of origin.

John Murray (Publishers)
338 Euston Road
London NW1 3BH

www.johnmurray.co.uk

*Professing themselves to be wise, they became fools,*
*Who changed the truth of God into a lie, and worshipped and*
*served the creature more than the Creator*

**– Romans i, 22, 25, King James Bible**

# ONE

## A Highway

The first round hit the engine block. A hood covered my face, but they hadn't bothered with headphones this time. I heard and felt the old petrol monster die, its V8 thrum replaced by tyres screaming as we drifted into the median of whatever road we were on.

When we came to a stop I could hear only two voices. The man in the front passenger seat was reporting to someone over a phone while the other to my right returned fire with a SAW light machine gun. The driver was probably dead, killed by the same weapon that had brought down the vehicle.

The SUV's interior and the hood over my face made it impossible to separate the gunfire. It seemed to come from all around us, the opposing fire pebbles thrown by an angry child when they hit the SUV's bodywork. There were still hostiles out there, but maybe they weren't hostile to me.

'Assailants unknown,' the man in front said into his phone. 'Request immediate reinforcements.'

An explosion jammed its hand into my chest and then imposed silence. Ringing ears, confusion. The drugs hadn't quite worn off yet. I thought about running, but the chains

1

hadn't gone anywhere. I was still alive, so I waited. If a bullet was coming, now would be the time.

The door across from me opened. I felt a hand, and then I was looking at a man wearing a ski mask, surgical gloves, chinos and an aquamarine golf shirt. His rifle was on his shoulder, at rest safe in the knowledge that everyone in the truck's interior was restrained or dead. Behind him was the desert – not the clean sand of a movie, but an arid expanse of little flora, a seabed minus the water – and beyond that what appeared to my disoriented eye both a rising and a setting sun.

The man put a light in my eyes and seemed satisfied with the way the pupils dilated. His own were a faded brown, determined to tell me nothing. The man didn't climb into the SUV; instead he unlocked my chains and shoved aside the corpse so I could get out. My late captor had been ventilated through the door he was firing from, some bullets meant for him coming to rest in the seat beside my head.

I climbed out, legs unsteady from the shot they'd given me and long periods of enforced idleness. There were four other men in the same uniform as my rescuer, an office that had decided to shoot up traffic as a team-building exercise. Three cars waited for them on the opposite side of the road. The other men stood a little apart and waited for their leader to finish with me.

'Are you Felix Strange?' the leader said.

I stared at him, and it wasn't because the man had spoken in Hebrew. I couldn't remember the last time someone had used my real name.

'Is that your name?' he said, switching to English.

I nodded.

He pressed a key into my hand and pointed at a motel in the distance. The man turned away and rejoined his subordinates before I had a chance to ask for a ride. I could see them putting their surgical gloves into a single plastic bag, to be destroyed along with the masks when I was out of sight. After the guns went the same way, they'd be another collection of nameless faces.

I began to walk. The motel was about a mile down the highway. I dragged my lead feet along the pebbled shoulder and noticed the lack of cars in both directions. The sun was brighter than I remembered, the light almost alien. The wind made up for it. It was a tepid breeze that could only be felt if you paid attention, but it was real, honest-to-God wind, not air filtered through the guts of a machine. I wondered where I was, which country, how long I'd been there – here.

After a while, I could see a sign identifying the buildings I was aiming for as the 'Restful Slumber Motel'. The embossed plastic keychain said someone had reserved number nine.

I walked.

A parking lot encircled the motel like a moat. Past it was a veranda that connected the buildings; tile, stucco and sharp-edged plants from a thirsty climate. If someone in the office saw me, they didn't come out to say hello.

I opened the door expecting a thrown-fist or guns-drawn welcome, but the room was empty. There was a double bed, nightstand, and a wardrobe built into the wall. On the night-stand was a phone and an old flip calendar. I laid it face-down, not yet able to believe that I had been gone so long.

A shoulder holster was draped over the coat rack beside the wardrobe. Resting inside was a forty-five pistol with the serial number burned off. I felt the weight and checked the action. It wasn't mine, but it would do.

In the wardrobe were two pressed white shirts, half a dozen ties of varying taste, and one dark suit. In a pocket of the jacket were car keys and a roll of hundreds of respectable size. In the other was my medication, pills red, green and blue. The only thing my benefactor had forgotten was a decent hat.

The last item in the room lay on the bed in plain sight. It was the picture of Iris, the only one I'd ever had. It was from just after she'd dragged herself from the streets, long before I knew her, when the scars of a short misspent life were still fresh.

I sat on the bed. The cover was chenille. I pinched it between my fingers and thought of her. When I closed my eyes, I didn't see the girl in the photograph, but the woman I'd first seen in New York turning heads and disrupting traffic. Iris had worn a tan trenchcoat and her dark hair long. At the time she'd worn sunglasses, but I'd rubbed those out and replaced them with her beautiful grey eyes.

I was a private investigator at the time, and Iris a spy for a bunch of deranged moral hypocrites. I'd tailed her around Chinatown and then chased her halfway across Central Park before I even knew her name. It was complicated, then almost as much as now.

The photograph was rough around the edges, one corner smudged by my hand. I'd rubbed it between my thumb and forefinger for what now seemed like my entire life, hoping it would grant wishes I knew wouldn't come true. I turned the picture over, then thought better of it and placed it in my inside pocket. Someone wanted me angry.

Fisher Partners – the for-profit secret police whose guest I'd been until recently – would be responding to their dead employees' calls for help. They wouldn't search this place for a while. The reasonable assumption was that I'd been whisked away, not forced to walk a fucking mile of highway. I could linger for a while in room number nine.

4

Iris had written me a note before she was kidnapped by Fisher Partners' man in New York, Peter Stonebridge. I hadn't managed to return the favour, occupied as I was trying to kill everyone involved, especially the man known as the Corinthian. They still had her, somewhere, but now was a good time to write some things down before my second chance ended with handcuffs or a loaded gun.

I wanted to try to explain to her what had happened, how I'd gone from being a shamus in New York to what I'd become. The hotel's complimentary pad didn't look like it had enough paper for that, but I picked up the branded Biro next to it and started anyway.


Iris:

You told me not to look for you, that you wanted me to be somewhere where I could be happy, healthy and pissing someone off. I passed up the chance to leave the country, so I guess I only managed the last one. I couldn't let you go.

The Corinthian led them to you. He sold the information to Fisher Partners, just like he sold anything else he could get his hands on. The price was high because of my history with Stonebridge. They used you to get to me, and it worked.

I didn't expect to live this long. It's been pretty confusing, sweetheart. I knew I couldn't find you, but I knew where the Corinthian was. I thought if I killed him, and the Fishermen contracted to kidnap you, it would make a difference.

The prob

The phone rang. I drew my new forty-five in its direction before I realized I was being an idiot. The phone kept ringing. I put it to my ear.

'This is Jefferson,' said a voice I'd never heard before. 'We have work to do.'

# TWO

## Eden Hotel and Casino, Babylon, Nevada

*Three years earlier*

I came to Las Vegas to kill a man. It was my bad luck that he was the owner of this hotel and proprietor of a criminal empire. I comforted myself with the thought that, as powerful as the Corinthian was, his enemies were even worse than mine.

'Bust,' the dealer said, just as I sat down at the table. The schmuck to whom the bad news was directed – a portly Malaysian man in track wear, sweat on his brow from the exertion of losing money – gave me the stinkeye like I'd brought his bad luck with me. I considered it a fair trade for the gift of his stupefying BO.

The Eden was the newest, most opulent casino in Babylon. The whole building was based around the biblical story from which its name had been lifted: earth tones covered the walls and the paths between the tables decorated with foliage that was surprisingly real. I wouldn't have thought that the first, unspoiled home of humankind would be a natural environment for games of chance, but it was a probably a mistake to think anyone even noted the decor on their way to the tables.

Las Vegas had been a serious problem for the rulers of America. As fundamentalist Christians supposedly laying the groundwork for Christ's return, the Elders weren't big on gambling as a pastime. They'd taken the dice out of board games years ago, and possession of a set of poker chips still carried a fine.

The Elders' movement, the Revivalists, insisted that gambling broke up families, distracted people from their Christian mission, and was clearly forbidden by scripture. The problem was that the Elders needed currency, and convincing people to fork out for the privilege of watching blinking lights and spinning wheels was an easy way to raise it.

The circle was squared by creating the legal no-man's-land I was currently standing in. The Elders had carved out the heart of Las Vegas – taken the Strip and enough of the surrounding streets to include McCarran airport – and turned it into a reservation of sin. They'd christened it the Las Vegas Special Economic Zone, but everyone knew it as Babylon.

American citizens were forbidden from trying their luck at the tables, but foreigners were encouraged in every possible way to endanger their immortal souls. The rules were a fig leaf to shield the Revivalists and their Elder masters from obvious charges of hypocrisy. It also justified direct administration by the federal government, so it wouldn't have to share the tourist dollars with the city and the state.

The Revivalists had surprised everyone with how much sin they'd pushed to the margins with a quiet word and a gun. Maybe that was the real reason the Elders had created Babylon. There could be no madonnas without whores or faithful without heathens, and here in Babylon were walking, talking examples of the latter. To have the belief wasn't enough; only opposition from some force, however nebulous, made the feeling real.

More likely it was just the fucking money.

The name on the driver's licence in my pocket said Peter

Braithwaite. I wouldn't use my old name now, even if I could. I'd buried Felix Strange in New York City. It was the only place he belonged.

I played a few hands and was up fifty bucks by accident. The five dollar table had a good view of my real interest: the casino's VIP elevator. It was the only way up to the suites, and from there to the penthouse and the Corinthian. Two heavies guarded it at all hours, and the approaches were covered by half a dozen cameras that I could see. After that I'd need a key.

The upstairs was a big blank on the map in my head. I'd hung around the all-night bars where the help went to get away from the tourists, pretended I was one of the many no-hopers looking for work. The busboys, valets and cleaners I'd spoken to kept *omertà* to a man. They might know their employer's pedigree, but it was more likely they were just desperate to keep one of the few decent jobs left in the country.

I'd figured it would be possible to take him on the outside, even if he was surrounded by his usual entourage of bodyguards. If I could see the cars they used, get a sense of his security detail's order of battle, maybe I could do the job with a home-made ticket to Kingdom Come. I'd spent a week playing with my small fortune, gambling just enough to be inconspicuous while I waited for the Corinthian to come out of his tower. He hadn't obliged me once, and I suspected that he'd gone Howard Hughes since his luck had turned. If the Corinthian did leave the penthouse, it was through secret paths known only to him.

The final insult was that Babylon was the only place in the United States that prohibited guns except by special licence. It went without saying that the Corinthian's men would have that piece of paper next to their sidearms. Right now my arsenal consisted of a roll of quarters and a steak knife someone had left unattended.

I decided to cash out before my luck changed. To get to the cashier, the management had made sure I crossed half the casino floor, ignoring the temptations of roulette, black jack, craps, pai gow and a dozen other games I didn't recognize. Between the cashier and the front door were ranks upon ranks of slot machines, a terracotta army of one-armed bandits. They were less profitable now that Grandma couldn't get to them by bus.

I went outside to get the casino out of my head so Babylon could fill it with a different kind of noise. After the zone had been created, they'd ripped down the giant screens that once hung over Mott Street and installed them here. The elaborate light shows set to music condemned the Strip to live an eternal, neon twilight. I had trouble believing the sunlight was real, even in the middle of the afternoon.

In the distance was one of Babylon's entry points. Tourists flew into McCarran, stayed long enough to lose more than they could afford, then flew back out the same way. The land entries were for Babylon's workforce, desperate Mexicans mostly replaced by desperate Americans willing to work in a paradise free of unions and labour rules. Every day they filed past Babylon rent-a-cops who checked their work IDs with the warmth of East German border guards.

You could buy an employee badge for around a hundred bucks. If actual police had been manning the checkpoints, they might have noticed that there was a ratio of about five IDs to every job. It was almost as if the incompetence was deliberate.

Merrymakers packed every inch of pavement around me, chattering and drinking from souvenir glasses made for giants. They wore souvenir T-shirts to match the glasses, tube tops, jeans and whatever else was comfortable. The Strip had always had pretensions to class, as long as it didn't cost them money. The Eden encouraged its guests to dress up in the evening, but that didn't mean they turned away the shorts-clad sea of humanity coming through the front door.

They were just average Joes looking for nothing more than a good time, and maybe that was why I couldn't stand them. I was the only man in Babylon not interested in drawing a pay cheque or throwing it away. I suppose you could say I was self-employed, though what they said about lawyers representing themselves was just as true for private detectives.

By the third day I'd decided that this is what the end of the world would look like. There would be no great prayer vigils, the smug chosen looking down on the universe's end from their skybox in heaven. People would flock to temples of pleasure, not wisdom, for one last turn on the fiddle while the world burned.

I thought I'd seen Iris a few times in Babylon, the back of a head in the crowd, a glimpse I could never turn fast enough to see. The illusion hadn't lasted very long. The few dames making an effort couldn't steal a mark on her elegance, and were I to question every one who passed by for the next hundred years I wouldn't find one with her humour, courage or gift for infuriating me. The only good part of this Wurlitzer for sex fiends and the maths-illiterate was that its cacophony stopped me from hearing her voice – as I had on the way here when the train had passed through particularly desolate country – whispering at my shoulder, pleading with me to tell her where she was.

My wandering took me, as it always did, to the New York New York Casino and another nightly episode of masochism. The Manhattan skyline had been rebuilt into a false-front stage set, complete with rollercoaster. They'd turned the greatest city in the world into a cross between a model village and an amusement park, all for the glorious purpose of separating people from their money. It would save everyone a lot of time if the casinos just turned everyone upside-down and shook out their pockets as soon as they hit the front door, but I guess that approach would affect repeat business.

I walked through an entrance built like the ones at Grand Central, the only part of that august terminal they'd chosen to rip off. Inside the genuine article, between tracks twenty-six and -seven, was a wall of the missing: names and faces of people who had gone out one day and never come back. These weren't runaways or custody battles but the 'clients' of Fisher Partners, detained or killed for the Elders on a contract basis. Each Elder had a financial stake in the company. The more people they ordered disappeared, the more money they made for themselves and the company's director, General Simeon Glass, US Army, retired. Had some brave soul re-created the memorial here, the foreign clientele wouldn't have even understood what it meant.

Every minute I spent in this simulacrum of a city stole a little of my true memory. These fun house streets were pushing aside my recollection of the real, living thing, a concrete dance floor on which a pas de ten million was enacted to music that never stopped. Another week here and the only thing left in my head from more than a decade in New York would be stock photos of the Brooklyn Bridge.

I swallowed my medication and chased it with a New York microbrew that was my only indulgence. I'd been cautious about taking my pills in public for the first few days I'd been here, until I saw a man blowing luck on a pair of dice from his oxygen tank. I'd had another seizure a few days ago, woke up sweating and confused in my little hotel room. It was pure luck that it had happened while I was inside. The next attack could be at one of the tables, or out on the Strip.

My days here in Babylon were the shrinking eye of a coming storm. Sooner or later what I'd run from in New York would catch up with me. I could only hope that the Corinthian would emerge from his tower before that happened. I couldn't find Iris or reach Glass alone, but there were others debts I intended to pay while I was still able.

When the beer and my appetite for self-flagellation were both exhausted, I returned to the Strip. A gang of touts worked both sides of the Strip's pavements. They handed out escort cards, shuffling them against their palm when sticking them in people's faces wasn't deemed annoying enough. I found it a little shocking, just for the novelty of seeing it done on an American street. I ran the gauntlet, hands in my pockets, mind on other things.

I was outside the Bellagio when I realized there was something in my breast pocket. I thought one of the touts had slipped a card inside, and had half a mind to go back and explain a few things about personal space until I dug out the offending article. It wasn't a card at all, but a ticket to a performance by comedian Ricky Mann at the Luxor that started in two hours.

Someone wanted to say hello.

# THREE

## The Luxor, Babylon, Nevada

The Luxor's Blue Room was built ten years ago to look like it had already been there for fifty more, a cash-in on the retro craze that had swept the Strip since it became Babylon. Booths of dark purple leather were arranged in a semicircle, candles on the tables so people could see their dates. An old-fashioned condenser mic stood alone on the raised white parquet stage. It was mostly for atmosphere, since there would be only one man on stage tonight. Cocktail waitresses navigated the narrow channels between the booths, switching on their smiles whenever instinct sensed proximity to a tip.

I cast my eye over the nearly full room. Most of the people I could see I discounted immediately: foreign tourists, too soft and content to have anything to do with a person like me. They held hands across the tables, in intense and distracted ways, waiting for the show to start. Some proffered cameras to the waitresses so the night could be preserved and carried home. These couples had so many shared memories they needed records to keep track of them, a problem I wished I had. The whole scene was a little maudlin, but schmaltz, like adversity, was easier to take when you were with someone you loved.

I still didn't have a weapon worth the name, but I doubted the invitation had come from Fisher Partners. They wouldn't have bothered with the subterfuge. Time is money, and theirs could be better spent murdering or kidnapping others for profit.

I had only one good friend, and he was on the wrong side of the Atlantic. Benny and I had served in the Airborne together in Tehran. After the war we both ended up in New York, Benny as an agent of the FBI, me as a private investigator. The sickness I came back with meant the only person who would employ me was myself. Now Benny was gone, a political refugee hiding out with his family in Israel. His name was on a Fisher Partners list, just like mine.

I'd covered my trail from New York to here: switching trains, driving rental cars, always paying cash. Anyone following me would have thought I was running for the border. That was the trail I'd wanted them to follow, but maybe I hadn't arranged the breadcrumbs as deftly as I'd thought. I was having trouble seeing clearly these days.

A man waiting in one of the booths was weathering his forties with more than the usual style. He wore a linen suit of enviable cut and had managed to hold on to all of his hair. The man was fit rather than strong, a body developed by exertions as a youth and kept during the intervening years by an act of will. His skin was an olive darker than the tablecloth, his eyes as grey and expressive as concrete. They settled on me for less than a second with a sort of calculated blankness that I recognized.

Before he left, Benny had told me about a friend of his in Israeli intelligence who was working in America. He went by the codename Gideon. I hoped that was who I was looking at. Otherwise I was going to need that steak knife after all.

I walked over, dodging waitresses unbalanced by drink trays and their measurements. The man showed no awareness of my approach other than watching the empty stage at an angle that kept me in his peripheral vision. His fingers hovered over a malt whiskey, with another set aside for the empty seat. I doubted he was expecting the prophet Elijah. I couldn't see a gun, but then again I couldn't see under the table. I sat down anyway.

The man raised his glass, and before it returned to the table a pack of Lucky Strikes torn in half had appeared on its surface, exactly halfway between us. I added the half Benny had given me. They were a perfect fit.

'Gideon, I presume?'

'The legendary Felix Strange.'

'You do realize that in order for someone to be legendary, they have to be dead first?'

'Benny said you were a ray of sunshine.'

Gideon nudged the untouched drink towards me with a finger.

'It should be your brand.'

I took a sip. It was.

A wave of applause rolled over the audience as Ricky Mann took the stage. Born Richard Mankiewicz, the name had been changed for the sake of the marquee, not to hide his obvious Semitic heritage. His hair was a burning bush – red and brown in a thick tangle – and he had the stubble to match. The hair gave him a few inches of height he badly needed, but that small body projected enough energy to power all the lights in the building.

'How's everybody doing tonight?'

Mann pretended to play with the microphone while he took a bead on his audience.

'Man, am I glad to be home. Well, almost home. You'd think this would be the first place our Dear Leaders would have ploughed under and sown with salt. Instead I'm playing three shows a week in this fucking zoo.'

On being compared to animals, the audience burst into a chorus of whistles and self-congratulatory applause.

'Benny says Shalom by the way,' Gideon said.

'I doubt those were his exact words.'

'"Tell that schlemiel to get his ass out of the country before I go back and kick it out myself," or words to that effect.'

'He's safe?'

'He and his family are firmly in our bosom.'

'Do your American counterparts know?'

'Even a married couple keep secrets from one another.'

Our marriage with Israel was starting to look more like a suicide pact. Gideon wouldn't be sitting with me unless some people in the Holy Land had the same idea.

'And Cassandra?'

Cassandra was a retiree from the now-defunct CIA. Benny and I had smuggled her out of the country so she could tell the world what Fisher Partners was up to. Now that I'd met Gideon, I was getting pretty sick of all these codenames. Only spies and pop stars thought having a single name was a good idea. Benny was different; I knew his surname but never used it by mutual agreement.

'She's in Europe somewhere, singing as loud as she can,' Gideon said. 'The world intelligence community is currently running around like frightened children. They spend half their time gossiping about how deeply other agencies were involved and the other half terrified that their cooperation will be exposed. The Brits are particularly worried; I hear the streets in Vauxhall Cross smell of panic urine, but I don't know how you'd tell the difference.'

'Do you think it will make a difference?'

'As a Chinese official once said about the French Revolution: "It's too soon to tell." Everyone's holding American agencies at arm's-length for now.'

17

The Israelis had never really liked the Elders, considering they believed that all Jews were destined for conversion or annihilation during the Second Coming. What mattered was that the Elders were willing to expend an unlimited amount of American blood and treasure to help the settlers realize their dream of colonizing Judea and Samaria. It was the most cynical of alliances, but one that had worked until recently.

'It's a funny thing for the Mossad to do,' I said, 'help drive a shiv into the back of their only ally.'

'I guess it depends on how you look at it.'

I waited. Gideon didn't continue. Instead he pretended to give his full attention to the stage.

'I gotta tell you, when I was younger, I didn't pay much attention to politics,' Mann was saying on stage. 'I thought Adamson was a power tool, not the President. So when I got a call from the government about the Holy Land, I thought I'd won some kind of contest.'

Ricky had been one of many celebrities who had finally made good on their oft-repeated threats to leave the country. In his case it had been more out of necessity than pique. Bits like the one he'd just started had scientifically proven that the Elders lacked a sense of humour.

'How did you know I was here?'

Gideon sighed. 'Couldn't we just skip this bit? It's fucking tedious.'

'Humour me.'

Gideon warmed himself against the impending boredom with the last of his drink.

'You aren't the reason I'm here. One of our people happened to spot you feeling sorry for yourself.'

'They tried to sell me on the Settlements like they were a Florida timeshare: great views! Great deals! All you can eat

18

shrapnel!' Mann said. 'When the guy threw in free travel, I knew something was up. When the nice Gentile says get on the free train, Jews have learned to be a little sceptical.'

'If I'm not the reason,' I said, 'then why are you here?'

'If you mean this quasi-federal whatsit, I should be asking you that question. We've been in Babylon a hell of a lot longer than you have. If you're asking why I'm in this chair, then the answer is I'm meeting a new friend for the sake of an old one. Benny said we would get along: mutual friends, mutual interests . . .'

There it was. Gideon's fan dance was finally getting to a point.

'You have an intimidating CV, Strange,' he continued. It was obvious he meant it was intimidating because the accomplishments that impressed him also scared the hell out of people. 'I didn't quite believe Benny's stories about you until I'd checked them out myself. I know only five men who could pull off what you did, and you'd have to catch two of them on the best day of their lives. Where have you been hiding all these years?'

'If you touch me under the table, I'll scream.'

Gideon laughed. 'We both know what you told Benny, about going to find this woman, was a white lie to make him feel better. You aren't naive enough to think you can actually find Iris.'

The name still hurt, and Gideon would know that. He was sounding the depths of my hatred, seeing what I was capable of. Whatever he had in mind for me was neither intelligent nor safe, but probably no worse than what I had planned for myself.

'And what, exactly, is our shared interest?'

'The Corinthian,' Gideon said. 'You want to kill him, and we want him dead.'

'The Revivalist pencil-neck called me selfish,' Ricky was saying up on stage. 'Yeah, I guess it is really self-centred, not wanting to move to a different country. It's incredibly fucking uncharitable for me not to play my part in the end of the world.'

Gideon's statement was unusually forthright for a member of the intelligence community. There was no talk of 'liquidation', 'wetwork' or other euphemisms.

'Why is Israeli intelligence so interested in killing the Corinthian?'

Gideon shrugged. 'When it comes to that man, there are so many reasons you can choose one for me.'

'Seriously, though, I'm excited as hell about the Rapture. Have you heard about this?' Mann said to the audience. 'You people live in sane countries, so I can't be sure. When I talked about this in Amsterdam, they thought it was some kind of sex toy.

'The Rapture is when all the believers are lifted up to heaven – a miracle in itself; have you seen the size of these people? All the good Christians, not those Catholics or whoever, get a free space ride to heaven just before all hell breaks loose. I don't know about you, but seven years of murder and natural disaster might be worth it to get these fucking people off my back.'

I stared at Gideon and he stared back, completely unconcerned. This point was not negotiable: I'd never know the Mossad's real interest in this whether I rose from the table or not.

'So how's the assassination going?' he finally asked, as if I were trimming wisteria.

I related my various strategies to Gideon. Plan A had been the aborted mission to catch the Corinthian on the road. Plan B involved the other VIPs. A Russian oligarch, a Vietnamese tchockte baron and the dissolute son of a Cypriot shipping magnate were the current occupants of the Adam, Eve and Presidential suites, respectively. The oligarch would be protected to the hilt: he was Russian, rich and still alive. The Vietnamese entrepreneur lived at the craps table, so that left the prodigal son and his exhausted security. I considered waiting for the right strip club, sticking a gun in his face and explaining a few things, but even if that got me into the elevator the advantage of surprise and chutzpah wouldn't last long. I had a plan C in the works, but it hadn't developed beyond the need for high explosives.

'They are creative, I'll give you that.'

'Improvisation is one of my specialities.'

'You can't just kill your way to him. The place is bum rush proof.'

'Yeah, well, when you're a hammer everything looks like a nail.'

A waitress with an improbable bosom appeared. Gideon ordered another round and tried not to stare into the abyss of décolleté in front of him.

'Do you think there's some kind of bylaw that mandates necklines be so low around here?'

'Las Vegas tradition isn't legally binding, but it might as well be.'

'Sometimes I think the Rapture is already happening,' Ricky was saying. 'I must be wrong, there are so many assholes still here. But you know, friends of mine who stuck around, some of them are just gone. No warning, no note to the wife and kids, nothing. They weren't the people who were supposed to go. It's almost a Rapture in reverse. All these people I knew – know, for years, one day they're just gone.'

The audience wasn't sure where Mann was going, but the subject matter was interesting enough to distract Gideon and me from our conversation. Everyone stared at Mann, riveted even if they didn't know why. They could only sense what Gideon and

I knew: we were watching a man covered in petrol threatening to play with matches.

I hadn't been able to see the two men sitting at a booth near the stage when I first scanned the room. Their hair was cut short, and they dressed badly in a way that deviated from the tourist norm: cheap suits, white socks over scuffed shoes. They must be the plain-clothes department of the private security firm that policed Babylon. There were no real cops here, and it wouldn't be worth a Fisherman's time.

The Elders permitted a greater amount of freedom in Babylon than they did anywhere else. It was in their interest to pretend to the world that the First Amendment still applied. They might tolerate flesh and blasphemy, but the legal fiction that created this place hadn't made their skins one iota thicker. In case anyone was tempted to have too much fun at their expense, the Elders had paid men to sit here and remind performers who ran the country, and what they were capable of.

Ricky Mann knew who they were; he would have clocked them the first time he looked the room over. His eyes swept the audience again, but Mann was seeing something else. Maybe it was the person whose recent disappearance had left an open wound. I wondered if it was as deep as my own, and what he was willing to do to distract himself from the pain.

It was just as likely Mann was imagining what he would lose if he lay in the bed he'd been making on stage. The Revivalists would probably let him leave, but they'd make sure he never came back, and God help anyone left behind. Mann looked in the thugs' direction, and nailed them to the leather with his best showbiz smile.

'I guess I'm lucky they're all disappearing. I like my friends, don't get me wrong, but I owe most of them money.'

The audience felt they could laugh, now that Mann was back

22

on recognizable ground. He looked at the floor and smiled to himself, though it was a smile in name only. 'Yeah, lucky, that's what I am.' Then he looked up and went on with his set.

'A friend of mine in MI6 recommended Mann,' Gideon said. 'I had no idea he'd be so interesting. Do you think they'll retaliate?'

'I doubt it. He knuckled under in the end.'

The sum total of Gideon's reaction seemed to be bemusement.

'Now where were we?'

Before Mann had intervened, Gideon and I had reached a new stage of the courtship. He'd shot down my plans to kill the Corinthian, and we both knew I was going to ask what he had in mind eventually. A silent minute with my new whiskey was a way for both of us to pretend I still had some dignity left.

'I assume you have a plan.'

'Well,' Gideon said, unable to feign reluctance as well as I'd expected, 'we have half a plan, maybe two-thirds. Due to unforeseen circumstances, we are missing our shooter.'

'What happened to your original triggerman?'

Gideon looked like he was about to give me another non-denial, but then thought better of it.

'He was killed before he could enter the country. Long story, none of which I'm going to tell you. You have my word his death had nothing to do with this operation. He was a friend of mine and a damn good soldier, but prey to lady luck as all of us are.'

I had Gideon's word. I was about to find out how much it was worth.

'Give me the outline.'

'In two days the Strip will be celebrating the late President Adamson's birthday. The Elders lack the mental flexibility to see the irony, so they take it as a compliment.'

'And?'

'The streets will be full of drunk conventioneers using it as an excuse to get high, sideways and loop-de-loop. Babylon's tin stars will have their hands full. Response times will degrade.'

'That won't get me upstairs.'

'Getting up is easier than you'd think; it's getting back down that's the problem.'

'Are you saying it's a suicide mission?'

'Suicide. Now there's an ugly word to throw into a friendly conversation. It's not impossible. You just have a better than even chance of not getting out alive.'

'How much better than even?'

'You might get lucky,' Gideon said. 'After all, this is Babylon.'

I let Gideon wait. The reports he'd read had likely painted me as crazy, but I doubted they'd said I was stupid. Whatever he'd been told, we both knew I didn't have much choice. I couldn't do this piece of work alone, and I couldn't leave it unfinished.

'I'll need a weapon.'

Gideon smiled from ear to ear.

'I think we can do better than that steak knife in your pocket.'

He raised his drink. A clink of glass, and the contract was sealed.

'You know,' he said, 'when this is all over—'

The crowd erupted in laughter and applause. I hadn't heard the punchline.

# FOUR

## Eden Hotel and Casino, Babylon, Nevada

The Eden was the busiest I'd ever seen. Throngs of actual and pretend foreigners filled the tables and warmed the slots, determined to celebrate the birthday of a twisted, puritan Stalinist by drinking, gambling and fucking as much as possible. I'd been looking for a silver lining to Babylon ever since I got here, and I guess that would have to do.

Everyone was too busy having a good time or facilitating it to notice one more suit walk through the front doors and head directly for the elevators. I ignored the games and the women, making it obvious to the revellers who crossed my path that I was there on business.

'The Cypriot golden child has all the appetites you'd expect from the young, dumb and rich,' Gideon had said. I'd met him in the back room of a Korean barbecue place the day before to go through his half-to-two-thirds plan. 'He's expecting a package of party favours, and it's been arranged for you to deliver them. This isn't a street-corner operation you're fronting for: you'll be the last doctor on earth to make house calls. Dress smart, keep the Ps and Qs in view, and definitely wear that hat,' he said, pointing to my fedora.

Gideon took a leather briefcase from beneath his feet and put it on the table. 'This has everything you need. They'll frisk your kishkes better than a urologist and scan the briefcase for metal and explosives, but they won't open it. The casino's deniability must be protected.'

Two standard-issue security men guarded the elevator: line-backers in grey suits with sidearms and brush cuts. I put down the case and let them look me over.

'Good evening, sir,' the taller, older one said. I figured he was in charge. 'What suite are you visiting?'

'Presidential.'

I showed him the ID Gideon had provided.

'I'm expected.'

The older man mumbled into his hand mic while his subordinate frisked me. The partner was thorough, but he still felt the need to wand me down after to make sure. The only thing the metal detector turned up was a belt buckle and a pair of cufflinks he couldn't afford.

'This way, sir,' the older man said. He escorted me to the elevator and was kind enough to press the button. Before the doors closed I saw him talking into his wrist mic again, telling the men upstairs that I was on my way.

Gideon had opened the briefcase and set it between us on the table. The inside looked like the wares of a travelling pharmaceutical rep: a dozen plastic prescription bottles arranged in a square of grey foam. The bottles took up only the top half of the briefcase. Gideon removed the other section to reveal the grip and receiver of a killpiece.

'It's gas-powered,' he said, 'and made completely of ceramic and plastic. The metal detectors won't give you any trouble.'

'Are you sure this arts-and-crafts piece will do the job?'

Killpieces were compact handguns meant to be assembled

and vice versa. They were underpowered compared to normal handguns, designed for concealment before assassination.

'It's done the job more than once already,' Gideon had said, as he laid the rest of the pieces on the table. 'The elevator is new and fucking fast. You'll have ten seconds, fifteen tops, to assemble and hide the gun before you reach the suites. We aren't leaving this room until I see you do it in eight.'

I put the case on the elevator floor and got to work. The grip came out first. The receiver clicked into place on top. The bullets were in one of the prescription bottles, .32-calibre ceramic-composite pills. There was no clip: I had to hand-feed each one through the breech into the grip like an old bolt-action rifle.

The elevator was an express to the top, so I had only the count in my head to rely on. It told me I was running out of time. The recoil spring was packed into another bottle and the slide popped out of the back of the briefcase if you knew where to press. I put the recoil spring on top of the receiver and then the slide over the spring.

The elevator bell announced it was newer and faster than Gideon had believed. I stuffed the silencer in a pocket, the pistol in the back of my waistband (never wise when the gun lacked frills like a safety) and got the briefcase closed just as the doors opened.

I stepped into a small foyer. Three short corridors gave a little extra privacy to the suites, and space for the help to stand. All three doors were manned by more bodyguards from central casting, twelve in total. They didn't bother pretending not to watch my every move.

'There are no security cameras in the elevator or on any of the VIP floors,' Gideon had said. 'Privacy, yet more deniability, etc. They make up for it with a shitload of guards. You'll be eyeballed from the elevator to the Cypriot's front door and all the way back down. The guards downstairs will tell the ones upstairs when you're on the elevator up, and vice versa on the way down. Every step you take will be accounted for.'

I walked towards the Presidential suite and kept my face set to the distracted boredom of a man doing work he doesn't particularly enjoy. The Eden's nature-themed wallpaper seemed more menacing than tacky up here. It might have been the softer lighting, or the complete silence.

The Fauntleroy's head of security was Cypriot like him, maybe a cousin or a school friend. He was young, unshaven and hostile in a casual way. He spoke into his wrist mic as I approached, probably telling the men downstairs that I'd arrived.

I stopped three steps short of him and extended the briefcase as an offering. He took it, viewed its contents, then said something in Greek to his employer inside. I was dismissed with a flick of the wrist. I walked back to the elevator and resisted the urge to wave at the personal protection convention as the doors closed.

'The elevator hatch will be directly above your head,' Gideon had said. 'It's alarmed, but we'll take care of that.'

'Security will notice when I don't come back down.'

Gideon gave me the same smile he'd worn when I signed on with this crazy idea. It was the grin of a troubled child unwrapping a BB gun on Christmas morning.

'They'll be far too busy to keep track of one stray Dr Feelgood.'

I took a plastic earpiece from my coat pocket and put it in, now that there was no risk of it being seen. I stood in the elevator and waited. I had only a few seconds before the security outside noticed the elevator wasn't moving. Much as I wanted to break radio silence, it wasn't time yet. Gideon had better get on with it.

The power died. I was in complete darkness for a second before the emergency lights kicked in. I unlocked the hatch and pulled myself up.

Once Gideon had shown me the case, he put it by my feet and laid the penthouse blueprints on the table.

'This is the VIP elevator,' Gideon had said. 'The good news is that there's a hatch leading to the ventilation shafts next to the elevator's motor. The shafts lead right up to the penthouse. The original owners weren't international criminals, so they didn't plan against anyone crawling up with a knife in their teeth. The bad news is that they valued their privacy enough to give the Corinthian another escape route if you don't reach him fast once the alarm is raised. The penthouse has its own elevator that leads directly to the parking garage.'

'So I've spent the last week sitting on an elevator the Corinthian doesn't even use?'

Gideon shrugged. 'Last time I checked, you were fifty bucks ahead. The Corinthian has put most of his people out on the floor to make sure the big night goes profitably. There are four guards down in the parking garage, but he'll keep his personal detail light: two men on the front door, and only his new head of security, Maurice Wilcox, will be inside. The Corinthian doesn't like witnesses, whether they work for him or not.'

'The elevator sounds like my exit.'

'Only the Corinthian can use it when he's in residence, and I don't want you dragging around his severed head to get through the retinal scanner.'

'You sure about that? I can think of a few places where it would look great on a pike.'

'If you try to go through the parking garage, those guards will have a witness-free venue to dispose of you. If you go the other way, you'll be able to take advantage of the magic ingredient.'

'Magic ingredient?' I said.

I closed the elevator hatch behind me and started up the shaft's ladder to the wheel housing on top. The emergency lights weren't much to see by, but the darkness favoured me. I found a hatch at the top and climbed into the ventilation shaft. It was thin aluminium and didn't take my weight without protest. There was only enough space in the shaft to lie flat and shimmy forward.

'I'm in,' I said. Gideon had said I could use the earpiece once I was in the Eden's guts.

'Get a move on,' he said. 'You'll reach the vertical shaft any minute.'

True to his prediction, I nearly shimmied off the edge of a ten-storey drop. Metal rungs were bolted to the opposite side so some poor bastard could crawl around in here as a full-time job. I stretched over to grab the nearest rung, the bottom half of my body still in the other shaft, the rest above ten storeys of air.

'You don't have all day,' Gideon said.

I grabbed the rung and pulled the rest of my body out of the shaft. Then it was up two storeys and into another shaft for some more goddamn shimmying. I prepared myself to mourn the early death of yet another suit.

'You remember what comes next?' Gideon said in my ear.

'Fifty feet, and I'm above the guest bathroom.'

Fifty feet later, I was looking down through a grate at a white marble bathroom both cleaner and larger than the flophouse room I'd been staying in. I listened for signs of life and heard nothing. I pushed the grate out and pulled it back through the opening and out of the way. After a short drop, I was finally inside.

'The bathroom opens on to the main corridor,' Gideon had said, tracing the route over the plans with his finger. 'To your

30

right is the main entrance with the two bodyguards on the outside. On the left, the corridor ends in storage closets. There'll be an opening to your right that leads into the main room, with a living area closest to you and an open-plan kitchen at the far end. On the other side of the room is the doorway to the Corinthian's bedroom and private bathroom, but he doesn't spend much time in there. I don't think he's been sleeping well lately.'

'What about this?' I'd said, pointing to the floor-to-ceiling windows that formed the external wall of the main room and led to the balcony. 'Why don't we skip the rest and buy a high-powered rifle instead?'

'The surrounding buildings aren't tall enough to give us a decent shot, and the glass is one-way. Thermal imaging isn't enough to tell the Corinthian apart from his staff. Besides, I don't think a bullet from a mile away would be satisfying enough for you, considering your history.'

I hadn't known Gideon long, but the way he danced around things was already starting to irritate me. He knew my past with the Corinthian went further back than what had happened to Iris, and had said just enough to make it plain. Every spy I'd met loved to hint at how much they knew.

I screwed on the silencer then left the bathroom and turned right. There was murmuring on the other side of the front door, probably a debate about when the power would come back on. It was impossible to tell how many people made up the conversation. My pottery automatic held only five rounds, and as far as I knew there were four people in this penthouse I had to kill.

I opened the front door. On the other side were two bodyguards in the standard plain-clothes uniform. They turned towards the sound of the door, training and experience not stopping them from hesitating as they saw an unfamiliar man looking back at them from inside their employer's private apartments. I used that moment to shoot them both and close the door.

A lead insect travelling just below the speed of sound went past my face and tore a piece out of the door before it clicked shut. I caught a glimpse of a bald, sunburned head attached to a semi-automatic leaning around the corner leading to the main room. Maurice Wilcox had just introduced himself.

I distracted him with a shot and ran back into the bathroom. Wilcox tracked my dash with his pistol, punching more holes in the wood panelling. I was closer to his position now, but I had only two bullets left, and one of them was reserved. Wilcox put a few more rounds into the bathroom door for sport while I figured out what to do.

The shooting stopped. I risked a look around the corner. No bald head, and no gun.

I crossed to the other side of the corridor and inched towards the opening to the main room. If I were Wilcox, I would have sent the Corinthian into his room as soon as the power failed. He was probably lying in the tub in his private bathroom, unperturbed, waiting for his man to give the all-clear. Wilcox should have withdrawn from his place at the corner to somewhere in the main room where he could take a clear shot as soon as I poked my head around.

I got to the doorway without opposition. Now all I had to do was charge into a room I couldn't see where a trained man with the advantage of position was waiting to gun me down. I moved around the corner, ready to dive into the room at what according to Gideon's blueprints should be cover. I got a punch in the face instead.

Wilcox had been waiting on the other side. I got a hand on his gun arm before he could draw a bead, and he did the same on mine. We struggled for a second before I drove my forehead into his nose, the slick wetness of his blood on my skin. Wilcox began to fall, but instead of crumpling to the ground he went backwards, taking me with him in a judo throw.

I landed on a glass coffee table, and when it refused to support my weight, the carpeted floor. To my left was a long sofa the table had been in front of, and behind it the floor-to-ceiling windows that formed the back of the room. The Corinthian sat on the sofa right where the coffee table had been. I looked up at him from my bed of wood and broken glass with astonishment. He looked down at me for the briefest of moments, then back up at something only he could see.

From the floor I saw an upside-down Wilcox – even before I'd broken his nose, he had the brutal features of a former boxer with a middling record – reach for his gun. The frame of the coffee table had been solid teak, the lengthwise beams still intact. I grabbed one and stabbed above my head, right into Wilcox's gut.

He groaned and dropped his gun. That gave me enough time to rise. The beam was too heavy to swing so I used it like a spear. For a big man, Wilcox was light on his feet. We danced around his gun, my feints and thrusts finding only air.

I over-extended and Wilcox grabbed on to the beam. We played tug-of-war for a while. The Corinthian's eyes flicked between us, as if he were watching a tennis match between two minor talents he didn't recognize. Wilcox was a bigger man than me, and in this game size would eventually win out over intelligence. I waited until Wilcox pulled on the beam with all his strength, and then I let him have it.

Victory unbalanced him. Without my opposing force, Wilcox's own strength made him stumble backwards. I closed the distance with a hop, skip and a jump that put my right knee in the same space as his chin. The impact kept him moving backwards until he reached the window. It seemed to support Wilcox for a second, until gravity got a hold of his unconscious body and pulled it to the floor.

I grabbed Wilcox's pistol, and aimed it right between the Corinthian's impassive eyes.

# FIVE

## Eden Hotel and Casino, Babylon, Nevada

'I didn't expect it to be you,' the Corinthian said. 'I suppose I'm disappointed.'

The gun in my hand had no effect on him; I might as well have been holding a piece of modern art. He hadn't moved since I'd entered the room with an involuntary display of acrobatics.

'What do you want?' he said. 'Money doesn't interest you, and if you were here only for my life we wouldn't be having this conversation.'

The scale of the couch he sat on made the Corinthian smaller by comparison.

'Who told you where to find Iris?'

'Are you going to kill him as well? I'm afraid you're too late. Judases never seem to live long.'

'Why did you sell her to Stonebridge?'

I had a different history with Stonebridge, one that was equally unpleasant. During the war, I'd volunteered for service with Task Force Seventeen, a special group looking for weapons of mass destruction in Tehran. Stonebridge had tortured prisoners for information as a private contractor on the orders of General Glass, who commanded the task force. Ten years later

I found Stonebridge running Fisher Partners operations in New York and Glass controlling the whole company.

A flicker in the Corinthian's eyes told me he was wondering if my question was a joke.

'Finding people was my business. Stonebridge paid ten thousand dollars for the information. I only remember because it was above the market rate for a client of her importance. In retrospect, that should have given me pause; she turned out to be worth far more than the initial appraisal.'

The Corinthian didn't have to say that I was the reason Iris had gone from a single name on a long list to Stonebridge's number one priority. I'd stolen the list of people Fisher Partners had planned on abducting in New York, and Stonebridge had thought to use Iris as leverage to get it back. He failed. We both did.

'I don't know what more I can say off the top of my head; if you had told me you were coming I would have found the relevant paperwork.'

The main living area of the Corinthian's penthouse was more of a gallery than a room. The floor was wood and stained almost to black. Light came from panels in the wall, not lamps. Besides the coffee table I'd destroyed, there was no other furniture apart from the sofa. I wasn't expecting pictures of his great-aunt, but there wasn't a single object in the room that I could identify as belonging to him. The whole place was an anonymous showpiece, one more barrier between the Corinthian and the rest of the world.

'You haven't shot me yet,' he pointed out. 'You've had no qualms about taking life on a number of other occasions. Perhaps it has something to do with shooting an unarmed man in cold blood. If it makes it any easier, you're only finishing what you've already started.'

36

It was less than a month since the Corinthian and I had tangled in New York. When I'd pointed a gun at him the last time, he'd had the good sense to run. Yet here he was, serene as a martyr waiting for the kindling under his feet to be lit. It was a safe bet that the Corinthian hadn't found God. Maybe something had found him.

'What about the list?' I said. 'If it meant so much to you, why did you let us get away?'

The Corinthian brushed a microscopic bit of fluff from his jacket; he wore a gabardine suit fitted to him like a prophylactic. He might be a criminal sociopath on an international scale, but at least he knew how to dress.

'You don't think you escaped all on your own? As soon as Benny called the Mossad, they screened your retreat all the way to DC. It was irrelevant by then anyway. You sealed my coffin by giving the list to one of those Pentagon lackeys. Information is valuable only so long as it's scarce.'

'So you lost a profitable opportunity. I don't see how that's a death sentence.'

'Conditions in this country will change,' he said. 'Or, rather, they will change back. The Elders are a temporary phenomenon, a mass delusion.'

'That didn't stop you from working for them.'

'I did what any good businessman does,' the Corinthian said, 'followed the money wherever it led. My equal utility to all sides was usually enough to protect me from any hard feelings. The profit margin on those task orders was like nothing I'd ever handled: guns, drugs and diamonds didn't even come close. It was simply too good to resist, and for that reason alone I should have been more cautious. I've been told that, when the old America returns, my involvement with Fisher Partners will not be forgiven.'

'I have to say, I'm as surprised as you are.'

'Too many wives and children had become involved for people to remain rational. The list might have balanced the scales, or at least made me no longer worth the effort. Now I've alienated both sides.'

A ghost of a smile passed across his lips. I imagine he'd had a lot of time to sit in this expensive cage and appreciate the irony. Without the protection of the Elders or the Pentagon, everyone with a grudge now saw their chance.

'Why didn't you run?'

'I know better than anyone that it would be pointless,' he said. 'There is no mountain so high nor no village so remote that one of my enemies wouldn't find me. Even if I could find such a place, it wouldn't solve the underlying problem. I have lost my bearings, Strange. In my business, when that happens your life is sure to be misplaced as well.'

The Corinthian stopped speaking and cocked his head to one side, as if an idea of such great weight had fallen in that it made his skull lopsided.

'The Israelis sent you, didn't they?' he said. 'I can accept that.'

The sky behind him began to glow and burst as the fireworks display celebrating President Adamson's birthday got under way. The power was still off, the explosions back-lighting the Corinthian in the same neon shades that lit the sprawl of Babylon. One half of his face was for a moment cerulean, the other magenta, red and green, before the light faded and he returned to the half-darkness that was his natural aspect. The one-way glass allowed all the colours but none of the sound inside.

'You spared Stonebridge's life,' he said, not a plea but a minor point on which he wished his curiosity to be satisfied.

'Stonebridge was too dumb and small-time to wiggle out of his corner. With you I had to be sure.'

'You've had other chances to kill me.'

I knew he was thinking of that night at the Waterfront, his club in Brooklyn, when his goons had escorted Iris and me up to a private room to face the Corinthian's judgement. He'd seen the calculation in my eyes then, the arithmetic that had said I could throw him through a window before his minders returned.

'That was before you took her from me.'

'Don't lie to a man you're about to kill. This is for the others, the ones you found at my expense. Killing me won't make this Iris return, any more than it will erase what you did when you worked for me.'

The Corinthian straightened his back, sat up straight, got ready for what was coming.

'If you pull that trigger, just what do you think will change?'

'You'll be dead.'

I shot him twice and then checked for a pulse. The second bullet had blown out the back of his skull but I had to be sure. The windows were shatterproof but the bullets had left holes on their way outside. The sound of the fireworks and the fury of the world rushed in to touch the Corinthian at last.

# SIX

## Eden Hotel and Casino, Babylon, Nevada

'You took your time up there,' Gideon said, when I was back in the ventilation shaft.

'Unfinished business.'

'Well, it's put you behind schedule. Move your ass, the power is coming back on.'

True to Gideon's word, I could see light coming through the elevator hatch just as I reached it. I wasn't as concerned about that as the voices coming from inside the car. I would have to share the elevator this time.

Two heads looked up when I opened the ceiling hatch. One was the dissolute Cypriot who had already been so useful to me. The other belonged to an aspiring piece of arm-candy, who out of fear or simple reflex action gave me her best collagen smile.

'Against the wall,' I said, encouraging them with my ceramic gun. I'd brought it with me to keep it out of official hands. Wilcox's gun got a rubdown – a little pointless since my DNA was all over what was left of the coffee table – and was now resting by the Corinthian's body as a gift for forensics.

They did as they were told, giving me enough room to drop into the car.

'Okay,' I said, 'none of us wants to be here—'

Golden boy took that as his cue to make a clumsy grab for the gun. I don't know if he was trying to impress the girl or was high on the stuff I'd delivered earlier, but either way I gave him a shiner with my free hand for his trouble. The girl began to wail, until I made it clear that she was irritating an armed man.

'As I was saying,' I continued, 'none of us wants to be here, but if you do exactly as I say, you'll both probably live.'

I picked the would-be hero off the floor and stood him in front of the elevator doors.

'When those doors open, feel free to run,' I said to the girl.

'What about Mitzi?' she said in accented English.

'Mitzi?' I echoed. He twisted in my grasp and swore at her in Greek. 'Sorry, I'll need my new friend for a little bit longer.'

'They're waiting for you down there,' Gideon said in my ear.

'I know,' I said, and pushed the button.

Above the elevator doors was a monitor I hadn't noticed before. It displayed a news crawler, weather and classic cartoons. The three of us watched Donald Duck and waited for the faster-than-average elevator to reach the ground floor.

When the doors opened I saw nothing but trouble. Six guards had formed a semicircle around the elevator entrance. Alarms must have gone off when they'd been unable to raise their boss right after an unexplained power loss. Behind them, patrons gambled on as if nothing had happened.

The girl left the elevator at full scream. I'd hoped she would cause a distraction, or at least obscure their line of fire. The guards just let her pass, drew their guns and kept their eyes on the weapon I had to the back of the VIP's head.

'Look at it this way,' I said into the Cypriot's ear as I slow-walked him out of the elevator, 'when this is over, it will be a great story to tell the ladies.'

He replied under his breath, in Greek. The tone wasn't kind.

The girlfriend caused as much of a stir in the crowd as she had with the guards. Most didn't notice or care when she went running past, panic and screams not being unknown at the tables. The site of a flowering hostage situation in front of the elevators did get some attention, but no one knew how to react. A few people ran, but most just stared at me in surprise. Maybe they thought I was part of a new show.

When Gideon had said I had a better-than-even chance of not getting out, I thought he might also have been talking about the odds he'd hang me out to dry. I'd completed my mission, which from Gideon's perspective meant I was now just a walking bundle of liabilities. I knew the logic and had accepted it before I'd agreed to his proposal. If Gideon was leaving me for the wolves, it would be Benny I'd feel bad for. He'd trusted Gideon to keep an eye on me; if he sold me out Benny might be fool enough to think he should do something about it.

'If you're going to add that magic ingredient,' I said under my breath, 'now would be the time.'

A chip cart sat idle by a closed pai gow table. They were feats of modern engineering, fortresses on wheels. Two pit bosses had to provide pin codes and retinal scans simultaneously just to get one open. They could withstand drilling, explosives and incredible heat. Anything that could get through its proprietary skin would destroy all the chips it contained. It was practically invulnerable, at least from the outside. I should have been paying attention to the men pointing guns at me, but I'd never seen a chip cart left unattended before.

The explosion had been designed to be all bark and no bite. Panic rippled through the crowd, but it was quickly replaced by a mixture of joy and greed as thousands of chips erupted from the top of the cart and came down in a shower of plastic tender.

42

Pandemonium arrived without delay. The guards found themselves in a sea of people high on free liquor and easy money. It was impossible to keep a bead on their armed hostage-taker without putting bullets through paying customers.

I pushed my hostage to the right and went left, straight towards the epicentre of the cash explosion. People clambered over each other to get at the chips, spilling drinks and starting fights. The crowd held the security guards in solution, and nearly did the same for me. Anyone who got in my way I pushed in the direction of the money. They didn't seem to mind.

'Thanks for the distraction,' I said, bone induction the only reason Gideon heard it over the riot he'd unleashed.

'Just think of me as your circumcised genie. Don't head for the front entrance,' he said, just as I got within sight of it. A phalanx of men with big guns covered the three revolving doors that were the Eden's primary entrance.

'Take the escalator to your right.'

'I want to go out not up.'

'Trust me.'

Circumstances had already made the choice for me. The security guards had freed themselves from the treasure hunters and were heading my way.

I went for the escalators, cutting through the labyrinth of slots to slow my pursuers. Minor celebrities and popular cartoon characters glowed and rotated above me, enticing patrons with their frozen smiles. In my peripheral vision I saw the guards spreading out. The area was too big for them to encircle me, but they could herd me into a corner if I wasn't careful.

I was so intent on my pursuers I nearly ran over a waitress coming the other way. She wore the Eden's uniform, a costume made of stylized fig leaves that covered about as much as their biblical inspiration. She recoiled from me in terror, rightly afraid that the slightest impact would cause her to spill out of a dress already under incredible strain.

There were two obstacles between me and the escalators: a full craps table in front of me, and a guard in front of the escalator. They'd anticipated my route, and now the other guards were coming to cut me off. The players had stopped rolling long enough to watch the chaos, but the sight of a hundred-person scrum wasn't enough to make them abandon the table entirely.

When they saw me bearing down on them, only the boxman and the base dealers had the good sense to get out of the way. The stickman put up his hands and froze, even though my gun wasn't pointed in his direction.

The guard near the escalator saw me coming, but he made the mistake of drawing his weapon instead of moving. I jumped on to the table – scattering a two-hundred-dollar prayer on hard six with my left toe – kept going and leapt off the other side, my free hand finding the stick in the stickman's paralyzed hand and bringing it down on the guard with all the force of gravity and momentum. I stepped over his body and ran up the down escalator. The other guards weren't far behind.

Upstairs was the retail area. Commemorative plates, mugs, shot glasses, hats, shirts and anything else the Babylon skyline could be printed on were available for sale. If none of that appealed you could always get your picture taken with a stripper to bring home to the wife. There were more guards up here, but the crowds were still too thick for them to use their weapons. Word must have gone out on the wire by now. Pretty soon every one of the Eden's hourly police would be on my tail. At least news of the gold rush downstairs had made its way up here; I was nearly trampled to death by the stampede of people trying to get down to grab a piece of the action.

'Where the hell am I going, Gideon?'

'Head for the buffet.'

The shops gave way to a series of restaurants, segmented by cuisine and price. The Eden had the greatest pretensions to class of any casino in Babylon, but even they couldn't do away with that hallowed Vegas institution, the loss-leader buffet. A big queue was waiting in a snaking line defined by wooden railings, as if gluttony were a theme park ride. The queue was beginning to dissolve as rumours reached it of the money on the floor downstairs. They were too surprised at the sight of me running past to object when I cut in line, and kept quiet when they saw the armed retinue following behind.

'Everybody down!' I yelled at the dining area, so the goons wouldn't have to.

'There's a kitchen door by the Chinese,' Gideon said.

I dashed around the Mexican buffet – refried beans congealing under heat lamps, big trays of fajita mix, a mountain of tortillas – elbowing customers who were too stupid or full to get out of the way. The guards had grown desperate enough to take a few shots. It was the sight of their guns that got people screaming, not the sound of them going off: real gunfire always sounded different in the movies, and it took a second for the lucky civilians in the audience who'd never heard it before to work out what was going on. Other than scaring the hell out of a hundred people, the only thing the shots accomplished was nine-millimetre-sized holes in the egg foo young.

I hit the kitchen's two-way door at full speed. It swung in and caught a busboy coming the other way. I jumped over his body and legged it past a bank of cooks working a food assembly line.

'This ride better stop soon.'

'Lose the pursuit or it will.'

I turned the corner into the refrigerator area. Massive brushed aluminium units hummed their own tune. Under-chefs were working at the stainless-steel table in the centre, but the room emptied quick as soon as I arrived. The exodus slowed down my pursuers long enough for me to grab a frying pan from a rack and cosy up to the doorway.

I hit the first guard as he came through the door. The frying pan met his left knee and forced it to bend in a way nature hadn't intended. While he was rolling on the ground I leaned out and dealt ceramic death to the next man with the last two rounds in my gun. The other pursuers must have fallen behind.

An employee wheeled a room service cart into the room from its other entrance. She didn't scream or run at the sight of a panting, armed man, so I knew immediately that something was up. The woman opened the cart and beckoned me inside with her eyes.

'Do as the lady says.'

The cart was bigger than it looked on the outside. The woman mumbled Hebrew into her wrist and closed the door. A moment later I felt the cart begin to move. Shouts and confusion touched the cart and then passed it by.

We stopped. The woman was having a conversation, but I couldn't make out what they were saying. Short sentences. She was negotiating our way past security, which from the tone of their voices were verging on panic.

She said the right words and we were on the move again. More shouts, but they were of protest not fear. The casino was trying to reverse Gideon's largesse, and the punters weren't happy.

I heard the distinctive bell of an elevator. We were going down. It was a short trip, the car stopping almost as soon as it started. The engine noises and echoing acoustics said underground parking garage.

Hands lifted the cart and put it in the back of a vehicle.

Someone opened the cart door. I crawled out into the back of a van. The woman who had been pushing the cart was at the wheel, Gideon occupying shotgun. He had a laptop open on his knees – on the screen the frozen moment of me airborne off the craps table, stick in my hand and fedora still in place – and was laughing so hard I was afraid he would break something.

'A room service cart was the best the Mossad could come up with?' I said.

'It worked, didn't it? This is Shoshana,' he said, tilting his head towards the driver.

She said hello by starting the van.

Gideon turned back to the laptop. 'What possessed you to do that?'

'Instinct,' I said. 'I owe you for the extraction.'

He waved away my promise. 'You let me keep this, I'll consider us square. I could watch it until doomsday.'

'As long as you watch it with your pants on, we've got a deal.'

Gideon's new fit of laughter was Shoshanna's cue to get the van moving. I left Babylon in the best Las Vegas tradition: under cover of night, pursued by armed men.

# SEVEN

## Providence, Colorado

*Three years earlier*

Roy St James had chosen the New Life Evangelical Church as the place he would meet God. It was a small wooden structure of classic puritan design: an arched double door entrance, above it a large window filled by modest, clear glass, and a steeple to show parishioners the way. With the snow on the ground it could be a Christmas card from the last century. I didn't know when St James had left New York, or why he'd come here. I suppose there were worse places to die.

I'd bought the rifle and scope from an asthmatic old hunter at a gun show in Denver. Cash, no questions asked. It was a .30-06, a gun that had been killing mammals of all kinds for more than a hundred years. The silencer was my own design.

Last night I had walked the church's perimeter looking for the spot I now lay in. Snow had fallen all through the hours of moonless darkness, covering my tracks as fast as I could make them. Now the forest was calm, the sky clear and cold. A camouflage blanket kept me warm and invisible. I watched the congregation through the scope and waited for the service to begin.

After the Eden, we'd driven from Las Vegas to a private

runway in South Nevada. The driver got out at Gideon's unspoken signal, leaving only him in the front and me in the back.

'I'll be out of the country for a while,' Gideon said. 'Procedure and so forth. This is the part where I should convince you to come with me.'

'Doesn't sound like you're going to try that hard.'

'I'm smart enough to know my chances.'

Gideon passed back a manila folder.

'A bonus for a job well done. The four names that your numbers belong to.'

After Stonebridge had taken Iris, I'd tossed his flat in New York looking for anything that might tell me what they'd done with her. I'd found her task order, a sort of contract through which the Elders told Fisher Partners who had to disappear. The task order didn't have the names of the men who had done the work, just their employee numbers. I had known the Corinthian was involved, but had no idea who the others were until Gideon dropped them in my lap.

The dossiers inside were thinner than I would have liked: vital stats, a blurry picture, some known associates and their criminal records. It wasn't much, but it would be enough to get me started. Stonebridge had tried to cut costs like any other businessman. Instead of hiring professionals to do his dirty work, he'd found criminal scum willing to work cheap. Stonebridge had found out the hard way that you got what you paid for.

'This may not make a difference,' Gideon said, 'but those men are no longer Fishermen. They're not in a position to hurt anyone.'

'If Black September had disbanded after Munich, would that have made a difference to your predecessors?'

'That was different. We were trying to make an entire

49

generation of terrorists think twice about fucking with the Jews.'

'And what kind of message does it send when these four men are allowed to torture, kill and walk away?'

Gideon looked at me. He was trying to make up his mind about something, but I didn't know what.

'If you're still alive when I get back, I'll be in touch. The car is a gift. I wouldn't hold on to it for too long. There's some pocket money in the glove box—'

'I'm not a paid assassin.'

That look again.

'I'm not sure you know what you are,' Gideon said. He got out and slammed the door. I stayed in the back and watched him walk to a plane on the tarmac, leaning against the wind.

Inside the church, the congregation was singing. I was too far away to hear the tune, but most of the people could sing it without looking at their books. Judging by the number of times they had stood and knelt, we were nearing the sermon. After that would be the ceremony I was waiting for.

The pastor began to speak. My lip reading had never been very good, and I wasn't really interested in what he was saying anyway. I could guess the gist from what was coming: a few conversion stories from the scriptures, emphasis on it never being too late to come to God, something about the importance of forgiveness.

As he neared the end of his sermon, I saw the pastor beckon someone to the front. Roy St James rose and stood beside the pastor, uncomfortable in the first suit he'd ever owned in his life. Roy had cut off the mullet and scrubbed himself as clean on the outside as he hoped his soul would soon be. After the pastor had said a few more words, he left the floor to the newest member of his flock.

This was the moment I'd planned to shoot him. St James was standing in line with the window, speaking but not moving, as clear a shot as you could hope for. I'd found a good position, planned what would happen before and after the shooting down to the last detail, and then forgotten about the choir standing directly behind him. At this angle the bullet would go through St James and right into a middle-aged woman with blonde highlights.

So I waited. I let Roy tell his story, or at least the story he wanted his new brothers and sisters to hear. He had grown up in a bad family and run with a worse crowd. He'd stolen cars, sold drugs and spent time in jail. Roy would play up the degradation and violence because it would make his conversion more spectacular by comparison. The audience played along, scared and excited by sharing a room with a character from evening television.

In my head, I filled in the parts their new brother would leave out: after his last stint in prison, he moved out to New York to stay with a friend. The friend told Roy about a job that would pay good money for easy hours. The best part was that they were practically working for the government, so there'd be no cops to worry about. Roy would have asked how this was possible, and that was when this friend would have introduced him to Peter Stonebridge.

According to the task orders I'd found in Stonebridge's place, Roy St James was paid to assist in twelve kidnappings and four murders. All the 'clients' would have lived in or around New York. For this work Fisher Partners had paid him around thirty-five thousand dollars, a much better salary than the criminal sector offered, especially since he got it tax-free. Stonebridge had paid an extra bonus for a special job, St James' last. All that blood money would make a good nest egg for him and his new bride.

He was reaching out to her now, motioning the woman who was his salvation up to the front beside him. Beauty and the Beast had become something of a local sensation. A few hours at the only café in town had told me that the residents couldn't say much about Roy, but were full of loose talk about his new bride. She was a local girl, met Roy in Bible study if that could be believed. She was a few inches shorter and at least five years younger, a girl whose charm resided in her aura of stability and calm. After only three weeks they became engaged, the culmination of a whirlwind courtship of the type so beloved by romance authors and divorce attorneys.

Roy would be telling that story now. She was blushing, and the middle-aged woman in the choir blocking my shot was getting misty-eyed. I could see the congregation periodically raise their arms in jubilation, perhaps in response to Roy name-checking the Lord. His face was flushed and sweaty. He begged God for forgiveness, and promised that the love of Jesus and a good woman had made him a changed man.

I'd spent most of my adult life watching people lie. The tears in his eyes were genuine. So was the remorse, for everything, not just what he'd told the congregation. I wasn't so focused on my work that I couldn't appreciate how remarkable a turn-around that was. To go from agent of terror to reformed man in around two months was amazing, even for a religion that placed its faith in instant grace. Roy St James was a new man. I didn't care.

The congregation began to sing a joyous hymn. People swayed in the pews, threw their arms in the air and around each other. The choir moved from their positions behind the altar, walking down the outside aisles to dance and sing with the parishioners. Roy St James stayed where he was, his wife holding his left hand, the pastor his right. They sang and moved together, new tears on Roy's face, ones of joy for his new family and the new life they promised.

Half the congregation turned towards the window when it broke, perhaps expecting to see a rock or a bird. The rest saw Roy St James, still standing, still holding hands, a brand-new hole in his head. His death, like his salvation, had been nearly instantaneous. A few inches from my face, I heard the hiss of the spent casing melting the snow it lay on.

Sensible members of the congregation took cover, pulling screaming children and adults into the shelter of the pews. The pastor was yelling something calming to his flock while he looked in vain for some sight of me. Gravity forced Roy's body to the floor, and into the arms of his betrothed. Shock was giving way to grief and horror. She began to scream, embracing the meat that had once been her fiancé. The look on her face was the same as the wives of all the men Roy St James had helped destroy.

Wind and the broken window brought the sounds of panic all the way up the hill. I unscrewed the silencer for disposal later, and threw the rifle and the single casing into a hole in the frozen ground I'd dug for the purpose. A layer of snow and dirt would be enough to keep it hidden until I was gone. I wrapped the blanket around my shoulders and disappeared into the quiet hills.

# EIGHT

## South of Las Cruces, New Mexico
*Three years earlier*

'That's a lot of rod for one man.'

The waitress was at my elbow again, a pot of mature coffee sloshing in her right hand as she looked me over. Her nametag said 'Lorelei'.

I'd been thinking about Iris. I'd promised myself I wouldn't, but it was a promise imperfectly observed. Last night I'd been sitting up in a motel staring at the wall, no reason in particular. On the nightstand beside me was a bottle of whiskey, still wrapped in brown paper. I'd bought it with the intention of drinking myself into a dreamless sleep but found the thirst had deserted me once I got home. Alcohol would do me no favours in any case; drinking was supposed to make you forget, but the opposite happened in my case.

It was easier to focus on the names, the work at hand. I'd removed my plans from their context, split what I was doing into discrete parts with no wider meaning. As a whole I would have to consider what I was doing, its point, whether Iris would want me to do it at all. As pieces it was just another job: find, track, kill. I'd first learned the technique working for Task Force Seventeen and then perfected it over ten years of watching hotels and following cars. It was easier to think of what you were doing as pointless when the true aim was worse.

'Ma'am?' I said, coming back to the present.

'Your guns,' she said, gesturing with the coffee pot.

My family forty-five was in a shoulder holster, the same place it had been ever since I came back from Tehran. The new addition was on my hip: a beat-up thirty-eight I'd bought at a pawn shop in Las Cruces. The owner had been surprised I'd wanted something so reasonable, considering the region was swimming in high-powered weaponry, but a police special was exactly what I needed. It was common as dirt, and a revolver would keep all the casings with me.

'What do you need two pistols for?'

'As a man I knew once said: I like to have options.'

Lorelei upped the wattage on her smile to hide her confusion. She was a few years older than me and almost as tall. She could no longer hide the lines on her face, but in compensation she moved with an alluring grace that only an experienced woman was capable of.

'Me and Hector – that's the short-order cook – have got kind of a bet on about you. Hector knew there was something interesting about you the moment you walked in.'

Behind the counter I caught a glimpse of a sunburned face, prematurely old, scars on the left cheek not caused by acne unless it had wielded a two-inch blade. From the way he ducked behind the counter as soon as he caught my eye, I got the feeling 'interesting' wasn't the word he'd used. The vibe from me that scared Hector was exciting Lorelei, and I could do without both kinds of interest.

At the lunch counter, a biker called Zeke Reed was inhaling the daily special. He was big, tattooed, and let his mouth hang open when he chewed. His reputation said he had at least one screw loose and the history of violence that went with it.

Reed didn't know me from Adam, and I aimed to keep it that way. The conversation with Lorelei was attracting the attention of the restaurant right at the time I needed to be most anonymous. Reed may not have known me, but he might recognize the type. I couldn't afford for him to get suspicious and drug couriers, even dumb ones, leaned that way by nature.

Compounding my problems was another man at the counter who'd noticed Lorelei's attentions. He was a trucker in a work shirt with a Santa Claus girth that hid a fair amount of muscle. The daggers he was sending my way between bites of fried chicken suggested he was pining for the help. My arrival had disrupted whatever romantic back-of-the-cab sexual encounter he'd been dreaming about while on the road.

'I figure you must be one of those private security men on his way to El Paso,' Lorelei continued. 'Hector, on the other hand, reckons you're a gunslinger.'

She said it so casually, I had no choice but to laugh.

'Aren't I a hundred-and-fifty-odd years late for that profession?'

''Round these parts, you'd be surprised.'

Northern Mexico had been a free-fire zone for going on twenty years. The Liberty Wall that now watched most of the southern border had originally been dreamed up by fevered nativists afraid of brown contamination. It was only given serious attention after violence in Chihuahua got so bad it could be justified on national security grounds. Both nations managed the barrier, since both were interested in stopping something coming across. The Americans wanted to intercept drugs going north, the Mexicans guns coming the other way. There was also the flow of political refugees fleeing the Elders' policies that neither government wanted to talk about.

El Paso was now more of a garrison than a town. FBI, CIA, army and immigration all had large forces stationed there to keep the gangs on the other side of the river. Somewhere in the city there was also a regional office of Fisher Partners, watching for clients who ran for the border.

'The cartels are hiring American mercenaries?'

'That's the talk I've heard. Some pretty tough customers have passed through here on the way to El Paso, but I couldn't say they were hired guns for sure.'

Hector was still hiding behind the counter.

'So what are you then?' Lorelei asked.

'Passing through.'

My quarry had paid his cheque and was heading for the door. I dropped a few bills on the table, including a generous tip, and waited for him to leave first.

'No dessert? You won't find better pie in a hundred square miles.'

'I lost my sweet tooth a long time ago.'

'You ever find it again, you know where we are.'

At another time, I wouldn't have hesitated seeing just where Lorelei's invitation would go. She didn't hurt the eyes, and not many women these days had the courage to be unafraid of their desires when the penalties for displaying them too publicly had become severe. I bet Lorelei was a lot of fun. Too bad I was out of that business for good. I touched my hat in her direction, and started for the door.

As I drew level with the trucker, he began to rise. I guess he'd been having an argument with himself about whether he should challenge me, and he'd finally worked up the courage at the worst possible moment. I would have explained to him that he was the only one in the race, but I didn't have time. I put a hand on his shoulder and forced the Romeo back into his seat. His eyes were in danger of being swallowed by the greying forest of his full beard. I held his gaze. I didn't have to say anything.

His eyes dropped. I could feel surrender relaxing his whole body through my hand on his shoulder. In the reflection of the mirror behind the counter I saw the horror on Lorelei's face, the hand to her mouth. Maybe her fascination with bad boys had been cured.

Reed was already down the road by the time I got to my car. It was a sky-blue four-door sedan that I'd stolen from a long-term parking lot on my way south. My fake identity was still solid as far as I knew, but I'd rather commit grand theft auto than take the chance it was blown. Cars could be ditched, but a charge on a credit card would kick around for years, and it was only a matter of time before the Fishermen discovered my new name.

Reed turned off the highway into the desert. We were the only traffic on the road. Following him would have been risky if my subject wasn't a drug dealer known to sample his own product. He was what they called a functioning addict, in the sense that he could remember his own name and walk a straight line if called upon to do so at the right time of day.

Reed would lead me to the man I was looking for, Marco Gambi. The police presence in El Paso had made the Juarez drug corridor unprofitable, but the Chihuahua Desert was large, and the government far away. Gambi lived in a junkyard owned by his cousin, one of many smugglers' rest stops in the area.

Gambi had been one of Stonebridge's favourites, invoicing almost eighty thousand dollars for assisting in eighteen acquisitions and ten murders. The file was unspecific about his actual duties; according to its records, everything Fisher Partners did was a team effort. Gambi had come down in the world since then, to a trailer in a junkyard and grunt work for his cousin.

It didn't take long for the blacktop to give way to gravel. After that it became a ribbon of dirt called a road only because it was packed more neatly than the earth around it. I gave Reed miles of leash. There was a lot of country, and it was flat enough you could see almost all of it.

After twenty minutes of back roads I saw where Zeke Reed was going and stopped. The junkyard was a fortress of rusted sheet metal, all four sides enclosed and topped with ageing strands of barbed wire. It would have been a weird set-up if the Gambis had been above-board, as if they expected the muskrats hiding in their desert holes to come and scavenge for parts.

Reed stopped at the front gate. Through my monocular I could see an old-time speakerbox on the driver's side. Zeke pressed the button, said open sesame, and the gate slid back.

Most of the drugs coming from Mexico weren't the old narcotics. There was more money in knock-offs of patented medication, which they brewed up in small labs all along the border. Most of the merchandise was destined not for an inner city ghetto but the sunbelt that ringed the south of the country with suburbs and retirement communities.

I swallowed my medication and waited. Reed was here to pick up some product and drive it to market. The nature of his visit meant he should have been in and out, but after an hour I was still waiting for him to reappear. I didn't expect drug mules to stick to a rigid schedule, but I had the feeling there was a bigger reason for the delay than just both men running on junkie time.

With nothing to look at but sand and metal, my mind began to drift. I hadn't been sleeping well lately. Bad dreams. The first time it happened I thought it was another seizure, until fragments of the dream floated up from my subconscious.

They'd started just after Babylon, but it wasn't the Corinthian's death that weighed on my conscience. On that score alone I would have a sleeping competition with any baby on the planet. What I remembered came from the war more than a decade earlier. If I was going to have flashbacks, I would have expected them to come from the invasion. Back then it had been a real war, not the game of armed hide-and-seek it had become by the time I joined Task Force Seventeen.

Instead the memories were oddly mundane: stray images of the broken Tehran skyline, bound and hooded men, faces I didn't recognize. They qualified as bad dreams only because the task force's day-to-day work was the stuff of nightmares already. Seventeen tortured anyone they thought would lead them to the Iranians' nuclear stockpile, kid draftees and officers alike screaming the names of everyone they knew to make the pain stop. Then we'd go out and find them, and the whole process would repeat itself.

Officially, Stonebridge was a contractor doing interrogation. What that meant in practice was hanging detainees from the ceiling until they said what he wanted them to. My primitive Farsi meant I had to sit in on interrogations in between translating for the teams that went out to find more people to brutalize. Glass was a colonel then, President Adamson's golden boy, and he ran the whole show.

I wasn't really shocked when he started doing the same thing to Americans. I guess I was surprised it took them ten years to get around to it. By then Glass was head of the Department of Homeland Security. The only security the Elders cared about was their own, and the cowards came crawling to their war hero to make all the bad people disappear. When Glass created Fisher Partners he staffed it with veterans of Task Force Seventeen, and everything old was new again.

I'd helped Glass in Tehran, persuaded myself at the beginning that it would bring the war to an end. This time I'd been on the right side, but I doubted it had made much difference. Stonebridge was expendable, as were the men I was hunting. The Corinthian was a middleman who could be replaced. I'd give up all the others, even my own life, for one clean shot at Glass.

I was on this desert road because I knew I'd never have that chance. Cassandra's revelations about what Fisher Partners had been doing might make Glass an embarrassment, but they'd never put him in chains. I'd only gotten to the Corinthian because of the Mossad. They didn't like General Glass much, but that didn't mean they'd help me assassinate a member of the cabinet.

A few hours later, and Reed still hadn't come out. A wind began to blow from the south-east; it felt like Fisher Partners breathing down my neck all the way from El Paso. I'd already been here longer than I'd expected or wanted to be. Driving on interstates thick with highway patrols wasn't something I could get away with for ever. The unusual nature of Roy St James's death was already percolating through the layers of federal law enforcement, and word would reach the Fishermen eventually. It would take them a bit longer to put two and two together, but they weren't stupid. I had a lot of work to do before they finished their sums, and I wasn't going to let a drug-addled biker fuck with my schedule any longer.

Cameras covered the front gate, but not the perimeter. I drove the car right up to the wall, under a spot where the barbed wire was hanging off. I stood on the hood of the car and cut the wire. The fence was short enough that I got my hands on the top with a jump and clambered over.

Inside were acres of sand and twisted metal bathed in sodium light. Crushed cars were stacked ten-high, multicoloured towers that reminded me of the high roller stacks I'd seen at the Babylon. I'd bought a few drinks in nearby Las Cruces to see if I could scrape up any more facts about the man. The only thing I learned from his fan club, other than that Gambi rarely paid for his own drinks, was that his trailer was behind the office near the front gate.

At first glance, Gambi's home was difficult to tell apart from the wrecks. It was on blocks, rust creeping up from below, a colour that might have been green in another life. The dirty linen curtains were drawn, a little light bleeding through from inside. There was only one entrance, but at least the door was thin as shit. One determined kick nearly took the thing off its hinges. I was right behind the falling door, leading with the thirty-eight from my hip.

I had surprised Gambi and Reed sitting around the trailer's dining table. In front of them was a collection of pill bottles, the colours of the rainbow prescribed by doctors who didn't exist. Both men stared open-mouthed. Reed was deep into an open bottle of greenish pills. Gambi looked only drunk, though the current situation was sobering him up fast.

Beside the hillock of illicit medication was a tarnished revolver. The drugs had sunk Reed's brain into a five-second time delay. Information was just reaching it that an unknown man had a loaded gun in his face. Instinct told him to pick up the revolver, which might have been a viable option if he'd gone for it as soon as I kicked in the door. Reaching for it now was just a lazy form of suicide, but it took another five seconds for that judgement to reach his hand, which was already doing what muscle memory told it to.

I shot Reed in the heart. Gambi jumped back, but he was sitting on the far edge of the table, boxed in by the fitted seats. He might as well have been staked to the ground.

'Jesus, do you know who you're messing with?' he said. 'Nobody rips off the cartel.'

I took Reed's revolver, emptied the barrel on the floor and threw it through the window.

'You're the only one I'm interested in.'

It wasn't until Gambi realized I had come for him that fear reached his last functioning brain cell.

'What are you talking about? Nobody's interested in me.'

'976239,' I said, reciting his Fisher Partners employee number.

Gambi's yellowed eyes tried to jump into the greasy weeds of his dark hair. His skin had an unhealthy shine, and there was too much of it to begin with. He might have been in decent shape once, before drugs replaced jogging as his regimen. Now it looked like a smaller man had taken up residence inside his skin, keeping it warm until the real Marco Gambi came back. I had a feeling he'd be waiting a long time.

'Oh Jesus,' he said, taking another look at me. 'Stonebridge warned us about you. He talked about you like you were a fucking fairy tale.'

I resisted the urge to say boo. 'You weren't with him in Virginia?'

'I'm alive, aren't I?'

Benny and I had made contact with Cassandra in an empty suburb near Washington. Before we could get on the move, Stonebridge had shown up, then the Corinthian, everyone after the list of clients I'd stolen from Fisher Partners. When we left, after I'd beaten Stonebridge within an inch of his life and left him for his colleagues, at least a few of his goons were still alive.

'Who took care of the rest?'

'Management,' Gambi said.

He breathed the word rather than saying it. Gambi was more

afraid of the Fisher Partners board than the loaded gun in my hand.

'When Stonebridge didn't come back, we saw the writing on the wall,' he said.

'What happened to him?'

'You think I asked? He's gone, just like the others.'

'Like the others you disappeared.'

'Hey, hey, hey,' Gambi said, putting his hands up as if he could catch my words. 'I just drove, brother. That's it.'

I should have just shot him. That had been the plan. Whatever he said was untrustworthy: leave a gun pointed at a man's head long enough, he'll cop to being the Lindbergh baby. I suppose I wanted to hear him try to justify himself, since he was never going to be forced to do it inside a courtroom. I might even learn something useful if I could filter out all the self-serving lies and attempts to save his life.

'Convince me. Start with how Stonebridge recruited you.'

'I was in a cell in Jersey, looking at grand theft auto. I didn't do it, you know: profiling.'

'Sure.'

'Anyway, one day I go to meet with my no-dick public defender, and there's this other guy there. The way he's looking me over was weird, not like a fed, kinda faggy I thought at first. I said, "Who's this asshole?" and just then I realized my lawyer was sweating like we're in the middle of a Texas summer.'

'Stonebridge.'

'He said he could make the charge go away. Then he offered me a job. It was the strangest fucking day of my life.'

'And you just drove.'

'I was the fucking wheel man, I swear to fucking God,' Gambi said.

His eyes were more focused now, trying to stare at me

with something approaching sincerity. The result was sickly desperation.

'You're looking for that woman, right?'

I didn't show my hand by reacting.

'Stonebridge said he had a special job for us. He gave Leon—'

'Leon Becker?' He was another one of my names.

'Yeah, Leon ran the team. He gave Leon this address and a description, said the woman had to be taken alive, no rough stuff. It was weird, 'cause usually it was all paperwork, you know, task orders, but this was all verbal. We were supposed to keep it to ourselves, not talk to other Fishermen.'

I was finding it difficult to breathe.

'Where was the address?'

'It was a long time ago,' Gambi said, though it had only been about three months. 'Somewhere near Shea Stadium, I remember that.'

Iris had been hiding in a motel near there.

'We didn't go in the place. We were told to wait outside. She'd park somewhere else and walk there. That's when Roy and Leon grabbed her off the street. Or tried to.'

'What do you mean?'

'Lady saw them coming. She put two rounds in Becker with this thirty-two that seemed to come from nowhere. If Leon hadn't been wearing a vest he would have stayed on the pavement. Then Roy hit her with this tranquillizer thingie they used on tough jobs like that. One of those and she was out cold.'

'And after?'

Gambi shrugged. 'Standard procedure. They carried her into the van, cut off her clothes, wrapped her up in a diaper and a jumpsuit, and gave her another shot to make sure she stayed quiet.'

They would have put blacked-out goggles over her eyes and

noise-cancelling headphones on her ears, to complete her exile from the world.

'Where did you take her?'

'Some parking lot in Queens. We met another van from Transport, just like we always did. The weird thing was, Stonebridge was there to supervise the handover personally. He'd never done that before. And there was this other guy.'

'Other guy?'

I heard a rustle in the direction of the bedroom, which was separated from the main living area by a curtain. I swore at myself for not following my own training and securing the whole shitbox when I'd had the chance.

Gambi yelled something, but the words were erased by my two shots. I pushed the curtain aside. A young boy looked at me and the gun that was still pointed at him. He was maybe eight, dark hair, a face the shape of his father's. There was a hole in his chest just below the collarbone. He didn't call out to his father, or run. He just stood there, shock and innocence keeping him from falling down. We breathed at each other while I tried to understand what I'd done.

What happened next must have been simultaneous. My brain couldn't admit all the signals from my senses at once, had to process them in order. I felt the explosion first, the heat on my face, bits of grit on my skin. I saw a delayed image of the flash on the inside of my eyelids, eyes closed and shielded by my free hand. Last was the sound of a big pop, filling the air inside the trailer. I held my breath and made for where the entrance had been.

I tripped over the broken door and tumbled down the steps, trailing smoke and gasping for air. I was a little on fire. I rolled around in the dirt until my jacket ceased to smoulder.

Black smoke poured from the broken window and doorway.

The smoke tasted like black powder, but there hadn't been much of an explosion. The bomb had been designed to burn, maybe to erase evidence. God knows where it had been, or how Gambi had set it off. I doubted he was smart enough to plan ahead for a visit like mine.

Gambi was still alive. He'd been kind enough to cut himself on the glass when he jumped out the window. I could see a trail of haemoglobin breadcrumbs leading from the trailer into the steel forest of the junkyard.

The bare ground made the trail easy to follow. Crushed cars were stacked twice my height on both sides. If there was an order to how they'd been placed, I couldn't see it. I stepped around the blood trail, careful to keep it intact since I'd need it to find my way out. This place was a labyrinth. I guess that made me the Minotaur.

I could hear uneven steps ahead, scratches on metal in the night's silence. I didn't know where Gambi thought he was going; the junkyard's one entrance was in the other direction. He must have been hoping to lose me in the wrecks.

The sounds ahead stopped. I followed the trail another fifty metres, past two left turns and a right. We were in the part of the junkyard where cars waited to be crushed. They had been thrown around the ground in no particular order, unlike the passages of crushed wrecks I'd been chasing Gambi through. The blood trail stopped in the middle of the path. I waited and listened. Nothing.

I knelt next to the end of the blood trail, hoping for inspiration. I wasn't disappointed. There was a single blood drop just a little to the right, barely visible to the naked eye. I reached under the remains of an ancient Pontiac sedan next to me. When I got hold of his ankle and pulled, Gambi screamed like I was dragging him to hell.

He tried to grab on to the sedan, but whatever he'd reached for snapped off in his hand. He clawed at the dirt as I dragged him out into the open, tracing ten uneven lines with his broken fingernails. I dropped his ankle, and Gambi struggled to a kneeling position under the shadow of the thirty-eight.

'Wait, just wait. I have files, okay?' he said. 'You think I didn't expect this to happen one day?'

Gambi's heart was beating too fast. The pressure made him pant like a dog and tried to force his eyes out through their sockets. We happened to be near one of the big sodium lights that illuminated the yard. It made me feel like we were in a stadium, or a coliseum. The harsh white light traced every line and crater on the left side of his face, while the right was hidden like the dark side of the moon.

'I'll give them to you, tell you everything you want to know.'

'You don't know anything,' I said. 'That was the idea. Management expected this day to come long before you did.'

Gambi's nose was running, joining his eyes and mouth, his body pulling out every stop to delay what his mind was telling it would happen. A herd of promises and regrets came out of his mouth, one on top of the next, stampeding each other into incoherence. I drew back the hammer.

'Please, please,' he said, when the words slowed, hands clasped in front of him in an imitation of prayer. 'I don't want to die.'

I shot him in the head. He listed to one side like a sinking ship, then fell into the dirt. After that, he didn't move.

Sirens came to me, wrapped in the trailer's smoke. There was no way a patrol car would just happen to be passing this forsaken patch of ground. I must have tripped a silent alarm.

My stolen car was still on the wrong side of the fence. I walked back towards the office and the front gate, giving Gambi's still smouldering trailer and the small body inside as wide a berth as possible. The son was already dead, and going into the trailer to look for him would be kabuki for a disbelieving audience of one.

The state policeman reached the front gate just as I was leaving it. I saw the lights in the corner of my eye. I kept walking towards the car that was temporarily mine. I doubted my regular pace fooled anyone, but running wouldn't get me there before they got out of the car.

'Stop!'

A single voice, only one officer. I kept walking.

'Stop or I'll—'

It was a flinch, an automatic reaction. My arm went back, there was a shot. I saw only part of a tan uniform, a badge, Caucasian features blurred by peripheral vision. I didn't turn around, or break my stride.

More staties were waiting where the side road joined the interstate. They'd set up a roadblock, which struck me as a little silly considering there was nothing but space around us. I turned off into pure desert, the ground chewing the bottom of the sedan with rock and sand.

Three patrol cars broke away from the roadblock and gave chase. I was back on the interstate, but the car was making funny sounds from my nature tour and they were gaining fast. New roadblocks would be going up in front of me, ready to blow the tyres with road spikes or just gun me down if I didn't stop.

I'd manned some checkpoints in the early days of the war, trying to keep the highway between the airport and the city clear. We knew Basij militia were mixing with the refugees fleeing Tehran. Command was determined to avoid the mistakes of Iraq. We stopped anything and everything, pulled people from their cars if they didn't move, strip-searched on a hunch. We lit up a vehicle at the slightest provocation, and wondered why civilians were too stupid to slow down for the soldiers of an invading army.

If the police followed the same procedure that we did in Tehran, they'd start with a verbal warning. The first bullet would go in front of the car, though considering how fast I was moving they'd probably skip that step and put one in the grille. The next shot would go in my head. I decided that was a fitting way for me to die. I didn't remember believing in karma before. Now I guess I did.

I wasn't sure in what direction I should be fleeing. My decade as a pedestrian had been fine for Manhattan, but there was no way I could out-drive the officers chasing me. Give me ten city blocks and I could lose half the army in a foot chase, but I was out of my element in this wilderness. Behind me I heard a new sound interspersed with the sirens. Helicopter blades. There was no way I could outrun them now.

I guess I should have been more worried about my situation. I hadn't expected to live this long, so my imminent death wasn't much of a surprise. My real sorrow was the outstanding name on my list. After I found Gambi I'd gotten stupid, started to think I might actually find them all before the Fishermen got to me. It was the closest thing to hope I'd had left. Now all I had to do was make sure I wasn't taken alive.

In the distance I could see the roadblock I'd predicted, shimmering in the heat like a prophetic vision. A car blocked each lane with two more in support behind. I saw half a dozen sheriffs wearing standard-issue mirrored sunglasses readying their weapons. One yelled through a megaphone, and for some reason I was surprised it wasn't Farsi.

I stepped on the gas.

# NINE

## Our Redeemer Hospital, El Paso, Texas
*Three years earlier*

I was supposed to be dead. Instead I was in another damn hospital. I raised my head and inspected the damage. I still had everything I should, but my chest was bound and left leg elevated. A TV was on somewhere. My right hand was cuffed to the rails of the bed. I saw shadows through the glass in the door, probably law enforcement keeping an eye on me.

I'd promised myself I'd never spend another night in a place like this. I guess I promised myself a lot of things. I looked at the tubes in my arm and realized one of them had to be full of morphine. No one with my hospital record would be this relaxed.

The first time I surfed a bed long-term was just after the explosion in Tehran. I'd been shot up a few times before that, but it hadn't taken them long to sew me up and send me along. My wounds from that last mission in the city weren't much worse than the others but the doctors kept me around anyway, for observation they said.

It took about a week for the reason why I needed to be observed to make its way around the beds. The explosion in Tehran had bathed everyone downtown in ionizing radiation. They never officially said how many soldiers were affected, but it had to have been in the thousands considering how many of us were stationed in the heart of the city. I was confined to a bed long after they'd taken the shrapnel out of my leg, re-set the bone and closed the wound. Every day the doctors made their rounds and looked at me like they were waiting for something.

Then one day I was released. No explanation. It didn't take me long to figure out that we'd been pronounced healthy just in time to be marched around for propaganda purposes. I was in a big parade in Washington, another in New York. Everyone called us heroes, but the title was bestowed as a way of forgetting.

I stood beside every breathing man who'd pulled a trigger in Iran at the National Houston Memorial while our President laid a wreath for the cameras. He gave a long speech that said the Holy Patriotic Crusade was over. There had been no official surrender from the Iranians, but we were taking our ball and going home. The country was a wasteland and Tehran an irradiated ghost town, so there wasn't much left to blow up anyway.

The war was over, and there was no one more anxious than me to get on with life. Benny was joining the Bureau and I planned on going back to school. After that I didn't know; I wasn't yet twenty-five and already had a lifetime of things I wanted to forget. A week before I was to be given my discharge I collapsed outside a bar in Staten Island. They shipped me out to a Veterans' Administration hospital in North Carolina the next day.

That second time I was in hospital, we weren't heroes any more. Concern gave way in short order to pity and then a kind of dread, a hidden fear that I was contagious no matter what the doctors said. As for the lab coats, they went back and forth, speaking to us as patients one day then scrutinizing us like lab animals the next. We were problem children, and like all troubled kids that meant we moved around a lot.

I didn't find out there were others like me until we were in

Ohio. They put us in an isolation ward subdivided by wood partitions. I caught glimpses of other soldiers in other beds, tied down just like me, as I and they were wheeled from one room to the next. I guess it should have made me feel better, knowing I wasn't alone. I was too busy having seizures at the time to think about it much.

Three more hospitals in the US followed. I could usually figure out where I was from my bed: staff accents, an open window, the occasional glimpse of a television. They never told us where we were going. I didn't think it was security or my usual paranoia; they just didn't bother any more.

The last stop before I returned to New York was Okinawa. We were dangerously ill, but not so sick that they couldn't fly us halfway around the world. The doctors still didn't know what was wrong with us, but this time they said it in Japanese. The VA was already starting to lose interest. For the first few weeks they'd flown in experts from all over the world to have a feel around our insides. They'd made some educated noises, then fucked off to where they came from. The move to Japan was an excuse to transfer most of the specialists to other things. By the end it was Doc Brown and seven other stubborn, decent men and women.

I had a lot of time to think while I was on my back. I read as much as I could, which was a challenge when your arms were restrained all day for your own protection. They kept the TV on the Pentagon channel or other wholesome programming. If they'd consulted me and my fellow spastics, we would have gone with porn or at least light comedy, not constant speeches about shared sacrifice set to brass. That left hours killed slowly staring at the ceiling, trying to think about anything but the future. I ended up dreaming about the past, and that was even worse.

Then it was back to New York, with a move to the psych ward thrown in as a homecoming fuck you. I didn't argue that much. After so many weeks in hospital stuck on an endless cycle of seizures and morphine dreams, I was half way to crazy. The new doctors I saw told me it was all in my head. I told them to talk to the other doctors, the experts and their noises, but they didn't listen. It was the only thing they were supposed to be good at. It wasn't until later I realized someone higher up was covering their ears.

Just when I'd started to get used to the idea of being crazy, I woke up in this new room. No explanation, again. No mental cases, just an ordinary ward full of ordinary soldiers who'd lost limbs, eyes and other parts of the body, another in-between place where everybody was waiting to go somewhere else, home or in the ground. The windows by my bed looked out on to another wing of the hospital ten feet away, but I'd take what I could get.

Nobody seemed to know why I'd been moved. After three days I decided to write it off as a fuck-up that had worked out in my favour for once. Then I got the letter and a visitor, and began to worry what else was waiting around the corner. Bad things always come in threes.

My visitor was my old commanding officer, Simeon Glass. When I first saw him in the ward I'd prayed he was there for someone else, but I knew I wasn't that lucky.

'At ease,' he said to me as I struggled to get up.

'Sir,' I said. It was an automatic reaction.

'How are you, son?'

'Alive, sir.'

'I apologize for not visiting you the first time. I had a lot of flimflam in Washington to deal with.'

In Tehran, Glass had visited every man wounded under his

command and attended every funeral. The higher-ups in the Airborne had written letters, but that was about it.

The flimflam had been congressional hearings, and Glass was the carnival's main attraction. Task Force Seventeen had been publicly credited by the President as the unit that had 'found' the weapons of mass destruction in Tehran, even though no one had lived long enough to set eyes on them before they exploded. I watched Glass answer senators' questions with words Stonebridge had tortured out of an Iranian colonel. Those words had made Glass a general and a national hero, and I still believed that every one of them was a lie.

'How are they treating you?'

'Better, now.'

'I had you moved here as soon as I found out you were in the psych ward. You shouldn't be down there with the malingerers and the freaks.'

Glass sat down on the bed beside me. It was the second time we'd sat like this. The first had been when I was in the stockade in Tehran. He'd wanted something then. I wondered what he was after now.

'What do you know about the Holy Land?' he said.

'I heard we're knocking up condos over there. I don't understand why.'

President Adamson had regarded the book of Revelation as a policy roadmap, and founded the Council of Elders to carry it out. As soon as victory in Tehran had been declared, the Revivalists turned their attention to the Holy Land. They were encouraging every Jew outside Israel to return to their historic homeland, and offering them protection whether the Israelis wanted it or not. If you read the scriptures at the right angle, they said that once the chosen people had been gathered and the Temple rebuilt, Jesus would return to the earth, with a few earthquakes, locust plagues and frog thunderstorms for the unbelievers in between.

'The people elected the President, he wants us to be there, so we're gonna be there.' Glass took a cigar from his pocket but remembered where he was before he lit it. 'Do you think all those ragheads we were trading bullets with in Tehran have just disappeared? As soon as they get wind of what we're doing, every Jihadi in the hemisphere will be bearing down on Israel.

'There will be real amenities out there, real bases, less bullshit. It'll be like Iraq, not Iran. Too many civilians around. I'll need your investigative mind more than ever, Strange. The Israelis won't like it if we play by Tehran rules.'

He fixed me with that look, the one that had persuaded me to sign up with him and Task Force Seventeen. It said that I was better than my surroundings, that I was capable of much more as long as I had the right guidance. It was a look that commanded, and damn it if half of me didn't try to jump up and do what he said.

'Your country still needs you,' Glass said.

'Tell them that,' I replied, and showed him the most recent love letter from the Department of Defense.

'Personality disorder?' Glass said, reading from the page. That's what the Pentagon had decided was wrong with me. The seizures, vomiting and blinding joint pain were the result of a negative attitude. It was the second-longest way of saying fuck you I'd ever seen, after the paperwork from my mother's health insurance company saying her claim had been denied.

'First they thought I was sick,' I said. 'Then they decided I was crazy. Now I'm just an asshole.'

Crazy people got pensions, benefits and the drugs they needed. Assholes got the kerb, hard. I'd never wanted to be nuts so badly.

76

'I can fix this.'

'I don't need anything from you, sir.'

He looked up from the letter. Glass wasn't used to being contradicted, and the novelty brought him no pleasure.

'Talk to me, son, don't just sit there sulking like a child. Is this about your last mission?'

'I still don't understand what happened.'

'We won, that's what happened. I know we paid a high price for that victory. They were good men.'

They were always good men. I'd seen men die, but never heard it over the radio before. It wasn't any easier to take.

'That mission didn't make sense from the beginning, sir. If the Iranians had a weapon, why hide it in the middle of their capital city? Why set it off then?'

'There is no if, Strange, get that through your head.'

The voice of command. Its pitch was almost the same as the friendly voice he'd been using a moment before. The only difference was that you usually found yourself doing whatever he'd asked before you could figure out why.

'I don't know why the mullahs did what they did, and I don't care. What I do know is that we have hundreds dead and thousands more in hospital because of that weapon you're not sure existed. They turned one of our cities into a crater, and now their capital is a wasteland. That was the hand of God, plain as day. I know that doesn't cut much mustard with you, but whether it was Providence or karma I'd say the universe has a habit of kicking people in the ass when they most deserve it. You're like Job yelling into the whirlwind, son. You won't get an answer.'

Glass looked around and, seeing no medical professionals nearby, lit his cigar.

'The only problem here is your overactive mind,' he said,

rising. 'Your curiosity is useful, Strange, but without an outlet it turns you a little crazy. They've kept you on your back longer than a Tijuana whore; all you need is exercise and fresh air. I'll take care of this misunderstanding with the Pentagon, and you and your disordered personality can get back to work.'

It was typical of Glass to think the memory of everything I'd done with the task force could simply be walked off.

'The war is over, sir.'

'Son, you'd better unfuck that attitude PDQ. What are you going to do out there? The civilian world doesn't look too kindly on people like us, Strange. More often than not we end up in jail. That's not to mention the fact that if the doctors are half right about what's wrong with you, you'll need a lot of expensive care. It's a bad time to turn your back on your family.'

'I'll manage.'

Glass had another minute before the pall of smoke around my bed summoned an angry nurse. He was in no rush.

'Some day you're going to realize you have a lot to be proud of, son,' he said, as if my hospital bed was already a casket. 'When that happens, you know how to reach me. We've got work to do.'

Once Colonel and now General Glass walked away just as a nurse turned the corner. She wrinkled her nose at the cloud of toxic smoke, and scrutinized me for incriminating evidence.

'He went that way.'

# TEN

## Our Redeemer Hospital, El Paso, Texas

The door opening snapped me back to the present. Through the morphine I saw a man I didn't recognize standing in the doorway. He was big, a lot of muscle and fat squeezed into the uniform of New Mexico State Police. He had dark skin and small eyes, the face they were set in far from friendly. The nametag on his chest said 'Gutierrez'.

'You don't look that happy to be alive.'

He closed the door and pulled up a chair.

'I ain't surprised, considering the way you drove at that roadblock. Nobody who does that wants to live.'

'I'm a little vague on the details.'

Gutierrez didn't seem surprised by that either.

'You mean before or after you shot four people?'

'After,' I said. 'I remember that part.'

'One of our sharpshooters in the helicopter shot out your back tyres.'

'They can do that?'

'At the speed you were going, the physics weren't pretty. Your car swerved and began to roll. No one was killed.'

I heard the disappointment in his voice. I had a few images of a spinning blue sky, stray frames of a spliced movie. Between seeing the roadblock and waking up here was a chasm of lost memories.

We were in a private room facing the street. Once the state had a compelling interest in my death, they'd spared no expense keeping me alive. Outside the window, a bright sun shone on a street of semi-detached houses. It could have been New Jersey if it weren't for the palm trees, but then again everywhere outside New York reminded me of New Jersey. A flagpole stood in front of a fire station across the street, the flag of Texas lounging in the breeze.

'This isn't your state, officer.'

'The marshals are letting me spend a little time with you, on account of you shooting one of our own.'

'Did I?' The flashes of that statie in front of the junkyard's entrance came back to me. They were still out of focus; my mind had been on other things when I shot him. 'I didn't get a very good look at the uniform.'

Gutierrez struck the wall behind him. It was an involuntary motion, a gesture as thoughtless as the one that had put a bullet in his colleague.

'Extradition papers are being drawn up as we speak. If there is a God you'll be fit and healthy in time for your execution.'

'I already tried to self-administer the death penalty, officer. There won't be another execution, at least not in public. You'd need a trial for that.'

'You've got a lot of faith in your lawyer.'

The morphine haze receded for a moment, and I realized that Gutierrez hadn't used my name once.

'You don't know who I am, do you?'

'You supposed to be famous or something? I don't care what kind of friends you think you have—'

80

'You know that's not what I mean. You took my fingerprints, DNA, hell, maybe even a cast of my teeth while I was in dreamland, put it all in your system and got back nothing. Being an officer of the law of long standing, you know that's impossible.'

Gutierrez kept his eyes on me, took his time answering. 'I wouldn't say impossible. Odd, maybe. You could be a foreigner.'

'Their fingerprints are taken at the border.'

'We did find a passport,' Gutierrez said, ignoring what I'd said, 'best forgery I've ever seen. If your name's Braithwaite, then I'm Miss Junior El Paso. Refusing to give your name won't do you any good. We can still put you on trial, and sooner or later we'll figure out what your name is anyway.'

'When did you put my DNA through the system?'

'Beg pardon?' Gutierrez said.

'How long ago?'

'After you got out of surgery, five, six hours ago. You expecting a rescue?'

It hurt to laugh so hard.

'Have you figured out why I was at that junkyard, as part of this ironclad case you're building against me?'

'Drugs or money,' Gutierrez said. 'We've been watching the place for a while now.'

So that was how the police had arrived in such a timely fashion.

'Yet you didn't find either in the car.'

'That only proves you're dumber than you look. Now tell me your name.'

'I don't have one any more.'

I followed Gutierrez's eyes to the morphine drip hanging to my right. I could see what he was thinking: not torture exactly, not the way he saw it. It would be more like a withdrawal of care.

'I could tell you my name, officer, but there would be no point. Rumpelstiltskin is as verifiable a name as the one my mother gave me. I don't exist any more.'

'The woman who you widowed, the girl who will grow up without a father and a little boy would all fucking disagree.'

I felt the tension in Gutierrez's body, waves of it making the stale air hum. He was keeping control of himself, but it was a close-run thing. It had gotten wild out here: border jumpers, drugs and guns, open warfare. The Elders would have encouraged a lack of restraint in these parts long before those policies made their way east. Gutierrez didn't follow the crowd. He sat motionless with a decency and stubborn honour that had nothing to do with the uniform he wore.

That TV I'd first heard was actually in the room. I hadn't noticed it before because it was mounted in the top corner, and it took a long time to get my head in a place where I could see it. The White House press secretary was on the screen, tame reporters pretending to ask important questions, the secretary pretending to answer them. It had been a pantomime at best when elections still mattered. Now it was just a sick joke.

For the first time in over ten years they were discussing something that interested me. The title on the screen said: 'Head of Homeland Security Resigns'. They split the screen, put a picture of General Simeon Glass, Medal of Honor recipient, etc., next to the secretary where he belonged. The subtitles said something about him resigning for health reasons. It was a more plausible lie than the old saw about spending time with the family: Glass had never married, and a few years ago someone had shot him in the head.

Ever since I'd heard the news, I'd regretted that I wasn't the one who pulled the trigger. I would have done it properly, made sure the bullet went through his brain instead of in the face and out the neck. You could trace every scar on his face from the picture on the screen. Most other people would have tried to hide the shooting's legacy, but I knew he would have been as proud of his scars as of the medals on his chest.

It looked like the fallout from Cassandra had finally reached the front pages. It had taken its sweet time. I thought the Elders would have forced Glass out immediately if they were going to force him out at all. Maybe they were just telling the country now, or it had taken them this long to trap that consummate insider into a corner he couldn't get out of. It was a victory of sorts, but for some reason I didn't feel much like celebrating.

When it had been discovered that Glass was running death squads in the Holy Land under the noses of the Israelis, all they did was send him home. The highest price he'd pay for his failure to get Cassandra would be the forced retirement that I was watching. They'd pack him off to somewhere quiet where he could live off the proceeds of his campaign of terror in comfort, shuttling between restaurants, golf courses and resorts until the day Death came for him in his untroubled sleep. The stars wouldn't fall from his shoulders or the medals fly from his breast. He was as likely to see the inside of a cell as I was to leave the one I'd soon occupy.

A bullet in the head had only slowed the general's dread momentum; exile wouldn't even break his stride. Glass would play the retirement game for a few years, lie low and wait. Sooner or later, the leadership would be afraid or desperate enough to persuade themselves that they needed a man like him. Then they'd come to Glass, his crimes forgotten or ignored, and ask his help for the sake of the country, just like they did after he was kicked out of the Holy Land. I might have been on the way to hell, but at least I wouldn't have to see it happen all over again. Glass wasn't my problem any longer.

'You're awfully interested in the news for a man in your position,' Gutierrez said, following my eyes. I guess I'd been staring at the screen for a while now. He thought I was ignoring him, trying to mess with him somehow.

'I'm going to tell you a story,' I said. 'It will be better for you if you don't believe me. The man who lived in that trailer, Marco Gambi, used to work for Fisher Partners.'

Something in Gutierrez's face changed. It wasn't surprise or interest; it had nothing to do with me at all. He stared through me, pupils dilating in the light of an unhappy memory.

'I see you've heard that name before.'

Gutierrez wasn't going to tell me what movie had been playing in his head, so I continued.

'Gambi helped them take someone from me. It doesn't sound right when I say it that way, since she was never mine in the first place. The Elders ordered it out of fear, and he took her for money. I guess the reasons don't really matter. I came here to kill him, because I couldn't imagine a world where he'd ever be held accountable.'

'Are you trying to justify yourself?'

'Reasons and justifications are two different things. The boy I shot—'

For a moment I was struck dumb by memories: the look on the face of Gambi's son, the amazement that such things could happen, and then a dozen other dead eyes from the war, some I'd killed or maybe killed, the 'I' so easily becoming 'we'.

'The boy I shot, when I served we called that collateral damage. It was supposed to be a reason and a justification, but we knew better.'

'Treadwell.' The name cost Gutierrez some effort to say. 'That was the name of the officer you killed. He was a good man and my friend. You say you had your reasons for killing

**84**

Gambi. Maybe that's true. But what did my friend ever do to you?'

I forced my head back towards Gutierrez. I had to look him in the eye if he was going to understand what I was about to say.

'I shot your colleague because he was in my way.'

The morphine made Gutierrez appear faster than he was. I saw the rage in his face, then one blink later he was standing over me, gripping the rails of the bed, knuckles turning white. He didn't move or speak; he was too preoccupied in trying to find the right excuse for what he wanted to do.

'If you want to kill me, go ahead; your reasons are as good as mine were. You'd probably be doing me a favour. Just don't expect your revenge to make a difference. I've been taking that brand of medicine for months, and it's no better than the placebo. Fisher Partners will be along soon to take me to a place worse than any you could dream up. You can take your revenge, or we can sit here and enjoy what remains of the day.'

The rage in Gutierrez's face began to lose its edge. It wasn't forgiveness. Maybe all he'd wanted was a confession, or he had a better idea of what was waiting for me than I did. He sat back down, breathing hard, exhausted by his anger.

'I hope you burn in hell.'

I turned my face back to the sunlight, to a world I never expected to see again.

# ELEVEN

## Sleepy Head Rest Area, New Mexico
*Present day*

When Jefferson had called me in the motel room after my escape, the only thing he was prepared to talk about was directions. They'd pointed me to a rest area just off Highway 40, a little complex with a petrol station and a few covered picnic tables set back from the highway in case families wanted to pretend they were enjoying the great outdoors. It was anonymous and easy to escape from, facts that made them popular for clandestine meetings of all kinds. A few single men haunted the place, keeping their distance from each other. The Elders had declared open season on gays and lesbians ever since the Battle of Christopher Square. The worse things got, the more we heard it was the gays sabotaging the factories, persuading foreign companies to leave, and destroying the stock market with their homosexual mind tricks. Between that official persecution and the decency laws that tried to keep unmarried men and women apart, it had never been so dangerous to look for love.

A butch man waited at a picnic table near the grid coordinates I'd been given. I didn't think he was looking for a date. I could feel other eyes watching me as I approached and wondered if the man had been propositioned already. I would have blown him a kiss for yuks, but he might not get the joke before he drew the sidearm on his belt.

The man looked right through me, on the alert for tails and maybe back-up. When he was satisfied I was alone, he murmured something into the mic on his wrist and said nothing. We waited.

I was worried, but not about the meeting. I'd played games like this before. No matter what I'd said, I hadn't been able to get Gideon to be specific about what they wanted me to do. I knew the price was a man's head, but not who it belonged to. I didn't like walking into this blind, but I hadn't had much of a negotiating position in prison.

We waited. The day was bright, and I hadn't brought sunglasses. For a moment the light—

The room I was in was about twenty feet square, judging by the way my coughing bounced off the walls. Shackles bound me to an aluminium chair that was bolted to the floor. My bare feet recoiled from the icy concrete, but I had nowhere warmer to put them. It was dark except for a single light pointed at my face, and quiet as the grave.

'Roy St James, Zachariah Reed, Marco Gambi, and Officer Nicholas Treadwell.'

The voice behind the light belonged to Control, the shared name of all interrogators. Control intoned those names at the start of every one of our chats, a spell to get me to talk. He never mentioned the Corinthian. I wasn't sure if that meant they didn't know I'd killed him or they didn't care. I wasn't about to ask.

'Why did Jefferson tell you to murder them?'

'Jefferson didn't order me to kill anyone. I've never met him, I've told you that a hundred times.'

We called the place 'IF'. I was supposed to be in complete isolation but voices still reached my cell, the result of stuffing too many people into a prison built by the lowest bidder. One voice had claimed that a friend's late cell-mate had seen the letters stencilled on a door when his blindfold slipped. He thought it was part of a military designation, 'International Force', back when we still had a coalition of the willing. Others said it was just a short form for the guessing game everyone played, as in 'If the Poles are still happy about having secret prisons . . .' or 'If the days last so many hours, then we must be at such-and-such a latitude . . .' In the end, IF was as good a name as any other.

The first month or so was just abuse. Most of the time they had left me hanging in this room, naked and freezing. I had to stand until the joints in my legs swelled so much I couldn't manage it any more. Instead of falling, the chains kept me upright, the weight of my whole body on my arms until they nearly popped from their sockets.

When they decided I'd had enough they'd bring in a doctor to look me over. He'd pronounce me undamaged, and then they'd escort me to a yoga mat beneath fluorescent lights. I'd pass some time there, guards banging doors and yelling outside my cell to make sure I didn't fall asleep. Then it would start all over again.

I don't remember how I got here. All I had were dreams, stray pieces of memory that might not be my own. I remembered a hum in my bones. The vibration was the same frequency as a C-130 transport plane. The army had made sure I was used to the feeling. Maybe that was how I got here. Wherever here was.

Voices. I was hearing them now or remembering the sound. I couldn't tell. One belonged to Control, saying I was ready for phase one. The other said I was still recovering from a serious collision. I recognized the voice, one Control called doctor, but I didn't know from where.

'If Jefferson didn't order you to murder them, then why did you?'

'You know why,' I said. 'They worked for Fisher Partners, just like you.'

Silence.

'Prisoner 48326' – that was my new name – 'you have been observed with two known members of the Founder terrorist organization. That makes you a member of the same organization.'

'I don't know who Jefferson is.'

It was the truth. The only reason I knew the name at all was because I'd worked with two of Jefferson's agents, Cal and Jack, in New York. Jefferson worked for the Defense Intelligence Agency, the Pentagon's spies. He'd been running a network of veterans as a check on the Elders. If Fisher Partners had found me, I didn't like to think about their chances.

Cal had maintained operational security whenever he'd talked about Jefferson, and I didn't think Jack had met him. For all I knew, Cal had never met him either. Concealing his identity from everyone who took his orders would have been the smart thing for Jefferson to do.

'I find your ignorance hard to believe, 48326. We have irre-futable evidence of acts of treason against the Holy Republic of the United States of America.'

Someone had changed the name of my country without telling me.

'Traitors to the Republic and those who stand in the way of God's plan will find only suffering in this world and the next.' His voice had the flat, mechanical tone of a telemarketer. I think he was reading from a script, and it probably wasn't the first time he'd read it that day.

'The only hope for your life and your eternal soul is a full confession of your crimes.'

A square of light appeared. A guard framed in an open door.

'Take him for a bath,' Control said.

'Can't, sir,' the guard said. 'All baths have been suspended, pending a training review. We lost two detainees last week.'

I wondered how many people they 'bathed' here, and how often. When you lay someone on an incline and pour water into their mouth and nose, it shouldn't be a surprise when people actually drown.

'Fine,' Control said, irritated by the order and that he'd heard it in front of me. 'The pinball machine, then. Just get this detainee out of my sight.'

They had the bag over my head before I had the chance to say anything more. Two pairs of hands – the guard I'd seen and someone else's – each took an arm and half dragged, half carried me out of the room.

We were in corridors. They seemed endless to me because I never saw them, just felt the turning, right, left, right, left. They hadn't bothered with the noise-cancelling rig. I could hear our footsteps, a buzzer, muted small talk between the men transporting me and someone who passed us in the hall. Screams.

The bag came off. I remembered this room. We'd had a similar one in Tehran. The original design had used bare concrete walls, but that had caused skulls to crack too early. This room was the new model, walls covered in plywood to cushion the blows just enough so they could be repeated. I could see the marks of impact, in fresh red and older brown.

A towel, twisted straight, was looped around my neck from

behind. Someone wrenched the towel back. I had no choice but to follow if I wanted to keep breathing. He led me around for a bit, pulling the towel in one direction then another, my malnourished legs struggling to keep up. Eventually he led me into a kind of orbit, spinning round and round, faster and faster, him at the centre. Before my legs failed, the hands let go. I was suddenly free, and hurtling towards the wall head-first.

Stars, darkness, the floor.

Hands under my armpits, lifting me up. Hands steadying me. The towel wrapping around my neck, ready for another spin—

I blinked in the sunlight. I was back in the rest area with the heavy, waiting for Jefferson. He continued to watch everything and nothing, giving me the same level of attention as the bins nearby. If it had been a seizure then I would be on the ground and he'd have disappeared as soon as I started to twitch.

I looked at my watch. Less than a minute had passed. Whatever had just happened, I hoped the goon hadn't seen it. I'd never met Jefferson before, and burgeoning insanity would not be a good first impression.

A car arrived, drove right on to the grass and I seemed to be the only one who noticed. A man emerged from the back seat directly on to the concrete island, never once touching the grass or the light. He was Caucasian, middle forties, gut a decent size for his age. A Rorschach blot of sunburn decorated his bald head. He wore a golf shirt and chinos just like my Mossad rescuers, the forgettable uniform of the modern American man.

Jefferson shook my hand and gave me an MBA smile. I threw it on top of the pile of other reasons I had not to trust him.

'You look better than I expected,' he said.

'Our Mossad friends could have given me a ride.'

It was Gideon who had arranged the attack on the highway.

He'd shown up in IF one day, posing as a rabbi right under the noses of Fisher Partners. His actual role had been closer to Mephistopheles, giving me freedom in exchange for an unholy offer I couldn't refuse.

'They were under orders not to transport you. Someone might have seen.'

'Who?' I said. 'We were in the middle of fucking nowhere.'

Jefferson pointed up. There was no way I rated being followed by a glass eye in the sky. Maybe Jefferson was paranoid about it because he did.

'Before Fisher Partners got you, you were looking for some of their employees.'

'I found almost all of them.'

The only name left on my list was Leon Becker. He'd led the team that kidnapped Iris. The files Gideon gave me had pointed to somewhere in northern California, a small town whose name had been knocked out of my head in IF.

'Becker is dead.'

'How?'

'Three cars on the interstate. He died instantly. Pure, ordinary accident.'

I hadn't decided before then whether I was going to resume my pursuit of Becker or not. I hated leaving things unfinished.

'Why are you telling me this?'

'Call it a goodwill gesture.'

I didn't yet feel like calling someone I'd just met a liar to his face. Jefferson wanted me completely focused on whatever dirty work he had in mind. The way he looked at me, the tight smile, I could tell he regarded the information as a present, a debt to ease me into his pocket right from the beginning.

'I've heard you like to be direct,' Jefferson said, handing me a large envelope. 'I work the same way.'

A bundle of papers and photographs were inside: paper-clipped, cross-referenced, stamped 'Eyes Only'. A dossier.

'Hard copies?' I said. 'That's old-fashioned for the Defense Intelligence Agency.'

'I like paper,' Jefferson said. 'Time-consuming to duplicate, easy to conceal, and if I burn it properly no egghead will be able to recover it.'

I looked at the photographs first. Most of the shots were of parade grounds, kids standing to attention. They wore the pseudo-military uniforms of the Sons of David. The organization had been founded to prepare kids from the Christian colleges for war. In fact, they did so much preparing they never seemed to get around to being in the middle of one. Instead they patrolled Wal-Mart parking lots and issued spot fines for whatever their adolescent minds deemed was indecent. The Sons were the go-to organization for the rich and connected to hide their children from the wars they supported, now that the National Guard was deployed in the Holy Land.

'Why is the Pentagon interested in the Sons of David?' I said. 'Did it become a crime to dress up like the Hitler Youth?'

'The Sons have become something different since you've been away.'

He meant since I was in prison. It was nice to see there was a little delicacy left in the country.

Jefferson moved a photograph to the top of the pile. It was a poster, billboard-sized but home-made, mounted on the white-washed wall of a building that wasn't in shot. Most of the poster was a shot of the Dome of the Rock in Jerusalem. Written over it, in big red characters, was 'Where is the Temple?'.

'Are you collecting graffiti now?'

'This poster was put up six months ago at Zion Academy in Virginia. Do you know what that is?'

'Sure. It's the Eton of Revivalist education.'

Among the network of Fundamentalist schools the Revivalists had built, Zion had been reserved for the progeny of the elite. It offered full board to keep the little darlings out of the way, an opportunity to learn the importance of networking from an early age, and the personal guarantee of more than two hundred educators that their charges would grow up as twisted and humourless as their parents.

'This is what the campus looked like two weeks after that poster went up.'

The buildings had been in a style that could be called Neo-plantation: Roman glory mixed with nostalgia for a lost cause. That was before a brigade had done live fire exercises on the Zion grounds. The whitewashed columns that held up the entrance had been blackened by smoke and pecked by automatic fire. Windows were smashed and blown out and makeshift barricades blocked the visible entrances.

'A poster did all that?'

'It was the beginning of what they called "The Awakening". The entire student body ceased going to class or obeying their teachers. They said their authority was illegitimate, because . . .' Jefferson trailed off and flipped through the paperwork, 'because the teachers and their parents are products of a corrupt secular society.'

'I know the Revivalists aren't big on sex education, but didn't somebody tell these kids where babies come from?'

'In the next week, a few dozen other posters went up,' Jefferson said, ignoring me. 'The students held meetings, debates and rallies, all on their own. Sources told us the talks were focused on bringing their movement back to its true purpose.'

'Reviving the Revivalists?'

That explained the first poster. The Dome of the Rock was built where the Temple had once been. Demolishing the mosque had always been a big goal for the Revivalists: it was another step towards the Second Coming, and the destruction of one of Islam's holiest sites would enrage the world's billion-plus Muslims, no matter their nationality or politics. It hadn't been done for the same reasons, the last few voices of sanity prevailing so far.

Some of those voices would be Jefferson's bosses in the Pentagon. They weren't as excited as the Revivalists about setting the world on fire, since it would be their troops who would be stuck in the middle in the Holy Land.

'I'm guessing the damage in this photo was the aftermath of these kids learning the limits of free will?'

'When the Elders heard what was happening, they actually encouraged it. They told the teachers and administration to stand down, and gave the leaders of the movement their support.'

'Come again? The Elders don't tolerate defiance, even by their own children.'

'They thought they could harness the movement's energy,' Jefferson said. 'They said the events were examples of the Christian culture the Revivalist movement was trying to create.'

That made sense. The Elders had been so excited to see genuine enthusiasm for their policies, they hadn't noticed that it wasn't under their control.

'So what happened?'

'Like good students, they followed their logic to its natural end. If their parents and teachers were illegitimate, then so were the Elders. Once they started mentioning individual Elders as traitors to God, Stillwater contractors were on site within hours.'

'Why use mercenaries and not the police?'

'The Elders didn't want it to get out that their own children were turning against them. They managed to keep a lid on it better than we expected. Anyone they couldn't trust was dealt with.'

'It wouldn't be too good for morale if it got out the Revivalists were killing their own children.'

'They didn't. Stillwater set up a perimeter and tried to wait them out. The kids inside weren't as disciplined. The siege lasted forty-eight hours, during which there were sporadic exchanges of gunfire. After some of the students were killed, the Elders lost their nerve and offered everyone inside amnesty.'

'Amnesty?' I said. The word came out of my mouth like a curse. 'These sons of bitches are putting people in shallow graves for nothing more than inconveniencing them, and they offer armed rebels amnesty?'

'Had it been anybody else, I've no doubt every single one, regardless of age, would have gone against the wall. Like you said, it wouldn't have been good for morale if they executed their own children.'

'Funny how they only remember what Jesus said about forgiveness and compassion once their own flesh and blood is involved.'

I handed the photographs back to Jefferson. He hadn't conspired with Gideon to spring me from custody just for a history lesson. I couldn't see the other shoe right now, and that meant when it dropped it would probably land right on my head.

'I'm not sure what you're expecting to get from me other than schadenfreude,' I said. 'That I can provide in bulk.'

'After the amnesty, the students were released to the custody of their parents. Almost all had absconded within a week. Kids this pampered don't have the skill to do that on their own. We found some of them in the Deep South, travelling under fake names with forged papers. They've been moving through the country, going school to school, preaching the word of this boy.'

Another picture. A boy who couldn't have been more than twelve posed for an official photograph in his Sons of David uniform. He was slight, his hair so blond it was almost transparent. The eyes that stared back at the camera were a rich, dark blue. The last time I had seen eyes that young and full of conviction, they'd been staring at me from behind the iron sights of an AK-47.

'This boy is too young to shave, let alone have a word of his own.'

'And a child shall lead them,' Jefferson said. 'The boy's name is Joshua Reynolds. What he's saying is an expansion of what he said at Zion: the Elders are products of the old, secular world, and are unfit to be leaders in the new Christian era. That's why they haven't built the Temple, and why God has withdrawn His favour and protection from America.'

I skimmed Joshua's file. It was thicker than a kid's should be. His father had been a preacher and Revivalist bigwig, his mother a dutiful appendage of same. He was home-schooled until he came to Zion, grades near the top of his class until something happened when he was eleven. The file didn't give the details, just that the father and mother were both dead, and not from natural causes.

'You think this kid started the Zion standoff?'

'Started it, hijacked it, it doesn't matter,' Jefferson said. 'Joshua Reynolds is in control of the Sons of David now. More than a thousand young men, each one armed and trained by the state. Add in the girls and new converts old enough to know better, and we've got a small army under the control of a twelve-year-old boy.

'The Sons of David are moving through the country like an

old-time revival, gathering converts and stirring up trouble. The Joint Chiefs have decided the organization represents a threat to national security. Your first objective will be to infiltrate the Sons of David. We want to know who is providing logistics and support to the organization, and who Joshua is meeting with.'

'And then?'

'You will terminate Joshua Reynolds's command.'

It took me a second to decode the euphemism. I was out of practice.

'You want me to assassinate a twelve-year-old boy?'

'I'd been told Gideon was clear with you.'

'He's never clear about anything, and I made a deal with him, not you.'

'Gideon was only the middleman. I'm the one who can get you what you want.'

I didn't ask Jefferson if he was out of his fucking mind; it was a prerequisite to conceive a plan like this.

'They're kids, Jefferson. Paddle their asses and send them home. Why can't the most powerful military in the history of the world deal with a high school club?'

'That boy has already caused the deaths of several people, and they're getting more violent by the day. Joshua has been prophesying a "cleansing miracle". He hasn't let on what that means, other than the end of the Elders and the ascent of the Sons of David, but you can bet a lot of Americans will lose their lives when he sees it fulfilled.'

'You're not answering my question. Just arrest the little punk if he's so much trouble.'

'His followers wouldn't allow that without a fight. The Sons are stronger than you think, Strange; they exchanged fire with Stillwater for two days and didn't lose their nerve. If we try to arrest Joshua or roll up the organization, Waco will look like a fucking picnic. And it's not just kids.'

Jefferson put a photo under my nose, pushed it into my hands when I refused to take it. It was a shot of Joshua Reynolds on the podium at some kind of revival. In front of him was a line of bodyguards, but they weren't teenagers. At least half were my age or older. The third man from the right in the photograph interested me despite myself.

'I've seen him before,' I said, pointing the man out. 'I can't remember where.'

'You probably ran into him a few times in Tehran,' Jefferson said. 'You served together in Task Force Seventeen.'

I took another look. Jefferson was right.

'What the hell is he doing working for this kid? I thought he'd be working for Fisher Partners.'

'Fisher Partners has had some personnel problems lately, ever since they removed General Glass from the board. Half of the old Seventeen hands left with him.'

I couldn't remember the last time I'd heard good news. Glass's removal had been more damaging than I thought.

'So what the hell are they doing with this child prophet?'

'That's what we want you to find out.'

'Before I kill the kid.'

'Look, this is the course of action decided on by the Joint Chiefs,' Jefferson said, visibly annoyed that he was being forced to explain himself. 'The whole organization is built around his charisma. Take him out of action, the Sons of David fall apart. We regret what you have to do, believe me, but this way will cost the fewest lives.'

Jefferson was doing his 'good of the country' face. It was the first time I'd seen it on this particular mug, but I'd run into the expression before. I'd seen it on politicians' faces on TV and officers wearing it up close, that mask of grim resolution that said they didn't like whatever insane, cruel idea they were proposing, but they were willing to order the deaths of strangers in service of a weighty task. The task itself was never spelled out very well; it always seemed to be whatever was most expedient at the time.

'I'm sure the Joint Chiefs are shedding so many tears, the stars on their shoulders are tarnished,' I said.

I should have been outraged: that I'd been rescued for this, that they thought I was perfect for this operation, that the operation existed at all. Most of the indignation had been bled out of me in IF, like the old quacks who had opened up a vein to cure an excess of spleen. I wanted to scream about the fact that when the American military apparatus wanted a child dead, I was the first name on the list. I would be angry, except for that voice in the back of my head saying they had a point.

'Why me? I'm sure you had other candidates who didn't need breaking out of a gulag.'

'Our mutual friend in the Mossad is a big fan of yours. Gideon says what you did in Las Vegas was some of the best work he's ever seen.'

'And what does the Pentagon think about it?'

Jefferson shrugged. 'We wouldn't have gone to the trouble of killing him, but we're glad you did.'

'I'm flattered by Gideon's praise, but not enough to be your lone gunman. He told me I'd have to kill someone, but not another— but not a kid. I've played patsy enough for two lifetimes.'

Jefferson narrowed his eyes. It was a conscious display of anger; he did it with a lot more tension than there would have been if it had been involuntary, a sort of clenching of the eyes rather than his fists.

'We can put you back where we found you.'

'More likely you'd just put me in the ground. The answer is still no.'

I rose from the bench and made eye contact with the minder. He made no move to stop me. I guess that meant whoever was watching us would finish things with a bullet before I reached the tree line.

'Gideon was supposed to be preparing you for this operation, not turning you into a fucking peacenik,' Jefferson said. 'At least he told us the extra incentive you'd need.'

Another picture, held up before I could turn away. It was Iris, her face framed in the window of a house I didn't recognize. The picture had been taken from some distance with a powerful lens. I sat back down, let Jefferson put the photograph in my hand.

'That picture was taken two months ago,' he said. 'I think you're as surprised as we are that she's still alive.'

She had a house. She had a window. It was something.

'We'll find her again, it's only a matter of time.'

'And then?'

'That depends on you.'

'So the deal is, I whack the kid and you save the damsel?'

'I wouldn't put it that way.'

'Which part, the rescue or the child murder?'

Iris had changed her hair again. In this picture she wore it up. Maybe she always did when they weren't interrogating her. It was a silly thing to notice, superficial, and that was why I focused on it. If I started thinking about her, where she'd been, what had been done and what they planned to do to her, I might lose my mind before I could help her. I looked at the picture for as long as I could stand, then turned it over.

'I'll infiltrate the Sons and find out what I can,' I said. 'Before

I do anything more than that, I want proof that Iris is safe. Benny's word will be enough. After that, I'll hold up my end.'

'You'll make contact with the Sons of David in Kansas City,' Jefferson said, as if all that had come before had been a foregone conclusion from the start. 'They'll be arriving there in a week and staying at least four days, which should give a smart man like you enough time to find a way in. I suggest you use your condition.'

'What do you mean?'

'Joshua Reynolds has developed a reputation for healing. It's one of the ways he gets such big crowds, the accessibility of healthcare being what it is nowadays. He claims most diseases are caused by demons that he can drive out. A number of other survivors of Tehran have fallen under his spell.'

'My condition,' I said, repeating Jefferson's words back to him. 'Does that mean the Pentagon believes us now?'

'I misspoke. Alleged condition.'

I had the final reason why Jefferson wanted to use me. My syndrome would be the reason that I sought Joshua out. Later they'd use it as another sign of mental instability when they explained my actions after the fact. You had to laugh.

'What happens after I make contact?'

'You'll get further instructions. Since you've made some things clear, let me do the same. This woman you call Iris has been in their custody for years. Any intelligence value she had would have been exhausted long ago. The fact that she's still alive says the Elders think they can trade her for something. The fact that she's still in their custody tells us their asking price has been too high. This woman is an asset that is depreciating rapidly. It won't be much longer before the Elders decide that she isn't worth keeping alive.'

Jefferson studied his watch.

'That dossier contains everything we know about the prominent members of the organization. You have two hours to study it. My associate will not allow you to take notes. Commit as much of it to memory as you can; if your cover is blown, every single person in that file will want you dead.'

Jefferson left the folder with me like an unwanted child and walked to the edge of the picnic tables. He stopped just short of the threshold of shadow cast by the roof above us, afraid of the sunlight and the open sky it shone from.

# TWELVE

## Morning Star development, Kansas City

I hated the suburbs. I did eighteen years in one, and the stretch ended badly. Morning Star wasn't really a suburb, but a product of the infill between the various towns that made up the Kansas City metroplex. It was an on-the-way-to-somewhere-else place, a 'we-need-a-backyard-for-the-kids-and-this-is-what-we-can-afford' place. A place built on the settling of dreams.

The suit Jefferson had given me was too respectable for the role I intended to play. I'd changed into a pair of dirty jeans and a work shirt on my way over, but that wasn't quite right either. Like Goldilocks, I wanted something in between: respectability down on its luck, dignity without the means to maintain it.

Kansas City had suffered as much as anywhere under the Elders' faith-based economic policies. Jobs had been migrating overseas in great flocks for years, and it had only gotten worse while I was a guest of Fisher Partners. Morning Star and a thousand other developments like it had no shops or jobs nearby, a place gradually surrounded by nowhere until it was in the middle.

Yet the ghost of the American entrepreneurial spirit was still present in the long-abandoned strip mall that fronted the development on the highway side. His name was Bob, according to the cracked nametag pinned to his overalls. He'd taken over the ruins of a chain chemist, clearing out most of the debris but leaving the gang signs on the wall for colour. In place of the wrecked shelves and used condoms Bob had arranged clothes racks in almost straight lines. They came from a trailer I'd seen out back in the strip mall's now abundant parking.

When I came in the door, Bob eyed me with a mixture of merchant friendliness and hidden suspicion that must have been the professional face of frontier traders: eagerness to make a sale balanced against the fact that most of the customers were armed. The white ten-gallon hat Bob wore needed blocking, but it managed to shade his eyes even in the interior half-light.

'Afternoon,' I said.

His white head nodded as he took his thumbs from the loops of his overalls. He didn't reach for the gun behind the misshapen cabinet that served as his counter, just left his hands at rest and his options open.

'Afternoon. Something I can help you with?'

'I'm looking for a suit.'

'We got all kinds,' he said, pointing to two racks on the right side.

I walked over and began to browse. There were a few complete suits and a larger collection of orphaned jackets and trousers, all arranged in no particular order.

'You after anything in particular?'

'Something grey and deloused.'

Bob laughed. 'All my wares are cleaned regular. Have a sniff if you don't trust my personal guarantee.'

The clothes were all under plastic, and smelled clean enough.

I'd have to take his word. I found a pair of grey trousers that would stay together as long as I'd need them, and a jacket a size too big that almost matched.

I added a paper-thin white shirt and a ratty tie to the pile and brought them over to Bob. We haggled for a while, but it was mostly for form's sake. Bob watched me count singles and fives on the dusty cabinet, and I took my time doing it, saying goodbye to every rumpled note as if it were an old friend.

'Most folks like one article to match another,' Bob said of my selections, only after the sale was final.

'You'd have to stock some articles that matched first.'

He smiled. Bob was more at ease now that I was confirmed as a paying customer.

'How long have you been here?'

'A while. It ain't profitable for a man in my business to stay in one place for too long.'

'I guess you haven't heard of any work around here?'

I might as well have asked him about miraculous appearances of the Virgin Mary.

'I haven't heard of work around anywhere.'

I nodded, made sure to display my lack of surprise at the answer. I was pretending to be one of the country's many itinerant wanderers, and it was important to stay in character.

'Is anything else shaking around here?'

Bob shrugged. 'Families mostly. Everybody doing the same thing as you, looking for work and not stopping till they find it. We got some religious types hanging around as well. Not government, as far as I can tell. Kids. It ain't work, but they'll trade you a bowl of soup for an hour of sermonizing.'

'Sounds like work to me. They nuts or something?'

'Harmless nuts, if I had to say. I'm Christian to the core, you understand' – Bob's words were sincere, but even believers

106

made sure to cover their asses – 'but that's no reason to act the fool.'

'Amen. What about the people they're preaching to? Anybody I should avoid?'

'It'd be faster if we talked about the people you shouldn't. This place is full of the usual freaks and weirdos the road coughs up from time to time. You got gangs on bikes, gangs in trucks, families chasing a rainbow, fugitives, strays, runaways and unattached gentlemen of the road such as yourself.'

'That all?'

'There's a few home owners still kicking around. I reckon they'd provide the best conversation, if you could get more than one step on to their property before they took a shot at ya.'

'I guess those kids have got their work cut out for them.'

'Well, they got privation on their side. A hungry man will listen to just about anything.'

I thanked Bob, scooped up my new wardrobe and was halfway to the door before I turned back.

'I need a hat.'

Bob's smile was wide, and not just at the promise of more money in his pocket.

'A man who goes outside without a hat might as well be naked,' he said. 'Can I presume you're lookin' for something in the eastern line?'

'Cowboy has never been my style.'

'Each man to his own. I think I have just what you're looking for.'

Bob rummaged through a cardboard box at his feet and came out with a grey fedora.

'Try this on.'

The hat was pavement grey. The brim was frayed around the edges and the hatband was missing, but other than that it was in remarkable condition. This hat wasn't a sweatshop special, a novelty meant for a night of dress up and then discarded; this was a piece of honest-to-God gentleman's attire. Skilled hands had made it, and for that reason it had endured.

'Where did you get this?' I said, trying it on.

'From a dead man. It fits you perfectly.'

I couldn't argue. It fitted me better than the hat I had left behind.

'I hope you found the gentleman in that condition?'

'Estate sale. I get a lot of merchandise that way.'

'Much obliged,' I said. I paid Bob and shook his hand.

'You watch yourself around those do-gooders,' he said on my way out the door. 'Ain't nothing free in this world.'

I saluted with my new hat, and left Bob to the rag trade.

I changed out of my old disguise for Bob to find while I wandered into the development to survey the territory. This neighbourhood had been laid out solely for the benefit of automobiles: wide lanes that turned gently into cul-de-sacs and two-car garages. There was no pavement, so I took the cracked and uneven road, untroubled by traffic.

I'd been shadowing Bob's do-gooders for a few days. At first glance the Sons of David were just like any other gang: new recruits were put through their paces until they proved their loyalty. I didn't have that kind of time. I had to impress them, and a knowledge of scripture wasn't going to cut it.

The road led me to a small park, the architects' attempt to create a centre for a place that had none. It was enclosed on all sides by concrete, as if the grass was an infection that must be contained. There wasn't much left to quarantine anyway, just a patchwork quilt of dirt and brown grass like the lawns I'd passed, struggling to survive without human benefactors and their low-wage garden labour.

Bob had been straight about the local wildlife. They'd congregated around a water main meant for the park and the development's only traffic light. An oversight had left both working, and the flotsam of the road had attached a web of hoses and cables to siphon off as much water and power as they could. They knew I was there as soon as I turned the corner, and greeted me with as much enthusiasm as the arrival of the plague.

I saw the families first. There were ten of them, a defensive circle camped around the cars that kept them moving. The lucky ones had electrics or plug-in hybrids. They charged up with solar panels spread out on the grass and whatever they could steal from the grid. Most of the vehicles had been designed with a range no greater than the school run and commute that measured out a suburban day. They'd get no more than a hundred miles on electricity alone, but at least all they had to do was wait for the sun to come up. The others depended on ethanol, cooking grease and whatever else they could find. A lot of petrol cars were still on the road, but I didn't see any here. Between supply shocks and the collapse of the dollar, it was cheaper to fill your tank with liquid gold.

These migrants were the new Okies, only this time there was no California dream, no Big Rock Candy Mountain just over the horizon. They had once been the settled class of a mid-sized city, until the jobs dried up and they were left sitting on a mortgage worth more than the house they looked after for the bank. More than one family had decided to leave the keys in the mailbox and see what the rest of the country offered.

The answer had turned out to be not much. Decent jobs were thin on the ground everywhere, and day labour wasn't what it used to be. The Internet spread rumours of work and filled the positions with the same speed, information and money travelling too fast for flesh and bone to catch up. There was always the army if you were young, but the days when it was a real career were over. You'd end up dodging IEDs in the Holy Land right out of basic, for a three-year stretch that suddenly became five, then seven.

Not everyone was looking for work. A few had the look of the hunted, an aspect I'd now seen from both sides. I wondered who they were running from: Revivalist officials, their corrupt law enforcement friends, maybe even Fisher Partners. If it was the latter, then the price on their heads must not have been worth scooping up the poor schmucks hiding in plain sight.

The solid citizens wore casual wear ragged around the edges, attire for a day trip that had become indefinite. The children watched me with curiosity while their parents tried to figure out if the stray dog they were looking at was rabid. I eased their minds by ignoring them.

I didn't have that option with the bikers who had taken over the centre of the park. They were unorganized, no gang patches on their leather, in some cases no leather at all, just dirty work shirts. Not the sort of crowd you expected to see lounging under what was left of a gazebo. Their transport was a motley collection of choppers, racing bikes, scooters, anything that could propel two wheels in one direction. They were more of a motorized hobo infantry than anything resembling the Hell's Angels.

Their unkempt faces watched me like the families had, but there were different questions behind their eyes. I knew they were adding up the contents of my pockets, trying to guess if I was worth the trouble. A single man was a target for predators, another reason I'd made sure everyone could see I was armed.

As I passed, one of them stood and made a big show of staring: a burly lughead with an uneven red beard and no other hair to speak of. He might be their leader, groups like those tending to favour size over intelligence. A plaid shirt hid a bulge on the left side of his waistband that may or may not have been a weapon.

I didn't break stride, but I did turn my head enough to stare right back. I kept my pace even, unhurried, a signal to all that his attention was as worrying to me as the scrutiny of a meter maid. It wasn't strictly intelligent, and might have provoked him to make a point while his boys were watching, but I wanted to let everyone know who they were dealing with. The big man glowered, and let me pass on by.

I left the square and looked for a quiet place to await the arrival of the Sons of David. I found an empty back garden suitable for the purpose. The house it belonged to and all those around it were empty, weatherbeaten signs from defunct estate agents now serving as headstones to mark the suburb's passing.

I kicked away debris deposited by the wind and began to do a little kung fu. My time in IF had done more damage to my mind than my body, but at least I could do something about the latter.

The art had kept me alive in IF. After Gideon's intervention got me the luxury treatment, I was allowed outside for one hour a day to exercise unmolested. A young guard watched me practise punches, dislocating kicks to the knee, and fingers to the soft parts of the neck. Since I was a terrorist in his mind, God knows what he made of my little workouts.

The house I grew up in wasn't much different from the one I trained behind, or any of the others on this street. Mine was older, built as part of the postwar boom, affordable shelter for a nuclear family on a reasonable income. I'd hated it then, hated it with a passion, but now I can't for the life of me remember why. In those days I didn't have to spend my waking hours hustling up the money to buy medication, didn't have to worry about what would happen when the drugs no longer worked, didn't have to sleep with one eye open.

If I no longer hated the place I was raised, I wasn't nostalgic for it either. Other than my time in New York, I didn't have much to compare it to: I wasn't at university long enough to get the hang of it, and after that it was basic and then barracks in Germany. I guess my time in what was left of Tehran gave me some appreciation for the place my parents had chosen for me to grow up, but that would have happened if I'd been weaned on the far side of hell. Maybe it was because my whole childhood seemed curiously unreal now, a story that had happened to someone else.

I tried to find my way to the perfect kung fu state of mind: no mind at all. My head wasn't in the clouds or fixated on a single thing, but in the present and aware of its possibilities, without favouring a single one. I'd been forced to live in the past for years and saw nothing good in the future. If there was anywhere I could find a little peace it was here, in the immediate present. I trained hard for an hour, got some sweat on my new suit so it would smell like I'd lived in it for a while.

While I was in IF, Gideon had tried to prepare me for how much things had changed. I doubt I would have believed him if he'd told me the whole truth. There had been no great disaster, no bubble popping or market crash. Foreign news had called it a collapse of confidence, the air slowly but inevitably being let out of a balloon. Corporations only cared about the rule of law as far as property rights were concerned, but the people who staffed them had to live here, and watch their backs if they weren't whatever the Elders had decided were real Americans that year.

Gideon had appeared in IF one day without warning, right

112

around the time I thought Control had finally tired of me. When they led me to the first interview with my new rabbi, I thought I was walking towards execution. Instead I'd been led to yet another interrogation room. The guards pushed me inside and closed the door. Sitting across the table instead of Control was a man wearing a blue chalk-stripe suit, yarmulke and a fresh beard. I made the rational assumption that I'd finally lost my mind.

'Hello, 48326,' Gideon had said. 'I'm your new rabbi.'

'Gideon, why are you here?'

'I appreciate the difficulty of your position,' he said, as if we were discussing a bad mortgage, not the circumstances of my likely death. 'I'm here to offer you a way out.'

Gideon turned the manila folder my way. The page on top looked like a transcript, and the person speaking was me.

```
48326: Jefferson recruited me through Jack
    Small, who I didn't know very well at the
    time. We shared a hatred of the
    Revivalists, and that was enough for me.
    Jefferson was impressed with my military
    record and my willingness to do whatever
    was necessary.
```

'When did I say that?'

'This is a record of your time with the Founder Initiative. It's got action, intrigue, thrilling deeds and narrow escapes. Some of my best work, in my opinion. My only regret was that I couldn't work in a little sex.'

'Why are you trying to keep me alive?' I said. 'And don't say Benny. That excuse won't fly here any better than it did in Babylon.'

'Call it a bonus for services expertly rendered.'

'Bullshit.'

'We need to remind Fisher Partners why they thought you were valuable in the first place,' he said, ignoring me. 'You can't be left here to rot: you know too many secrets. If they don't torture you to death, and they'll do their best, then they'll kill you and be done with it. You're a Jew according to their rules, and because you're still here that's a problem for them. The ingathering of the chosen people doesn't extend to their corpses.'

'Then they'll kill me either way.'

'Not if we convince them that your value outweighs the risk of keeping you alive. We're going to make you a convert, in every sense of the word. When I'm done with you, you'll be a reformed man who has embraced his identity and his covenant with God. You'll be positively eager to go to the Holy Land and help bring about the Second Coming of a messiah neither of us believes in. The propaganda value will be too much to resist.'

'Good Jew or bad Jew, I'll still end up in the ground.'

'The photo op only works if you make the trip to the Holy Land alive. They'd never let you go free, but anyone Fisher Partners decides is sufficiently broken is sent to work camps in Israel. That includes all Jews in their custody. Those Settlements aren't going to build themselves, after all. It's what the management calls "win-win".'

The testimony he wanted me to give must be part of a disinformation campaign Mossad was running against the Elders, but that alone wasn't worth the trip. Gideon wanted me to do something. It was the reason he'd approached me in Babylon, and it was the only reason he'd be here.

'I don't know what you want me to do, but you can forget it. I tried playing hero, and a lot of people died or disappeared. I tried playing villain, and the result was the same.'

114

'I don't know why you're being so hard on yourself,' he said. 'You haven't been completely useless.'

'How so?'

'The unwelcome PR from Cassandra's revelations has split the Elders down the middle. One group wants to withdraw from the Holy Land and entrench their power in America. The other wants to accelerate the Holy Land project at any cost. They call themselves the Puritans and the Stalwarts, respectively. There's some scripture at the bottom of their dispute, but I fall asleep every time someone tries to explain it to me.'

So that was the Mossad's real problem. If the Stalwarts got the upper hand, the only way they could move their precious Holy Land project forward would be the destruction of the Dome of the Rock, at which point the entire Middle East would lose its mind.

'I guess that explains the Mossad's belated interest in democracy and justice.'

'Both factions have withdrawn to the Elders' personal retreat, Sinai,' Gideon said, again pretending he hadn't heard me. 'I'm told by reliable sources that both sides split their time between praying for a miracle and intriguing against each other. The Puritans have most of the federal agencies – Homeland Security, the FBI – under their thumb. The Stalwarts have a lot of pull with state officials, especially in the old South.'

'And the Pentagon?'

'It goes its own way, as always.'

I'm not sure why he expected me to be impressed by this. The Elders had been squabbling among themselves for years; this new round wouldn't change anything.

'Answer me this, Gideon: are Fisher Partners still a going concern?'

'I'm trying to tell you that the Elders are weakened, but—'

'Yes or no?'

'When you helped Cassandra, what did you expect would happen?' Gideon said, rising. 'Mass resignations, free elections, a fucking parade? Just how wishful was your thinking?'

'I didn't expect—'

'That's not how the real world works,' he said, cutting me off this time. 'You've seen enough to know that. There are few clear victories in intelligence, and almost all of them are secret. The point is your country is inching towards civil war, as is mine, unless we do something.'

'No, the point is that good people are rare, while assholes grow wild the world over. I traded one for the other. The minute I knew Iris was in danger, I shouldn't have let her out of my sight. I couldn't give a shit about the big picture any more.'

Gideon paced for a while. I could see the gears in his head working, searching for another line of attack.

'For the last time, Gideon: why are you here?'

He sat back in his chair, a little disappointed I was in no hurry to read his masterpiece. He gave me the same look he had in Babylon and at that private airport before we'd parted ways: the clinical eye of a naturalist examining a creature whose genus he was still unsure of.

'I'm here because you're the only man in this secret prison who thinks he's getting exactly what he deserves.'

A voice advertising hot food in accented English brought me back to the fading sunlight of Morning Star. Out on the street, an old Mexican man pushed a food cart, his sales patter a spell to make customers appear in the empty street.

It worked on me. I bought a breakfast burrito with extra hot sauce, though it was the wrong time of day. I trusted his eggs more than his mystery meat, and as Benny had once said:

'Anyone who trades pancakes for a sandwich is a schmuck.' I was sure the general principle held with Tex-Mex.

I had one more thing to do before I took up my cover. I should have done it as soon as I met Jefferson, but I'd been blindsided by a sentimentality I hadn't known was lurking in my character. I took the letter I'd started to Iris from a pocket and forced myself to read. Half of it was illegible, lines jumbled, the confession of a man expecting imprisonment or violent death in his near future. Writing it had been an act of desperation, but holding on to it was just plain stupidity.

Even if what I did in the next few weeks bought Iris her freedom, there was every chance we'd never meet again. There was no one in the country I could entrust the letter to. Most of its contents were known by Fisher Partners already, but maybe not the connection between me and Iris. As it was, this example of bad penmanship was a danger to us both.

I found an old flowerpot, lit a corner of the letter and dropped it in. It made a nice little flame for a while, then faded out. I poked through the ashes, made sure it had been burned completely. It was the last evidence I carried that I'd ever been someone else.

Maybe it was the suburban setting getting to me, but I found myself thinking about my mother. Cancer had taken her, and watching her die had taken my father. I wondered if there was some kind of genetic predisposition to being a true believer in my family. It had presented in my father when he gave all our money to some huckster prayer warriors to cure my mother. I ran screaming from religion, and right into the arms of General Glass.

My mother had been the smart one in the family. My father and I had expected miracles, from God and the US Army respectively. When she returned to the synagogue, all my mother asked for was a little peace.

The Sons of David wouldn't come until nightfall, when the migrants had settled down and they could move among their marks with greater ease. I found some abandoned plastic chairs in another garden, and set myself up to watch the sun go down. The burrito was far better than it should have been, the only nice surprise I'd had in quite a long time. Between the food in my hand, the sun on my face, and the calm that always followed kung fu, I felt almost human.

# THIRTEEN

## Morning Star development, Kansas City

I slipped back into the square just after nightfall. The streetlights had long since gone dark in this neighbourhood, and the migrants didn't waste their electricity when there was so much easy firewood to be had. The square was dotted by small fires and surrounded by even smaller figures, a mirror image of the night sky above them. The fuel came from trees felled in Canada, shipped to the Far East to be cut and shaped to Swedish design, and then shipped back across the Pacific so they could be chosen from glossy catalogues and assembled by American hands with copious swearing and confusion. The scene was almost beautiful, but only from a distance.

I chose a circle of unattached gentlemen of the road, as Bob had called them. Fellow lost souls. My arrival wasn't exactly greeted with joy. They didn't so much stare as look carefully around me. A word might provoke, a meeting of the eyes could be read as a challenge. They pretended I didn't exist until I made the first move.

I took a bottle of whiskey I'd found from my coat pocket. Everything else that was portable and of any value had already been stripped from the houses, down to the fixtures and copper wiring. I'd found the bottle by accident, inside a space between the floor and the bottom of a wardrobe that should have been empty. My guess was that a quiet alcoholic had lived here, emergency hooch salted away in case an intervention by loved ones cut off the regular supply.

I unscrewed the bottle's top, took a swig to show it was good, and then set it in the middle of the circle. After that, I sat down and didn't say another word.

The first one to accept the offering was a white man in his sixties. He reached for the bottle with a labourer's hands, outdoor work from what I could see of his weathered face. He took a reasonable swig, declared the liquor's bona fides with a grunt, and passed it to the left.

'Name's Felix.'

Everyone out here wore a false name, so I might as well use my real one. It was no more genuine than the others now.

'Vince,' the old man said. 'Thanks for the drink.'

'The fire's an even trade.'

We passed the bottle around for a while. I tipped the neck to my mouth long enough for a good pull, but only let a sip's worth into my mouth. I'd need a clear head tonight.

'This used to be farmland,' the old man said.

'Goddamnit, Vince, not again,' one of the others said, a heavy-set black man about my age. The general rolling of eyes told me this wasn't the first time Vince had brought up this subject.

'I'm just saying the land here used to produce something, Gary. Now it ain't for shit.'

'If this place was anything, it was pasture,' Gary said. 'More likely it was absolutely fucking nothing, like us.'

'I thought farmers were an endangered species,' I said.

'Aw Jesus, don't encourage him.'

120

'I had a few hundred acres in Oklahoma,' Vince said. 'The bank took it, but Taft Food Services already owned me. I planted what they said, got myself balls deep in debt to buy the machines they demanded. Say no, and your contract gets torn up. Wanna sell to someone else? Better ship your produce over six states to find another company, and they'd have their own stupid ideas. I wasn't a farmer; I was a goddamn food technician.

'When Adamson came in, I thought I'd get some relief. He wasn't one of those Washington sons of bitches, pockets full of Taft cash. He was an outsider, a simple God-fearing man like me. Finally, there was someone in that sewer who understood what we were going through.'

'Let me guess,' his friend said. Gary's sarcasm was mixed with sadness; he'd heard the story before, and lived through a similar one of his own. 'Nothing changed.'

'All the old bastard did was take away my pornography.'

Vince spat into the fire.

'We might as well be endangered,' he said. He seemed to like the idea. 'Me and the fucking spotted owl.'

'At least you're too old to be shipped overseas,' a young man to his right said.

'Yeah, lucky fucking me.'

'When did they bring back the draft?' I asked.

'Where you been, the moon?'

'New York City.'

'They don't draft us, at least not out in the open.' The fire showed me deep, dark eyes and a face thinned by the caprices of the road. He was no more than nineteen. 'If your parents are friendly with the local Revivalists, you're okay. You've got a good job maybe it's the same, but who the hell has one of those nowadays?'

'Party bosses and bailiffs, that's about it,' Vince said.

'The more of us they send over, the better the bosses look, is what I heard. They get together with the cops and recruiters and look us young boys over like turkeys round Thanksgiving. I used to think it was all talk, too much drink and idle hands as the good book says, until they threw my friend in jail for vagrancy.'

'You gotta be kidding me,' Vince said.

'Honest to God, saw it with my own eyes. Said having no visible means of support was a felony.'

'And they used to say it wasn't a crime to be poor,' I said.

'They put some papers in front of him, said it was the army or a cell. I lit out of town the next day.'

There was a round of general swearing as Gary refreshed the fire. It was a raw deal, but only one of many on offer.

'You think that's funny?' the boy said, catching a smile on my face.

'Jail or the army was how they got me. I did break a man's jaw, so I guess they had some cause.'

'Did the guy have it coming?'

'He was one of Bryan Binn's prayer warriors,' I said. 'He conned my father out of his money by saying he could cure my mother's cancer, then blamed her when she died.'

Another round of oaths as commiseration. The general opinion was that I should have put him in the ground, not the hospital. It wasn't the first time I'd told the story, but my mind had been reminding me of things with an unwelcome vividness lately. I remembered the grey of my father's skin, as if he were returning to the clay he was made of even as light remained in his eyes. I held his hand, told him it would be okay even though we both knew it hadn't been that way for a long time. He just looked at me, but I knew what he was thinking: he'd watched my mother die and it had driven him crazy, made him believe in fairy tales. I guess that was better than admitting he could do nothing. I tried to tell him it didn't matter, even if it did, but he was gone before they'd finished loading him into the ambulance, in a hurry to leave this world behind.

Vince gave me back the bottle. I took more than a sip this time.

'Which war you get roped into?' he asked, when I gave the bottle back.

'Iran.'

'I was with the Mississippi National Guard,' Gary said. 'Isfahan.'

'Tehran.'

Gary sucked on his teeth. The others didn't quite understand like he did. I guess the stories about how much fun we were having had gotten that far south.

'Were you there, on that day?' the young man asked.

I nodded.

'Believe me, Vince, there are worse things than being old.'

'If you don't mind me askin' a personal question,' Vince said, 'if you used to live in New York, how'd you end up here?'

'My past caught up with me,' I said. 'Or I caught up with it. We've been chasing each other in circles for so long, it's hard to tell who came out on top.'

We passed the time saying nothing in particular. An hour or so later, I saw four small figures appear at the edges of the square.

'Those the Sons of David?' I said, to see what the circle had to say about them.

'Yeah, that's them,' Pete the draft dodger said. 'They're always pestering us about something. Hide that liquor or it will be tonight's subject.'

'Kids that age should be in school,' Vince said.

The youngest couldn't have been more than nine, cheerful as only a child could be in these surroundings. The good condition of their simple clothes stood out compared to the hand-me-downs and mend-agains of the migrant children around them. They all wore the same approximations of clothing that had been the uniform of the Great Plains a century ago: denim cut to the requirements of work, not fashion, braces, shirts of unfinished wool in plain colours, something close to gingham. Someone had kidnapped a legion of farmers' wives and kept them in a sweatshop for a hundred years, the fabrics the only thing allowed to change.

I'd seen clothes of the same type, not in discount stores but upscale boutiques. They weren't in vogue out of simplicity and poverty, but for the same reason the fashions of fifty years ago had become popular in New York. Both were a message to the Revivalists, and a plea: I'm doing as I'm told, move on, look at someone else. At least the clothes back home showed a dame's figure to the best advantage.

'Crazy or not, I heard there was a bowl of soup in letting them run their mouths,' I said.

'Son,' Vince said, his voice suddenly full of the sadness of his previous tale, a weight so heavy it had taken gravity a few extra minutes to pull it out of his mouth, 'there ain't no fucking soup.'

Their leader was a girl of no more than sixteen. Her bearing immediately set her apart from the others, calm and prepos-sessed, sure of who she was when other girls her age could only pretend to such feelings. She had dark hair down her back, gangly teenage proportions, and eyes that caught the fire in a way that made divining their colour impossible.

Her name was Sarah Bright. I could see enough of her face to match it to the school photo in Jefferson's file. She had been a sophomore at Zion Academy, class president, Bible club leader, Miss Zion, head cheerleader. Being high school queen turned out to be great training for violent revolution when the Awakening came. She wasn't their leader, but she was one of the organizers, a sort of high priestess. In all the photographs Jefferson had of Joshua, she was never far away.

They approached a cluster of five families making a vat of stew. I could see the change in their faces from where I was sitting. The expression wasn't much different from the ones Vince and the others had worn the first time they saw me.

'Beg your pardon,' one of the fathers said to her, though she was only half his age, 'we've all heard the good news. Everyone round here is born again. Our faith is about all we got left.'

'I bring you tidings of a different kind,' Sarah said, not missing a beat. 'Just as the birth of the prophet Moses was a harbinger of the Pharaoh's destruction, we are here to bring you a prophecy of the Elders' passing.'

Suddenly all that could be heard was traffic on the highway, the pop and spit of the fire, and actual goddamn crickets to drive the point home. If there was such a thing as a grenade of silence, the girl had dropped one at her feet.

The migrants didn't greet this declaration with a rousing cheer and the distribution of pitchforks. The fear and unease that had arrived with the Sons jumped tenfold.

'You are afraid,' Sarah said, stating the obvious. 'We are all afraid. But we are also children of God. Is this what we were promised?' She opened her arms to embrace the whole decaying fantasy that surrounded us. 'Have we not accepted Jesus into our hearts? Have we not denied ourselves the pleasures of the flesh, and kept His commandments?'

125

The sudden epidemic of averted eyes told me the question was not as rhetorical as she thought.

'Haven't you wondered, brothers and sisters, why this is happening to us? Our seeds do not take root, our houses fall as if they are built on sand, and our children do not heed our words.' Her audience looked more like middle managers down on their luck and she was barely of childbearing age, but the general idea was clear. 'What have we done?'

She had their attention now. No one was ready to stick their neck out and agree with her, but they were willing to listen.

'The problem, brothers and sisters, is what we have left undone. What the Elders haven't built. The mosque of the Satanists stands defiant, as it did the first day President Adamson was chosen by God to lead us.' Sarah could only be talking about the Dome of the Rock. She didn't think to explain why their sainted Adamson hadn't destroyed it while he was President, or how an immovable pile of stone could defy anything.

'Do not despair,' she continued. 'We are here to give you something wonderful.'

'Then why don't we go somewhere quiet and you can give it to me?'

The offer came from that big red-bearded fuck I'd seen earlier. He stood at the edge of the circle with two of his friends, leering at the girl. The families withdrew as he came forward. Sarah's younger friends turned to stare, frozen in place, too young and maybe too innocent to know what to do. The young lady surprised everyone by standing her ground and keeping her composure. It would be smarter for her to run – it was the smart thing to do in most circumstances – but I was glad she had the courage to stay. What happened next would be for her benefit.

'Gentlemen,' I said, getting up, 'it has been a genuine pleasure.' I meant every word. It had been a long time since I'd passed a few hours in quiet conversation with men of decent character. I might never have the chance again.

'You aren't getting involved in that?' Vince said.

'It's a long story. Keep the bottle,' I said, 'and stay well back. This will likely get ugly.'

# FOURTEEN

## Morning Star development, Kansas City

I walked closer to Sarah and the man harassing her. No one noticed me approach; their eyes were fixed on the crime unfolding in front of them.

'Whaddya say?' he said, grabbing Sarah's arm. 'Since you're such a giving girl, I'll bring my friends along too.'

His back-up sniggered on cue. I wondered if they'd rehearsed this tired little act of intimidation beforehand, or if they could only manage one working brain between the three of them.

The salt of the earth she'd been preaching to melted away, children carried if they could not be dragged, young eyes turning to watch something they didn't understand. The civilians outnumbered these thugs, could have scared them off if even five of the migrants took a stand, but that wasn't how things worked out here. Concern for others, like charity, began at home and never quite made it out the front door.

'I don't think the girl is interested,' I said, from the edge of the firelight, 'and considering her age, you shouldn't be either.'

It took a second or two for him to grasp what I was saying. 'I ain't no kiddie fiddler. This is between me and the little woman here.'

'She isn't a woman, at least not by law.' New federal statutes had made the agent of consent the same as the drinking age: twenty-one. The change made several million young men guilty of statutory rape, but there was an exception in the law if you were married, even if the matrimony happened after the crime. 'Made an honest woman of her' was now a valid legal defence.

'Who the hell are you?'

I could tell he recognized me from earlier that day, and so did his friends.

'Nobody,' I said. 'Just a man who takes a dim view of pederasts.'

He turned from the girl and walked towards me, closing the distance so his size would make more of an impression. Up close he smelled even worse than I thought.

'You should mind your own business.'

'And you should move along before I make a citizen's arrest.'

The human trash in front of me had provided the opportunity I'd been looking for. A little derring-do in defence of a lady's honour was the perfect way to impress kids with a narrow education. Red-beard's friends were likely to move on once I knocked him on his ass. As for the leader, I'd done the maths, and he wouldn't be a problem.

That was the reason I hadn't drawn my gun: bare-knuckle justice made better theatre. It had nothing to do with years of incarceration and torture at the hands of bullies like this one, men whom I'd never be able to repay. It had nothing to do with the sleepless nights, the feelings of dread and panic that came from nowhere, the memories that, like uninvited guests, arrived without warning and stayed for far too long. Even if it did, this aspiring rapist had it coming.

The gang leader fixed his bloodshot eyes on me in what he

thought was an intimidating manner. I wished he'd hurry up and throw a punch already.

He stepped forward and started to throw a hook. I saw it coming as soon as he moved his foot. I stepped in, turning away from his punch, my left arm meeting his while my right palm arrived at his nose with the full weight of my moving body behind it.

The crack was audible. The man stumbled back, eyes watering, blood from his broken nose turning his beard a darker shade of red.

Nobody moved. His friends stayed where they were, looking between us and trying to figure out what to do. I had just enough time to see him draw a knife from beneath his shirt before the other two attacked me.

Maths never was my best subject.

I side-stepped to put one henchman in front of the other. The first, a fat thug in a state football jersey a size too small, took a swing before he realized the side of my hand was already in his neck. He stumbled into the other, a Latino man old before his time, fear sweat reflecting the firelight as he tried to backpedal away from me. They fell down together.

By the time I'd dealt with his clown entourage, the leader had wiped the blood off his face and was on his way over for revenge. The knife was part of kitchen set from a big box store. It was an insult to the steel it was made from, but it would part flesh all the same. There was less than ten feet between us. At this range my sidearm was about as useful as a fucking paperweight; there was no way I could bring it to bear before that knife was swimming in my guts. I would have traded the forty-five for my old punch dagger, even a sturdy tree branch, but nobody made an offer.

He was unsteady on his feet, and not because of blood loss. I may have been dumb enough to bring a gun to a knife fight, but at least I didn't show up drunk. The skinful of cheap hooch gave him strength and resistance to pain, but it played hell with his hand–eye coordination and his ego.

Red-beard came at me wielding the knife overhand like a maniac. He was faster than he looked; I got a hand on the knife arm but couldn't get out of the way in time.

We went down in a tangle. He ended up on top, the knife aimed at my eye. Sweat dripped on my face from his tangled beard, more red than orange up close, his eyes swollen with adrenaline and anticipated triumph. He was stronger and heavier, and I'd be dead if I let him use that against me.

I pushed his elbow in with mine and twisted his wrist the other way. He tried to fight me, but it was physics that won. He lost his grip on the knife, and I used the distraction to headbutt his broken nose with everything I had. He fell on top of me screaming, all that cheap booze not enough to numb the pain. I rolled him over, grabbed the knife and stabbed him one, two, three times in the carotid. The screaming stopped.

I stood up, leaving the knife in his neck. The whole dirty business had taken only a few seconds. I glanced over to the fire where I'd been sitting. Vince and the others had taken my advice and disappeared. The man's accomplices had been too busy untangling themselves to do the same. They looked up to see me standing not far away, hands still red with the blood of their leader. The men pushed themselves away from me with their hands, so desperate to run they were afraid to spend the time to get up. I wiped my hands on the dead man's shirt and let the others go. There was enough blood on the ground already.

I walked away. I didn't want to appear too friendly, or too eager. The latter would make them suspicious, and a hard-won convert was the most treasured kind. I didn't want the civilians to see the triumph that found its way from his dead eyes into my own, an infection we'd both contracted from the handle of that knife.

'Wait, please,' she said from behind me.

I stopped, turned back with a show of reluctance. I hadn't had much time to see her during the fight. She was more beautiful than I'd first thought, enough to make any man uncomfortable once he realized how old she was.

'Like the Samaritan who did not turn his face from the man dying by the side of the road, so you did not walk away from me in my hour of need.'

I didn't know what a parable of a man showing kindness and mercy to a total stranger had to do with my justifiable homicide on her behalf.

'I am called Sarah,' she said. 'I am in your debt for the courage you showed today.'

'Forget about it,' I said. 'I just don't like seeing that sort of thing go on, that's all. I didn't think it would get out of hand.'

'Modesty becomes you, but we both know only a man with a good heart would have done what you did.'

I looked at the ground and said nothing.

'Are you hungry?' Sarah asked.

'Everybody's hungry.'

'Our camp, Zion, isn't far from here. We'll be having dinner soon.'

'I appreciate it, but—'

'I'm sure you've heard things about us,' Sarah said. 'Some of them might even be true. If you come with me, I promise a good meal and no more talk of the Lord than you can take. Let me say thank you.'

Sarah held out her hand. Her smile was warm and genuine. It had been a long time since someone looked at me that way.

I took her hand, and let Sarah lead me to the Sons of David.

# FIFTEEN

## Zion, the Sons of David camp near Kansas City

We drove to the camp in an old station wagon, Sarah behind the wheel. The children who'd been with her sat in the back and stared at me. I could hear their furious whispers, trying to work each other up to ask me a question. I watched Kansas City's vestigial suburbs go past while I figured out what I was going to do.

If the migrants in Morning Star had looked like a Boy Scout camp from afar, Zion resembled an army on campaign. Huge, floodlit white circus tents stood in neat rows. Four young men manned the entrance. They carried sub-machine guns and wore the same uniform the Sons of David had issued them, but all the insignia had been removed.

'Who's this?' their leader said to Sarah when he saw me. He was a tall kid still having trouble driving the new body hormones had given him.

'He is my Archangel Michael,' Sarah said. 'This stranger saved my life tonight.'

'No shi— seriously?' he said, catching himself just in time.

'I'll tell you all at dinner.'

'Thank you, Sarah.'

He bowed a little to her, which she took as a signal to drive on. I'd noticed the other boys had been careful not to look at Sarah directly, and it was more than just adolescent shyness around a fine specimen of the opposite sex. Jefferson's file was right. My escort was a big deal around these parts.

'Shall I introduce you as Michael?' Sarah asked me as we parked. It was her way of pointing out I still hadn't told her my name.

'My name is Peter,' I said, reverting to the first part of the alias the FBI had given me. I'd have to think up a new last name.

'That's a good strong name. As Jesus said to that Apostle: "upon this rock I will build my church; and the gates of hell shall not prevail against it." Dinner is starting soon; I'll introduce you to my brothers and sisters.'

She led us down the street formed by the tents. Everything I could see was clean and new, a big change from the make-do-and-mend world I'd seen on the drive to Kansas.

'You've got a nice set-up here,' I said. 'Who pays for all this stuff?'

'The Lord provides,' she said, and didn't specify whether that was by credit card or air drop.

Everyone we passed was around Sarah's age. I didn't see a single person older than eighteen. They wore the same pioneer chic, everything pressed and starched within an inch of its life. Like the guards, each teenager returned Sarah's greeting with a bow or a shy version of their standard greeting: 'And a child shall lead them.'

'I can see what you're thinking,' Sarah said.

'I'm wondering where all the parents are.'

'They would say we've left, run off. We say they're the ones who have run from Jesus, and we refuse to follow them.' She smiled. 'I am not as good at explaining all this as Joshua. When he speaks to us after dinner, he will make it all clear.'

Joshua. Before I had a chance to ask her more about him, we arrived in the centre of the camp. Hundreds of kids of varying ages were milling around, not doing much like it was the only vocation they'd ever known. Tables had been set up in front of a raised stage to feed them and hundreds more. Almost all the kids over twelve were armed, and a few under that were packing as well.

Behind the stage was a complex of tents closed off from the others and guarded by men closer to my age. That must be where Joshua held court. 'We are like the Israelites,' Sarah was saying. 'Twelve tribes that shall be called to heaven before the end begins. We eat, pray and sleep beside our brothers and sisters, as Joshua has taught us. I have the honour of being of the tribe of Levi. Tonight you will be my guest.'

I still wasn't used to the odd way that Sarah talked. Sometimes I thought I was listening to a professor of divinity who'd led a very sheltered life. To hear those words coming from the mouth of a girl too young to vote was as mysterious as it was unsettling.

'Where do I sit?'

'I'll be up at the high table with Joshua,' Sarah said, indicating the single long table that sat on the stage. 'You will sit with my Levites. Don't worry, they'll take good care of you. There's one more thing: I need your phone.'

'Why?'

'We don't allow phones in the camp. Joshua says they're an unlocked gate through which evil forces may enter.'

I had a vision of Satan dialling numbers at random and seeing who picked up.

'The guard would have taken it from you at the gate,' she

finished, leaving unsaid the fact that he didn't was because I was with her.

'When will I get it back?' I said, handing over the phone with a great show of reluctance. I couldn't appear too eager to do what she said.

'If you leave the camp, the guard will return it to you.'

Sarah called over a few girls her age. She began to whisper to them and the teenager finally appeared. Her posture changed, her movements frantic with the fear of what had happened and its excitement now that it was safely past. I could read the whole tale on the faces of her audience.

'Come to the tent behind the stage after dinner. The guards will expect you.'

Sarah set off with a wave, while her friends came over and surrounded me with their bright eyes and untroubled faces. I knew they intended nothing but kindness. That didn't stop my nerves tingling with the desire to run or fight as soon as they boxed me in.

'I'm Martha,' a blonde girl of about fifteen said through the pink braces on her teeth. 'We just want to thank you for what you did for Sarah.'

Nobody ever thanked me. It was disorientating.

Martha took me by the hand and led me towards a table near the stage. She and the other girls talked to me the whole way, asking if I was hurt, then where I was from, what I did, how I'd come to be in the Morning Star development when Sarah had come along. I kept my answers short and stuck to the Braithwaite identity, improvising as little as possible in case this chat came back to haunt me later. Their attention, and admiration, was focused on me the whole time. It was too efficient to be spontaneous – alternating questions, staying on a single topic, almost never talking over each other – but I could feel real sincerity behind it on account of what I'd done for Sarah. Maybe I'd just been in prison too long.

The table we sat down at was everything Sarah had made it out to be. Plates were heaped with fried chicken, rolls, sweet potato and some salad here and there. No one at the table touched the bounty in front of them, chatting away and patiently waiting for grace to be said. I wondered if any of them could remember the last time they'd gone to bed hungry. The kids back at Morning Star wouldn't have taken long to answer.

To transport and prepare this much food was an impressive feat of logistics, not to mention the tents, electricity and water. Whoever was running the back office of this operation, it wasn't these teenagers. I was damn sure they weren't paying for it either.

An organ blasted through the speakers near the stage, and everyone rose to their feet. Joshua came from his compound with an entourage trailing behind. Sarah was by his side, as well as an honour guard of young men in Sons of David uniforms. A man my age was last, by inclination rather than status judging by the relaxed, confident way he walked. He looked ex-military despite the easy pace. I hadn't seen him in Jefferson's file. He was the right age to be a Task Force Seventeen alumnus, but I had never served with him. As they mounted the stage, he turned and looked in my direction. I held his eyes, let him examine me. Whatever he was looking for, I hoped he didn't find it.

Joshua came to the front of the stage so we could all get a good look at him. He was a handsome boy, tall for his age, blond hair left curly and wild like a cherub's. It became obvious as soon as he spoke that puberty had not yet reached him.

'Brothers and sisters, we owe the bounty you see before us, as we owe everything, to our Lord. May He give us the wisdom to see how blessed we are. Amen.'

The brevity of his grace was a shock. I'd braced myself to resist the chicken's aroma all the way through a long sermon. As soon as Joshua sat, we did the same. The girls continued with their questions between bites and exclamations about the quality of the food. I didn't think Sarah had told them to investigate me: there were no snares hidden in their words. The questions were an excuse for me to talk about myself, something everyone loved to do. I relaxed, even smiled a little in spite of myself. I could only imagine how effective it would be on someone who didn't have a hidden agenda, a person who was just lonely and used to being ignored by everyone.

While we were eating, a group of teenagers pushed carts loaded with food past the dining area, towards the camp's entrance.

'Who's getting takeout?' I asked Martha.

She laughed far more than was justified, another element of the red-carpet treatment I was receiving.

'That's for the tribes. Many lost souls come to us for spiritual and material comfort. We do our best for them. They help us in return.'

'I don't see them here,' I said, looking around.

'Oh, they don't stay in the camp. Only Sons of David eat with Joshua.'

'And their guests,' another put in quickly.

My next question was drowned out by the organ. Joshua was standing at the front of the stage again. This time we didn't get up, just fell into a reverential silence. Joshua was smart enough to schedule the sermon after dinner, when his audience was full, content and not inclined to move.

'Brothers and sisters,' he began again. His voice was high even for a young boy's, but it wasn't shrill. Someone had taught him to project his voice over a crowd.

**138**

'We gather here in the shadow of our Lord.' The happy murmurs told me this bedtime story was a particular favourite. 'Not only in the shadow of His protection, but of His coming. We see the signs all around: earthquakes in Asia, the Roman empire reborn as the European "Union", the armies of Muhammad ready to join with the Russian Bear against the Holy Land.'

I hadn't been keeping up with current events lately, but I was pretty sure that if Russia was poised to lead a coalition of Arab nations in an invasion of Israel, I would have heard about it. More likely Joshua was talking about them protesting against our Holy Land project, which they'd been doing since it had started ten years ago.

'We see the signs, but the "Elders"' – he said the name like a playground taunt – 'turn away. The forces of Satan stalk this land, corrupting all they touch, and the Elders do nothing. Jews in our own nation ignore their covenant with God, and the Elders do nothing. The Temple lies under a pagan shrine, and the Elders do nothing. They dream only of their own comfort in this world, and kill or drive out the Godly ones they find. As Chronicles says: "And there are gathered unto them vain men, the children of Belial. Have ye not cast out the priests of the LORD, the sons of Aaron, and the Levites, and have made you priests after the manner of the nations of other lands?"

'The Bible commands us to honour thy father and thy mother. But we cannot love our parents and let them sin against their Lord at the same time. The Elders have made them Pharisees, clouded their minds with luxury and gold. As Jesus said: "He that loveth father or mother more than me is not worthy of me."

'Our parents were born into a fallen world, a cesspool ruled by lust and liberalism. The Great Adamson saved them from that lake of fire, saved them so they could give birth to us, the first pure generation and this fallen world's last. We love our parents, as we love all sinners. They kept us from the evils of the secular world, and now we must show them how far they have gone astray.

'We are the twelve tribes John the Revelator saw sealed as the servants of God. Judah, Reuben, Gad, Aser . . .' At the mention of their tribe's name, a group of tables gave a mighty cheer, like they were at a baseball game. 'Nephthalim, Manasses, Simeon, Levi' – my section erupted – 'Issachar, Zabulon, Joseph and Benjamin. One hundred and forty-four thousand chosen people, and we will be their vanguard.

'They call us wayward. Jesus said: "For I am come to set a man at variance against his father, and the daughter against her mother, and the daughter in law against her mother in law." They call us pagan. To the Elders, I say only what the good book says: "And now ye think to withstand the kingdom of the Lord, in the hand of the sons of David?"'

It was a strong finish. The cheers made my skull rattle, and they didn't stop until Joshua had left the stage, retinue in tow. After he left they served peach cobbler. It wasn't half bad.

# SIXTEEN

## Zion, the Sons of David camp near Kansas City

After the meal I went to the entrance to Joshua's compound. The two men guarding it, both in their forties, had to be ex-Fishermen. They didn't ask who I was, just took my sidearm and frisked me for any other toys: the thoroughness of the search meant they were looking for bugs as much as weapons. One pointed to the largest tent in the complex and watched me walk towards it.

The same man who'd been in Joshua's entourage met me at the tent's opening. He resumed his examination up close, so I returned the favour. He was thin but I could see muscle filling out his unadorned army surplus uniform. He had Semitic features, with dark hair and darker eyes. A line of scars started at the collarbone and worked its way up the left side of his neck.

'Shrapnel?' I said.

'Mortar.'

'They always land in the damnedest places.'

'Yes, they do.'

'Thomas, stop playing guard dog and let Peter inside,' Sarah said from inside the tent.

He stepped aside and let me pass.

'Peter, this is Thomas Bloom,' she said. 'Don't mind his manners; he takes Joshua's safety very seriously.'

'Is this our hero?' Joshua said, lifting his head from Sarah's lap, where she'd been stroking his hair. 'Thank you for coming to Sarah in her hour of need. I don't know what I would have done without my big sister.'

It was a term of affection; there was no resemblance between them. He stuck out his hand, but didn't get up.

'It was no big deal,' I said, taking Joshua's hand. It was baby-soft.

'I told you how modest he is,' Sarah said. 'He fought off three armed men.'

'Only one was armed.'

'Weren't you scared?' Joshua said. There was a new light in his eyes, the excitement any twelve-year-old boy feels at tales of heroism and violence. Bloom was the only other person in the room who had an understanding of violence. I got the feeling he was waiting to see how much I'd embellish the tale.

'You don't have time to be scared in a situation like that.'

What surprised me was how little it had affected Sarah. According to Jefferson's file, she was the daughter of some big-time White House aide. There had been layers of money and hired protection between her and the world right from the cradle. Tears would have been the normal human reaction to being threatened with rape by a stranger, especially after the danger had passed, but I saw no evidence of them on her face. She might be in shock, but I didn't think so. If she could treat the incident lightly, then maybe the siege of Zion Academy had been worse than Jefferson had let on.

'Where did you hit him first?' Joshua asked.

'The nose.'

'Show me. Thomas, you stand in for the servant of Satan.'

**142**

Bloom didn't bother hiding his sigh. I showed Joshua the palm strike I'd done to the redhead's face. After that he insisted on going through it all, Thomas and I re-enacting every detail, right down to where I stabbed the man.

'That is so cool,' Joshua said, right after I'd delivered the final stab to the neck. 'Could you teach me to do that? I did some boxing in school.'

'It takes a long time to learn,' I said as Thomas and I got up, playtime over. 'You look pretty busy right now.'

Joshua grinned.

'Can we show him?' he asked Sarah.

'It isn't a secret.'

Sarah stood up and opened the curtain at the back of the tent. On the other side I saw computers and a microphone in a small booth, a recording studio in miniature. Joshua beckoned me to the computer, a child ready to display a triumphant report card. There were four monitors, the first of which had a map of the country decorated with coloured dots, the majority clustered in the south and south-west.

'What am I looking at?' I asked, so Joshua wouldn't explode before he told me.

'The Awakening,' he said. 'The greatest, and last, revival in the United States. Each one of these dots represents a place where the pure generation has awoken to its responsibilities to God.'

'And you lead them all?'

'I wouldn't say I lead them,' Joshua said. He was still learning how to simulate modesty. 'I am in contact with every group.'

The other monitors showed that contact. There were emails from supporters and websites dedicated to Joshua. The monitor on the bottom right had a slideshow of marches, riots and posters inspired by his word as its screensaver.

'There must be thousands,' I said. What was happening was even bigger than Jefferson let on.

'By the time we reach Houston, thousands more will have heard my broadcasts.'

'Houston?' I said. He must have meant the National Houston Memorial. The city itself was still an irradiated no-go zone. The memorial had been built on its edge, a place for the nation to mark the city's passing every year. 'What happens when you get to Houston?'

Joshua only smiled.

'Speaking of broadcasts, we have one soon,' Sarah said.

'Now?' Joshua said, in the tone of any child being told to do his homework.

'It's important, Josh, the people need your message.'

'Fine. You must stay with us tonight,' he said to me. 'It's the least we can do.'

'I'll walk you to the tent,' Bloom said.

I was sure he wasn't doing it out of a desire to make me feel welcome. We moved towards the tent's entrance, Sarah holding the curtain open for us to pass. As we left, I heard Joshua ask if they were going to speak to Father. Sarah didn't seem to hear, just smiled at me one last time and let the curtain fall back into place.

'I gotta ask,' I said, when we were out of the tent, 'how did you end up with these kids?'

'You mean, because I'm almost twice their age, or because I look like a Jew?'

'Now that you mention it, both. Joshua didn't seem that keen on Jews still in the USA.'

'I'm here because these kids need looking after. Just because they aren't talking to their parents doesn't mean mom and pop aren't shitting bricks.'

144

'Are they the ones paying for all this?'

Thomas shrugged a yes.

'Do the kids know who you work for?'

'They don't like to think about it, but they aren't stupid. They know the money has to come from somewhere, whatever they say about the Lord. Always amazes me, how much people can lie to themselves.

'As for the second part, my parents were never that Jewish. They found Jesus when I was eight, and I got baptized along with them. I'm these kids' favourite kind of Jew: a Christian.'

'Same here,' I said with a laugh. It was almost true.

It was a short walk to the guest tent. We stopped in front. I could tell Thomas had more he wanted to say.

'I could use some help out here,' he said. 'There aren't enough adults to go around, and you've seen what happens when I rely on teenagers for security. I can guarantee you three squares a day; the spread you saw tonight is typical. We're supposed to be in this for our final reward, but I always manage to throw a down payment or two to my boys along the way. You seem level-headed, and from Sarah said you can handle yourself. Both qualities are in short supply around here.'

'You run this show?'

'Not in the way you think.' Bloom had gone cagey. 'Really I'm just another employee. Joshua decides where we go and what we do. I'm just here to keep the wheels from falling off.'

'So you're kind of like a roadie?'

Bloom laughed. 'Close enough. Interested?'

'I could do worse,' I said.

'In this economy, you most definitely could. Sleep on it,' he said, shaking my hand again. 'No hard feelings either way.'

I watched Bloom walk back to Joshua's tent. My guest accommodation was a small tent furnished with a cot and a foot locker.

I swallowed my medication with some water from a canteen they'd left for me. I could hear voices from what seemed like all over, the exuberant sounds of the young. I couldn't make out the words, but they didn't matter. I waited for the voices to die down, or at least go far enough away.

When I felt confident no one was nearby, I went rooting around in my underwear. Jefferson had known about the no phones rule and given me something so we could stay in contact. It was small enough that I could have stashed it anywhere, but I figured my pants were the safest place in the middle of people terrified of any hint of homosexuality.

I found the earpiece, removed the plastic cover and stuck it in my ear. It was smaller than the earpiece Gideon had issued me in Babylon, yet it somehow worked like a satellite phone. I'd never used a piece of kit this sexy before. I guess being the Pentagon's crazed loner had its occasional perks.

'Report,' Jefferson said, the way normal people say hello.

'I'm in.' The earpiece worked using bone induction, so I could whisper and Jefferson would hear me as clear as day.

'Have you made contact with Joshua?'

'Yes. The security around Joshua is a big contrast to that of the rest of the camp. He's got a detail of at least four armed men – ex-Special Forces most likely – around him when he's on the move. When he's at home you can add in the permanent guards watching the inner compound as well.'

'So hit him on the move. What about during one of his endless sermons?'

I pictured tonight's dinner. I'd had my pistol during Joshua's sermon, but there was no way I'd have been able to hit him from the table I was sitting at.

'He's too far away to hit with what I've got, and they frisk anyone who gets close within an inch of their life. Even if I

146

pulled it off I wouldn't get ten feet before his entourage dropped me.'

The silence on the other end of the line told me that consideration was a distant second in Jefferson's mind.

'I'm sure you'll think of something.'

'I thought you wanted me to find out who was backing the Sons of David.'

'And?'

I got the feeling that Jefferson was still more interested in ending Joshua as a problem than finding out who was behind him.

'Joshua's head minder is a man called Thomas Bloom. I didn't see him in your file, but he looks military so you should have a service record.'

'We'll take a look.'

'Bloom claimed he'd been hired by some worried parents. He wasn't specific with names, but he did say that's where the money came from.'

'They were the first people we suspected,' Jefferson said. 'We've been digging into their financials for the last few weeks and haven't turned up a thing. If they are funding the Sons of David, they're hiding it well.'

'Could the parents, even if they're big-time Revivalists, afford all this?', I thought of all the food that had been served out tonight. I may have been in a tent, but it was large and came with a padded cot. The set-up was closer to a gentleman's idea of roughing it than a military campaign. Add in all the vehicles and the fuel to run them and you had a very expensive roadshow.

'That's for you to find out.'

'Joshua mentioned something about a father. He couldn't have meant his own.'

Jefferson's file had had only the highlights, but it had been unambiguous about his being an orphan.

'Do you know anything more about his parents than what was in the file?' I asked.

'Not really. There was some scandal there, but I don't know what. Any foreign gossip site should have more.'

'I'll see what I can find.'

'You'd better come up with something soon, for your girl's sake,' Jefferson said. 'Or you could just do what you're supposed to.'

I didn't need to be reminded of why I was doing this, and Jefferson knew that.

'If you're so desperate for this kid's head, why don't you use a drone?' I said. 'A missile from a thousand feet up is the way the Pentagon usually solves its problems.'

'Gideon thinks you're funny,' Jefferson said. 'I don't. Call me again when you have something worth reporting, like the fact that Joshua is dead.'

The line went quiet. I hid the earpiece, took off my shoes and lay down. I closed my eyes, but sleep didn't come. Jefferson's mention of Gideon called the Mossad agent up in my mind like an evocation.

'*Sh'ma Yis'ra'eil Adonai Eloheinu Adonai echad,*' Gideon had said to me, tracing the Hebrew with his finger.

'*Sh'ma Yis'ra'eil Adonai El*— Fuck,' I said, and pushed the Torah away. Gideon and I had been at this for weeks. Learning Hebrew was one part of his project to turn me into a model Jew. My parents had had me circumcised when I was born. It had been for health rather than religious reasons, but at least I had that part covered.

Whatever Gideon had said to Fisher Partners had changed my

148

circumstances completely. I was given food and water on a regular basis. The lights actually went off in my cell. I hadn't been interrogated by Control or anyone else since Gideon showed up. Even the guards treated me better, though they couldn't resist a shove every now and then. I didn't take it personally. Everyone had a quota to fill these days.

'I'm still waiting for you to develop some enthusiasm, Felix,' Gideon said.

'You're wasting a lot of time on my account. I would have thought the Mossad would keep you too busy to fly out here twice a week.'

Gideon smiled at my latest attempt to learn where we were. After weeks, he still wouldn't admit how he got to IF, let alone where it was.

'If you don't want to study, then are you ready to tell me why you're so intent on committing suicide by private military contractor?'

'I didn't think you'd care.'

'Don't be like that,' Gideon said, pouting from behind the pious beard he had grown for his cover. 'You know I'm curious by nature, and teaching you Hebrew isn't the most interesting job I've had.'

'If you're so bored, why don't you find someone who isn't in custody to do your dirty work?'

'It has to be you,' he said. 'You're exactly what the operation calls for, assuming your stability isn't in question.'

'Stability?'

'Well, you did kill several people before a long period of torture and incarceration. It's a natural concern.'

'You weren't concerned about my stability when I was killing for you.'

'You didn't kill for me. You don't kill for anyone.'

That was a question in a statement's clothing. I pretended to read Hebrew instead of rising to the bait.

'I'm your rabbi. You can tell me anything.'

'Jews don't do confession, remember?'

'Humour me. There's not much entertainment around here unless you're a sadist,' Gideon said. 'Maybe if I ask the question another way: why didn't you go with Benny to Israel?'

'I had unfinished business. You know that better than anyone.'

Gideon shook his head. 'Straight-up revenge doesn't cut it. You're too smart for that.'

'Since when did vengeance have anything to do with smarts?'

'You didn't know what to do with yourself after you killed the Corinthian. You didn't expect to survive.'

'Says who?'

'Said that lost look on your face the last time I saw you. You might as well have drawn me a fucking map.'

'Do rabbis swear?'

Gideon shrugged. 'Mine does. The point is, just going around killing people isn't your style, even if they have it coming. So I'll ask you again: why didn't you go with Benny?'

I said nothing. Somewhere down the hall, a metal door opened, briefly, and then closed.

'I got all day,' Gideon said. 'We both do.'

The extractor fan buzzed.

'I knew no one would be punished for what they'd done, no one important anyway. If the atrocities ever did come to light, you and I both know Glass and the Elders would never face charges. The good of the country and all that shit. The Fishermen I killed were worthless, but that doesn't mean the others won't hear and wonder if there's someone else like me out there. Maybe I should have hanged their bodies at the crossroads where they sold their souls, just to make it clear.

Gideon looked at the ceiling for a while. I guess he was trying to decide if he believed me.

'Not good enough.'

'Not good enough?'

Gideon picked up the Torah and hunted through its pages.

'I believe Deuteronomy is applicable here,' he said.

'That's the first time I've heard that in conversation.'

Gideon found the passage and turned it to face me.

הָוהִי דָליחְנִי רֶשֵׁא רְצָרַא לוּבּג-תֵא תְּשַׁלשׁוּ דֶּרְדַה דְל וְיכָּת ג
חֵצ-לָכ הָמָשׁ סוּנָל, הָיהוּ דְיהֹלֵא

והֵער-תֵא הֵכּי רֶשֵׁא     יָחו הָמָשׁ סוּנֵי-רֶשֵׁא חֵצְרָה רַבְּד הֶזו ד
סְשׁלשׁ למְתמ וֹל אֶנשׁ-אל אוֹהוּ, תַעַד-יִלבּב.

וְזַרְגַב וֹדָי הָחְדְנוּ, סֵיצֵע בּטְחַל, רֵעֵיב והֵער-תֵא אֹבָי רֶשֵׁאוּ ה
סוּנִי, אוה: תֵּמָו והֵער-תֵא אָצָמוּ וְעָה-וֹמ לְוַדַבָה לַשָׁנוּ, וְעָה תְּרְכֵל
יָחוֹ--הֵלֵאָה-סֵירָעֵה תַחַא-לֵא.

I held out my hand for the Bible. Gideon demurred.

'If you want me to learn this moral lesson inside the next six hours, you'd better hand over the translation.'

According to the plagiarists who had worked for King James, it went something like this: 'Thou shalt separate three cities for thee in the midst of thy land . . . which the LORD thy God giveth thee to inherit . . . that every slayer may flee thither. And this is the case of the slayer, which shall flee thither, that he may live: Whoso killeth his neighbour ignorantly, whom he hated not in time past.'

'Sanctuary,' Gideon said. 'You were offered it in Israel, and you refused.'

'I didn't kill those men by accident.'

Gideon stroked his beard – a new affectation he was still getting the hang of – and let my mind fill the silence. He must know about the boy, Gambi's son. It would have been in the police report.

'Maybe you should read the rest of that chapter,' I said. '"But if any man hate his neighbour, and lie in wait for him, and rise up against him, and smite him mortally that he die, and fleeth into one of these cities: Then the elders of his city shall send and fetch him thence, and deliver him into the hand of the avenger of blood, that he may die . . . And thine eye shall not pity; but life shall go for life, eye for eye, tooth for tooth, hand for hand, foot for foot."'

I closed the Bible. Gideon watched me, as he always did, behind the false front of his eyes.

'I killed a child, Gideon. I've killed boys before, but they were pointing a gun at me and we were both victims of circumstance. If I try I can say the same thing about Officer Treadwell, but not the kid.' I saw him again, standing in that little room with the holes in his chest, staring at me. 'I don't even know his name.'

'His name was Michael,' Gideon said. 'He was in the wrong place at the wrong time. You want to call me a bad rabbi and an even worse person, go ahead, but we both know that's how it was. Reasons don't often enter into it, and when they do they rarely make sense.'

I shook my head, so hard Gideon became concerned.

'I always thought I hated the war, but I must have been lying to myself all these years, because I loved it so much I made one of my own. I had more cause for violence than we'd ever had in Tehran, but the result was the same: a lot of killing for nothing.' Iris was still missing, maybe dead. The fishers of men still went about their work, my quarry appendages they'd already cut off before I killed them.

'The world came at me, I used to come back harder and fuck

the consequences. I spent so much time in Tehran telling myself I was different, and then one day I turned around and found them looking at me in the mirror. Maybe that boy shouldn't have been there, but neither should I, and only one of us had a choice. Everything Glass said about me was right, Gideon. I belong in here. We all do.'

He finally had his answer. With his curiosity sated, I fully expected Gideon to leave me here to rot.

'We Jews don't go in much for redemption,' Gideon said. 'That's the other guy's racket. I can't undo that kid's wounds any more than I can cure you. What I can offer is the one thing you really want: something more to do than just roll over and die.'

The fact that I was in a tent in Joshua's camp made it obvious who had won the argument. I'd shot a child by accident, and now I'd just met the boy that Gideon and Jefferson wanted me to kill in cold blood. I'd wanted a second chance, and now I had to live with the consequences.

# SEVENTEEN

## Zion, the Sons of David camp near Kansas City

I accepted Thomas's offer the next day. I expected guard duty, babysitting of one kind or another. Instead I was put to work doing manual labour: unloading boxes from trucks and fetching anything that needed to be carried somewhere. It was honest, if unskilled work.

I loved it. All I had to think about was getting box A to point B, no questions, no grey areas. These days of lifting were the first stage in my absorption into Joshua's flock. It was called 'The Humbling', that old Protestant idea of the nobility of work. Our teenaged foreman reminded us the first day that making a living by the sweat of his brow was God's punishment on Adam after the Fall. The pain of childbirth was Eve's, but the girls got off with cooking rather than forced pregnancy.

In the meantime I tried to figure out what I was carrying and where it came from. The what was pretty innocuous: food, toiletries, essentials for a small town on the move. The where were regional wholesalers so desperate for the Sons' large orders that they drove them to Zion at their own expense. I memorized a few licence numbers, but they wouldn't be enough on their own for Jefferson to figure out where the money was coming from.

I didn't see Thomas for a few days. He had left the camp but no one seemed to know where he'd gone. One morning he showed up in a truck while we were unloading boxes of paper. Instead of flagging me or my fellow humbles over to deal with the truck, some of his guards showed up and did the unloading themselves.

They weren't new recruits like me. Thomas had said he was shorthanded when it came to muscle, so it made no sense to have those guys doing manual labour. They unloaded half the truck, then Thomas told our foreman to deal with the rest. I made sure I was the first guy available. The boxes were made of wood and stamped with the name of a National Guard armoury.

Their contents became plain as soon as I was told where to take them. The Sons had a firing range set up on the other side of the dining area. I'd wanted to give it a look over, but until now I'd had no reason to be there. When I delivered the ammunition there were about a hundred Sons engaged in shooting practice and close-order drills. I had to admit, for a bunch of teenagers their discipline was impressive. Jefferson had said they'd held out against some of the country's best mercenaries for two days. Now I could see why.

I'd seen people like me deliver all manner of things to Bloom and his people before; if those crates had held just bullets they would have let us do the lifting. For the moment I'd have to assume that those other crates had come from the National Guard as well. They could be surplus munitions but I doubted it. The only way I was going to figure out where all this stuff was coming from was to nose around Bloom's office.

That was going to be easier said than done. The place was either occupied or guarded twenty-four hours a day. I needed something damning to slow Jefferson down, convince him that killing Joshua would cause more problems than it solved. The best way to do that was to find out who was controlling him. Hopefully they'd be bigger game than a deluded boy.

I went back through the dining area just in time for lunch. It was a communal affair, like all meals. The tables outside were already filling up when I got to the kitchens. They were set up along professional lines even though they were in tents. One of these penitent women was frying something. The smell was familiar for some reason.

Control held an automatic against my head. It had been recently cleaned, the smell of gun oil still fresh. I could smell another kind of oil, grease on Control's fingers, definitely fast food, the residue of his lunch, or dinner, or breakfast. There were no days here, let alone mealtimes. I wondered what burger joints had franchises in secret prisons, what pizza chains delivered to a place that didn't exist. The gun to my head didn't stop my mouth from watering.

'Nothing,' Control said, looking in my eyes. 'That's what fascinates me about atheists who resist. Moslems, I understand,' he said, pronouncing it with an o like a fucking Crusader, 'they think they're going to paradise, to be with their virgins and the pimp God who'll give the women to them. Completely wrong, Satanic, but understandable at least.

'Atheists, on the other hand,' he continued, grinding the barrel of the gun into my skin in case I'd forgotten it was there, 'are a mystery to me. You honestly believe there's nothing waiting for you after I pull this trigger, and yet you resist.'

Control gave me the same impersonal smile he'd used to start our initial interviews. I was used to seeing it on the faces of waitresses and shop assistants, muscles in the face contracting under the demands of a training manual rather than emotion.

156

I couldn't remember the first time he'd let me see his face. For the first few weeks Control had been just a voice behind a light, talking about my supposed crimes while gravity, water or bare hands destroyed my body. No questions, no attempts to elicit any real information. Maybe the whole thing was done just to show me who was boss.

One day I was taken from my cell. A medic looked at my wounds. They gave me food my stomach rejected after starving for so long. I was brought back to the same room they always did their work in, but this time there was soft lighting and a human Control waiting at his desk. He was in his mid-twenties but looked older: straw-coloured hair thinning at the crown, heavy black bags under his eyes earned by substituting caffeine for sleep. I wanted to think it was what he did in this place that kept him awake, but that was probably true only in the sense that he was overworked. Control's body was lumpy rather than fat, his young metabolism keeping the natural consequences of a bad diet and sedentary work momentarily at bay. I thought he looked like hell, and was glad there was no reflection of myself to compare it to.

His wardrobe was the same business casual that Stonebridge had worn when he did interrogations in Tehran. I'd tried to count the passage of time by the change in the colour of his golf shirts but lost faith in Control's commitment to good grooming.

'Atheists are the most arrogant people on earth,' he said. I sensed the beginning of one of his long, boring monologues, a funny way of trying to get someone to talk. 'Their self-belief is so strong they see themselves as the centre of the universe, and the only way to do that is to murder God.'

'Are you doing a correspondence course in philosophy in between having people tortured?'

'The Comedian,' Control said. 'That's what the other 'gators call you. You've got a little fan club.'

I didn't think Control was holding a gun to my head out of anger, or even as a tactic to get me to talk. His voice was academic, almost distracted. The gun was there to satisfy a point of curiosity.

'Most of our clients fall back on something pretty quickly: faith in a pagan God, family ties, even their own importance. You wouldn't believe how many people I've had in here who demand I call this official or that secretary, try to tell me that it's all a big mistake. God, those idiots make me laugh,' he said, but didn't.

'I know everything about you, 48326. I know you've got nothing, no one, certainly no God to watch over you, yet you've held out longer than most. Your reckless, nihilistic individualism has brought you here,' he continued, fresh pressure on the barrel the only sign he still knew I was there, 'and yet your pride is so strong that you believe you can stand alone against both God and the Republic. What do you think your stubbornness will get you?'

'Nothing. If I help you, I'll have to live with it. I can't count on a bearded man in the sky to forgive me.'

The woman who'd been frying, bacon as it turned out, was looking at me. Nobody else was, so hopefully I'd been quiet. I smiled at the woman and walked back to the tables with very careful steps.

I needed to sit down. I heard grace recited, saw people around me chatting and filling plates, but none of it seemed real. I knew what was happening. It had nothing to do with the condition I'd picked up in Tehran, at least not directly. These were flashbacks, not seizures.

'Peter?'

Sarah was standing over my shoulder. It took great effort not to jump out of my skin.

'Not eating?' she said, pointing at my empty plate.

'I've lost my appetite.'

She sat down beside me. Sarah was the last person I wanted to talk to right now. My head was so scrambled I wasn't sure what I would say. I realized for the first time that I was alone at the table. Lunch was already over.

'Thomas told me you'll be staying with us.'

'I could use the work, no offence.'

Sarah smiled. 'I think there's more keeping you here than just a job.'

Unemployment was around eighteen per cent last I'd heard, and that didn't include all the people who'd given up and gone off the grid. These days there was no such thing as 'just' a job. I doubted that Sarah had ever wanted for anything, and wouldn't understand how powerful a motivating factor want could be. I decided to go with the angle Jefferson had suggested.

'I heard Joshua can heal people. Is that true?'

'People say Joshua can do many things.'

She waited for me to say more. Sarah may have been the only person in this camp who knew when to be silent.

'I came back from the war with this, illness. There are others. We were all there when Tehran was hit with that weapon. Ever since then I've had these attacks, of nausea, joint pain and finally seizures.

'The Pentagon did nothing for us, pretended it was all in our heads. I heard through some others like me that Joshua could help us. Is that true?' I asked again.

'Joshua doesn't heal sickness, not the physical kind.'

'You mean he's a psychiatrist?'

Sarah laughed. 'We consider ourselves advanced, Peter, but there is so much wisdom we have forgotten. We pretend not to believe in demons any more, even though they are all around us. Science has usurped that authority, as it has so many others. Now demons are nothing more than chemical imbalances that can be fixed by drugs, not cast out by the word of God.

'Jesus gave to His disciples power against unclean spirits, to cast them out, and to heal all manner of sickness and disease. God has granted the same gift to Joshua. The Gospel of Mark tells us that Jesus met a man whose son was possessed by a demon, and "wheresoever he taketh him, he teareth him: and he foameth, and gnasheth with his teeth." Does that sound familiar?'

So I wasn't the first.

'I know ever since Tehran, you've been asking yourself why you are sick, why it had to be you. The question you need to ask yourself is: is there a demon inside you, Peter?'

I didn't know how to answer that.

A teenage girl ran up to our table, tapped Sarah on the shoulder and said Joshua needed her.

'I hope we can finish this conversation soon,' Sarah said, getting up. 'I believe what you told me, Peter, but I don't think that's why you're really here.'

Sarah left arm in arm with the teenage girl, smiling at me over her shoulder. Things had not gone exactly as I'd planned.

# EIGHTEEN

## The High Plains, Nebraska

We'd stopped in an empty field off Highway 80 just before nightfall. The adult tribe members had spent most of the night setting up stands and a place for Joshua to speak. The Sons of David hadn't fanned out to spread the good news, so I wondered what was up.

I'd been with Joshua's circus for about three weeks. I had been allowed to retrieve the car Jefferson had given me from Morning Star so I could join the vast convoy of camp followers that tailed the Sons of David. I was glad they hadn't asked me to ride with them. I had my medication close at hand, and could make tracks if my cover was blown.

My 'Humbling' was over. Much as I'd enjoyed moving boxes around, I needed to get close to Thomas, and, by extension, Joshua. I had hoped that my initiation was over, that they'd just give me the decoder ring and let me get on with it. Instead I spent a week listening to a kid talk about the Bible.

'My name is Jed,' he'd said on the first day. 'I am here to help you navigate the tricks and traps of this sinful world, and lead you to the light.'

My first impression was that this kid couldn't navigate his way out of a supermarket parking lot. He wasn't a day over fifteen, all skin and bone, one of those kids who could eat twice his weight without any noticeable effect. He was our shepherd, sponsor for a spiritual AA. The whole group was men, the flocks segregated by sex, everyone Jed ministered to older than him. The old man of the group was fifty-five, the youngest nineteen. All had fucked up their lives in one way or another, so I didn't have much trouble fitting in.

'Everything you need to know about life is in here,' he had said, holding up a Bible. 'God gave us the complete manual for all of creation. All those scientists, professors and politicians who have been telling you what to do your whole life, who have been telling you you're stupid, are just trying to control you. The truth is simple: "For God so loved the world, that he gave his only begotten Son, that whosoever believeth in Him should not perish, but have everlasting life." And "the fearful, and unbelieving, and the abominable, and murderers, and whore-mongers, and sorcerers, and idolaters, and all liars, shall have their part in the lake which burneth with fire and brimstone." That is all you need to know.'

Despite his earlier declaration, we spent the next week studying whatever passages Jed had decided to take out of context that day. The schedule was gruelling: up at dawn, study until noon, group study and hymns after lunch, evangelism training, and more verses after dinner until they told us we could go to sleep. I didn't have a free minute to hear myself think, and was so tired I couldn't think of much anyway. That was probably the point.

It reminded me of basic training, only with more boring lectures and less physical activity. The army broke you down and then put you back together in their image. It might not sound like the sort of thing people would seek out, but the members of

162

my group were eager to be broken. They'd had the chance to be masters of their own fate and had made a hash of it with a combination of bad circumstances and worse judgement. Our prayer sessions – group therapy in disguise – were one long chronicle of addiction, abuse, broken homes and bad marriages, one thing leading to another in a merry-go-round of despair. It wasn't hard to see why my new brothers and sisters were so interested in a fresh start, a chance for someone else to take the wheel of their lives and steer it properly for once. You didn't have to look sideways at a recruiting poster to see the army offered the same thing.

The schedule had put an end to my snooping for the time being. Every hour of my day was monitored and accounted for, and even if I'd had the energy to look around I was never left alone long enough to do it. I still didn't know who was funding the Sons, or what Joshua was planning. The average Son didn't know who ran things or how and had no interest in finding out. Willing ignorance was the best form of operational security there was. That meant I still had nothing for Jefferson. It had taken only one meeting to figure out that he wasn't a patient man.

This morning they'd let us sleep in, the sun already climbing in the sky when the ram's horn they blew over the PA woke me from a dreamless sleep. We assembled around Jed as we had every day since this forced march into the light had begun. I looked at the other groups and saw that they shared our confusion.

'I have good news,' Jed said. 'Today is the day you've been waiting for.'

It took us a moment to figure out what he was saying, our minds still clouded by lack of sleep and food. The shouts of joy erupting around us finished connecting the dots. Our new lives began today.

I hadn't known when it was coming, but I was less expectant than the others. Thomas Bloom had pulled me aside a week into the programme and let me know what was coming.

'We're going to make you a father,' he'd said to me.

'Come again?'

'Keep your pants on,' Bloom said with a grin. 'It's only a title. Sarah told you about the tribes. They're organized into families, so they can go out and proselytize and the like. The kids do most of the talking. A mother – that's what Sarah was doing – keeps control of the kids. The father does what fathers do.'

'Kick ass when necessary.'

'Now you're getting it.'

'Will I be working with Sarah?'

'Joshua has insisted she stay close to him after what happened. We'll find you a nice family. Hands off the mother though.'

'I don't play with kids.'

'That's what I thought. Now, there's one more thing you have to do.'

'Please tell me it doesn't involve more Bible study.'

'Naw, it's sort of an initiation. It won't be hard to figure out what they expect. Talk about the war; these kids will love that. One piece of advice,' Bloom said, 'don't lie to them. They want you to spin things a little, but not make them up. These kids may not know much about the world, but they can spot a false convert a mile off.'

The shepherds led their flocks to the area between the stage and the stands. Sons of David strolled around with clipboards, making sure we were all present and accounted for. One of them spoke with Jed for a few minutes, working out the order in which our souls would be saved.

After half an hour, they organized us into rows facing the stage. It stayed empty for a good long time. The sheep stole glances at each other, unsure what to do. No instructions had been given. We wanted to speak, move and relax, but no one wanted to be the first.

The horn blew again, this time behind us. An organ beside the stage started up, and the sound of martial drumming blasted out of the PA. We turned to see the Sons of David marching into the stands, white robes over their uniforms. As each row filled, they turned in our direction and marched in place, the bleachers reverberating from a thousand boots striking them in perfect time. When the last row was in position the drumming stopped, and they saluted and sat down as one. Any drill sergeant would have been proud.

If there was one topic that could rival hell for sheer repetition, it was the white raiment. It was proof we were in the right club, a get-out-of-hell card spun into pale cloth. After our lesson in the simplicity of life on the first day, the next passage Jed quoted was from Revelation: 'He that overcometh, the same shall be clothed in white raiment; and I will not blot out his name out of the book of life, but I will confess his name before my Father, and before his angels.'

'What do you think that means?' Jed asked.

There was a long silence. It took a few more days before the flock realized that these questions were not invitations to thought or discussion, but pauses so we could repeat what we had been told.

'The people who wear the white thingy have eternal life?' the nineteen-year-old kid said, playing with the long sleeves of his shirt to make sure they were still hiding the track marks on his arm.

'Raiment,' Jed said, delighted to correct him. 'It's like a robe, only biblical.

'"What are these which are arrayed in white robes? and

whence came they?"' he continued from Revelation. '"These are they which came out of great tribulation, and have washed their robes, and made them white in the blood of the Lamb. Therefore are they before the throne of God, and serve him day and night in his temple: and he that sitteth on the throne shall dwell among them. They shall hunger no more, neither thirst any more; neither shall the sun light on them, nor any heat."'

Jed closed his Bible and let the words sink in.

'So how do we get the white raiment?' another asked.

It was one of the rare times that Jed kept his mouth shut. He looked at each of us in turn with an expression of smug wisdom he must have copied from TV. It wouldn't be the last time I had the un-Christian urge to wring my shepherd's neck.

After their performance, the Sons of David did nothing. We followed their eyes back to the stage, and were surprised to find people there. Twelve men were arrayed on either side of an empty throne. These were the Patriarchs, the leaders of the twelve tribes, and I'd be damned if they weren't Task Force Seventeen to a man. I didn't think I'd served with any of them directly but I tried not to look at them anyway, afraid of recognition even in a crowd this size.

All that was missing was Joshua, and he didn't keep us waiting much longer. He ascended the stage with his entourage following behind, Sarah closer this time. Only Bloom was missing from the line-up. I wondered where he was, and how he'd been lucky to avoid all this. Sarah helped Joshua climb up on his throne. When he was comfortable, another member of his entourage positioned a microphone nearby.

'Welcome to the first day of your new life,' Joshua said. The amplification somehow made his voice sound more childish than it did in person. 'And it cannot come too soon. The forces

166

of Satan lay siege to this world, and every day they grow closer to breaching its walls. You are being baptized on the ramparts, warriors for Christ in the last days.'

With a wave of his hand, Joshua bade the ceremony begin. Two Sons of David removed a part of the stage to reveal a small wading pool in front of Joshua's throne. The first shepherd led the first of his flock up to the start of their new life.

The lucky lady was in her forties, a heavy bottle blonde of a type popular in the West, easily able to play Joshua's mother if ever called on to do so. The initial part of the ceremony was the confession. She turned to the audience and began her tale.

Her confession and those that came after had an eerie similarity to them, and not just because many of the sins were the same. The shepherds had massaged the narratives, through overt guidance and unconsciously by their lambs figuring out what they wanted to hear. Jed had done the same for us.

After her short tale of woe was finished, the oaths began. They were led by her shepherd, a slight brunette of about fourteen with horrible posture.

'Do you swear to spread the word of the Lord our Saviour?'

'Spreading the word of the Lord is the most important job you'll ever have,' Jed had told us. '"Whosoever therefore shall confess me before men, him will I confess also before my Father which is in heaven. But whosoever shall deny me before men, him will I also deny before my Father which is in heaven."

'What Matthew is saying is that evangelizing is essential for your entry into heaven. As Joshua tells us: "no man reaches heaven alone."'

'But how do we do that?' one of the flock asked. 'I never sold nothing before.'

Jed's eyes lit up. The question was so timely I wondered if it was a plant. He got us to partner off, one playing the erstwhile sinner, the other the righteous proselytizer trying to lead their ignorant ass to heaven. Jed flitted between the groups, encouraging the confused, suggesting scripture, and giving notes on our performance.

What made these sessions different from the proselytizing I'd heard for the last ten years was that the Sons of David's central gimmick – that they were the pure children of the Revivalist revolution – meant that adults like us couldn't offer salvation directly. Instead, we spread news of the glories of Joshua and the evils of the Elders in order to steer our marks to the children who could actually save souls. We were a sub-franchise, the hype men for the Sons of David evangelical machine.

We played these games every day, for hours. It didn't take long for me to regret the fact that the Bibles they'd given us didn't have any sharp corners I could stick in my eyes.

After he'd felt we'd had enough practice, Jed made us perform in front of the entire group. When it was my turn, I was partnered with the young man of the group, an ex-heroin addict named Tim something. Considering what he'd been through Tim was still a pretty good kid, guilty only of being lost and desperate like all the others. He played the evangelist that day, while I played the unlucky sap forced to listen.

'Do you want to know the secret to eternal life?' Tim began, staring at his feet. It was the most common opening.

'Excuse me?'

He repeated the question.

'I already go to church.' We'd been taught that this would be the most likely obstacle a convert would put up. It was the first thing that father had said to Sarah in Morning Star, the religious equivalent to 'I already gave at the office.'

'Church alone won't save us from the fires of the End Times,'

Tim said, on cue. 'Have you studied the vision of John the Revelator? He says only those who have been sealed by the Lord will be spared.'

'More feeling,' Jed stage-whispered to Tim from the sidelines.

'Only Joshua, the child prophet of the last days, can lead us safely out of the fallen world the Elders have made,' Tim practically yelled, interpreting feeling as volume.

'Why?'

Tim stared at me. It was kind of amazing no one had thought to ask that simple question during the interminable hours we'd been doing this, but then the true objective had always been to perform as expected, not to perform well.

'Why what?'

'Why this kid Joshua?'

Tim began to stammer. Jed glared at me.

'We are the first pure generation, untouched by the corrupt world falling apart around us,' Jed whispered to Tim, who struggled to repeat it. 'As Isaiah says: "And I will give children to be their princes, and babes shall rule over them."'

'There are lots of children. Why him?' It was stupid what I was doing, but I couldn't help myself. 'I think that's the first question people are going to ask,' I said to Jed.

'Listen,' Jed replied, beginning to stammer himself, 'Joshua has been anointed by God. He is the only one who sees what must be done to bring about the Second Coming.'

He hadn't really answered my question, and the flock, tired and half-brainwashed as it was, knew it. Jed struggled for something more to say, until a horn blast over the PA signalled it was time for dinner.

'We'll finish this tomorrow,' Jed said, before heading off with unseemly speed. The next day Jed seemed to have forgotten the question, and none of the flock had the courage to remind him.

'Do you swear to abstain from fornication, onanism and all the pleasures of the flesh?' the girl continued with her older lamb.

Jed had pounded away at this theme, though it was obvious from the way he talked about it that he understood fornication only in the abstract.

' "For this is the will of God, even your sanctification, that ye should abstain from fornication: That every one of you should know how to possess his vessel in sanctification and honour." '

Jed looked up at the sound of a giggle suppressed too late. He met a circle of innocent, attentive faces.

'Guys, this is serious,' Jed said in a plaintive voice. 'We're talking about your immortal souls here.'

'I have a question,' a fat Latino guy in his forties said. He'd never said anything before, and wiped his bald head while we recovered from the surprise of him speaking. 'What if you're married? Is fornication okay then?'

I was pretty sure fornication meant sex outside marriage, but I didn't have a dictionary handy, and watching Jed ape a learned man was the most fun I was likely to have all day.

'Joshua has thought long and hard on this question,' Jed replied. Whoever had giggled before kept control of himself this time. 'The Lord teaches that the only purpose of fornication is procreation. But is procreation still moral, knowing that the next generation will not see adulthood before the End Times?' It was clear Jed had memorized this, like most of the other things he told us. 'Joshua believes it is no more right to cease having children because of our Lord's imminent return than it would be to stop eating for the same reason. So yes, you may fornicate.'

'Do you swear to follow Joshua, the last Prophet of the Lord Jesus Christ, and like the Apostles obey his commands?'

'I do,' the bottle blonde said, perhaps still unsure what ceremony she was taking part in, as she knelt and swore allegiance to a twelve-year-old boy.

Her shepherdess dunked her head into the pool with as much violence as her young arms could muster and then stuffed the robe over her head as soon as she came up sputtering for air. The flock's newest member was presented to the crowd, dazed, happy and sopping wet.

The whole ritual took barely five minutes, but there were a lot of us to get through. The Sons of David were careful to keep the ceremony on track, interrupting penitents with the beginning of the oath if their confessions dragged and getting the converts off the stage as fast as humanly possible. Even then the ceremony went on for hours. I was surprised the teenagers in the stands tolerated this much boredom.

Only the occasional hymn broke up the assembly line. They were the same hymns the Elders inflicted on the country through mandatory morning and evening prayer on all radio and television stations, the hymns that would have been the Sons of David's only music when they were at their religious schools. The lyrics were childish and the songs atonal, some Elder having ignored the entire history of classical music in deciding that melody was a recent invention of the devil.

I sang the words and tried to imagine I was somewhere else. Each day the feat was harder to perform. At the start it looked like it would be easy to ignore material so insulting to my intelligence. I let my mind wander while Jed rambled, thinking about things I'd read, old movies, the cases I'd worked in New York that had been odd or interesting. I let the other me, the eager convert, sing the hymns, repeat the dogma, drive my body from one place to the next while its absentee landlord thought of happier times.

Turns out I didn't have too many good memories to hide in.

The long hours and skipped meals – random 'fasting' that we were required to perform with little or no explanation – made it hard to keep the two selves apart. Sometimes I'd snap back into my body during the middle of a hymn, confused for a moment where I was. Even worse were the moments when I realized I'd been happily following whatever lies Jed was spouting, no other thoughts in my head. Repetition could make the silliest ideas persuasive if it went on long enough, the words sinking past the sceptical mind to the lower depths of the subconscious.

It was a lesson I'd been forced to learn more than once, first in IF, now here. The mind could starve, just like the body. Keep it hungry long enough, and it will eat whatever is in front of it.

The young heroin addict was in the queue before me. He was shy but Jed's pep talks had given him some confidence, at least until he got on stage and the size of the crowd slapped him in the face.

'Two years ago, my parents disappeared,' he began, then stopped. Jed gave him some encouragement. 'One day they were just gone. No note, didn't take luggage or anything.' He stopped again. I wondered if the young man had spoken about this before he came to the Sons of David. His words weren't polished like the ones that came before. He'd started out with Jed's plan, but the emotions were still raw, and they tolerated no convenient structure.

'I was so angry and alone. That's when I started taking drugs. I was angry with everyone, my parents, the police when they wouldn't help me, God when I believed in Him. Mostly I blamed myself. I thought I'd done something wrong, driven them away.

'One of the children found me in an alley, brought me to Joshua. I didn't care what he said at first, but the more he spoke . . .' His voice broke. 'He said it wasn't my fault. I'd been born into a sinful world, I didn't have a chance. My parents – he said it wasn't my fault. They'd brought it on themselves, he said. You see, they were atheists.' Jed rubbed his back in some kind of commiseration. 'And God punished them.

'But Joshua told me I was different. God had a plan for me. I'd be dead if it wasn't for Joshua. He's given me hope.'

Jed dunked the young man to great applause. From what Tim had said on stage and in our group, it sounded like Fisher Partners had paid a visit to his house. Maybe his parents had been taken because they were atheists, but I doubted that alone would have been enough unless they were suicidally loud about it. More likely they had pissed off the wrong person, or their name was spelled like someone else's. Joshua had relieved the young man of his survivor guilt by blaming the other victims.

It was finally my turn to be saved. Jed led me up the stairs like all the others. Joshua perked up a little when he saw me. He gave a big smile, and seemed eager for my confession to begin.

Here was the template of confession: start with your former life. Make it sound as bad as possible, the more sensational the better. Don't go on for more than half a minute. Then relate in detail a point when you needed help the most. It could be the rock bottom of an addiction, the death of a parent, some other trauma. If you're lucky enough not to have that kind of material, relate a time when you had to face your own mortality and fear of death. That's another minute. The last minute and a half is the change, the moment you felt the Holy Spirit enter your heart. The fear of death lifting is important, the joy of His presence even more so. Connect these feeling at the end to Joshua, emphasize his role as the earthly embodiment of this hope in some way.

That was all I had to do. An entire spiritual life in around three minutes.

'When I was in the army I ran with a bad crowd, drank too

much and fornicated a lot,' I began. 'I knew nothing of God, thought people who cared about Him were crazy.'

I realized halfway through the first sentence that I was reading from the confession Gideon and I had cooked up in IF. Gideon had made me say it until I could recite it backwards, so I decided to run with it. All I had to do was change which God redeemed me at the end.

'I fought in Tehran,' I said. I could feel the crowd's ears perk up. 'So many people died who didn't deserve it, if anyone does, just bad luck. I thought if there was a God, He couldn't care less what happened to us.'

I kept to the schedule, and moved on to my dark night of the soul. Jefferson said there were fellow sufferers in the flock, so the syndrome was a natural choice.

'I was on patrol the day Tehran died. When I found out there was something wrong with me, all I felt was anger. I had no one.'

The sun came out from behind a cloud, and for a moment I was blind. When my vision cleared, it was klieg lights, not the sun, that bore down on me. I was in a big dark place, a hangar I'd guessed at the time. There was no bar, no wooden panelling, no pale imitation of a real court that you saw in the military commissions they televised. A single long table, twenty feet away. I could see eight silhouettes sitting on its far side, eight shadows cut from the blinding light behind them. I was shackled to a metal chair. It was always a metal chair.

'I didn't see the point in living.'

I'd told those men how the syndrome had made me angry, how I'd blamed the Elders and God through them. I said I'd wanted to do anything I could to hurt them, to hold back the cause of the almighty creator. That's why I'd stolen the Fisher Partners list and helped Cassandra escape. I swallowed my pride and apologized for the only good things I'd ever done in my life.

174

I didn't say sorry for killing their thugs and errand boys; I didn't beg for forgiveness for killing that child. They weren't interested in either. They wanted to see one of their enemies, broken and in chains, admit everything they said and did was right.

I'd told them what they wanted to hear. For Iris.

I was back on the stage. I had been gone long enough for an expectant silence to gather around me. Had my story been more typical they might have just hustled me off the stage, but they held out hope for more talk about war and destruction.

'I've seen so much death,' I said, off script, trying to carry on, 'some of it at my own hand. It has to mean something. There has to be—'

I couldn't finish. I didn't know what to say. I looked past the stands, the children in their robes of snow, to the high plains and the endless horizon. It looked unfinished, a place God had forgotten to grace with typography before he rested on the seventh day. I could be imagining all this. I could be one shift change away from waking up back in IF, staring at the fluorescent ceiling, waiting for Control to summon me for more fun and games.

A hand shoved me head first into the water. I heard Control's voice, bored, waiting for his next coffee break, saying, 'Who is Jefferson?' over and over. Water went up my nose. I didn't struggle. After I'd fought them the first time they pretended to drown me, I knew it wouldn't do any good.

I came back into the light. Jed held me by the shoulders, grinned so I could count all the teeth I wanted to knock out of his skull.

'Wait,' Joshua said, as Jed readied the white raiment. He rose from his throne and took the garment from Jed's hands.

'This man came to us a wanderer, as many of you have,' Joshua said, turning to address the crowd. 'But this man came on the wings of Providence. He shed blood for one of us when he didn't even know her name. God has sent this man to protect us; he has earned a new name for a new life.'

I knelt before Joshua so he could place the robe over my head.

'Rise, Gershom, the stranger,' Joshua said. 'Rise and join your new family.'

I did as he asked. At Joshua's bidding, the crowd greeted me with applause fit for a conqueror. I wore the jersey of the righteous now.

# NINETEEN

## The High Plains, Nebraska

I woke up staring into Sarah's eyes. The shock that must have been in my eyes wasn't mirrored in her own. I was shivering, and not just because I was on the cold ground and wrapped in a layer of sweat.

I sat up and saw a circle of Sons of David rubbernecking me. When I looked at them they shuffled their feet and couldn't meet my eyes, not used to the car accident staring back. It had finally happened. I'd had a seizure in public.

Bits and pieces of the near present filtered back into my mind. It was the morning after my baptism. That boring ceremony had been followed by the squarest party in human history: no booze, no music that deserved the name, dames in unflattering dresses and men in worse suits. It's what my flashbacks would look like if I'd done my tour in a suburb in 1955 instead of Tehran.

'They said you were having convulsions, and came to get me,' Sarah said. 'This is your sickness, isn't it?'

I nodded. My throat was so dry I could barely talk.

'Water.'

Sarah raised her hand and someone put a bottle into it. I drank half of it in one go.

'Do you need your medication?' My pills were in her hand. I didn't bother to ask how she'd known where I kept them, or that they existed at all. Eyes were always on you in this camp. I took the bottle but not the pills. My medication was to stop full-blown seizures which I couldn't wake up from, not these little earthquakes that I seemed to come out of on my own.

'How long was I out?'

'They found you a few minutes ago.'

I might have been in convulsions for a while before then. I couldn't tell if the seizures were getting longer or not: their only witness was too busy shaking to take notes. I could be like this for years, and then have my heart give out or a blood vessel pop in my brain during a seizure. There would be no warning.

'Brothers and sisters,' Sarah said to the crowd that had gathered. 'You heard our brother Gershom's confession last night. You know how much he has sacrificed for this country, yet you see his affliction. The evil that stalks this land does not spare the righteous any more than the wicked. The only protection in this world lies in the arms of the Lord.

'When you believe yourself too good or too pure to fall victim to the devil, remember Gershom. This is what a demon looks like.'

Sarah's words made it clear there was no more entertainment to be had. They dispersed quickly, as people a little ashamed of themselves often did. I was about to get to my feet when Sarah stopped me. She put out a hand to check the temperature of my forehead. The touch was so kind I had to stop myself from flinching in surprise.

'You should rest,' Sarah said. She helped me up but didn't let go.

'I can walk.'

'I know,' she said, and supported me with her arm anyway.

178

We shuffled off to my tent in Joshua's compound. All eyes followed us, and for the first time they weren't all focused on Sarah. I didn't appreciate the change.

'Do you mind if I ask you something?' I said.

'Not at all.'

'Why aren't you' – I had no clue what sixteen-year-old girls did these days – 'cheerleading or something?'

Sarah laughed. 'I was a student, and a cheerleader, until we blew up my school.'

'Well, I did fantasize about that a lot at your age. What I mean,' I said, trying to find a way to ask this question without letting on I'd read her file, 'the way people talk about you, it sounds like you had everything. Why come out here and do this?'

'Faith.'

'Nothing else?'

'That's all you need. Besides,' she said, 'the only point of going to high school is to go to college. The only point of going to college is to have a career. Why have a career when the world is ending?'

'That's not very optimistic.'

'I think it's very optimistic,' Sarah said. 'This world is dying; you know that better than I do. Before I'm your age Jesus will have returned, and in place of this world that kills the innocent and takes the ones we love, there will be a kingdom free of pain and want. The end of the world is the best thing that could happen to me.'

'If you really believe the world is going to end, why go to all this trouble?' I said, indicating the camp with my hands. 'Why do anything at all?'

'There is still time to save souls, and they last for ever.'

We reached my tent, and Sarah helped me sit on the cot.

'Do you mind if I ask you a question?' she said. 'Who is Iris?'

I forced myself not to react. When you work in the business of meeting people on the worst day of their lives, when only heartbreak or prison was waiting around the corner, you learn to ignore pain. After a while, your own looks the same as anyone else's.

'You said that name.'

'During the seizure?'

'No, just as you were waking. Is she your wife?'

I had to laugh. 'That would be news to her.'

'How did you lose her?'

'I didn't lose her. She was taken.'

'By the Elders?'

I nodded. It was the truth, and even better it was what Sarah wanted to hear. They hated the Elders almost as much as I did.

'Do you know why?'

'They don't need a reason.'

Sarah shook her head. 'What was she like?'

'Why are you asking?' I said, letting some of my anger show. I didn't want to discuss Iris with a girl who wouldn't understand.

'You asked me if Joshua could heal you.'

'And you said that wasn't my real problem.'

'I said this sickness wasn't the real reason you are here. There is a demon in you, Gershom,' she said. 'I'm sure of it now.'

'So I heard.'

'I'm sorry if I embarrassed you, but we are a family, and that means we have no secrets, especially when one of us is in need. Joshua can help. He has cast demons out of other men like you. The point is, Joshua can heal your body, but this,' she said, putting her hand on my chest, 'this belongs to God. Only He can heal the pain of the Elders taking Iris.'

My relationship with Iris, such as it was, could be measured in

180

hours, and a good percentage of that had involved following criminals and dodging bullets. I had images mostly, some good phrases.

'I don't want God to heal that pain,' I said. 'It's mine. It reminds me that I love her. They can't take her away from me as long as I have it. You wouldn't understand,' I said to Sarah. 'You're too young.'

'Joshua says the same thing about his father,' Sarah said, 'and he's younger than me.'

'I guess it's not a happy subject,' I said, not sure how much it was discussed, how much I was supposed to know. I'd already shown a lot of dangerous free-thinking tendencies and didn't want to pile it on.

'No, but Joshua doesn't want to forget any more than you do. He told me there was a demon in his father. It destroyed his mother, his father and nearly killed him. His father reminds him why he was called, what we are all fighting for. His old and his new father.'

'New father?' I said.

The first time I'd met Joshua I'd heard him and Sarah talking about someone who couldn't be his dead, biological father. No one had mentioned him since then. She couldn't be talking about Thomas; it didn't fit with the way I'd seen them both order him around.

'You're a lot like him,' she said. 'Maybe I think that because you were both in the military. That makes people different. Neither of you takes advice very well. I can't count the number of times I've begged him to stop smoking those awful cigars, but he just pats my head and keeps on with his indulgence.'

There was a feeling crawling up my spine, a mixture of understanding and horror impossible to describe.

'What's his name?' I said. 'Maybe we served together.'

'He's just Father,' she said. 'I think he said once that he was in Iran, and then the Holy Land. That's where he got the scars.'

I couldn't breathe.

'He won't tell me how. I guess he looks scary to people who don't know him, but I can see the kindness under his scars, just like you.'

Sarah looked at her watch and rose.

'I should go. So much to do. Do you need anything?'

All I could do was shake my head. I was too busy holding on to myself, trying to breathe and not react to what she'd said at the same time.

'Get some rest,' she said, hugging me in a motherly way even though I was twice her age. 'You'll be yourself again in no time.'

Sarah left. I think I said goodbye, but I wasn't really paying much attention by then. There was only one person Sarah could be talking about, only one man who fitted that description. The dirt underneath my feet seemed thinner, liable to blow away at any moment and leave nothing but empty air.

It was Glass. Of course it was.

# TWENTY

## Near Topeka, Kansas

I was on my feet a few minutes after Sarah left. I found Thomas near Joshua's tent and said I needed to leave for a while to take care of a medical problem. I was surprised when he didn't put up a fight. Word of my seizure had probably gotten around, and maybe he trusted me a little more now that I'd paid my dues with the Sons of David.

More likely Bloom didn't care that much. He gave me the day off and some grid coordinates outside Denver. The Sons of David were on the move. I'd worry about that after I made a house call on a doctor.

I put in the earpiece and tried to raise Jefferson when I was safely on the highway. I had to go through two of his subordinates before I convinced them to put the big man on.

'Is it done?'

'If the kid was dead, I would have followed that procedure. We've got a bigger problem.'

'Bigger?' Jefferson wasn't in the mood to believe me.

'I've figured out who's supporting Joshua and the Sons,' I said. 'It's General Simeon Glass.'

There was a long pause at the other end. I began to worry that we'd lost the connection.

'That is unlikely.'

'Unlikely fuck! It's the only way this freak show makes sense.'

Jefferson didn't say anything so I soldiered on.

'I spoke to Sarah Bright this morning, Joshua's surrogate big sister. She's in your file if you don't recognize the name. She told me about his new father: he's a military man with a fucked-up face who smokes cigars.'

'There are four generals on my speed dial with war wounds and a fondness for Cohibas.'

'And how many of them were patrons of the Sons of David?' I said. 'Wasn't it Glass who gave them the power to harass people when he was Director of Homeland Security?'

'It was an Elder policy. He just implemented it.'

'What about the Task Force Seventeen vets guarding Joshua? How did they end up with the Sons?'

I couldn't believe I hadn't thought to ask the question before. I would have kicked myself if I wasn't driving.

'After they resigned from Fisher Partners, the majority of Glass loyalists went to another private security company called EduSafe. They're a subsidy of Stillwater that primarily guards schools and a few of the new Christian universities. The rest joined up with Stillwater and went to the Holy Land for irregular duty.'

That meant kidnapping and assassination, Seventeen's old tricks.

'Was EduSafe guarding Zion Academy at the time of Joshua's Awakening?'

'They had the contract.'

So Stillwater was being paid to protect Zion right up to the point they were paid to storm it. No wonder they were one of the only companies in the nation that was growing.

'These guys are ex-Special Forces, the only marketable set of skills left in this economy,' I said. 'Mercenaries who go to the Holy Land get much better salaries, and then combat pay on top of that. The numbers should be reversed. Why would they sell themselves short?'

'Maybe they were tired of combat.'

I laughed. 'You didn't serve with these guys. The day that any of them tire of combat is the day peace breaks out all over the world.'

'What's your point, Strange?'

'Glass put his own people in the movement for a reason.'

'Glass didn't put his people anywhere, because he doesn't have any. He's retired, Strange. The biggest conspiracy he's probably involved in is bribing his way to a better tee-off time.'

'You could have killed this idea at the beginning if you'd told me what Glass has been doing,' I said. 'You didn't because you don't know, do you?'

There was another silence.

'He sits on a few boards, vacations, lobbies like every other retired general. That's what he's been doing lately, meeting with people in DC.'

'Who?'

'I don't know and I don't care. Answer me this, Strange: why would Glass tell some of his old soldiers to take jobs with EduSafe?'

Now it was my turn to clam up.

'I was afraid of this,' Jefferson said with a sigh. I think he was trying for paternal, but it came out as plain condescension.

'Afraid of what?'

185

'At the beginning of this operation doubts were raised about your stability. Gideon assured us you were fit for duty.'

'How stable do you have to be to put a bullet in a twelve-year-old?'

'You keep harping on about that.'

'Well, excuse me for expressing some concerns about the idea.'

'All you've given me so far is conjecture, Strange. You worked long enough in intelligence to know that isn't good enough. Do you have anything definitive tying Glass to the Sons?'

'Not yet.'

The line died. I pummelled the steering wheel so I didn't destroy the earpiece I still needed.

The house Doc Brown now lived in was aggressively ordinary: a two-storey square of red brick on a street of identical models. No flourishes. It was the perfect house for a man who wanted to lose himself in a crowd.

Brown had been part of the team of doctors investigating what had happened to soldiers like me in Tehran. He was there from the beginning, and ended up heading the project by default when no one else seemed to give a damn. He had helped develop the cocktail of drugs that had kept me out of the hospital ever since, just before the Pentagon shut down the project. I pretty much owed him my life.

On the other hand, he had helped Fisher Partners torture me for about a year.

I stepped up to the green front door, no screen attached. I was about to put my finger to the bell when I heard his voice from inside the house.

Again, the room.

Time moved slowly in the empty light. Maybe it didn't

move at all. I hadn't seen a clock since the hospital in New Mexico. None of the personnel here wore watches, probably by decree, but had I managed to see one the hands wouldn't have made much sense. There was no day or night here. No rest.

Sometimes I put a hand on my heart and tried to count the beats. One, two, three, four . . . so many meant a minute had passed, then another. I couldn't keep count for long.

The paint on the walls of my cell was cheap. I marked time with interrogations. When I heard the door opening, I tried to scratch a line with my untended fingernails. Sometimes I was fast enough.

They didn't always take me to this room. Sometimes they took me out for what they called exercise. The yard was a square of corrugated iron. Sand and gravel under my feet. I was kept blind, a guard leading/dragging me around the edges. They added extra restraints first, still expecting me to break free and scale the sheer iron walls. It was just another way of running us down, but at least I got some fresh air.

I found something on my right arm. Maybe it was yesterday. Fresh track marks just below the bicep, three little holes with angry red haloes. My skin smelled of disinfectant. I didn't remember them administering anything, couldn't recall needles or figure out what would have been in them. Sodium pentathol maybe, or some other concoction a snake oil salesman had convinced them was a truth serum. We'd tried drugs in Tehran, but the results hadn't been what Glass was looking for. We got a lot of gibberish, ravings, flashbacks of what we'd done to them pouring out of their opened minds.

The light was bright. It was always bright.

The door opened. It wasn't Control. Standing in the doorway, framed by the light of the corridor, Doc Brown wore a white lab coat and a shocked face pointed in my direction. The guard closed the door behind him, locking us both in.

Brown put his case on Control's table and opened it. He took out a pen light, a blood pressure monitor and a stethoscope. He put the monitor around my arm, and refused to meet my eyes while he pumped it up.

'Doc . . .' The sentence died there. I had so many questions, but I didn't have the strength to push the words from my brain to my mouth.

Brown couldn't help but look at me then. I knew he'd been trying to keep my existence at arm's length ever since he'd entered the room. It wasn't easy to forget about someone while you were looking at them, but it could be done. I was a malfunctioning device, not a person, something that could be fixed without thinking about how it got broken in the first place.

'Sip,' Brown said as he held a bottle of water to my lips. 'Gulp and your body will throw it back up.'

I did as I was told. Before I came here, I hadn't realized just how goddamn delicious water could be.

'How do you feel, Felix?'

'Take a closer look and guess.'

Brown nodded, to himself more than me.

'What are they doing to me?' I asked, rolling my head in the direction of the track marks.

'I told them you wouldn't remember. The fucking sadists never listen.'

He blinked at his own words and looked around. The fucking sadists in question were probably listening right now.

'Are they trying to hook me on something?' I said.

As an answer to my question, Brown took the case from the table and showed me the rest of its contents. Inside were bottles of my medication and syringes filled with the drug that kept the seizures under control. That's what I'd been injected with. I only needed to mainline the stuff if I was in the middle of a full-blown seizure. I wondered how many I'd had – or been forced to have. The track marks wouldn't tell the whole story.

'I told them it wouldn't make them more cooperative, but they wouldn't listen,' Brown said, again more to himself than me. I was arriving in the middle of an argument he'd been having with himself for a long time.

'Them? How many others have the syndrome here?'

'I can't tell you.'

Brown put the stethoscope against my chest for a while. Whatever he heard, it seemed to satisfy him. On his right arm was an old military watch, leather band damp with Brown's sweat. The smell of the leather . . .

Arm restraints: a different chair. Struggling, no, convulsing. Control's voice, distant, yelling questions. Burning, burning in my whole body. Dry heaves. More questions. Screaming, screaming, screaming . . .

'Strange.'

Doc was yelling in my face, shaking me.

'When did you get here, Doc?'

Brown shone the penlight in my eyes, stared at the pupils as if they contained my fortune.

'They thought it would make you easier to control,' he said. 'I told them all it would do was destroy your body. You can't threaten a man with something he can't remember.'

I had again overestimated Control's intelligence, something I didn't think was possible.

'Now they worry that you've been permanently damaged.'

'Is that why you're here?'

'I'm here to make sure you won't embarrass them. Have you been taking your medication regularly?' Brown said.

'You're kidding, right?'

He wasn't exactly. Out of it as I was, I could see the strain on his face, the desperation to keep this just another consultation.

'Who did they threaten, Doc?'

Brown didn't reply. He gave me more water, and fed me pills between sips. I counted five.

'Your full complement of medication,' he said, 'plus some vitamins and a placebo. You could use the sugar.'

When he was done feeding me pills, Brown packed up his case.

'You're in better shape than I expected,' he said. 'Assuming you had some food and they let you sleep, it might only take a few weeks to start feeling like a human being again.'

'That's about as likely as you getting your hair back.'

Brown smiled, the most he could muster in the surroundings. When he began to turn away, I grabbed his arm with what little strength I had left.

'Doc, please, tell me what they want me to say.'

I was standing on his porch. The front door was open. My finger was near the bell, I might have pushed it. Doc Brown stood in the open doorway. He didn't say anything either, just waited to see if I was real or a manifestation of his conscience.

'Hello, Doc.'

I recognized the look on Brown's face, that mixture of surprise and resignation. He had been expecting a day like this one for a long time, but was still caught off guard when it finally showed up.

'Are you here to kill me?'

'Darling, who's at the door?'

Behind Brown I caught sight of a good-looking woman in tracksuit bottoms and an old T-shirt, pure surprise on her face

190

without Brown's taint of anticipation. Unlike Brown, the more his wife looked at me, the more fearful her wide brown eyes became.

'Is there somewhere we can talk?' I said to Brown, ignoring her. It would be best for everyone if I did.

'Who are you?'

Brown's wife moved towards me, but he stopped her.

'Cheryl, let me handle this.'

'Handle this, my ass. You're one of them, aren't you?' she said to me, trying to get in my face from behind Brown's broad shoulders. I had thought she was his wife, but now I wasn't sure. I didn't see a ring on her finger or his.

'Why can't you leave him alone? Hasn't he done enough?'

Brown closed his eyes for a moment, and I caught sight of the despair he was wrestling with.

'He doesn't work for Fisher Partners.'

Cheryl was not a stupid woman. As soon as Brown said those words, she understood how we knew each other, at least in the present.

'Oh my God.' That was all she could say.

'We can talk in the garden,' Brown said. 'Take the side entrance, I'll meet you there.'

I left him trying to explain things to Cheryl.

The back garden was loved by at least one person. The lawn was mown, two flower beds in bloom against a high brick wall. Lamps in the flower beds gave enough light for me to find one of a pair of wooden garden chairs and sit down.

After Jefferson had hung up on me, I'd spent the rest of the morning driving south-east into Kansas. Doc's place was outside Topeka near Silver Lake, another development, this one healthy enough to take a few boarded-up properties in its stride. I'd known he was here when I went to Kansas City to make first contact with the Sons. I hadn't seen the point in visiting then, and I'd lacked the courage anyway.

Now I had a good reason and was working on the courage part. The drive had been five hours give or take, and I spent most of it trying to figure out what I was going to say to Brown. Now, sitting on his garden furniture, I still hadn't made up my mind.

Brown came out of the back door and took the other garden chair. We stared at each other.

'I thought you were married,' I said.

'I was. How did you find me?'

'Your clinic has a website.'

He laughed. 'I guess I wasn't hiding that well.'

'Were you trying?'

Brown shrugged. 'I was, but boredom got the better of me. I had to open the clinic. It's all small things: broken bones, minor burns, the occasional fracture or rupture. It's good honest work, getting normal people back on their feet.'

'Why Topeka?' I said. 'Last time I checked you were working for some biotech firm.'

'They went overseas,' Brown said. 'They were too scientific for the Revivalists' liking. That's not how I . . . ended up doing what I did. I was still technically part of the ready reserve.'

'Fisher Partners is a private concern.'

'The distinction doesn't mean much any more. The firm wanted me, so they found a way.'

'Because of your special knowledge?'

Brown nodded. He was one of the leading experts on my condition, though that distinction had been more of a millstone for Brown than an accolade.

'That special knowledge was the reason the Pentagon had kept me at arm's length. All of a sudden I'm in demand.'

192

'How many of us were in IF?'

'If?'

'What did you call it?'

'The official designation was Camp X-Ray,' Brown said. 'I never found out where it was. They blindfolded us before each trip, the whole nine yards. I think it was more than just a single place.

'To answer your other question, I treated fifteen patients. There may have been more. Their thugs didn't know how to handle you. They wanted to know how your condition could be leveraged in an interrogation, and wanted to make sure none of you were inadvertently damaged beyond use.'

'As opposed to being deliberately damaged.'

Cicadas sang somewhere. I was surprised there were cicadas in Kansas, but I didn't know why.

'I asked you a question earlier,' Brown said.

'I'm not here to kill you, Doc.'

The answer didn't seem to bring him much peace. I don't think he would have minded terribly if I'd shot him right then.

'I wouldn't hold it against you if you did.'

It was my turn to laugh.

'I have it coming,' he said, almost a protest. Why he was trying to convince me, I didn't know. 'You try to tell yourself that you're still doing the same job, still patching people up. But there, I was fixing people so they could be more effectively broken. When they wanted to know how far to push someone, how much more they could take, they consulted my medical opinion.'

Brown rubbed his bald head.

'Most of the doctors were civilians, some other medics on loan like me. We stood in the back and pretended to be professionals, like we had no part in what was happening. We'd tell ourselves it's just another experiment. Where did they think those thugs got their techniques in the first place? How did they know which sounds were effective for disorientation, the uses of sleep deprivation, the effect on the mind of extreme temperatures? Professionals like me, that's how.'

Every time he used the word 'professional', Brown got angrier, most of all at himself.

'You were there against your will.'

'So what?' Brown said. 'We both got the same lectures in the army, we know what the "just following orders" defence is good for. I turned my Hippocratic oath inside out. That's all that matters.'

'I'm not here to put you on trial, Doc.'

'Then why are you here, Felix? My clinic doesn't have access to your medication—'

'It's not that. I need to know something.'

Brown sat back in his chair. The lights had gone off in his house, but I could see the curtains on the first floor move where his girlfriend was keeping vigil on us both.

'Do you remember when we met in New York?' I said. 'I showed you a video of me having a different kind of seizure, a smaller one that I came out of. It was a while ago, before I, before they—'

'I remember. You're still having the small seizures.'

It was just my luck they came in different sizes. The medication regimen Doc had developed had kept the symptoms under control for ten years. A few months before I drove into that roadblock in New Mexico, I'd started having a different type of attack. The seizures I'd had while in hospital were crippling, even life-threatening, whereas these new attacks were similar to epilepsy, convulsions that came and went on their own.

When I'd asked Brown about them in New York he hadn't been able to tell me what was happening. Peter Stonebridge, the Fisher Partners man who had taken Iris, shared my condition. He'd told me about a study the Pentagon had done on us and then buried. He'd also told me that none of us lived past forty, but Stonebridge had had every reason to lie. We'd been engaged in a contest to see who could beat the other senseless, and he was a sore loser.

At the time I hadn't paid much attention to what Stonebridge had said. I figured I wasn't more than a few months away from a violent death, so even if Stonebridge was right it wouldn't matter. Things had changed.

I told the whole story to Brown, about the Pentagon study and my life expectancy. Brown kept silent throughout.

'Is a single word of what Stonebridge said true?'

Brown spent some time lining up words in his head before he spoke.

'They gave me access to that Pentagon study,' he finally said. 'Once it was a matter of more effectively torturing people instead of helping them, the national security concerns went away.'

'What did it say?'

'What Stonebridge told you about the report was broadly correct. It wasn't definitive, Felix. It's all correlation, not causation. No one has been able to identify why it's happening.'

He didn't say people had been actively discouraged from trying.

'Then tell me one of us has lived longer than you expected. Has someone made it to forty without mysterious heart attacks or unexplained strokes? Give me just one anomaly, Doc.'

It was clear from his expression that Brown couldn't. He looked down and played with his hands, a nervous tic I'd never seen him do before. There had been a question in the back of my mind ever since I'd found the website for Brown's clinic, one I'd been trying not to ask.

'Fisher Partners let you go because your special expertise isn't needed any more. All the others are dead.'

'Not all of them died of natural causes.'

Telling me that several men with the same condition had been murdered rather than succumbed to the syndrome was Brown's way of cheering me up.

'Was it those small seizures?' I said. 'The ones the medication can't control?'

Brown shook his head. 'I learned only one useful thing in that place. Those fits aren't the same thing as the full-blown seizures. They're a side effect of the medication, not a symptom of the disease. It's like someone with Parkinson's; the uncontrolled movements are a side effect of the drugs that allow them to move at all.'

'Is that good news?'

'I don't know.'

'Is there any way I can control those small seizures?'

'Stop taking the red pills.'

That obviously wasn't an option.

'Any way to predict when they'll happen, at least?'

Recent events had shown just how extraordinary my luck had been so far. One of these days I'd have a seizure at the wrong time and never wake up at all.

'You'll have good days and bad days. I can't say any more than that. Why are you asking about all this, Felix?'

'If I'm going to die, I figure I should know.'

'You don't act that concerned.'

Brown paused. I could see there was something he'd wanted to say for a while, and was finally getting around to it.

'The way you talk about your condition, it's like you're looking for permission to do something.'

'I've already given myself permission,' I said. 'I just wanted a second opinion.'

Brown was too smart to ask me what I was up to, and I wasn't going to drag him further into trouble than he already was.

'For what it's worth, I'm glad to see you,' Brown said. 'I never thought they'd let you go.'

'They didn't exactly. Don't worry,' I said, 'I don't think anyone's looking for me. Besides, you can't look for someone who never existed. They saw to that.'

I stood, and so did he.

'If I forgave you, Doc, would you believe me?'

There were tears in his eyes. I hadn't noticed them before.

'I'd sure as hell try.'

I offered him my hand.

'The only reason you were there was because you tried to help us. If you'd acted like the others and walked away, they never would have drafted you. We've both followed orders we shouldn't have. Let's leave it that.'

Brown took my hand. It was the last time we'd see each other.

# TWENTY-ONE

## Near Denver, Colorado

I followed the coordinates Bloom had given me to the new Sons of David campsite. It was almost impossible to tell the tent city had even moved, at least from the parking lot. The layout was exactly the same, everything in its ordained place.

Bloom was in the parking lot, loitering next to a van with eight Sons of David. He called me over with a whistle.

'You sorted out your woman problems?' was the first thing he said to me.

'It won't get in the way again.'

'We got some others with the same problem, and I depend on them. I hope I can do the same with you.'

Bloom turned back to the Sons. As soon as they saw his eyes on them they snapped to attention. At his nod they got into the back of the van. He gave the same nod to me.

'I'm not babysitting today?'

'I got more important things for you to do.'

We drove out of the camp in a convoy. There were two other vans like ours and a larger one, a police surplus paddy wagon, bringing up the rear. No one spoke, so I didn't ask any questions. Bloom ran his operations on need to know, just like the people who had taught us both.

I'd been looking at Bloom in a new light ever since Sarah told me Glass was involved. Thomas must be his eyes and ears in the camp, Glass's shadow that stayed behind while he was in DC. I wondered if Bloom had said anything to Glass about me. I didn't think he'd recognize me just from a description by Bloom. With any luck Glass assumed I was dead.

I'd looked for any change in Bloom's body language but hadn't seen anything. I'd have to assume my cover was still in place for now. If they were going to off me in the desert they wouldn't need a convoy this big. That didn't mean I felt good about sharing a vehicle with Bloom and eight armed teenagers.

The drive wasn't long. We were hustled out as soon as the van stopped, on to the main street of a small town. A business nearby was called the 'Point Pines General Store', so I guessed that's where we were. The street was deserted and so were the shops, the general store empty even though a sign advertised it as open.

The Sons of David formed into ranks and stood at attention.

'I'm going to give these knuckleheads their marching orders,' Bloom said to me. 'You stick around. Okay, kids,' he yelled at the Sons, 'you all know why you're here, so get it done without pissing your pants.'

Several suppressed grins. I think they enjoyed his disdain, felt tougher to be under a leader who held them in contempt.

'Grubner, Matheson, Polchik, Darby.'

Four Sons stepped forward. They wore red armbands on their left biceps, which I guess made them the sergeants. He gave them grid coordinates like they were on a scavenger hunt. He also gave them names, which gave me a bad feeling about what they were scavenging for.

With another yell from Bloom, the Sons dispersed into their

teams, armed and in high spirits. Three of the Sons remained under Bloom's personal command.

'Is this some sort of exercise?' I asked Bloom.

'You could say that. Come on,' he said. 'We've got an errand of our own.'

Bloom led the way down streets as empty as the one we'd arrived in, quiet residential avenues full of frame houses barely older than I was. Occasionally I saw the curtains in a window rustle, caught movement in the corner of my eye. The townspeople were here, they were just staying out of our way. Whether it was because of the guns we carried or the reputation that preceded the Sons, I didn't know.

We turned a corner and saw our first citizen. He was in his forties, paunchy and unremarkable, a man you passed and never thought about again. He was holding a small dog, groomed and pampered, probably his wife's. The little rascal had run out the front door, and the man had tried to grab him and get back inside before we showed up. I guess he wasn't the lucky type.

'Morning,' Bloom said.

The man turned white and dashed back inside his house. The Sons laughed, remarked they didn't think a fat old man could run that fast. I didn't find it so funny.

The house we stopped at looked just like one of the deserted properties I'd walked past in the Morning Star suburb. The windows had been boarded up, a hopeful 'for sale' sign leaning on the wild lawn. The paint on the outside was chipped in the oddest places, as if the house had been rolled down a hill before coming to rest here. The Sons went around the back while Bloom and I went to the front door. He drew his gun and I did the same by instinct.

'Don't bother,' Bloom said, as I raised my hand to knock. I saw him squaring up to the door and got out of the way.

He sent the door inside with a single experienced kick. We moved straight into the smell of stale air and older sweat. A man had been sleeping in a recliner in the front room until we kicked down his door. Shock had overtaken him before he could get to the duck gun, sawed to half length, resting at his feet among old pizza boxes and empty bottles of beer. Bloom aimed the gun at his chest and shook his head. The man put up his hands.

He was in his late thirties but looked older, hair full and curly but shock white. His skin had the unhealthy pallor of a man unfamiliar with sunlight, the anti-tan I'd been sporting before my rehabilitation had begun. The undershirt trying to cover his hairy chest looked like it had been worn continuously for a month. His eyes were bloodshot with fear and last night's drink.

That hangover had probably saved his life. If he'd been any faster getting to that gun, he might have hit one of us. With a shotgun at this range you could be pretty generous with your aim. Even if he'd been lucky enough to hit both of us, the Sons of David who came crashing in through the back door a minute later would have shot him down before he could reload or flee.

'You're late,' Bloom said to the kids as they came into the room. He pulled the man to his feet.

'Please don't kill me,' the man said.

'Shut up,' Bloom responded, tying the man's hands behind his back.

'What the hell are we doing here?' I asked.

To the Sons, this question was near blasphemy, but Bloom just gave me a look I knew all too well. It said: we are here because I've led us here.

'Check the rest of the house,' he said.

I went upstairs. The house was big enough for a family, but all the rooms save one were empty. The man downstairs must have been squatting here. His bedroom was a single mattress on a bare floor, surrounded by what looked like the debris of his previous life: clothes stacked in one corner, papers in another.

I examined the papers first. The man must have had a reason to hold on to them when he'd let so many other things go, including himself. I picked up an envelope with a Denver postmark addressed to a family in the old way: Mr & Mrs Bernard Landsman, the woman no more than an appendage of the man. Inside was a brochure, the glory of the Holy Land on thick glossy paper.

They'd been shoving propaganda like this through the letter boxes of every Jew for a decade. Colour photo spreads showed pious men in synagogues, wrapped in talliths and hard at prayer. For the worldly there were visions of big cars and bigger houses, the walls that protected them always out of shot. The extra-worldly got buxom Jewish goddesses standing in front of them, ready to fill their houses with children and the smells of Shabbas dinner. It was a hologram of a dream, the scene changing depending on the angle, an illusion no matter how you looked at it. The last picture was of Tel Aviv, the capital they'd be discouraged from settling in, with an outline standing on a street corner. Above it were the words: 'Why aren't you here?'

I rummaged through the pile and found a dozen more, still in their envelopes, the same Denver address on the front. I couldn't understand why he'd held on to this junk mail. If he'd been thinking of emigrating, one would have been enough. The postmarks were never more than a month apart, a steady drip-feed of suggestion even if the Elders were careful not to threaten Jews out in the open. Aside from the Revivalists themselves, they were practically the only group in the United States that still had that privilege, though it could be revoked for individuals of both camps at any time.

I dug in the pile some more and found my answer: a different envelope, addressed only to a post office box in Point Pines. Inside was a letter in a child's hand, margins crooked, letters growing and shrivelling depending on how excited the kid was by the part of his new home he was describing. The back was a drawing of three figures: a boy and a girl the same size as the stick-frame house drawn behind them, a mother with brown hair and blue eyes towering protectively over them all. In the background, between the top of the mother's head and the bright yellow sun above, were grey rings that could only be barbed wire.

The Landsmans were relatively safe, wherever they were in the Holy Land. Access to Settlements was strictly controlled, and they were under armed guard twenty-four hours a day. The occasional mortar or rocket might fall near them, the occasional man might be shot at the front gate for walking the wrong way, but they were as safe as you could be in an armed outpost.

Now I had to wonder why Landsman hadn't gone to the Holy Land with them. His life here certainly wasn't an appealing alternative. Landsman's name could be on a Fisher Partners task order, his family allowed to leave because there was no profit in forcing them down the same hole they'd reserved for him. It was all the more reason to head for the border and try to rejoin them outside the country, as Benny had done.

Maybe Landsman was just stubborn. That I could understand.

'Hey, Pete,' Bloom called from down below, 'what are you doing up there, playing with yourself?'

I stuffed the child's letter into a pocket. It wasn't much, but after where I'd been, I knew how important the little things could be. I came downstairs with a brochure in my hand. Bloom and the Sons were waiting.

'I found some papers up there.' Landsman, who had shrunk

into himself, looked up at my face. I could feel him trying to read what I'd discovered. 'Just some junk mail, it turns out.'

'We're here to collect, not investigate,' Bloom said, and gave his prisoner a shove.

'I didn't do nothing,' the man said to himself, over and over again. It didn't stop us leading him out the door.

We'd barely cleared the front yard when we heard shots a few blocks over. The Sons of David stopped cold, mouths agape. I got on the move, stopping only long enough for Bloom to throw me his radio.

'Call in if anyone gives you trouble,' he said to my back.

There wasn't anyone around to give me trouble. I'd have expected that the sound of gunfire in a place like this – what passed for middle class nowadays, peaceful until we'd arrived – would attract at least some attention. It was nuts to walk outside or peer out the window after you knew someone was shooting but people did it all the time, a privilege of living in a place where lead in the air was a relative novelty. People learned to stay indoors when it was a fact of life.

I found three Sons of David standing in a back yard. They were staring at a boy curled up on the lawn holding his stomach in. He was their age, could have sat next to them in school. The little soldiers watched him bleed. One was repulsed and tried not to show it, but the other two were fascinated, especially a football type with a mess of brown hair. He had one of the red sergeant armbands on. I think Bloom had called him Darby. The grin on his face told me he was the shooter.

The three straightened up when they saw me. I doubted they knew who I was, but they'd seen me talking with Bloom before the mission began, and that was enough to make it clear I was to be respected.

'He had a gun, sir,' the shooter said to me, pointing with his

204

sub-machine gun at a rifle lying near the boy's left hand. 'He was interfering with our holy duty.'

'Get back to the vans,' I said. 'I'll clean this mess up.'

Darby hesitated, not sure now just how much authority I had. I stepped forward and hoped he'd give me an excuse to do something. Instead he turned away, taking his companions with him.

As soon as they were gone I knelt by the kid. The shot had found his stomach. I lifted him as gently as I could to look for an exit wound in his back. The bullet was still in there somewhere.

I laid him back down and put his knees upright. I remembered it from one of our interminable lectures during basic, some officer saying it reduced pain and shock, and prevented internal organs from being further exposed. I grabbed the Swiss Army knife on the kid's belt and used it to cut away his denim shirt, now soaked with blood. The wound was bad. It shouldn't have been that severe considering the gun the Son had been carrying. It was a crazy thought, as if there were someone to whom I could appeal while the evidence was bleeding on my hands.

'Hey, look at me,' I said to the kid, tapping his face, trying to get him to focus while I cut a strip off his shirt for a dressing. He didn't listen to what I was saying, but his eyes rolled in my direction.

'Are you here to take my daddy away too?'

He was lucid now, as lucid as he could be. I tried to ignore what he'd said and lifted him just a little so I could get the improvised bandage around his chest. The words stuck in my head, especially 'daddy'. It was a childish word, one he'd have been embarrassed to use in front of his friends. I tied the bandage lightly, careful not to put pressure on the wound.

When darkness fell across the boy, it took me a second to

realize what it was. I looked up to see an older man pointing a shotgun at me from three feet away. The bleeding teenager I was kneeling in front of could only be his son.

The father didn't pull the trigger. He was trying to figure out what I was doing, but the sight of so much of his son's blood was making it difficult for him to think clearly.

'Do you have something we could use as a stretcher?' I asked.

He lowered his gun, but didn't answer my question. I motioned with my head towards the pick-up truck in the drive.

'I don't want to move him, but they might come back.'

The father snapped out of his daze. I saw his wife poking her head out of the cellar where they'd been hiding just enough to see what had happened and weep. He yelled at her to bring the ironing board. I took the feet and the father the head while his wife got the car started.

'They're all over the main street,' I said to him when we had the boy loaded. 'Get him to a hospital any way you can.'

The father climbed in the back to hold his son's hand while the mother put the truck in gear.

'It should have been me.'

It was all the father said to me. Only when they were on the road did I stop to think about what had happened before I'd arrived. I didn't know why the Sons had been after him; they probably knew as much about him as I knew about Landsman. I couldn't figure out how the parents had found their hiding place while the boy had taken up arms. I'd never know. The way he'd looked at his son, I knew the father would call himself a coward whatever the circumstances had been.

I knelt on the ground and tried to wipe away the blood on my hands. The grass took the moisture but not the stain, or the smell. I closed my eyes and tried to go somewhere peaceful. It didn't work.

'Pete?'

It was Bloom's voice on the radio.

'What's the situation?'

'Everything's fine,' I said.

'Well, get back here then. We're moving out.'

I stood, began to put one foot in front of the other, and did everything I could not to think.

# TWENTY-TWO

## Between Denver and Colorado Springs, Colorado

Bloom dismissed me as soon as we got back to camp, so I was spared slow-walking our prisoners to wherever they would be held. I didn't know what they had planned for them, but I didn't need to see any more to convince me that Jefferson had been right about the danger the Sons of David posed. I had to find some alternative to putting a bullet in Joshua that Jefferson would be happy with.

The best way to do that would be to get into Joshua's little situation room. Hard evidence was the only way Jefferson would be persuaded. I had hoped being baptized into the tribes would give me more freedom in the camp. What being a member of the family meant in practice was that I was never more than five feet away from someone else. It was one of Joshua's commandments that we look out for each other's souls, which meant privacy was seen as disloyal. There was no reason for you to be alone except in a toilet stall; we were one and had better act like it.

What made it so bizarre, and at the same time easier to take, was that it didn't feel oppressive. Everyone I passed smiled and called me Gershom, the name Joshua had given me. I may have been surrounded, but it felt like being surrounded by friends. It was difficult to reconcile the smiling faces of children clutching toy Apostles with the look of triumph on the Son who had shot that teenager a few hours ago.

Something big was afoot. All day I saw the proselytizing groups – children led by their teenage 'parents' – on the way to the parking lot. Members of the flock were hard at work erecting the stage in a nearby field, but unlike the initiation no bleachers went up with it. When I asked what was going on, most of the people were too caught up in their sacred mission to do anything but smile and carry on. Those who answered said only, 'Revival,' as if that single word explained everything.

The sun was halfway to its rest when a boy came to me with a message from Bloom. I followed the messenger to a makeshift holding area. People of all ages sat on the ground, shackled to one another like a chain gang. There were a lot more of them than the ones we'd taken; other teams had been at work in other towns. Any fight they'd had in them had died during the hours of anxious waiting. They stared at the ground and kept the sobbing to themselves.

Instead of a cell, there was a wall of Sons of David. They ringed the detainees, guns at the ready, at least a few hoping they'd have an excuse to use them. Bloom stood some distance away talking with subordinates, master of the whole awful scene.

'Pete,' he said, calling me over. I wondered why he refused to use the name Joshua had baptized me with. I guess he'd decided there was only so much bullshit he could take. Too bad his tolerance for violence and the misery of others wasn't as low.

'What's going on?' I asked. 'No one seems inclined to tell me.'

'You're about to be a part of the best dog and pony show this side of Washington. Did you handle detainees in the army?'

'A little,' I said, not wanting to admit the full range of my experience. 'What do you want me to do?'

'Keep an eyes on these unlucky bastards,' he said, motioning to the people on the grass, 'and an even closer watch on their guards. These kids can get way too excited.'

'I guess it's a good thing they've got guns then.'

Bloom shrugged, as if excitable teenagers with automatic weapons was a fact of life.

'In a little while we'll need to move the detainees to an area behind the stage. The kids know where it is. I want you to make sure they don't slap anyone too hard along the way. Understood?'

I nodded.

'I get the feeling you got one more question.'

All day I'd been expecting a SWAT team to descend on the camp, if not a full FBI dragnet. Kidnapping a few dozen people in broad daylight tended to get the attention of the authorities. As dangerous as it would be, I'd been hoping the law would show up; I preferred the idea of being in the middle of an armed standoff than what Jefferson wanted me to do.

'What about the cops?'

Bloom laughed. I hadn't realized I was making a joke.

'The cops don't bother us, not with our friends. They haven't got the balls.'

Before I could ask who our friends were, Bloom began yelling at the Sons. He told them in no uncertain terms that I was in charge, then walked off and left me to manage the horror show. I was thankful Darby, the teenage shooter from earlier today, wasn't one of the guards. For the most part the Sons of David behaved themselves. Any time one of them got the urge to kick a detainee, he'd find my eyes on him. The mantle of Bloom's authority restrained them, as well as the threat of reciprocity I made sure was clear.

After a while Bloom called in over the radio and said to get the prisoners moving. I told them to stand first, hoping they would

210

get to their feet before the Sons gave them any help. Most of them got the message, but I had to restrain a guy from beating a man for the crime of being old and a little stiff.

A Son led the way while I kept an eye on the column. Those we passed greeted us in the same way they'd been saying hello to me all day, as if we were on a stroll instead of frog-marching a chain gang of terrified human beings.

I kept my eyes on the Sons of David. The only thing I could do for the prisoners was prevent them from being on the receiving end of their minders' high spirits. Landsman was near the middle, keeping his head down like everyone else. A figure near the back caught my attention: from between curtains of blonde hair I caught glimpses of a face I recognized. I let the line walk past me until she was parallel.

'Martha?'

She started at the sound of her name, shock raising her head for a moment before fear forced it back down.

'What happened?'

Martha wouldn't stop crying long enough to say. She had been the leader of the cheering squad Sarah had assigned to me when I first arrived. I'd thought Martha was one of Sarah's best friends judging by how they'd treated one another. I wanted to ask her again how she'd ended up on a chain gang of sinners, but I had to break off and stop the same Son from hitting the same man for the related crime of walking while old.

We reached the backstage area without too much mistreatment. A cross-section of America within a reasonable drive had gathered in a large crowd out front. They had the expectant mood of an audience promised something spectacular. There was no way I could add the spectators, Joshua and the prisoners in front of me together and come up with anything good.

Even a few years ago, a show like this wouldn't have attracted half as many people. The media had been cautious with the Revivalists ever since they came to power. All the big networks were part of conglomerates, as were the cable companies. Nobody wanted to lose millions of dollars over something as trivial as artistic integrity. The Revivalists had gone after the news first, but it was already so compromised it took a while for anyone to notice. Cable and satellite held out the longest. They didn't challenge the Elders directly, just imported shows and carried foreign channels that weren't to Revivalist taste.

There were ways to get around the censorship even after the companies had given in. Satellite dishes were still allowed – too many televangelists depended on them. It wasn't hard to point them towards foreign signals. In the last few years the firewalls and jammers hadn't gotten any more sophisticated; people were just less inclined to take the risk. I'd noticed the change on the way up to Kansas City. People had been disappearing for years by then. Citizens must have assumed that the Elders had developed some new surveillance technique, and didn't want to watch TV and their back at the same time.

A gaggle of teenage girls descended on the prisoners while I was watching the crowd. I was about to step in and prevent some new outbreak of violence when I realized that the weapons in their hands were powder, lipstick and eyeliner. A few of the detainees were startled into resistance, but that only gave the delighted Sons an excuse to raise their weapons. The resistance stopped almost as soon as it had begun.

The girls set to work making sure that the fear and mortification on the prisoners' faces weren't lost under stage lighting. They also added a few touches along the way, making their subjects more fearsome or comical according to printed instructions. One of the girls dragged a full bin bag behind her, from which she extracted props to finish off the look her sisters had

212

started: placards to hang around their necks, funny glasses and false ears, a large burst-vein nose that she put on a dark-haired man while others tied an apron around his waist.

They spent a lot of time on Landsman, again according to instructions they consulted and argued over as only a group of teenage girls could. They transformed the accumulation of exhaustion and fear that darkened his face into shadows around the eyes and an emphasis on the brow that made him look more scheming than broken. From the prop bag came an Old Testament beard and wide-brimmed black hat, side locks attached.

Landsman barely noticed his makeover. He was lost in his own world, expecting nothing from this one but pain and humiliation doled out according to a logic he would never understand. I knew that mask; I had worn it myself once. It hadn't disappeared when it had been lifted from my face, just transferred to another. Now the unlucky recipient was standing in front of me.

When the girls moved on I went over to Landsman and made a show of inspecting his restraints. Landsman stared straight ahead and didn't seem to notice. While I was fiddling with his cuffs I slipped the letter I'd taken from his squat into his hands. Landsman knew what it was as soon as he touched it, the feel of the paper, the folds he must have run his fingers over a hundred times. The small act of kindness startled him like a gunshot. He had the presence of mind not to say anything, but thanked me with his eyes. I checked some of the other prisoners' cuffs for form's sake, and pretended not to notice.

When the girls reached Martha I expected some reaction. As a personal friend of Sarah's, she must have known some or all of the girls now bearing down on her with drawn cosmetics. She tried to speak as they approached, but stopped as soon as the rouge touched her face. I saw a little recognition in the eyes of some of the girls, but that feeling never reached the rest of their face, let alone their hands. They worked on her the same way, applying more make-up than they had on the others. When they were done, the frightened girl had been transformed into a pantomime whore, a special mascara applied so the effect wouldn't be spoiled by her tears.

Orders came down to move the prisoners to the wings. Organ music, better songs than I was used to hearing to keep the audience entertained, filtered through from the front. It merged with the sounds of the prisoners marching, a shuffle-clink that was familiar.

I was in a hallway. There was a hand on my shoulder, and my hand on another's. We were deaf and blind, one leading the next. If a man fell, the chains around our ankles would drag us all down with him. We would do this step-clink shuffle until stopped by an order. The guards would subdivide us into smaller lines of pew length and then lead us into church.

We didn't sit until everyone was in place and the minister had arrived, a mark of respect only he could see. The headphones were removed, but not the chains or the blindfold. Perhaps they were afraid a secret cabal would plan an escape through a series of coded blinks. They certainly treated any cough of the wrong rhythm as an attempt at conspiracy. I wish they'd kept us deaf as well as blind; silence was preferable to the sermons.

The pastor was a mean old bastard in the fire and brimstone mould. He had a sandpaper voice that could reach around the whole room and grab it by the neck. I never saw him, but I always imagined a short man twisted smaller by time, white hair to match skin that was paler than ours, black, black eyes. He was the kind of man who would lecture to slaves about the Israelites and not blink twice.

'Each one of you bears the mark of Cain,' he began, 'and

214

without the personal intervention of the Saviour you have spoken against, worked against and sinned against, each one of you will burn for ever in hell.' They were big on tough love in IF.

The services weren't on a regular day at a fixed time. I only became sure of that once I had Gideon's visits to measure them against. I knew when it was day or night now, sometimes even the hour. No matter what time the service, the voice was always the same. There had to be more of us than could fit into this room, which meant the old man waited while guards brought in captive congregation after captive congregation, screaming the same words at different blind faces until the sun had set. Maybe he went home after that, to a family that bore him as their cross. The alternative was that there was more than one of him, and that thought was even worse.

Pretending to be a good Jew hadn't exempted me from these services. Either the paperwork had been messed up or the authorities were hoping my religious awakening would go all the way to Jesus. There were a few compensations. The pew under me was real varnished wood, a tactile novelty in this hell of fibreglass and steel. I liked running my hands on the seat's underside, where the whorls hadn't been polished away. The room must have had large windows; sometimes I could feel sunlight on my face even if I couldn't see it. They were letting me out for exercise by then, but the feeling was still rare enough I remembered it every single time.

I ignored most of what the preacher said. It was always about repentance and confession, and the consequences of resisting either. It would have been easier on all of us if he'd had a little of the faith and forbearance he so readily prescribed. He wasn't so deluded that he thought men brought to him in chains were interested in what he had to say. He fucked with us instead, breaking off in mid-sentence to start a hymn or demand we get

**215**

on our knees, just to see who was listening. I tried to separate a part of myself to monitor the flow of bullshit and let the rest wander free.

Gideon had said I thought I deserved to be here. I guess he was right. I had once delivered enemies into the hands of men like these. Now I had been delivered into theirs. If it wasn't karma, it had to be irony. The men whom I had wronged, they couldn't laugh at what happened to me in here, or commiserate over it, or decide I'd had enough and forgive me. They couldn't do much of anything. It would easier to think that my suffering meant something, instead of just adding to the oversupply of that commodity in this world. I wanted to believe. I knew better.

'And when—'

An organ began to pound us from the front. We got to our feet together, pulling up anyone who was too slow. They only ever played about ten songs. We opened our mouths and sang. God help you if you didn't sing.

# TWENTY-THREE

'Sir?'

A large girl was standing in front of me. She was speaking, half to me and the rest into a headset. She wore a look of smug efficiency and too much acne make-up.

'Are these the penitents?'

Another euphemism. Detainee might be more accurate, but it didn't have her word's flavour.

'Yes, ma'am.'

'Move them to the side there. I'll tell you when they're needed.'

The Sons of David prepared to accomplish this with yelling and gun butts. I got everyone's attention and persuaded the prisoners to step to the left on my command. Once in position, they waited in much the same attitude as when I'd first seen them: seeing nothing, expecting the worst.

We were in the midst of what could only be called a high school talent show. A children's choir rehearsed nearby, as well as kids dressed as the Statue of Liberty, George Washington, President Adamson, pilgrims and a bunch of other costumes I didn't recognize. The theatrical atmosphere gave me some hope for the prisoners. I didn't think lynchings had musical accompaniment.

Joshua took to the stage with a bombastic introduction. He wore a new costume for this performance: his old Sons of David uniform. All insignia had been removed like the others'. A pair of old aviator sunglasses shielded his eyes from the lights. All Joshua needed was a chest full of medals he'd given himself to complete his Little Generalissimo Hallowe'en costume.

Bloom wasn't among the retinue, but Joshua's security had doubled. Despite what I'd said to Jefferson, I couldn't help myself looking for weaknesses in his protection detail. I'd thought of snatching the kid as an alternative to killing him. With him in custody I might be able to persuade Jefferson that a trial would be more effective than making the boy a martyr. Right now I could see no way to neutralize the guards, get a hold of Joshua and then spirit him out of a camp filled with his supporters. If I didn't think of something soon, Jefferson would insist I follow through with the original plan.

'Good evening, brothers and sisters,' Joshua said. The plants in the crowd – new members of the flock eager to prove their devotion – clapped until the people around them did the same.

'You expect me to speak of our Saviour, and I will. You want to see a show, and you will. But I am here to give you so much more: I am here to give you answers.'

The crowd offered no more than polite applause, clearly interested in the first two over the third. Joshua was serene. I wondered how many times he'd done this schtick in front of crowds this size. Twelve years old, and already he was the consummate performer.

'Do you remember when President Adamson was elected? I was a little young' – his smile got a few easy laughs – 'but I know you do. Our nation was wounded and grieving for Houston. The forces of darkness were on the march all over the world. But one man didn't run, he stood up to be counted by God and the whole world.

'Adamson was our saviour, and he promised us a Godly administration. He promised us freedom from the taint of liberalism, feminism and Islamism. There would be no more tolerance of unwed mothers and their bastard children or homosexuals recruiting in our schools. The liberals who wanted to surrender to the terrorists and offer them therapy would be swept away. America would be a nation of strength again, not afraid to confront the armies of Muhammad and Satan. Adamson promised us an administration that would do everything in its power to bring about the glorious return of Jesus Christ and His thousand-year kingdom on earth.'

He had the crowd's attention now. Words like 'Adamson', 'strength' and 'Satan' all produced strong Pavlovian reactions. They were cheering, not for Joshua, but for the America they had been promised, the city on the hill that was always just past the horizon.

'Our President didn't live to see the promised land. Perhaps it was a mercy. He didn't live to see the reign of his disciples, the so-called Elders.'

Joshua's attack on the Elders produced in the crowd the same reaction as Sarah's words in Morning Star. The audience had spent years talking about the Elders behind their hands, looking at the people around them and wondering if they could be trusted. Even something as mild as 'the so-called Elders' was cathartic in the circumstances. They hung on Joshua's every word now, wanting to see just how far he'd go.

'Jobs go overseas. Businesses sell sex to women and children. Homosexuality and Islam run rampant. Foreigners defy us in the Holy Land and all over the world, laughing at our troops and treating us with contempt.

'And what do the Elders do about it? They tax us, tax us, and tax us some more. Their corrupt officials rob us blind, and where does the money go? They say it's for rebuilding the Temple. Do you see a temple? Do you even see a foundation? We ask these questions, and the Revivalists say we aren't true Christians.

'Once, it was a fact acknowledged the world over that Americans were the greatest people ever to tread the earth. Now look at us. Look at what we've become.'

The people who'd come for a cheap evening of distraction finally began to realize what they were in for. Tears were already falling, but they were for personal stories of the kind we'd confessed at our baptism. It was the alchemy of Joshua's words that transformed these tales of ordinary woe into something greater, an epic story where the crowd's private failures became part of a cosmic battle between good and evil.

I'd known the boy could speak ever since his after-dinner speech to the Sons. Now I wanted to know who was writing his speeches. There was no way a twelve-year-old could understand what it was like to work your whole life for something and then watch it slip through your fingers.

'Our enemies are emboldened and our friends worried. The Revivalists and the Elders who lead them have turned away from God. He in turn has withdrawn His protection and favour from America. We refuse to do His bidding, and for that we are being punished.

'As the Lord said unto Moses: "thy people, which thou broughtest out of the land of Egypt, have corrupted themselves. They have turned aside quickly out of the way which I commanded them: they have made them a molten calf, and have worshipped it."

'The Elders are our golden calf. We worship them because they have made us afraid to do the work of the Lord. No more. If we restore God's faith in us, He will shower His favour upon the nation. We will do what the Elders refuse to: finish the work of President Adamson. We will rebuild the Temple, we will remind the Jews that their place is with the Lord in Israel. We will cleanse this nation of homosexuals, harlots and pornographers. As the Lord said: "my wrath may wax hot against them, and that I may consume them: and I will make of thee a great nation."

'We must return to God before it is too late. This corrupt world is dying; our only hope lies in the next. As Moses destroyed the calf, so too must we cast down the Elders!'

The crowd was on its feet, whole families screaming and clapping at their hidden desires laid bare. Before tonight, I hadn't understood what really scared Jefferson about this kid. When preaching to the converted he sounded like any other cult whackjob, the kind that had been ranting in fortified compounds since before I was born. I thought his age was the only novelty, but what made Joshua special was a charisma that convinced ordinary people that what he said was reasonable and correct, no matter how crazy the words.

'Are you ready to stand with me? Are you ready to destroy the enemies of America?'

Those questions sounded a little ridiculous when asked in a voice that hadn't yet broken, but the crowd disagreed. I didn't need a programme to know what would happen next. Joshua had made them as mad as hell, and now he was going to provide lambs for ritual slaughter. Lambs I had brought to him.

The girl with the headset ran up and began to gesture at three of the prisoners. They were the man with the fake nose, the professor and a man they'd forced into bicycle shorts and sleeveless spandex. I oversaw their separation from the others and walked with them all the way to the edge of the stage. The girl shoved the prisoners into order with the exasperated air of a teacher keeping control of a school pageant.

'I present to you the enemies of the American people. As Elijah said to Ahab: "I have found thee: because thou hast sold thyself to work evil in the sight of the LORD."'

That was the cue for two Sons to bring the professor on stage. The audience had no idea who he was, but they saw the tweed, the glasses and the mortarboard and screamed bloody murder.

'This man, this "educator", thinks he's better than you,' Joshua said. 'He thinks you're stupid because you didn't go to Yale, that you're a fool because you believe in God, and a hick because you drive a truck. These are the values he teaches to children.'

Boos and a few wrappers hit the terrified man. A few times during the list of charges he'd tried to open his mouth to defend himself, but any words had been lost in Joshua's amplified voice.

'But for his know-it-all attitude, this professor is the stupidest of all. He thinks we are descended from apes. He calls all those fancy ideas he rubs in your face human knowledge. Well, who needs that when you have this?' Joshua said, holding up a Bible. 'This is superhuman knowledge. This is heaven and earth, light and dark, right and wrong, all in one easy volume. This is the only knowledge you need.'

One of the Sons took off the mortarboard and fitted the scared old man with a dunce cap. He looked ready to faint so they held him, a boy on each side, and let the crowd do its best to prove the theory of evolution by making animal noises in his direction. He was dragged off stage only when their enthusiasm waned.

222

The man with the false nose was dragged on next. I didn't know what the game was here, and neither did the crowd.

'This man is a slave master,' Joshua said. 'He catches men in his net and never lets them go.'

The crowd was still confused. Was Joshua saying he was gay?

'From noon to morning this man pushes a drug: alcohol. His bar leads to violence, to fornication, leads husbands away from families and into the arms of death and Jezebel.'

There was a definite gender imbalance in the screaming that followed. The women went at him almost as hard as they had at the professor, though I doubt that meant they were above a few drinks at home. As for the men, their symbolic condemnation showed that many husbands hadn't so much been led to the bar as gone there seeking asylum.

Joshua sensed immediately that he was on to a loser. Rather than drawing out the charges as he had with the first victim, he got the Sons to dump a few beers over the man for a little comic relief and then hustle him off.

He was replaced by a succession of villains: real, imaginary and bizarre. Girls that the Sons found attractive were dragged under the spotlight and shamed as sluts. Only Joshua didn't see that this was as much an expression of hope on the part of the men as it was derision from the women eager to prove their virtue.

The man in bicycle shorts and a few others were branded sodomites. The Sons' idea of a gay man was a mincing, lisping fool, so how they'd settled on these men I had no idea. At stake was more than humiliation; they'd made sodomy a federal crime while I was inside, and this crowd yelled their willingness to settle the charge with a lynch mob right there and then. As for the guy branded a Satanist, complete with a placard of a pentagram hung around his neck, as far as I could tell his only sin was looking like a drummer for a heavy metal band.

'And now a special example,' Joshua said. 'An example of sin that pains my heart to its depths, because it comes from one of our own.'

They pulled Martha past me. She tried to reason with the Sons holding her, called the teenagers by their Christian names. They didn't seem to hear, as indifferent to her pleas as they had been to all the others. They dragged a girl they must have spoken to, known, spent at least a little time with, out into the spotlights and a crowd seething with displaced anger.

'Do you know why you're here?' Joshua said in a paternal way to a girl only three years older than himself.

Martha didn't respond. She was stunned by his presence and the yelling of the crowd. Since Martha was a teenage girl, they'd already started calling her a whore; Satanists and gays weren't nearly as exciting as the idea of young feminine flesh passing itself around.

'Bring up the witnesses.'

A Son and a hatchet-faced woman were escorted on to the stage. Joshua approached the woman first.

'Good sister, will you tell us what you saw?'

The woman was wearing heavy make-up, almost as heavy as the clown face they'd put on Martha and applied with about the same skill. I got the feeling the woman had done it to herself ahead of her big scene.

'I was walking back to the tents after dinner,' the woman began, lines rehearsed. 'I saw a shadow out of the corner of my eye. I thought it was a terrorist.'

'In a way, it was,' Joshua said. His interjection confused her until he put a hand on her shoulder.

'That Jezebel had cornered this poor boy against a trailer. "I

**224**

know you want it,"'' the woman said in her best imitation, not of a teenage girl, but a breathy femme fatale. The combination killed every erection within a square mile.

'She took his hands and put them all over her young body, fluttered those eyelashes of hers. She shook everything she had at him. "Take me now," she'd said as she undid her jeans and—'

'You swear you witnessed all this with your own eyes?' Joshua said, disappointing the crowd by stopping her before she got to the good part.

'I swear.'

'Young man, can you tell us what happened?'

'I knew Martha as a sister.' He wasn't as rehearsed, stammering over his words from remorse or a simple lack of nerve. 'After dinner, she asked me to help her, um, move some things.'

'Go on, I know this is difficult,' Joshua said.

'She led me behind this trailer, put herself close to me. I immediately became, um, afraid for my soul.'

I heard one or two laughs, stifled but still audible in the silence. It was nice to know there were a few working brains out there, even if they didn't want to draw attention to themselves.

'I told her we must be married in the eyes of God,' the boy said after prompting from Joshua. 'That it was sinful and wrong. She said she wanted me and didn't care. If this good woman hadn't shown up, I don't know what would have happened.'

I looked around for a six-year-old to show a little scepticism, but the children were as enraptured as the adults in the audience. Some of Joshua's helpers hung a sign around Martha's neck that said 'JEZEBEL'. She was close to passing out; two Sons had to hold her up so the crowd could scream at her.

The detective in me couldn't help but wonder what had really happened. Perhaps Martha and the boy had been into some heavy petting when the killjoy found them. Or maybe the woman had seen them smiling at one another and decided to take out the waste of her own life on a young couple whose happiness she envied. This charade had probably gotten her more attention than she'd had in her entire life. The boy had sold out his Juliet for one reason or another, safe in the knowledge that there was no male equivalent to the whore of Babylon.

Whatever had happened, it was clear I was the only one who actually cared. Everyone backstage was as focused as the audience on the melodrama out front. Whether it was from general piety or delight at the entertainment, I couldn't say. More likely the spectators didn't draw a line between the two. With their attention so diverted, it was a golden opportunity for me to snoop around. I didn't want to be there for Landsman; I'd seen enough already.

The camp was almost empty. Everyone was at the revival, as participant or spectator. Ignoring one of Joshua's performances would have been evidence of disloyalty, not that any of his fans needed extra motivation to see him. His section of the camp was empty except for a few guards in front of Joshua's tent.

I walked past the guards, seemingly on my way to my own tent. Once they were out of sight I doubled back and crouched down beside one of the tent pegs, pretending to fumble with my shoe. I stayed there for a minute, listening. No voices came from the other side of the canvas. I untied the rope from the peg. It gave me just enough slack to lift up the tent and crawl inside.

The room I emerged into was familiar from the glimpse I'd seen that first night. There was the computer and sound equipment for Joshua's broadcasts, the monitors dark this time. In another corner were the same National Guard crates Bloom had taken possession of. I opened one with a crowbar someone had left nearby for the purpose. Inside, packed up snug on beds of straw, was brick after brick of plastic explosive. In the right hands there was enough here to bring down a large building.

'It's a good crowd tonight,' Bloom said from Joshua's audience chamber next door. I guess that answered the question of where he'd gotten to. 'They're getting bigger every show. The kid's got them eating out of his hand; it's only a matter of time before he goes national.'

He paused while the person on the other end of the line responded. I couldn't hear the other voice, wanted to know if it was Glass. If they caught me right now it wouldn't matter whether I was right. I replaced the lid on the crate but couldn't pound the nails back in place without Bloom hearing it. I hid behind the desk that held the computer and listened to half of Bloom's conversation. From the gaps between his words, it was clear the other end was asking the questions and in control.

'The cops have been no trouble. They know we've got friends upstairs, and we're better armed than they are anyway. It's the feds I'm keeping an eye out for, just like you said. They won't hit us in front of these people. If they try their luck, it will be on the road.'

Bloom didn't seem too worried about the possibility. I got the feeling he had more up his sleeve than just C4.

The other person asked Bloom a series of questions that elicited only binary responses. Voices passed by the tent, laughter and high spirits. I shrank against the desk, not that it would do any good. I'd be found as soon as someone entered this room, and talking myself out of it would be next to impossible.

'The shipment arrived yesterday,' Bloom said, finally offering a larger answer. 'Everything is accounted for. Flite isn't crazy about the quality of the detonators, but he says they'll do.' The other voice said something and Bloom laughed. 'Wormwood is on schedule, sir. I'll contact you when phase three is complete, but you'll probably hear about it on the news first.' They shared another laugh, then a formal goodbye.

I got out of the tent the same way I got in, tying the rope back to the peg in case someone smart walked by. My car was in the camp's lot. The camp itself was mostly empty, but not deserted enough for me to risk the earpiece. Joshua's entertainment would last long enough for me to get to the car and warn Jefferson. Whatever they were up to, it sounded worse than what I'd already been an accomplice to that day.

No one challenged me on my way there, just gave the usual smile and greeting. I returned it in an efficient manner, tried to give off the vibe that I was on some important errand for Bloom. Everyone I passed was content to judge a book by its cover and let me go on my way.

I opened the car and got my medication. It was my alibi, and I needed it anyway. The lot was deserted, but I still crouched between the cars. Jefferson answered the phone himself after four rings.

'We need to meet,' I said, before he could ask if I'd killed Joshua.

'There's nothing more to discuss.'

'The Sons of David just kidnapped a few dozen people and are currently parading them in front of a crowd,' I said. 'I think we have something to discuss.'

'If you're so concerned about those people, then do your job.'

There was no emotion or surprise in Jefferson's voice. I imagined him sitting in an office in the Pentagon, headset nibbling on his ear, crumbs from lunch still hidden in his shirt. This was the man I would depend on for my life if things went south.

'You knew about the revivals, didn't you?'

'They don't exactly keep them a secret.'

'What do these assholes have to do to get arrested?'

'I told you it wasn't that simple. Part of my assignment was discrediting the Sons, but they're doing that just fine on their own. We've got eyes on them all the time, to make sure things don't get too out of hand.'

'They shot a kid today. I guess your eyes missed that.'

'The more people hate and fear them, the easier your job is.'

Now it was my turn not to be surprised. The Sons had been so open about what they were doing, crimes in front of a crowd of thousands, I knew they had to have some kind of protection, even before Bloom had said they don't worry about the cops.

'Who's protecting them, Jefferson? Glass doesn't have that much influence.'

'For the last time, Glass has nothing to do with the Sons. Stop chasing your tail and hold up your end of the bargain.'

'The Sons of David are planning something a lot bigger and a lot worse than the side show they're putting on now.'

'And what's that?'

'I don't know exactly, but it involves a lot of high explosives.'

Jefferson's bored monotone finally changed.

'Explosives?'

'C4. I saw bricks of it with my own eyes. That's what was inside those National Guard crates.'

'You don't know what it's for?'

I'd finally gotten Jefferson's attention, right around the same time I'd run out of answers.

'No idea. Isn't it obvious now that the Sons of David are a front for something else? We'd better find out who or what is using these kids before a federal building is vaporized on your watch.'

Jefferson took his time answering. Every second he delayed left me open to exposure. He was lucky I couldn't reach through the earpiece and shake an answer out of him.

'Look into it. Your primary mission is delayed, not aborted. Is that clear?'

'Gershom?'

I stood up, hoping the earpiece was too small to be seen in this light. Sarah was three rows over.

'What are you doing out here?'

'I forgot my pills,' I said, closing the distance before she could, palming the earpiece along the way. I held up a bottle from my pocket like a child at show and tell.

'You won't need these much longer,' she said, taking the bottle from my hand.

'What do you mean?'

'Come on,' Sarah said, taking my arm and leading me back towards the stage. 'You'll miss the big finale.'

# TWENTY-FOUR

## Between Denver and Colorado Springs, Colorado

By the time we returned to the backstage the last prisoner was being dragged out to face the crowd. He was the poor man's devil, a harried figure in a cheap suit and a pair of red plastic horns. I figured him for a lawyer.

'Do you know who this is?' Joshua asked.

The question was clearly rhetorical. The crowd went nuts as soon as the spotlight fell on him. There couldn't be that many tailors in the crowd as outraged as I was at the quality of his suit.

'I think you've seen him before, or you know someone who has. This is Matthew Reilley, supervisor of Vice Prevention and Suppression for all of Denver.'

I'd heard the Office of Vice Prevention and Suppression mentioned in whispers and oaths ever since I got out. It was another head of the Revivalist bureaucratic hydra that had grown while I was in IF. From what people had said they sounded like the third iteration of the Elders' morality police, after the Committee of Child Protection had failed and the Sons of David had turned against them. From what I'd heard, they weren't a police force themselves, just a bureaucracy with investigators. They outsourced the dirty work of arrest to local cops, but they were always on hand to inspect their victim's property.

Asset forfeiture laws used in the War on Drugs were suddenly found to apply to all manner of other vices as well. If you lived with two unmarried women to whom you weren't blood-related, you were a pimp running a brothel. A friendly poker game in somebody's kitchen became an illegal casino operation. The properties on which these wicked crimes took place became fruits of a criminal enterprise, and thus eligible for seizure and sale, the money disappearing into the office's coffers. Promotion was determined by how much vice, measured in dollars, was suppressed, just like drug warriors were judged by the street value of the drugs they could put in front of the cameras. America was a meritocracy, after all.

'What does he have to do with me?' I asked Sarah.

'Nothing. Your part comes next.'

'Have you still got my medication?' I asked. 'I may not last that long unless you give it to me.'

She showed me the pills and then hid them with a smile, as if she were playing peekaboo with a child.

'Have patience, Gershom. And faith.'

My head had started spinning halfway to the stage. I felt like a record that was beginning to skip. The tingling in my nerves said a seizure was coming, but that didn't make any sense. The regular seizures were kept at bay by the medication. The new seizures, the infrequent attacks caused by that same medication always came without warning and left just as suddenly. I didn't know what was wrong, but I needed the pills Sarah had before my brain could no longer entertain the question. I wasn't ready to take them from her by force, but I didn't want to think what I'd be capable of in an hour or two.

'Confess your sins.'

'I have indulged my own greed.'

To the audience out front, his mumbled confession might have looked genuine. I was backstage, and could see the gun against his back.

'I have aided and abetted the Elders in their theft from the working men of this nation. I have worked against God and His word. I humbly ask forgiveness from America and its protector Jesus Christ.'

The crowd rejected his apology by surging forward. The Sons of David pushed them back, brandishing their weapons. I was amazed all this heightened emotion hadn't yet got anyone killed.

'This is the corruption that is destroying this nation,' Joshua said, grabbing Reilley by the hair and lifting his head to the crowd.

I thought Joshua might give Reilley to the mob then and there. He'd raised their anger and hate to a point on the far side of delirium; I didn't see how anything less than blood would satisfy them. Instead, Reilley was dragged off stage, and Joshua faced the mob he had created alone.

'We live in a world beset by demons,' Joshua said. 'They are in every city, every street and every house. I have shown you only a few of the faces they hide behind. These creatures urge good men to blasphemy, violence and sexual licence. They cannot be negotiated with, reasoned with or appeased. I know you understand this, because each and every one of you fights these demons every day.

'But I am a child, you say. What do I know of fear, greed or lust? On what road have I met these demons?

'My father was a preacher. I'm sure a few of you still remember him from the Holy Ghost Network. I grew up on the road with my parents: auditoriums, tents and little church halls were my playgrounds. If there were six men on a street corner, my father would call it a meeting and preach. He was the one who taught me to stand here, unafraid in front of a crowd of strangers, and spread the Word.

'My dear mother, on the other hand, was a shy person. She didn't display herself the way some preachers' wives do. She knew she was needed at home, not out strutting in front of the TV. She told me that I was one of the pure generation, the fruit of Revivalist labour. The Lord had a destiny for me, she knew it from the first time she saw my face. It was my responsibility to be ready when the Lord called, to study the Bible and keep myself pure. I thought it would be easy, but my father had one lesson left to teach me.'

I saw pain and a sort of expectation on the face of every Son. A few of the girls began to cry, but they were tears shed in anticipation, not a reaction to what I was seeing. Only Sarah seemed unaffected; or, rather, a kind of joy still shone in her face, a mile away from the pain of her brothers and sisters.

'He'd been carrying on behind my mother's back. The lights and the adoration of the crowds had let a powerful demon into his heart. That demon wanted money and power. That demon wanted women, and it dragged my poor father from one slut's bedroom to the next to satisfy itself.

'My mother knew, of course. She could see the signs. She spent every night on her knees, praying to God harder than she'd ever done before. Still it carried on. One night, when she had almost lost hope, the Lord sent her a vision.

'She saw me. I was wreathed in this incredible light. My whole body shone with it. She knew it must be the Holy Ghost. I stood over my father. She sensed he had been in great pain, but was now at peace, the demon gone.

'My mother woke me in the night. She told me her vision. I was a child – like so many of those the Lord chooses to work

234

through, I didn't understand. My mother knew what to do. She brought me before my father, and told him his salvation was at hand.

'The demon laughed in our faces. He laughed the way all sinners do, when they believe they are far from the eyes of God. The demon grabbed my mother. I tried to separate them, to make the man and woman who had brought me into this world love each other like I thought they always had. My father recoiled from my touch. My own father.

'The demon did not fear a six-year-old boy. It was the Holy Ghost inside me, the light my mother saw. I told that demon, in a voice not my own, to come out. It would live in my father no more. The demon and the Holy Spirit struggled. Then there was a flash, the sound of thunder. My father fell. The demon had gone, and taken my father with him.'

Joshua took off his glasses, so the crowd could see his tears. I got the feeling they were genuine, even if they'd been summoned on demand.

'When the police found my father's body, what could we say? What lawyer, what judge, even one of the Elders' supposedly Christian men, would believe our story? My mother was blamed, his infidelity the motive. She died in prison. The last time I saw her, she said, "Joshua, the Spirit is in you. You have been chosen to cast the demons out, to lead the last pure generation into the final days. When the Lord returns, your work will be done. When the Lord returns, we will be a family again."

'When someone tells you that joint is harmless, that what people do in their bedrooms is their own business, that they're not hurting anyone,' he said, dragging out the last word, 'tell them my story. I am an orphan of that victimless crime.'

Joshua closed his eyes and walked into his own world for a moment. Grieving women called out his name as if they were his mother. There wasn't a dry eye in the whole audience. It was just a story, I thought, but the pit that had opened in my stomach said otherwise.

'I don't know why I was chosen,' Joshua said, opening his eyes and making a show of wiping away his tears. 'I was just a boy. But God has made me a messenger, and what I have to tell you is this: when you struggle with yourself, you do not struggle alone. Your battle with lust and despair is part of a great war that began when time itself was young. Each one of you is a soldier in the holy army. Some day soon, the general Jesus Christ will return, and our private struggles will become the last great battle for heaven and earth. As Revelation says: "And I saw three unclean spirits like frogs come out of the mouth of the dragon, and out of the mouth of the beast, and out of the mouth of the false prophet. For they are the spirits of devils, working miracles, which go forth unto the kings of the earth and of the whole world, to gather them to the battle of that great day of God Almighty."

'I am a messenger, and what I have to tell you is this: hope is not lost. Our general is coming. That is the message I was chosen by God to spread across this nation. The Lord needs America; we are His sword, His shield, His homeland. We are in the last days; the signs are all around us. We cannot lose faith now. I am here to give you hope with words, and with these childish hands.'

Joshua held up his palms to the crowd, who began to cheer.

'That's our cue,' Sarah said.

'Cue for what?'

She led me out on to the stage. I wouldn't have been able to make it myself. The world was spinning, or perhaps I was, the effect was the same. When the crowd saw me, they neither cheered nor demanded my blood. They hadn't been told what to think of me yet.

By the time we reached Joshua I was beginning to shake. Neither he nor Sarah seemed worried that I might fall apart in front of them and hundreds of people.

'I need my pills,' I whispered to Sarah, too weak to grab them now.

'The man you see before you is a hero,' Joshua told the crowd. 'He fought valiantly in the Great Patriotic Crusade, risked his life to avenge the atrocity of Houston. We are here today because of people like him.'

The audience cheered the halo Joshua's words had woven around my head.

'When you fight a man, you may be cut, you may be shot or burned. This man fought the armies of Satan. His wounds are invisible, deeper than mere flesh. This man fought demons, and he returned with one in his heart.'

The front row of the crowd, which had boiled over while Reilley was on stage, moved back a little. I often had that effect on people, but I was too delirious to laugh about it now.

'The Elders discarded these brave Christian warriors when science said there was nothing wrong with them. What does science know? You only need eyes to see that this man is sick, only one book to tell you what is wrong.' Joshua brandished the Bible again. 'This hero needs healing that no doctor can provide.'

The crowd was silent now, expectant. Whatever Joshua was going to do, I hoped he was about to get it over with. I had a lot of convulsing and slipping into a coma to do.

Sarah stood me up in front of him. Everything swayed. Joshua's face was wrong somehow. Everything was out of focus except his face, and it was bathed in a light whose source I could not see. He raised his hands and smiled.

'By the power of God, creator of heaven and the earth, by all

His angels and archangels, by the power of our Lord Jesus Christ, I command you begone!'

With that last word Joshua struck my forehead. It felt like a bolt of lightning. Every muscle twitched at once, my breath caught in my throat. The world stopped. I fell, and kept falling, the stage floor a mirage that receded the more I approached. I saw the faces of the crowd gazing rapturously at Joshua: adults looking to a child to lead them. They must know as I did, deep in their head if not their heart, that this was insane. Yet they set aside their own minds, and were glad to do it. A dream was better, no matter what kind.

I fell into Sarah's arms, the smell of detergent and lipstick. I lay still. The shaking was gone.

'You are free now,' she whispered in my ear, her hair falling across my eyes like a shadow.

'Who will be healed?' Joshua asked.

It was the last thing I heard. It was darkness, not the storm of convulsion, that came to save me from a sea of grasping hands.

# TWENTY-FIVE

The smell of death: burned bodies, torn bodies, blood in the air. Over that smoke, powder, oil and insulation on fire. I recognized the bouquet. A battlefield.

I was standing in what was left of a street. Low buildings had been shoved close together before high explosive toppled one on the other. What was left of the grey walls was covered in writing, a label on an air-conditioning unit in the middle of the street. Farsi. I was in Tehran.

A buzzing in my ear. A little American voice, coming from a piece of plastic. I pulled it out and looked at it. The little voice inside told me to advance.

I had returned to hell.

Benny motioned to me from behind a hand cart further up the street. I ran over, the kit on my back a familiar if not comforting weight, the rifle loose in my hands.

'Where the hell are we?'

'Do you see a sign?' Benny said. 'They're telling us to go up that street, so that's what we're going to do.'

Up close, I realized I was talking to the Benny I remembered, not the one I knew. Here was the kid straight out of Brooklyn via basic training, unmarried, not yet a father or a fed. He was younger, as happy-go-lucky as you could get in a war zone, but not naive. We'd already seen too much by then.

'I don't suppose the sergeant said why.'

Benny grinned at me from beneath a layer of dirt and soot. 'Let's go.'

We advanced. Our sergeant was out front, a man I recognized but couldn't remember. We went slow, cover to cover, climbing our way up the street more than walking. No one spoke but the radio, and it managed to make a lot of noise without saying anything.

It was happening again. I remembered every word that Benny said, and what I said in response. The street, the soldiers who I didn't recognize any more now than I did then, I could draw it all from memory. It was all the same, or at least it was what I remembered. That meant I knew what was coming.

It was near the end of the invasion, but only the beginning of the war. What was left of Tehran's defenders had gathered in the old bazaar. It was the only way to Khomeini Mosque, all other routes blocked by rubble and mines. The bazaar was an ancient labyrinth of small shops and covered arcades, a defender's dream. We'd sent some architects in B-52s to remodel the place from a thousand feet, then brought in the artillery for advice on decorating the interior. The tons of TNT we'd dropped had only multiplied the places to shoot and hide, made it impassible to trucks but still too narrow for armour. It was a fortress, and we had been ordered to lay siege.

The Iranians were essentially trapped in there, but command wanted us to go in and root them out anyway. Later I would hear that the order had come from President Adamson himself. I guess he had visions of us raising Old Glory on the dome of the mosque just like the Soviets had flown the hammer and sickle

240

from the ruins of the Reichstag, and he'd wanted it in time for the anniversary of Houston. At the time, we were told this would be the end. Losing the mosque would break the Iranians' will to fight. Take this one patch of land and we'd be home by Christmas. I didn't know that day that I'd be stuck in Tehran for years after, fighting over a city we had already declared conquered.

A few shots ahead. We stopped while forward elements looked for the sniper. Benny looked back at me but didn't say anything. He was one step ahead, behind the second storey of a warehouse that had fallen into the street. I wanted to warn him, run over and drag him back. I couldn't. I was a passenger in my own body. I couldn't even turn my head in a different direction than I had on that day.

There was an explosion ahead, then 'incoming' in my ear. I covered my face. Explosions. A shower of grit. My ears ringing, black smoke. The ambush was happening, again. Martyrs and snipers in front to slow us down, mortars already zeroed on our position. Shells falling, screams lost in the explosions. It would get worse.

The radio was dead, or I couldn't hear it above the ringing. I forced myself to stand, move through the smoke towards the place I'd seen Benny. I found him on the ground, holding his side.

'What happened?' I yelled.

'What does it look like? I got shot.'

Our sergeant was dead. I knew the other bodies nearby were marines only because of their tattoos. I didn't see any friendlies up ahead, and there was still nothing on the radio. I found out later that, for a moment, Benny and I were the vanguard of the US Army. It wasn't a position anyone held for long.

'What's that?' Benny said.

'What's what?'

My ears cleared enough to hear something I didn't quite believe the first time, and dreaded the second.

'They're singing,' I said. I didn't know enough Farsi to understand the words then. Later I didn't want to know.

'Time to go,' I said, lifting Benny on to my shoulder despite his howls of protest. I could already see figures in the smoke, too many to be friendly. The song finished, and with one last 'Allahu Akbar' they charged. I remembered the whole world slowing down so I could see kids running towards me, carrying cricket bats, chains, knives, anything that could open veins and bash in skulls. Later I had time to think about that moment, teenagers rushing soldiers with automatic weapons, armed only with what could be found in the average kitchen. The Pasdaran were behind them, waiting for us to chew up their youngest generation so they could mop up whoever survived.

I was too busy running to think of any of this until later.

I had Benny on my left shoulder. I fired behind me as I ran, shooting one-handed from the hip, not slowing down to look back. The rifle went dry and I threw it away. I drew my sidearm, my uncle's forty-five. I risked a look back, but didn't fire. There were too many for it to matter.

A kid about seventeen in a shirt that had once been white came within a few steps. He had an old hatchet raised above his head. I shot him and didn't stick around to watch him fall. My legs were heavy, Benny even heavier. Smoke was in my lungs. I couldn't breathe. I saw the alley through a haze of sweat and smoke tears. They were still coming. Two hacked at a dead soldier, maybe alive when they'd found him. Artillery fire, beyond danger close, tore up the air around us. It killed Basij, but it didn't slow them down.

I felt something kick me in the ass. I stumbled, fell to my

242

knees, turned to see a woman old enough to be the kid's mother holding an old Soviet pistol. She had emerged from the remains of one of the metal shutters that used to protect shops during the night. She was as surprised by what she had done as I was. I shot her before she had the chance to fire again.

My legs weren't working right. I could crawl, but I couldn't move Benny.

'You still alive?' I said.

'Fuck,' was all he could manage in response.

The Basij were still coming. Too many to count. I wondered what the adults had said to them, how they'd convinced these kids to throw away their lives. I raised my gun and waited for them to come within range. I'd been too high on fear and adrenaline to realize I was probably going to die. I just fired, and kept firing.

Hands on my shoulders. I hit out at the hands, tried to crawl on top of Benny to protect him. I couldn't bring the pistol to bear. I struggled and screamed but the hands were on my arms now, English in my ear, voices telling me they were friendly. Machine-gun fire, close and going downrange.

I screamed for a medic. They told me I'd been shot. I didn't listen. I screamed for a medic. My friend was wounded.

I awoke in Joshua's tent. It was bright outside. Joshua was there, staring at nothing. The uniform, sunglasses and stage make-up were gone. He wore a pair of old jeans and a dark hoodie, and almost looked like a normal twelve-year-old boy.

'What happened?' I said, sitting up.

'I tore a demon from you,' Joshua said. 'I've only met one that was more powerful.'

'Your father's?'

'I don't like telling that story,' Joshua said, pulling his knees up to his chest. 'Every time I think it will hurt less, but it doesn't. I wish I didn't have to.'

'Who's forcing you?' I asked, but he didn't seem to notice that I had spoken.

'Do you ever feel compelled?'

'Compelled?'

'I have a calling.' Joshua stopped. I think it was the first time I'd seen him struggle to find the right words. 'It's hard to explain. It's not voices or anything stupid like that, just a feeling. I've had it ever since . . .' He went silent again. 'It's the Holy Spirit, telling me what I have to do.'

'How do you know it isn't a demon?' I asked, probably unwisely.

Joshua laughed. I guess I'd made a joke.

'Have you ever felt like that?' he said.

I tried to think of the exact moment I'd decided to kill the men who had taken Iris. Maybe it had been the wall of faces at Grand Central, the names upon names of the missing, or that warehouse, with its room of bare iron beds waiting for more detainees. I'd had difficulty explaining myself to Gideon because it had never been a conscious decision. By the time I'd reached Grand Central, it was the only thing I could do.

'There was a time when I was in the army,' I said, choosing to tell an older story. 'We were going out on this mission to look for nuclear weapons. The whole thing was wrong, probably a trap that was going to get everyone killed, but I insisted on going. At the time I thought it was to prove everyone wrong, even if it cost me my life. Now I think I had to be there. It was where I belonged.'

'And you survived,' Joshua said.

'I was the only one.'

'Would you still go?'

'If you mean would I be able to stop myself from going?' I said, 'the answer is no.'

'You were spared from death for a reason, Gershom,' Joshua said. 'Perhaps an angel is guiding your steps, the way the Holy Ghost guides mine.' If there was such a thing as an angel, the only one that would be guiding steps like mine was the fallen one Joshua had claimed he'd pulled out of me. 'I think you were meant to help me reach Houston. I know with every fibre of my being that that is where I belong.'

Among my arsenal of half-baked plans, I'd hoped I could find a way to convince Joshua not to finish his tour. Looking in his eyes, I knew the only thing that could stand between Joshua and Houston now was a bullet.

'I'm so tired, Gershom,' he said, closing his eyes. 'Tired of fighting demons, tired of looking at this world. Why stare at the trees or admire the stars, when everything I see will turn to ash before I am a man? This world is already dead, it waits only for our Saviour to put it down. I pray every night for the Lord to free me from this impatience, but it is a test He has decided I must bear. We are so close to Judgement, Gershom. I know I will not be raptured with the others. My place is on this earth, carrying a sword for my God. I will see the mountains crumble, the seas turn to blood, all those sinners who sneer at our purity burned, poisoned, hacked to death and torn apart.'

Joshua smiled and the boy was gone again, replaced by something I couldn't name but had learned to fear. I was glad I couldn't see what was going on behind his closed eyes.

'It will be a glorious day, and my work will be done.'

'What happens when we get to Houston, Joshua?'

'A miracle.'

He stood up suddenly, as if he'd just heard the Holy Ghost calling him.

'I'm glad we had this chat, Gershom,' Joshua said, and then he was gone.

I stood on unsteady legs, the sounds of Tehran still ringing in my ears. The guards who'd made sure that I passed the night here were outside, part of a group that had gathered near the front of the tent. I walked out into the blinding morning, still not quite believing where I was, and where I had been.

A circle of Sons of David and a few older converts had gathered around a single dead bird. It was a sparrow, light grey, resting peacefully on its back. There was no sign of what felled it, no blood or buckshot. It looked asleep. The crowd murmured around me, trying to divine the bird's meaning.

It was a morning thick with ill omens.

# TWENTY-SIX

## Between Denver and Colorado Springs, Colorado

A panicked Son ran into the middle of the circle examining the bird.

'The cops are here,' he said between gasps to everyone, so afraid he didn't know who to report to.

The Seventeen men were already forming an armed perimeter around Joshua's compound. Bloom seemed to appear out of nowhere, directing a few of the soldiers with a nod.

'I thought you said the police wouldn't give us any trouble.'

'They aren't the police,' Bloom said, as he dialled his phone. He was calling Glass for instructions, I was sure of it.

A minute later a throng of Sons and converts came towards us, cattle driven by the news of whoever had arrived. They were looking for Joshua for advice and comfort. I looked at the boy and he wasn't scared at all. Sarah stood by his side and both waited patiently for what was coming.

Behind them I saw why the boy had said cops, and why he'd been wrong. Eight men in dark suits strode down the path, protected by an entire FBI SWAT team. The suits were feds of one kind or another, I couldn't be sure. The SWAT team was kitted out for trouble: assault rifles, full armour, dark sunglasses. I found myself being unexpectedly optimistic. Maybe somebody was finally going to do their job so I wouldn't have to do mine.

'Who's in charge here?' said the lead suit. He was one of those strange Peter Pans, older than he looked, probably still went by the nickname his frat brothers gave him. He scrutinized the crowd with obvious disgust, unable to see anyone worthy of responding to his question.

'I lead these souls,' Joshua said, stepping forward.

The suit laughed. 'I'm not interested in a show, son. My name is Eddy Fulsom, and I'm the Assistant US Attorney for Colorado.' He spoke to Joshua as if the boy were a small dog. 'I need to speak to the adults holding Matthew Reilley.'

That was the Revivalist official Joshua had brought on stage last night and humiliated. I hadn't realized they still had him. I wondered what Joshua had planned.

'I have the blasphemer in custody.'

'On whose authority?' Fulsom said.

'God's.'

Nobody laughed.

Fulsom took a deep breath. 'Listen, kid, if it were up to me every single one of you would be in federal prison. Instead, I've been instructed' – it was clear from Fulsom's voice that he didn't enjoy the experience – 'to offer you amnesty if you release Reilley to me and disperse immediately and permanently. If we find more than five of you in one place after today, they will be arrested. You've had your fun. Now go home.'

Joshua was unmoved. I could see his followers, even those double and triple his age, drawing strength from the boy's defiance.

'Everyone here is a traitor to the United States of America,' Fulsom said, enraged that he wasn't getting his way, more childish than Joshua. 'Disperse or you will be held.'

248

Still nobody moved. I could sense the SWAT team getting antsy. The Seventeen men showed the impeccable discipline I would expect. They watched the agents with a deceptive passivity, ready to kill if they made a move. Fulsom was outnumbered right now, but he was a representative of the Justice Department, a weaponized bureaucracy that could swallow the Sons of David without spoiling its dinner.

Bloom had been on the phone during the entire confrontation. I couldn't hear what he was saying to Glass, whether this development had been anticipated. He only stopped talking when another Seventeen man whispered something in his other ear. He pulled the phone from his head long enough to talk to the soldier and swear loud enough that I could hear. When he got back on the phone, Bloom was talking twice as fast.

The news began to make its way around the soldiers. At almost the same time, I saw the head of the SWAT team listening to his earpiece and Fulsom getting his own ear whispered into. Something big was coming in our direction.

'This is your last chance,' Fulsom said to Joshua, though he sounded like he was the one in a hurry. 'Hand Reilley over.'

Bloom hung up and came closer to Joshua.

'Reinforcements?' I said to him.

'Not sure yet.'

It was another motorcade. They'd stopped outside the western edge of the camp and approached the rest of the way on foot as the feds had done. The composition was similar to Fulsom's party, uniforms orbiting a nucleus of suits, but the uniforms were different. When they got close enough I saw the logo of the Colorado State Police.

Fulsom and the FBI both worked for the Justice Department, a federal institution. Colorado State Troopers answered to the state, which I guessed was represented here by the suits they were guarding. As the lead suit got closer I saw some of the civilians giving him a second look. He was recognized, but not by me.

The second group stopped in front of the entrance to Joshua's compound as Fulsom's had. The two groups were separated by a no-man's-land of less than fifty feet. The way Fulsom and the other man stared at each other, I wondered if either remembered that we were still there.

'Lieutenant Governor Auerbach,' Fulsom said. He was stating a fact, not offering a greeting.

Auerbach was older, fatter and greyer, but had made up for it by bringing more goons.

'This is a Justice matter,' Fulsom said.

'A Justice matter in my state,' Auerbach said, as if he had ownership instead of a largely ceremonial position due to political connections.

'I'm serving a federal warrant, you have no standing here.'

'The state of Colorado will not stand by while you attack an American hero.'

There were some spontaneous cheers in the crowd, but they were short-lived. The words should have made the connection between Joshua and some of the Elders clear, but I wasn't sure. Bloom and the others hadn't greeted Auerbach's people as friends. Auerbach could be here on the orders of one of the Elders, as an opportunist or even a true believer. At least I knew where Fulsom stood.

Auerbach turned his attention from Fulsom and spoke to Joshua for the first time.

'We've followed your progress with great interest, son. We think you are just what this movement needs to renew itself. There are some very important people who have come to Denver to meet you.'

The movement was the Revivalists, which both sides claimed to be a part of. I wondered if the important people included an Elder.

'God has called me to Houston.'

Auerbach's smile was high and tight.

Fulsom laughed. 'Are you going to get out of our way now, or do you want to join these criminals in chains?'

'The boy is coming with us,' Auerbach said.

'The Elders are the same as the world that created them,' Joshua said. 'They cannot be renewed, only swept away.'

'And a child shall lead them,' someone said in the crowd. The words set off a tidal wave of Pavlovian response. Every man, woman and child chanted at the two groups of officials, over and over, without variation. The FBI watched the crowd, thumbs tight on the safety of their rifles, finally realizing just how surrounded they were.

The state police reacted about the same way. The suits from both parties weren't used to inconvenience, let alone physical danger. Every repetition from the crowd nudged them closer to the edge of panic. Joshua's minders drew closer. Like me, they scented trouble.

A helicopter's blades churned the air somewhere out of sight. I turned my eyes to the sky, and that's why I didn't see the first shot.

The fifty feet between the two groups became a killing field. Joshua's bodyguards surrounded him while Bloom directed fire at the two groups of officials, who in turn were firing at each other. Caught in the middle was a large crowd of all ages with nothing but canvas to take cover behind.

Some of the crowd were Sons of David. Once they started firing with their state-issued sub-machine guns, both the feds and the police began to fire on the crowd as well.

I drew my gun but didn't know what to do with it. I couldn't help anyone in the crowd. The bodyguards were still holding the compound perimeter. I had no interest in shooting any more police or federal officials, and wouldn't have wanted to try with so many bystanders already in the line of fire. I tried to stay close to Joshua but it was impossible when he and Sarah were ringed by so many men. Bloom led them away from the front of the compound, but not a full retreat. I saw him look up and followed his eyes.

The helicopter I'd heard had arrived. It was military, armed, twin rotors with open side doors for troop loading. I thought the Pentagon had finally come to its senses until I saw a man standing in the helicopter doorway. He wasn't wearing a uniform, and he was bringing one of the helicopter's miniguns to bear.

I hit the ground as I heard the whine of the minigun's electric motor spinning the barrels up. The minigun tore through everything in front of Joshua's compound, fed, state and bystander. Thousands of red-hot shells fell on the tents below, setting them ablaze.

The helicopter stopped firing and hovered above Joshua. A cable dropped, and a moment later I saw Sarah being winched up, Joshua in her arms. I followed their progress and saw a new face in the helicopter window that I couldn't quite believe.

General Simeon Glass. I had to be hallucinating; Glass never got his hands dirty. Yet there he was, riding co-pilot, still in uniform, face still scarred and twisted. He looked down at the hell he had unleashed – the fires spreading through the camp, the bodies around the front of the compound, the dead and dying of all ages – but I don't think he saw anything at all.

I think I screamed. Not fear, but raw, uncontrollable hatred. I screamed, but no one could hear. Then the helicopter was gone.

That left me in the middle of a burning camp. The survivors of the federal and state delegations had long since entered full retreat. I saw Bloom withdrawing in good order with the last of Joshua's bodyguards. Bloom thought I was dead, more likely didn't care either way. I shadowed their retreat.

The smoke was covering everything. I could barely see and breathe even less, stumbling over ruins, debris, bodies. I followed their silhouettes, then what I thought were their silhouettes.

Hands grabbed me from the smoke. We struggled. I knew where my enemy's neck was, based on the arm he had on my shoulder, and was about to dig my fingers into it when I heard a voice.

'Stop struggling, you big baby.'

The voice, not the words, stopped me dead. That gave the hands the opportunity to get a respirator over my face.

The smoke cleared, and I saw something I'd never expected to see again in my life: Benny, and from behind a respirator his shit-eating grin.

# TWENTY-SEVEN

## Near Denver, Colorado

In short order I found myself in an SUV with men in ski masks, and for once it was a good thing. We left the Sons of David camp a battleground being consumed by fire.

'What the hell are you doing here?' I said.

'It's good to see you too.'

'You should be in the Holy Land. If Fisher Partners finds out you're in the country—'

'They don't know I'm here, and I won't be here long enough for them to find out. I've only got one job to do, then it's back to my duplex and the tyrannical rule of my elder daughter.'

'Elder?'

'Rachel was born six months ago,' Benny said, handing over a photograph. 'She doesn't do much besides eat and shit, but she's a good kid.'

'Mazel tov,' I said. 'If I had known, I would have brought cigars.'

'Buy her something nice on her bat mitzvah, and we'll be square.'

Benny took a pack of cigarettes from his coat, lit one up and smiled as only a back-sliding ex-smoker could.

'This is how you celebrate the birth of another child? Maybe the cigars wouldn't have been such a good idea after all.'

'Yes, I know I quit, and yes fuck you,' Benny said.

The camp had disappeared in our rear-view by then.

'Where are we going?'

'Airstrip.'

I waited for him to add something to that single word. Instead he pulled out a phone, holding up a finger to forestall any argument or curse words that might come from me.

'I'm with him. Yeah, he's fine. Listen, he wants to know where we're going. I think I should tell him.' Benny listened to the other party for a while. 'I know I lost, and I also know you cheated,' he said. 'I saw you do coin tricks for three months in Haifa, don't tell me you didn't make it land heads.' Another pause while Benny tolerated the other person talking. 'Okay, fine, go fuck yourself in the meantime,' he said, then hung up.

'Gideon?'

'Never play games of chance with the Mossad. Looks like you'll have to wait until we get to the airfield.'

'Could you at least tell me why the FBI and those Staties were trading rounds?'

'The country is staring down the barrel of civil war, from what I've been told,' Benny said. 'Back there . . .'

'Yes?'

'You didn't shoot any feds, did you?'

'I don't think so. Why?'

'Why? You might have plugged someone I know.'

'They shot at me first. Besides, it's not your Bureau any more.'

Benny didn't argue that point. We let the tarmac go past, looked out the window though there wasn't much on the other side.

'It is good to see you, Benny.'

'Yeah, I know.'

We got to the airstrip a little while later. It was a regional one in the middle of nowhere, a place for hobbyists and the odd duster to land. The whole compound consisted of a single airstrip, small tower and a low prefab building for administration. There was only one plane on the tarmac, a C-130 military transport. Waiting beside it were Gideon and more of his Israelis, their faces covered even from their allies.

'We meet in the oddest places,' I said to Gideon as we shook hands.

'This place is a step up from the last one.'

I'd be the last person to argue with that.

'Now can you tell me where I was being held?'

'No idea. Scout's honour,' he said, when Gideon saw I didn't believe him. 'They blindfolded me and everything.'

'Can I tell him why we're here now?' Benny said.

'I didn't want Benny to give you the good news unless I was there.'

'Good news?'

I was, of course, suspicious.

'We found Iris,' Benny said, as Gideon opened his mouth. He shot Benny a look. Benny grinned in response and walked off, still talking over his shoulder. 'We'll rescue her as soon as I get back from the can.'


The cargo plane shuddered like the magic fingers of a hotel bed. I was strapped in to the fold-down seat next to Benny, with Gideon and two Israeli paratroopers on my left.

'Are you going to tell me where we're going?' I said through the headphones we all wore, the only way of communicating above the sound of the propellers.

'It's about time,' Gideon said. He took a small cylinder from one of his pockets and projected what looked like blueprints on to the far wall of the plane. They showed two floors of a roughly L-shaped building I didn't recognize.

'This is our target,' he continued. 'Galilee Farm.'

Beside the blueprints came several photos of the compound and the grounds. The main building was a sprawling affair only possible in this part of the country, where land really was as cheap as dirt.

'It was owned by Elder Barnabas Lee until he died six years ago,' Gideon said. 'He donated it to the Heifer project in his will.'

It had a fancier name than that, something about the Temple, but everyone called it the Heifer project. A completely unblemished red heifer had to be sacrificed as part of the ritual to consecrate the new Temple, should they ever build it. A network of ranches all over the country had been involved in a government project to breed a suitable animal.

'Why don't we see any cattle?'

'The Elders shut down the project and moved all likely candidates to Sinai, as part of their wider freak-out. Now the farm is used in the network of detainment facilities under the Elders' personal control. This area,' he said, pointing to the bottom of the L with a laser, 'has been made into offices for Fisher Partners. The stables are a garage where they load and unload prisoners.' Gideon pointed to the top of the L, the biggest single room on the plans.

'We believe they're being held on the first floor—'

'They?' I said.

'I'll get to that. There are eight bedrooms on the first floor. It's the most fortified part of the building, only accessible by two staircases behind reinforced doors.'

'If the ground floor is so heavily guarded, why don't we go in via the roof?' I asked.

'The windows on the rooms have been sealed; anything less than an angle grinder won't get through them, and they're alarmed anyway. We've found an easier way through the ground floor.'

'Assuming we get past the sentries,' Benny said.

'I'd get to that if you two would shut up,' Gideon said. 'There are two sentries on the front door, another near the garage, one on the roof and another at the rear of the building, with four more patrolling the grounds nearby.'

'What about inside?'

'Two more in the front, maybe four more roving inside. Infrared images suggest that they spend most of their time in the offices, but we don't have anything better than that.'

More photos appeared on the plane's wall, pictures of fields of long grass left to their own devices, grazing land for all the cattle the ranch no longer had. The only sign of a human presence were the cameras mounted on tall poles all over the pasture.

'It's about five acres of private property in every direction from the main building. As you can see, almost every inch of it is covered. That goes double for the road entrance, which is manned by four guards with a machine gun and anti-vehicle spikes. We don't know what the standing orders are in the event of an attack: they could kill the hostages as soon as they see the strike team, or if they think they'll lose them to us. Either way we need the element of surprise.'

'That's not mentioning that a bum rush would give them time to prepare a hell of a defence,' Benny said.

'It will be impossible for ten of us to get to the building without raising the alarm, at least by normal means.'

'Normal means?' I said.

One of the many questions Gideon had refused to answer until we were in the air was strapped to my back. The fact that I

258

was in a plane with four other ex-paratroopers kitted out the same way should have told me what they had planned.

'The field behind the barn lost three cameras in a storm,' Gideon said. 'They haven't been replaced yet. We land there and advance around the barn to the main building's veranda.'

'What kind of ranch has a Mediterranean-style stone veranda?' I asked.

'One built by nouveau-riche shitkickers,' Benny said.

'We take out the sentry on the roof and the one guarding the veranda, plus the camera that overlooks it. That clears our way into the sun room, which is usually empty during the day. From there we go to the kitchen. It has a staircase that leads up to the first floor. Once we have them, we go back out the way we came. Another team will be in position to smash through the front gate and extract us.'

'What do you want to do after lunch?' Benny said to me.

I was more concerned with why Gideon kept using the plural when describing who we were being sent to rescue.

'What about Jefferson?' I said. 'I'm surprised he's allowing this. I haven't held up my end yet.'

'It's not his operation.'

That meant the Mossad was running things. Jefferson might not even know what we were up to.

'Who are you after in there? The Mossad doesn't like me enough to throw this kind of party.'

'Just be glad it's being thrown at all, Strange.'

'Okay,' I said. 'I'll trust your word, again. Besides, I'm already on the fucking plane.'

'That's the spirit.'

Benny coughed and nodded to Gideon. He was puzzled for a moment, then swore in Hebrew.

'I almost forgot.'

Gideon removed the shoulder holster he was wearing and threw it over to me. Inside was my old forty-five. I'd never expected to see it again after IF.

'How the hell did you get this?'

'When it comes to Fisher Partners, everything is for sale.'

The pistol had seen my grandfather and uncle through two wars, then had the misfortune of being passed down to me in time for another.

'If he could marry that gun, he would,' Benny said to Gideon as if I wasn't there.

Fisher Partners had erased the records of my birth, where I went to school, my time in the army. They'd taken my name off the lease to my office in New York, removed any records that I'd ever been there. None of my former clients would say otherwise. When someone disappeared people knew not to talk about it, and they hadn't liked me much in the first place. In a way, this gun was the only physical record left of my existence.

'It is the longest relationship I've had.'

'That is sad,' Gideon said.

I think he meant it. I didn't get a chance to ask since someone else was already talking in Gideon's ear.

'Stand up and hook up,' he said. Unlike jump school, there was no ten-minute warning this time.

We stood and hooked our static lines to the cable that ran along the length of the aircraft. The line would open our parachutes as we stepped outside for a little air. Gideon called out an equipment check. We made sure our bits and pieces were in place and sounded off that this was the case.

Gideon opened the door. His men would be going first, followed by me and then Benny. He called out the minute warning. I found myself thinking about jump school, the last time I'd

260

done this. The memories were surprisingly fond, even if it reminded me that I hadn't done any of this in about ten years.

Gideon gave the signal. His men jumped.

'Man, this is going to be fun,' Benny said, slapping the back of my helmet.

'There's something wrong with you two,' Gideon said, as I stepped up to the door. I didn't have the chance to respond. I was next in line to throw myself at the sky.

# TWENTY-EIGHT

## Near Three Points, Arizona

One thousand, two thousand, three thousand, four thousand. That's how long it takes for the canopy to open. Four of the longest seconds of my life, back in jump school and now. In that moment, I am aware that I am just a hairless ape in a part of the sky where I don't belong.

The canopy opened. I knew the others were in the sky somewhere. In a little while I'd land on enemy ground, probably be shot at, a better than even chance of being killed. I'd go back to doing the stupid things that had me so useful to the wrong people. In the sky I was free and unaccountable to anyone as Adam in the Garden, before he got stupid and decided he needed company.

I rolled into the ground and gathered up my chute. By the time I was done, the rest had done the same. We gathered around Gideon in the long grass of the fallow field. We didn't hear any alarms or fire directed that way. If we were lucky, that meant we still had the element of surprise. The other possibility was that a trap was being prepared for our impending visit. We waited while Gideon swept the barn with a monocular to make sure it was clear.

'What is that?' I said to Benny, noticing for the first time the gun on his back that he'd brought in addition to the assault rifle we all carried.

'Auto-shotgun,' he said, with a grin wide enough to touch both coasts. 'I brought it for close encounters of the fuck you kind.'

Gideon signalled us forward. The barn was empty but covered in cameras so we had to crawl around it. I didn't see the main building until we reached the edge of the lawn, the only difference between it and the field we were in being the length of the grass. There was a sniper on the roof and a guard patrolling in front of the sun room's sliding glass doors, just as Gideon had said. Between the guards and the camera on the roof that covered the entrance, it looked impenetrable from the outside.

We waited for a while and watched the two guards, the sun setting behind us. This place may have held high-level detainees, but it was also in the middle of nowhere. I doubted this secret prison had been attacked by a stray dog in the last few years, let alone a paratroop assault. It was natural after a while for even trained men to begin to look to their comfort more than their readiness, to be lulled into a dreamless sleep by routine. The man on the ground, nothing more than a silhouette to my naked eyes, was one of the sleepwalkers. You could set your watch by the time it took him to walk across the doors and turn for another pass. That Swiss regularity was going to get him killed.

When he started his next patrol, one of Gideon's men shimmied across the lawn. That ridiculous stone veranda was going to give us our way in. It obscured part of the ground from the camera, and allowed our man to come up right against its side. The line that connected the camera to the house's security system happened to be there as well. Gideon had told us in the plane his friend was going to 'fuck with it', which I hoped meant something subtle. After a minute, Gideon got news over the radio he liked.

'Yithzak, if you please.'

The two men fell as if by the hand of God. One moment they were standing, not thinking about much, the brain in a lower gear after hours on duty. Now those brains were all over the veranda and the roof, respectively. I had no idea where the shots came from, and asked Gideon with a look.

'You'd be surprised what drones can do these days,' he said, and pointed up. It was a pity our guardian angels couldn't follow us inside.

The soldier who had cut the camera vaulted over the railing of the veranda and began to do the same to a pane of the sliding door's glass. Gideon hadn't told us to advance, which made me think there were more cameras being disabled inside. When his man opened the door from the inside, Gideon gave the signal. We crossed the lawn at a low run.

With the light outside failing, the sun room was dark, unlit and unoccupied. It was actually a sunken living room upholstered in white carpet. I got the feeling one of the Elders' wives had built this whole place to her tastes, which had been frozen in time around 1973. No wonder they'd donated the farm to the cause.

There was no door between the sun room and the kitchen. Gideon put me on point. I poked my head inside and found it as empty as the sun room. We watched the entrances while one of Gideon's men examined a reinforced door that led upstairs. It had a card reader and what looked like a number pad. He produced a card and typed in a number with the nonchalance of a man who was actually supposed to be here.

I took the lead up the staircase. It was a fucking miracle we hadn't been discovered yet, one that I didn't trust to last for much longer. Gideon handed me his monocular, and I turned it to infrared. There were only two people upstairs, and they were both in rooms reserved for Fisher Partners' special guests. I poked my head over the threshold and found the hallway clear.

It was lit by covered lamps set in the wall, plain wood with faded squares where family portraits or other inconvenient pictures had once hung. Gideon went right past the door containing the first warm body to a room at the end of the hall. Knowing his priorities, I tried by gesture – I was afraid if I opened my mouth I would yell – to ask if the other glowing silhouette I'd seen through his monocular was Iris. He understood my question, and shrugged.

I was about to reply with an equally simple gesture when a toilet flushed inside the room. The door was thrown open before I could move away, and I found myself staring into the eyes of a heavy-set, unshaven white Fisherman holding the door knob in one hand and his undone belt in the other. I couldn't say for a million dollars who was more surprised.

I could say who recovered first. Back when I was growing up upstate, my sifu had taught me a little move that came from the Shaolin. He called it a leopard palm. Fold the first and second digits of the fingers over the third, rather than make a complete fist. That meant the middle knuckles were the point of contact, not the heavy ones on the hand. He had called it the difference between a knife and a club. At the time I had thought it was pretty bad ass, and had dreamed of when it could be used to show up another teenager and impress some dame still wearing braces. None of my scenarios, no matter how far-fetched, had ever looked like this.

The punch landed on the neck where I wanted it. The Fisherman's windpipe collapsed, which would prevent him from doing any inconvenient screaming. He collapsed on the floor of the little room, his struggle to breathe dislodging the earpiece he had worn. I put it in my ear, and heard voices reporting the discovery of the guard on the veranda and urgent demands for a report from the man I'd just silenced.

'Jig's up,' I said.

'Ya think?' Benny tried to say. The words were lost in the sirens that went off all over the compound.

Gideon spoke into his radio while his two men dispensed with their fancy toys and kicked the other door in. The room the guard had emerged from had a double bed with brass fittings and burgundy sheets, all to match a carpet of the same hue. Portraits of cattlemen and horses shared wall space with a water-colour or two, the light in the en suite bathroom still on, a fan audible in the gaps between the sirens' call humming away what the Fisherman had left inside. This place was a B&B you could check into but never leave.

'They're coming up the way we came,' I said, repeating what I heard in the earpiece.

'Watch the stairway,' Gideon said, and went back to yelling Hebrew into his radio.

Gideon's men finally broke the door to the other room and rushed in. I heard an exclamation in an older woman's voice, and they re-emerged, one of them carrying a woman of about sixty still trying to articulate her situation in Hebrew. The second was on his way down the other staircase. Gideon told Benny to follow. I held the other staircase until they were done.

'Where is Iris, Gideon?' I said.

'She's here somewhere,' he said, as if she were a lost set of keys.

'I'm not leaving without her.'

266

The door downstairs opened. I threw a grenade down the stairs for them to play with, and followed Gideon the other way.

The Mossad man was shooting down the hallway, while his partner carried the now screaming old woman. If we didn't get out of this stairwell, all of us would soon be dead.

The soldier holding the woman threw something over his friend's head, and in a few seconds I could see wisps of smoke in the door frame. Gideon signalled that we were going through the offices. It was a better escape route than the front door, and the most likely place Iris would be after the cells. If Iris was here at all.

The hallway was about ten feet across. We took it at a low run, each in turn, the man behind firing blind into the smoke to discourage whoever was firing blindly back. In the office hallway I worked myself to the front while the Israelis kept trading shots with the Fishermen they couldn't see.

The offices themselves were subdivisions of what had been larger rooms, walls formed by plywood partitions with thin wood and glass doors. No one had emerged from them to check out the Armageddon happening outside. If we were lucky, that meant they'd poured into other parts of the farm as soon as the first bodies had been discovered.

I kicked the first door into an empty room. I had just enough time to see a desk and a map of the Continental United States before someone shot me through the wall. Two bullets of a large spray hit the back of my vest. I dropped to the ground as the Fishermen in the offices unleashed hell. They didn't bother coming into the corridor, just shot through the plywood along the length of the hall.

'Benny,' I said, crawling back into the hall, trying to get my breath back. 'Suppressing fire.' I turned to see Benny step into the hallway, the auto shotgun in his hand. I had just enough time to cover my head.

Benny swept the entire hallway on automatic, hundreds of balls of buckshot tearing through walls, windows and anything else that got in their way. Plywood, glass and bits of paper showered down on me from everywhere. It was impossible to hear over all that gunfire, but I could have sworn I heard Benny laughing.

When he finally stopped, so did any opposing fire. The Fishermen were either dead or as disorientated as I was.

'How's that for suppressing fire?' Benny said, throwing away the drum clip on the shotgun and loading in a spare.

'Amazing. Please don't do it again.' I struggled to my feet.

'We'll go out through the last office,' Gideon said.

I wasn't listening. I checked each of the destroyed rooms in turn, afraid of what Benny's enthusiasm might have done if Iris was in here somewhere. I got halfway down the hall before I heard a crash outside. Through one of the office windows I saw an SUV driving through what remained of the barn doors.

I crossed through the office, stepping over the body of a Fisherman in a suit holding a pistol he could no longer use, and dived out the window Benny had already shattered.

'There's a firefight going on over here,' he yelled at my back.

Outside I dropped to my knees and drew a bead on the SUV. It was tearing away as fast as it could. Iris was in that car. I wasn't much for signs or premonitions, but I knew it as much as I'd known anything in my life. I had but a few seconds before it would be out of range. She was in that car, and if I didn't stop it I'd never see her again. I looked through the scope on my rifle, the sounds of the battle behind me receding away. There was just the target, wind and gravity.

268

The first shot went wide but the second and third hit the rear right tyre. The driver lost control and fishtailed over the gravel drive, the top-heavy SUV bowing to physics and tipping on its side. I stood and began to run.

More Fishermen had emerged from the front doors. I was aware of them shooting at me, Benny and the others returning fire from the offices that ran along the L of the building. It felt distant, something happening on a nearby television. I could only see the SUV on its side, one wheel still spinning. I barely noticed it when a Fisherman, one of the men who must have been patrolling the grounds, popped up from the field and took a shot at me. I put a round in him, barely seeing the target, still watching the SUV.

Not much was going through my head, other than the thought that Iris had to live. I'd fucked up enough things in the past three years, gone the wrong way and done the wrong thing so many times that I was owed one right move. I didn't care what happened to me; it had never been that high on my list. I was going to pull one survivor from this wreckage of a life, even if I had to dig through the rubble with my bare hands. Nothing was going to stop me from finding her. Not a goddamn thing.

I reached the SUV just as a Fisherman was pulling himself out of the driver's side. He was dazed, bleeding from the head, just conscious enough to register the butt of my gun before it made contact with his face. I caught him before he fell back into the SUV, hauled him up and threw him to the ground.

'People are still shooting at you, by the way,' Gideon said over the radio.

I didn't care. I jumped into the SUV. There was an unconscious Fisherman still belted into the passenger side. She was handcuffed behind him, eyes covered with just a blindfold, restrained like I had been except for the leg irons. I was holding her before I could open my mouth. She flinched and then began to struggle for her life.

'It's me,' I said in Iris's ear, unable to think of anything else. 'It's me.'

I took off the blindfold and we were looking into each other's eyes, not in our memories, not in dreams good and bad. I could see she was thinking the same thing, her tongue stopped dead by shock and the weight of all her questions. We had time for one kiss before we had to run for our lives.

'I've got Iris,' I told Gideon over the radio. 'Where's the cavalry?'

'On their way. Stay near the car. We'll be along shortly.'

I poked my head out of the car to see Fishermen from the front entrance still firing into the offices. The main house was on fire, the sun room judging by the smoke. Gideon and the others were coming out of the window of the furthest office along, the old woman still over the masked Mossad's shoulder. There was another pillar of smoke in the distance behind us. That must have been the remains of the front gate. I jumped out of the SUV and yelled at Iris to do the same while I covered her. We took shelter behind the vehicle.

'Handcuff key?' she asked.

I shrugged.

'Give me your sidearm at least.'

I handed her my pistol and we kept our heads down.

'Friends incoming,' Gideon said, so I didn't engage the two black SUVs coming towards us even though they were indistinguishable from the one I'd just shot up. They went past us to where Gideon and the others were taking cover on the edge of the building. Gideon's men loaded their package into one while the men inside shot at what was left of the opposition. Benny and Gideon jumped in the other. The first vehicle did a wide

**270**

arc and then took off at top speed, not waiting to see how the rest of us were doing. Whoever that old woman was, she was worth more than everyone else put together.

The second SUV stopped and Iris and I piled into the back, Benny already sitting behind the driver with Gideon riding shotgun. We tore off after the first car. The Fishermen tried to give chase, but they were on foot and soon out of range. Somehow we were all still alive.

'Did you set the building on fire?' Gideon said to Benny from the front.

'No,' he shot back, indignant, as he lit a cigarette.

They argued some more, but I didn't hear the rest. I had my arms around Iris, my grip relaxing only enough to take the key from Gideon and get her handcuffs off. I held on to her and she to me, each refusing to let the other go, afraid to find out one was just a fragment of the other's dream.

# TWENTY-NINE

## Circle F. Motel, West Texas

The motel was the first time we'd stopped since leaving Galilee Farm. We'd taken a crazy series of dirt roads, switching back and trying to see if anyone was on our tail. So far pursuit had been nil. The motel itself was deserted, a business someone had walked away from once the bank took possession. It had a main office and eight rustic-style cabins, one of which Iris was using to clean herself up. I was outside with Benny and Gideon. The two Mossad operatives in balaclavas had taken the old woman to parts unknown.

'I don't suppose you're going to tell me who that woman was?' I said to Gideon.

'The mother of a good friend, and an honest-to-God civilian.'

'The Fishermen were holding her on behalf of some Settler fuckwads in the Israeli government,' Benny added. 'They've taken a few important hostages to keep people under control. What?' he said, when he saw the look Gideon was giving him.

'I guess that plan worked out real well for them. Are we staying here for the time being?'

'For the time being,' Gideon said.

'As for you,' Benny said to me, lighting up yet again as he

272

nodded his head in the direction of Iris's room, 'time to claim your reward.'

'A little tact, please,' Gideon said.

'What? He just jumped out of a plane and fought his way through a small army to rescue her. That's gotta rate a blow job at least.'

I left before I could be drawn into yet another of their arguments. Iris was in the shower when I let myself in. The room was old and neglected. Iris had left the windows open to air the room out. I took the dust cover off the bed and found an old print on the blanket beneath. From what I'd seen of Galilee Farm, I had to admit that the room I'd just rescued her from was probably more comfortable than this one. It seemed right that we meet here, in another place that wasn't.

I took off my hat, then my holster, draping the latter over the headboard, always in easy reach. The jacket went over a chair. In the fridge was a bucket of ice and a bottle of whiskey – a note saying 'You're welcome' in Benny's handwriting attached to the neck – and two glasses on the table. I poured myself a double, drank it down and poured another before I felt like I could sit down.

The bed was tired and uneven, but it would do. I lay down and stared at nothing in particular, which in this case was the wall. I'd dreamed of this moment, asleep on the road and in delirium in IF, dreamed because I could never believe it while awake. I'd told myself she was dead, cut those parts out of myself so I could do what I thought I needed to, never expecting to live more than a month or two after she'd been taken. Now I was alive and she was here.

I was the dog who'd finally caught the car.

I turned my head to see Iris standing in the bathroom doorway. I hadn't heard her turn the shower off, wondered how long she'd been watching me. She wore only a towel, her hair still a little wet.

She came over and without a word straddled me on the bed, just looking at me.

'Your suit's getting wet,' she finally said.

'It'll live.'

She ignored me and unbuttoned my shirt. 'My God,' she said, when she saw the scars on my chest.

'I was hoping you were going to say that when I took off my pants.'

'Who did this to you?'

'Circumstance. They're old wounds, most of them anyway. Let's talk about something else for once.'

She waited.

'We've been in this situation before.'

'And?'

'I want you to know I have no expectations.'

'No?' she said with a raised eyebrow.

'Hopes. Definite hopes.'

'So I can feel.'

'What can I say,' I replied, 'part of every man is an optimist.'

'I've had a lot of time to think,' Iris said, 'it was practically the only thing they allowed me to do. I thought about Isaiah, my work for him with the Crusade. I thought about you,' she said, running her thumb along the line of my jaw. 'I made some decisions.

'Brother Isaiah saved my life. I felt if I questioned what he'd taught me, I was being ungrateful. I hid my doubts from him and myself. When I met you' – by which she meant when I followed her in Chinatown and then chased her down in Central Park – 'things just got worse.'

'I tend to have that effect.'

274

'I tried to put it out of my head after I left New York. Brother Isaiah was dead, and that made it even harder to go against him. That's why I went back to Guyana. I knew I could do some good there, something concrete I could touch and know was right.'

'But you came back.'

'I felt like I had no choice. I don't know why. I couldn't stay out of trouble, any more than I could figure out what to do with you.'

'You could have asked me. I would have made a few suggestions.'

'When they first took me, I thought I'd be dead inside a week. Instead they gave me a lot of time to think about what I'd done wrong.'

I could have said the same thing, word for word.

'I finally realized I was demanding too little of God. I could not believe that a creator who made the heaven and the earth, the creatures within, a being capable of forming a universe full of inexhaustible wonder and mystery out of nothing, would then spend all His time haunting our bedrooms. It demeans Him. That's why He gave Jesus to us; it was a desperate attempt to get us to see that it's our happiness He wants.

'My God is not a lawyer or a private eye. My God does not meet an act of love with punishment. It is not our vices that fail Him, but our hatred.'

She was waiting for me to say something. I wasn't thinking too clearly. The adrenaline in my system had been replaced by fifteen-year-old whiskey, but that wasn't the main problem. I think it had something to do with the sound of her voice, the beads of moisture on her thighs, or the fact that the towel around her seemed to be growing smaller.

'Is this a long, theological way of saying I'm going to get laid?'

'There's no I in team. Now shut up and turn out the light.'

I did as I was told.

Later we lay awake, Iris staring at the ceiling, me staring at her.

'What happens now?' she said.

'Give me ten minutes, I'll see what I can do.'

She threw a pillow in my direction without looking.

'I mean the near future.'

'Gideon and Benny will smuggle you across the border. You'll be held by some people for a while, but Benny will be there to make sure everyone plays fair. It won't be for more than a few days.'

'And then?'

'That's up to you. You can go wherever you want after that, as long as it isn't the States.'

Iris lay back, stretched her perfect legs over the crumpled sheets. Except for the hair, she looked almost the same as the last time I'd seen her in New York, or at least what I'd imagined she looked like when I was undressing her with my eyes.

'All that time to think, I never considered a life after prison, or whatever they call it. I didn't think I had a future. They moved me around a lot in the first six months. Every time they chained me up and put me in a car, I thought it would end in a shallow grave. I was terrified the first time, afraid I'd piss myself.'

'That happens more often than you'd think. That's not a confession,' I said when she smiled at me, 'I'm just saying it's understandable.'

'Did you think the same thing, when they had you?'

'I wasn't usually conscious when they moved me. It was hard to tell if I'd been moved at all. All the rooms looked the same.' I didn't want to tell her that in my case it had been as much of a hope that it would end that way as a fear.

**276**

'The second time was easier. It shouldn't have been. It was just as dangerous, probably more so. Every time they transferred me the fear was a little less, like a drug I was developing a tolerance for. When they came for me today, I was sure it was for the last time. It wasn't any different; the Fishermen are sticklers for procedure, and they followed it to the letter. I just knew for some reason, and the weird thing was I didn't really care.'

'It's over now,' I said, moving so she had to meet my eyes. 'The Fishermen will never be within a square mile of you ever again. What happens now is your decision. You sounded happy in Guyana; you could go back there.'

Iris shook her head. 'If I sounded happy, I was being economical with the truth.'

'I didn't catch that.'

'We were pretty busy at the time, remember? The Crusade changed after the Elders kicked us out. They acted more like a regime in exile than a community of believers. Isaiah had moved the organization back to America against his better judgement. The Missions and Isaiah's prominence had given them a taste for power. Our entanglement with the Elders had cost Brother Isaiah his life, and all they could think about was coming back.'

A Mission had been the Crusade's fancy word for showing up in a city and outing a bunch of people on national television. It must have been more fun than it looked.

'Supplies for the clinic started becoming irregular, then stopped altogether. I had to go all the way to Georgetown to figure out what was going on; the leadership had decided to move everything to the capital months before, which should have been the first sign something was wrong. I found out they were cutting all development aid and most of the missionary work. They were building a war chest, trying to bribe Guyanese officials into letting our people go to America under diplomatic cover.'

'I guess they got tired of playing White Man's Burden.'

'My colleagues may have been a little ignorant and condescending, but the Guyanese we worked with were willing to put up with a little condescension in exchange for healthcare. What makes them different from the celebrities who fly over and cry for the cameras?'

'Worse hair? I don't see what the problem was,' I said, before she realized I hadn't apologized yet, 'they should have just come back to the States. There are a lot of people around here who could use some healthcare.'

'The Elders would never allow it. After what happened with Brother Isaiah, we were the enemy. They wouldn't let us back into the country even if we were simply there to do charity work. Helping those the Elders didn't would only make them think we were challenging their authority or trying to embarrass them. The Crusade had lost interest in helping people anyway. All they could think about was getting back in front of American cameras. Every time I raised it with them, they said everything would be solved in the next world. Brother Isaiah understood the problem the way Jesus did: eternal joy is no excuse for present suffering. I told you I met him in a soup kitchen. He wasn't there for any cameras.

'When they told me that our people were disappearing in New York, I jumped at the chance they offered to find them. I knew it was part of their plans to return to America, but I didn't care. Some of the missing had been my friends, and I could persuade myself I was doing something good.'

'Why didn't you tell me any of this at the time?'

'I didn't know they were actually running a blackmail ring. When you suggested it, I thought it was your dirty imagination.

The leadership had some crazy idea about building a web of dirt so strong the Elders would have no choice but to let them back in. I guess I must have suspected it, now that I think about the way I bit your head off when you suggested the possibility. I didn't want you to know the Crusade had turned out to be as corrupt as you thought. I guess you can gloat now.'

'I never gloat when someone I'm fond of has her heart broken.'

I got up and made her a whiskey with ice, the only option in our under-stocked mini bar. I poured another for myself, since I was up.

She took a drink, looked over the glass at me. I could see a question in her eyes that she didn't want to ask.

'What is it?'

'You're not going to like it.'

'I don't like much.'

'I'm trying to figure out why you came to save me.'

'Do you really want to look that gift horse in the mouth now?'

'It's not like we know each other that well.' She saw me look at the unkempt state of the bed. 'We didn't know each other that well then, and now. Sex isn't the same as telepathy. That rescue was too big for just me. Explain how you pulled it off at least.'

'Gideon – you met him in the car?'

'He was leering at me, if you count that as an introduction. Or was he the one swearing into his phone?'

'That was Benny.'

'I'm glad I could finally meet him. I can see why you two get along.'

There was a backhand to that compliment, but I couldn't see where it was.

'Gideon had an interest in an old woman being held with you. Did you ever meet her?'

'They didn't let us socialize. People were always coming and going, usually crying and pleading both ways.'

I could see where her mind was going and tried to distract her with a kiss. It half worked.

'So this Gideon likes you so much, he tells you where I am and brings you along out of the goodness of his heart?'

'He's Mossad. He has a karma mortgage that would make your eyes water, and wanted to make a down payment. Can we leave it at that?' I asked, already knowing the answer.

'What have they made you do?'

I didn't answer.

'What are they going to make you do, then?'

I told her about Joshua and the Sons of David. She asked me why they hadn't been arrested, why they were being allowed to run wild, all the questions I'd asked Jefferson. I answered her as best I could, trying to keep from her the full extent of the deal I'd made with Jefferson and Gideon. She outfoxed me, as she always did.

'They want you to kill that boy, don't they?' She drew the sheets tighter around herself, as if that horrible idea was a presence in the room.

'I've tried everything else, but Jefferson will only be satisfied with Joshua's head.'

'And until he's satisfied, I'm not going anywhere.'

'That's about the size of it.'

'Do you really think they'd kill me if you didn't go through with it?'

'There'd be an argument, and to be honest I'm not sure the right people would win. At the very least they would withdraw their protection, which is pretty much the same. You made enemies while working for the Crusade of Love.'

'They don't have to know where I am, especially if we run together.'

I imagined a man poring through phone records, CCTV footage, bank statements. He would be one of a group shadowing everyone we had known, watching and waiting for just one person to fuck up. There was always a parking ticket, a chance meeting, a stupid phone call.

'They'd find us,' I said. They'd find us, just like I'd found so many others.

'Listen to me,' she said, moving her naked body closer to mine, taking my face in her hands, 'I don't want you killing anyone on my behalf.'

'It's too late.'

That startled her, and she let go. She was still in the grip of a temporal confusion caused by her confinement. Iris had been kept inside for years, no TV or radio, just nights and days that hid behind one another, as indistinguishable as identical twins. The world had changed while she'd been in her en suite cell.

'The men who took you, I—'

'Murdered them?'

'Killed them. They were combatants as much as anyone I faced in Tehran.'

I told her about putting a bullet in Roy St James on the first day of his new life. I told her about the Corinthian in Babylon, how he'd sold her to Stonebridge and finally ended up on the wrong side of a deal. I told her about executing Marco Gambi while he pleaded for his life, and the child I'd shot in the next room. I lost my voice after that.

She held me for a while. We didn't say anything. She might have been shocked; in a way, Iris had seen me at my best during that week in New York, opposing a clear enemy who deserved it six ways from Sunday. I'd never told her what I did in Tehran. If I had, she wouldn't be so surprised.

'Was there something I said or did,' she finally said, 'that made you think I'd want you to do that?'

'They never would have paid for it. Who knows how many others they kidnapped and killed?'

'So you put on a fucking cape? It doesn't make any sense.'

'Of course it doesn't make any sense. None of this does, least of all the fact that I love you, and I'm not even sure I know who you are.'

The word dazzled Iris a little, surprised her to hear it floating from my lips in her direction. When I had first come to this room, I thought I'd be able to leave without telling her. I'd always taken pride in my lying, not just the inventiveness but the persistence that was really the key. With her it all went the other way. That's why I had already told her so much, why I would tell her everything.

'I don't have a future, Iris. If I do this, then you—'

'Wait,' she said. 'What do you mean you don't have a future?'

I tried to tell her about Doc Brown and my piecemeal prognosis, but she kept interrupting with questions like a cop trying to poke holes in an alibi. I pressed on, not sure how long my nerve would hold out.

'Why didn't you mention this earlier?'

'It would have spoiled the mood.'

When I was finished she sat back, let her eyes sink shut. She sat that way for a minute or two. It was a lot to take in.

'I don't believe you,' she said. 'Not that I think you're lying, you or your friend. The evidence isn't conclusive, you said that. You decided to take it as a death sentence, but I won't. It isn't certain, so there's hope. There's always hope.'

'Sure, why not,' I said and smiled, for her.

'Even if you're right—' Iris stopped. I could see her groping for words. 'Even if you're right, do you want to throw away what's left out of spite?'

'It's more complicated than that,' I said, but didn't know how to continue.

'Talk to me,' she said, 'don't just make up shit you think I want to hear.'

'I'm not going back for the kid.'

When I saw Glass in my mind, it wasn't the most recent glimpse I'd had of him in that helicopter. Instead, I saw him in his makeshift office in Tehran. He sat behind a salvaged desk in what had been the Tehran University Central Library, a hole in the ceiling encircling his head with light. I remembered him staring down the barrel of his cigar, taking apart with his eyes whoever happened to be in front of him.

'The man I'm going to kill is named Simeon Glass. He was my CO in Tehran, a retired general now. He ran a task force in Iran looking for weapons of mass destruction by any means he felt necessary. Then he killed people in the Holy Land, and finally came home to run Fisher Partners.' I could see the name alone get to her out of the corner of my eye, but Iris tried not to show it. 'I know you haven't met him, but you can learn all you need to know by the trail of bodies he's left behind.

'Ezekiel White threatened me with prison unless I investigated the death of Brother Isaiah. The Corinthian was much smarter, let poverty and the fear of my disease do most of the work. But Glass' – I stared out the window, not because I was interested in the empty lot beyond but because I couldn't look at her – 'Glass made me believe I was meant for something greater, if you can imagine that. I followed him of my own free will.

'That's why I'm responsible for him. He wouldn't have been able to do what he did if there weren't people like me willing to follow him. If Glass is caught this time, they'll send him into exile. In a few years he'll return with another group of lost boys willing to do what he says.

'Joshua once asked me if I'd ever felt compelled. I have to end things between Glass and me. I know that. Everything else I say is just an excuse after the fact.'

'There's nothing I can say, is there?'

'Could I have said anything to make you leave the first time?'

'And look how well that turned out,' she said, rising and coming to me. 'Maybe it's time to learn from someone else's mistakes.'

'I am. The Pentagon, the Elders, the Israelis, they all let him go. I won't.'

'You think what I'm responsible for doesn't haunt me?' Iris said, turning me to face her.

'It's different.'

'Fuck you it's different. I ruined a lot of people's lives. You were the one who told me that, and you were right. Who knows how many people died after being called out by us, killed themselves or worse? Do you think it would make a difference if I went on a killing spree too?'

'I want you to be safe somewhere. I want you to be happy.'

'You can't make me be happy any more than I can make you stop,' she said. There was a kind of despair in her eyes, but it wasn't for herself.

I held her close, because I needed to be near her as much as I couldn't face that look.

'We've lost so much time, and now we're wasting what we have talking about what's happened. Isn't there anything else?' she said.

'Tell me about when you were a boy. A memory that doesn't involve guns, or hospitals, or fear. Tell me about a restaurant you like in New York, or a joke Benny told you. Tell me about a fucking vacation.'

Her head sank on to my chest, the weight easing us both back down to the bed.

'Tell me anything.'

# THIRTY

There was a soft knock on the door some time after dawn. Iris was asleep, and I was watching her between naps. I went for the gun on the nightstand until I heard Benny whispering from the other side.

'Jefferson's here.'

I'd been awake the last hour or so. Bad dreams again. I was on the third floor of a half-destroyed building. Some members of Task Force Seventeen had carried me up there after a mine had taken a chunk out of my leg and killed one of them. One of us, at the time. It was my last mission for Glass, the day Tehran joined Houston as another city of the dead. I'd heard the rest of the team be ambushed and killed over the radio, but it wasn't the screams or gunfire I'd heard when I woke up sweating. It was Glass's voice, a single question over and over: 'Where is the package?'

I shook the dream from my head and pulled on some clothes, careful not to disturb Iris. I wanted her to enjoy the first night's sleep of her new freedom.

'How angry is he?' I said, pushing Benny back from the doorway as he tried to get a look at Iris sleeping inside.

He whistled, but not at what he'd seen. 'When he mentioned your name, if I hadn't known better I would have thought you got his daughter pregnant.'

'I knew Gideon hadn't told him about the rescue.'

'Need to know,' Benny said, and couldn't stop himself from grinning. 'We'd better get to the office. Those two are dancing as we speak.'

The same goon who had been waiting in that rest area stood guard outside the motel's dilapidated main office. He gave no sign that we'd met before, or that we were meeting now, just let us walk past while he watched the road. I could hear Jefferson's anger from the outside, but not his words until I opened the door.

'. . . incredible fucking breach of protocol,' he was saying, his bald head scarlet with angry blood. Gideon was unmoved. 'You have no fucking authority to conduct an independent operation on American soil, let alone one that endangers a DIA oper—'

'When was the last time you spoke to your superiors?' Gideon said, his quiet voice cutting through Jefferson's outrage.

Instead of answering, Jefferson turned on us.

'You shouldn't be here,' he said to me.

'Hello to you too.'

'Gideon and your FBI friend ran that little operation without telling me.' Jefferson's anger had crashed hard against Gideon's indifference, leaving only a sour petulance.

'I'm right here, asshole,' Benny said.

'I wouldn't believe that you'd rescued Iris unless I saw it with my own eyes.'

'That was their point. Mine was that you haven't lived up to your responsibilities.'

'We aren't here to discuss the past,' Gideon said.

He and Jefferson had moved the furniture in the office to one side and replaced it with a large table. Laid out on top was a series of aerial photographs of a complex in a desert. I thought I recognized the largest building at its centre. Around it were tents. Below them in the photograph were what looked like two semicircles of vehicles. Above was empty desert.

'Maybe you'd like to know what Joshua has been up to while you went behind my back,' Jefferson said, pointing to the photographs.

'After the shootout in the camp, Joshua and his close entourage were flown to the Houston Memorial.'

That was the building I recognized. The tents must be the other Sons of David.

'There were two different flavours of cop there,' I said. 'Were they too busy killing each other to stop them?'

'Too busy calling for reinforcements.'

Jefferson pointed at the two vehicle crescents. I looked closer and saw sirens on top of the inner group, the outer one black sedans and large vans.

'State police from Arizona, New Mexico and Texas are holding that line,' he said, pointing to the first. 'They're trying to convince Joshua to join the Stalwarts, the Elder faction that's pushing to build the Temple. Joshua hasn't given in yet. They'd much rather co-opt the boy and his movement, but if he defies the police much longer they'll probably raid the monument. FBI and DEA agents,' he said, pointing to the outer crescent, 'would like to crush them both, but for now they're containing the situation.'

It was a concentric Mexican standoff. Sooner or later someone would get scared or stupid, and then God knows what would be unleashed.

'You mentioned the possibility of civil war the first time we met. I have to admit I was sceptical.'

288

'Right now it's still at the proxy war stage. The south-west is contested territory.'

'Contesting, that's what I saw in the Sons of David camp?'

Jefferson turned the laptop he was working on my way. I had seen Joshua's footage of Awakenings happening all over the country, but what I saw on the screen was much worse: two Nevada State Troopers ambushed in their car with automatic weapons-fire, an assistant secretary of State found in a shallow grave with his whole family in Virginia, an entire Homeland Security tactical team shot up in Santa Fe.

'Some agencies have lined up behind specific Elders, others are battlegrounds. Revivalists are killing under orders, on spec hoping to be noticed, and settling scores of their own. It's a complete fucking mess.'

'Which side is Fisher Partners working for?'

'Both. We know the Elders are in contact with their private armies. This is just the beginning. When they decide to fight for real, it will be the worst political violence this country has ever seen.'

'Worse than Reconstruction?' I said. 'Worse than the Civil War?'

'Blood in the streets in every city in America,' Jefferson said. 'You'll have to take my word for it.'

Benny and Gideon were silent. I guess they'd heard some of this before. I looked at the photographs again. There was only one group missing.

'I don't see any soldiers.'

'The Joint Chiefs have decided this is a civil matter, at least for now.'

'Their asses getting sore on that fence?'

Putting down organized rebellion was their job. So was defending the constitution, and they hadn't done much of that for the last ten years. The state police wouldn't be here without the support of their governors. Those same governors had authority over the National Guard units of their states. When they called them up, told the units in the Holy Land to return, the Pentagon would have no choice but to respond.

'This is your doing, Strange,' Jefferson said. 'None of this would be happening if you hadn't thrown away a golden opportunity to complete your mission.'

'Don't lay this at his door,' Gideon said, before I could tear Jefferson's head off. 'He tried to warn you about Glass and you wouldn't listen.'

'I thought he was hallucinating. You were as worried about his mental state as I was,' Jefferson said, petulant again.

'Why does everyone suddenly believe me?' I said, instead of responding to this latest crack. I hadn't gotten around to telling him what I'd seen in the camp, and before that moment had expected him to dismiss it anyway.

'After the attack on the camp, Bloom went on a mission of his own.'

He queued up a video on his laptop. Before he started it he looked at Benny.

'You aren't cleared for this.'

'Give us a minute,' Gideon said to him, before he could respond in his own style.

Benny shrugged and walked outside.

The video showed an office park surrounded only by scrub and desert. The area was flat for miles, only shrubs and a few cacti breaking up the perfect blankness of the desert.

The camera zoomed in to show Bloom standing near a group of SUVs talking to his men. They were kitted out for a serious field trip: rifles, body armour, all the accessories of a modern land warrior.

'Where is this?'

'Off Highway 10.'

'Who builds an office park in the middle of the desert?'

'It's about half an hour's drive from Fort Huachuca,' Jefferson said.

That was the headquarters of military intelligence, a major artery of the national security apparatus from which profiteers could feed. The building in front of me had to house contractors of some kind, the lack of branding or even a logo announcing they were intelligence as much as their location. What these white-collar spies would want with Bloom, or he with them, I had no idea.

'I don't suppose you're going to tell me what company has offices there, or what they do for the government?'

'No.'

A suit came out of the building and Bloom showed him some papers. He went inside with the suit and a squad of his men. The rest formed a perimeter outside. The way they positioned themselves – only two at the highway's mouth, a few sneaking around the back while the rest kept their eyes on the front door – told me they were more interested in people going out than coming in.

If I had to guess – and I did – I was watching a secret arms deal. The Sons of David had to be funded somehow. Glass didn't have Fisher Partners' lucrative contracts any more, and he wouldn't finance the carnival out of his own pocket.

Jefferson advanced the video about twenty minutes, during which nothing happened. Nobody took that long to conduct illegal business. Just as I was about to press Jefferson, I saw a flash in one of the windows. It was easy to miss on poor-quality video taken in the middle of a desert afternoon, so someone in there obliged me by creating a few more. I was trying to decide between camera and muzzle flash when a body exited a third-storey window.

It was the perfect elevation for death by falling: high enough to kill, not so high the unlucky bastard had time to think about it before he was a bloody mess on the strip of concrete around the front entrance. I think he'd been mostly dead before he fell anyway; the window had been shot out, and the bullets had to have gone through him before they reached the glass.

The men outside didn't look that perturbed by what had just happened. Some of the first squad came outside and got some crates I recognized out of the truck. They held the explosives I'd seen in Joshua's tent. Two others picked up the body and brought it back inside. Bloom was still in there, and I still didn't have a clue what they were doing, but at least I knew what the explosives were for.

Less than ten minutes later, Bloom and his men exited the building. They brought nothing with them that I could see. The convoy drove off, and five minutes later the building collapsed in on itself in a controlled explosion.

'We followed them right back to the Sons of David,' Jefferson said.

'What the hell are Glass and Bloom up to?'

'We don't know,' Gideon said, speaking for the Pentagon and the Mossad.

'I might be of some use in this conversation if you'd tell me what that building used to contain.'

Jefferson sighed, but he did rise from his chair and make a call. He spoke too low for me to hear, but I guessed he was asking for permission from his superiors, whoever they were.

'It was a subsidiary of Janus Intelligence.'

Janus had been the biggest intelligence contractor for Task

Force Seventeen. They were the ones who had provided Stonebridge and assholes of a similar calibre.

'Last time I checked, Glass and Janus were friends. What was this subsidiary doing?'

'Analysis of satellite imagery for the Pentagon and the National Reconnaissance Office.'

'They must have stolen footage of something, then. Can you find out what they looked at, even with all the evidence destroyed?'

'The office was plugged into the secure intelligence network. They accessed hundreds of images that day.'

'What about after Bloom arrived?'

'Thirty images were delivered automatically to their servers. The office made no requests of its own.'

Jefferson handed me a stack of yet more photographs. This must be an average day for him: analyzing, collecting, manipulating, but always from a distance. He could order a thousand-pound bomb dropped on a corner of the Holy Land on the way to pick up his kids from school. He must resent these little field trips, even more so because it was on account of me.

In the pile were photographs of a suburb of Berlin, parts of Jakarta, a street in Nairobi, plus several more of American streets in Chicago, Seattle, Amarillo and other cities I didn't recognize. I wondered how many spy satellites had been re-tasked from defending American citizens to keeping an eye on them. One photo in particular got my attention.

'Is this what I think it is?'

Jefferson nodded. The photograph showed a complex of buildings that had been built in three stages. The first had been a farm, with stables, a barn and a large house. Then had come what looked like a suburban megachurch air-dropped into the middle of nowhere, a large amphitheatre with some offices growing like a tumour from the side. Around them both had been constructed a full military base, with an airfield, helipad, barracks, and a ten-foot wall topped with razor wire.

'Sinai.'

It was the Elders' vacation home, headquarters and fortified bunker all rolled into one.

'How long have they been holed up there?' I asked.

'The better part of a year.'

'Both factions?'

'Yes. God knows what they're doing in there. Peace talks, maybe.'

Jefferson didn't seem too thrilled with that idea. If the Pentagon was making a move, they wouldn't want to do it against a united enemy.

'You think Glass has something planned against the Elders?'

'There's no love lost between them now. They pushed him out of Fisher Partners after Cassandra aired our dirty laundry to the world.'

'A campaign of kidnapping, extortion and murder planned at the federal level qualifies as something more than soiled drawers, don't you think?'

I looked at the photograph again. The barracks housed the Elders' own Praetorian Guard, a brigade of men hand-picked for their loyalty. What really protected them was shame and fear. No one wanted to admit the obvious, that the country had been run by twelve idiots so badly for so long. The fear came from the deals people had made over the years to get along. The Elders would have spread the blood on their hands to as many others as possible. It was the DC way, and it ensured that the entire political class had an interest in keeping them out of the dock.

This photograph, taken from space, was the closest I would

ever get to the men who had destroyed the country and ruined my life.

'I don't suppose—'

'No,' Jefferson said.

Gideon laughed.

'It would be the best solution, if things really are as desperate as you say. Jets accidentally drop daisy-cutter bombs all the time.'

'That wouldn't be wise.'

'No, God forbid someone be held responsible.'

'You think I don't want to see them swinging from the nearest tree?' Jefferson said, his bald head reddening again with anger. 'They've crippled the nation I've spent my whole life trying to protect. Because of them, the military is at breaking point, the country is in chaos, and we're an international laughing stock. They need to be removed from power.'

'But not brought to justice.'

'You know a trial would tear what's left of the nation apart. I want to see those men punished, but I want America restored to its proper greatness even more. We have to do what's best for the country.'

'We always do what's best for the country,' I said, 'not its citizens.'

'None of that concerns you, Strange. You still have a job to do.'

'Are you out of your mind? The Sons of David are kidnapping and assaulting people, and you've got Bloom on tape knocking over a fucking intelligence contractor. Just what do these assholes have to do before you'll stop them?'

'I told you before, arresting them was never the point.'

Jefferson's intransigence was becoming fucking ridiculous. Glass was the keystone of the Sons of David, not Joshua.

Without Glass's money, organization and bloody purpose, Joshua would have been just a charismatic, damaged boy.

'Why do you really want Joshua dead?'

Jefferson didn't say anything. This time he looked at Gideon.

'You think I don't have the clearance?'

'I know you don't.'

The firmness of Jefferson's voice was a bigger surprise to Gideon than the answer. This wasn't a tantrum.

'Give me a moment with my operative.'

Before he left, Gideon raised his eyebrows at me in warning. He didn't know what was going on, and that worried a man like him.

'You don't understand the Beltway, Strange,' Jefferson said when Gideon had left. 'Family and connections have always counted for more than they should, but ever since the Elders took power it's been practically feudal. Where a man comes from is important, and so is where his children go to school. An ambitious man always covers his bases.'

'So someone used his children for networking purposes. What's your point?'

'Do you remember the pictures I showed you of the first Awakening, the one Joshua led?'

'Sure.'

'I told you people died in the siege. Some of them were students.'

I laughed. I don't really know why, nothing about the situation should have been funny.

'Whose child died?' I said. 'A senator's? A general's?'

Jefferson said nothing.

'Looks like I'm an instrument of straight-up, old-fashioned revenge.'

'You do have previous experience.'

In the short time Gideon had been outside, he'd managed to get in an argument with Benny. I couldn't make out the words, just Benny's combative tone. Gideon's masked soldiers stood to one side, watching like a Greek chorus.

They'd found a folding table and two chairs from somewhere and set them up on the pavement. They sat down, elbows on the table, getting ready to arm wrestle over a point of honour.

'Do the others know about this?'

'No, and they don't need to. Don't bother looking for help from them. The Mossad wants Joshua out of the way as much as we do.'

'Can't bring yourself to say assassinated or even dead, can you?'

'The deal is the same, Strange. We'll hold Iris in escrow until your end of the deal is verified.'

I wanted to tell Jefferson not to talk about Iris as if she were collateral, but that was exactly what she was.

'What assurances do I have that you'll release her?'

Jefferson didn't waste time being offended. 'The Mossad have agreed to broker the deal. Is that good enough for you?'

'Benny never leaves her side.'

'That's already been arranged.'

'What about Glass?'

'We'll deal with him and his men when we roll up the Sons of David.'

'How?'

'We've got Bloom and the others committing an act of treason on tape. The trial will be a formality.'

'And Glass?' I said, pressing him because I knew the general wouldn't be among those others.

Jefferson rubbed his bald head, which didn't distract me from his discomfort. He was almost sheepish. It was a look I never expected to see on his face, and it filled me with dread, then anger.

'You're going to let him walk, aren't you?'

'Not walk. Exile, maybe.'

'Maybe? Jesus Christ.'

I'd thought I'd have to deal with Glass on my own, but the fact that Jefferson had said exactly what I'd expected only made me angrier. I kicked the table. That didn't help. I put my foot through the yellowed paper on the wall, but that didn't work either.

Jefferson's minder poked his head in, gave a questioning look to his boss and a hard stare to me.

'It's okay.'

'Not that you'd be able to do anything about it if it wasn't,' I said to the bodyguard, holding his stare.

He grunted and went back outside.

'Simeon Glass is a retired four-star general. He's plugged in to just about every military contractor and national security agency in Washington. The fact that he was President Adamson's favourite means something even now. If you destroy the Sons of David, Glass will be powerless anyway. Focus on Joshua.'

'What happens if Glass is there, and happens to fall down while I'm nearby?'

'Stop getting your panties in a twist over an opportunity you won't have. Glass will be in Washington by now. He's safe there.'

'Safe from you, at any rate. Suppose you're right. We shut down the Sons of David and Glass is sent into exile. Do you really think he'll accept that, and live out the rest of his life on an American Elba?'

He didn't reply. I made for the door.

★

Gideon and Benny were waiting outside by the cars.

'What did he say?' Benny asked, concerned about the tantrum I'd had inside.

'Does the Mossad want Joshua dead as much as Jefferson does?' I said to Gideon.

'The Sons of David aren't good for the Jews, of any nationality. We want the organization destroyed, not the boy. Jefferson hears what he wants to.'

'What did he say?' Benny repeated.

I guess Gideon hadn't told him. He knew what was coming, and chose that moment to make himself scarce.

'I'm going back in, Benny.'

'Who do I punch?'

'It's my decision.'

I saw the punch coming, but I figured I deserved it.

'I don't know when you developed this appetite for punishment,' he said as I picked myself up. 'It wasn't there when we were in the Airborne: you were angrier than a dickless man in a whorehouse, but you didn't have this recklessness. You've got Iris, you've got a way out, and the Israelis will take care of both of you. For once you've got everything you need. What is your fucking problem?'

'I don't have a choice, Benny,' I said, rubbing my jaw. He could still throw a decent right. 'Gideon may like us, but there's nothing Iris and I can offer his superiors that's worth the cost of protecting us.'

'We can figure something out.'

'I already have. That's why I have to go back in.'

'Glass.'

I didn't have to say anything.

'How many times does that man have to ruin your life before you'll stay away from him?'

'The Pentagon won't hold him accountable. That leaves me. You know better than anyone why, Benny. I can't leave this unfinished.'

Benny caught the finality in my words. I hadn't meant it to be there, but I guess I was already thinking of myself in the past tense.

I told Benny the rest. He didn't say much, didn't argue the way Iris had. I'd joked about almost everything with Benny over the years, but not what happened to me in Tehran. He'd heard me talk about Doc Brown, knew what he'd done for me. I trusted the Doc's opinion, and Benny trusted mine.

When I was done Benny was silent for a long time. He kicked the dust since it was the only thing nearby.

'Does she know?'

'She knows.'

I think he'd prepared himself for this before. I certainly had. I'd never known exactly what was wrong with me, when it would get worse, so I'd had no choice but to be a Boy Scout about it.

I imagined Iris rising early, taking a bus in a bright land, maybe Israel, a bus that ended at a hospital, then a room, then me in a bed in that room. I could see the restraints on my body, the machines gathering like carrion eaters. I'd be insensible half the time, in pain the rest, staring at the ceiling when she wasn't there, waiting for the burst blood vessel, the heart attack, the final seizure. I knew this was my future, as much as I knew that Iris would hold my hand to the end.

'I'm never going back to a hospital, Benny. And I don't want her to watch me die.'

Benny swore again, just on general principle.

'I'm sorry, Felix.'

Benny wanted to say more, but by then Jefferson had emerged from the office, underlings scuttling out behind him to get things ready. Gideon had a lot of connections but no real authority. The assault on the farm would already have put one of his feet off the reservation. He could advise, but no more. The show was Jefferson's again.

He gave me a nod, his face a mask of grim determination though he wouldn't be in a hundred miles of hostile fire. My second coming had been arranged.

# THIRTY-ONE

## The Liberty Wall

It was time. Iris and I had said nothing on the way to the border. We'd done all that in the motel room, done it as best we could anyway. I don't think I'd made her understand why I had to finish things with Glass any more than she had been able to make me understand why she'd loved Isaiah like a father.

Gideon and Benny were in the front. They'd been arguing about whether baseball or football was the better sport. The debate could be summarized as Gideon arguing that football was the most beloved sport in the world, played and obsessed over by kids on the streets of Sderot, Seoul and Kinshasa, and Benny pointing out that it was fucking stupid. The discussion didn't improve much from there. When Gideon suggested that it was Brooklyn's fault the Dodgers left – a calamity that had occurred in 1956 – I thought I would have to jump into the front seat to stop Benny from drawing a weapon.

The rendezvous point was a patch of bare ground a few miles north of the Juarez checkpoint, one of the few legal ways left into Mexico. The Elders had used the chaos in northern Mexico to expand and accelerate the network of fences and sensors that had been creeping across the southern border for the last two decades. It had grown into what became known as the Liberty Wall, a monstrosity composed of ten-foot-high razor-wire fencing, guard towers and motion sensors, patrolled by drones and humans alike. Between the opportunities for cronyism and propaganda it had given the Elders, now that I saw it I was surprised it wasn't a hundred feet tall.

Jefferson and his men were already there when we arrived. Their car had Department of Defense plates, the heavies in uniform this time. They'd have an ID and maybe a change of clothes for Iris in the car, just in case Customs weren't suitably awed. Jefferson was still in plain clothes. Maybe that meant he was a civilian. I'd probably never know.

When we got out of the car Jefferson didn't react, his sunburned face annoyed behind dark sunglasses.

'What an asshole,' Benny said to us as he grinned and waved at Jefferson, not really under his breath.

'I'll go see about the arrangements. Don't test Jefferson's patience,' Gideon said to me, and I knew it wasn't just about the present. It sounded like a warning, but the words came with that same searching look he'd turned on me the first time we met in Babylon. He'd broken it out once in a while since then for no reason I could understand, other than it made me uncomfortable. 'Good luck, Strange. I'll pray for you.' We shook hands.

'You mind if I say goodbye first?' Benny said to Iris. 'It'll be shorter, no tears if this big baby can keep control of himself, and definitely no tongue.'

'Be my guest,' she said, and gave us some space.

Benny hummed and hawed for a bit, no real words coming out.

'This is more awkward than a junior high school dance,' he finally said.

'We've done this before,' I said, but we both knew it wasn't the same as last time. 'Thank you for coming, Benny.'

'Are you kidding? Most fun I've had in years. It's my wife who's at home with two small children. She deserves the combat pay, not me.'

'Has she forgiven me?'

'She never really blamed you.'

The way she'd acted the last time we met, you could have fooled me.

'Miriam knew a loudmouth like me was destined for the chop eventually, she just wanted to rough up the messenger a little.'

'I want you to take this,' I said, offering him my forty-five.

'Fuck no,' he replied, stepping back with his hands up like it was radioactive.

'Swap at least.'

'I know what that means, you drama queen. Your grandfather and your uncle came back from their wars. You'll come back from this.'

I offered again with no effect, and had no choice but to put the gun away. I watched Jefferson and Gideon talk by the other car. I thought they might be arguing, the way Gideon was smiling and Jefferson wasn't.

'We both know how well this will probably end. If I don't succeed, what will Jefferson do with Iris?'

'She'll be of no use to him,' Benny said. 'He'll have no reason to hurt or help her.'

That's what I was afraid of. Jefferson wasn't going to leave Iris in a shallow grave, but he might leave her by the side of the road. Fisher Partners would look for her, if only to protect their professional reputation. Even if they didn't, Iris had no shortage of enemies of her own.

Gideon had said he only wanted the Sons of David destroyed. He wouldn't take Joshua's continued breathing personally.

'What about Gideon?'

Benny got a little awkward, which was a lot for him.

'As much as I like Gideon – and I don't like him that much – he'll think the same thing. We'll figure it out,' Benny said. 'From what I've seen the dame can handle herself. I'll watch her back, just like I watched yours.'

'I've been thinking about Tehran lately.'

'No wonder you've been in such a shitty mood.'

'It was when I was locked up. I couldn't help thinking what my life would have been like if I hadn't met Glass. Maybe I would have turned out all right, like you did.'

'Just all right?' Benny said, but he wasn't laughing any more.

'Back in New York, you said I was going to get tired of thinking up ways to kill myself. I promise this is the last one.'

Benny knew odds were it was one stop too late.

'You said you don't want to die in a hospital. Fine. Even if Brown is right, you've still got a few years left. Spend them with Iris. If they try to take you to the hospital, just give me the word. I'll hit the ambulance with a bus myself.'

I thanked him for the offer.

'I never would have made it this long, hell, I never would have gotten off that bed at the VA if it wasn't for you,' I said. 'That's why I'm going to hug you. I'm telling you now so you can prepare yourself.'

'Aw, Jesus,' he said, but by then I had him. 'Whatever happens, I'll keep Iris safe. Now get the hell off me.'

I let him go. There was nothing more to say.

'It's been an honour, Benny.'

'Fuck your past tense. I'll see you again.'

Benny smiled, and he almost believed it.

After that he walked over to Gideon and the others. I knew he would honour the promise he'd made, that Iris would never leave his sight, especially now that he'd seen how she looked. I waited until he was saying something impolite to Jefferson to put the cigarettes I'd stolen from his coat pocket into one of my own. If I was lucky he wouldn't notice the theft until they were on the road. He'd find it funny, once he stopped swearing.

I walked over to Iris. She tried to smile at me, but that just turned out to be the opening her tears had needed.

'Don't cry,' I said, doing my best to comfort her, still not very good at it even after the crash course last night. 'Things aren't as bad as they look. Hell, we should both be dead considering what we've both been through, me at least five or six times.'

'This is you cheering me up?'

'We're lucky, that's all I'm saying.'

'I don't feel lucky,' Iris said between sobs.

We didn't say anything for a while, and we didn't try. Jefferson could stamp his little feet.

'You're angry, you have a right to be. I'm not asking you to forgive me.'

She tried to speak but I held her tighter, looking for words but only interrupting with silence.

'Just don't forget me.'

'You foolish man, what makes you think I ever could?' Iris said, and kissed me to set my mind at rest.

'We're almost out of time,' she said, turning in my embrace to follow my eyes to Jefferson.

'Almost. There's one more thing I have to know,' I said.

She was intrigued. We'd already told each other so much.

'I still don't know your last name.'

Iris whispered in my ear, then let me go. I watched her walk towards the other car, burned every second I could see her into my mind. They got into the car, Benny at Iris's side, one last look in my direction before she disappeared inside. They drove towards the border, the car kicking dust across the perfect horizon.

It was supposed to keep out drugs and terrorists, but when the Liberty Wall had gone up foreign commentators had compared it to the Berlin Wall, meant to keep people in not out. It had turned out that way, whatever the original intent. I looked at those guard towers, the wire shining in the morning, and I didn't think of escape. I belonged in this asylum.

# THIRTY-TWO

## National Houston Memorial, Texas

They said the world had changed after Houston. They'd said the same thing after 9/11. I guess they'd been right on both counts, but to me it just seemed like new excuses for old crimes. If this was a new world, then I was returning to the place where it had been born.

The National Houston Memorial had been built right on the edge of the exclusion zone; that way services had the irradiated desert as a background for the cameras. It was why the feds and police had surrounded the memorial on only one side. They didn't think anyone was crazy enough to approach from the irradiated side. That was why I was going to walk right in.

The Department of Energy maintained a facility nearby and a network of sensors inside the exclusion zone to monitor the fallout. Jefferson had commandeered one of their trucks. He said the edge of the exclusion zone was barely affected at all, cordoned off because the wind occasionally blew in dust from deeper inside the fallout area. That hadn't stopped Jefferson from issuing full radiation suits to the driver and me. I wasn't that concerned. I'd already been dosed once before, and the second time couldn't be any worse.

They let me out deep in the desert so no one would see my approach. The wind had been picking up since the morning. It was strong enough to ground most aircraft and keep me hidden in the swirls of flying dust. I navigated solely by GPS, barely able to see, the wind covering my footsteps as soon as I made them.

I walked for maybe an hour. It felt like being on the moon. I was surprised how relieved I was when I saw the outlines of the memorial and the fence that marked the edge of the exclusion zone. The fence was ordinary chain link, the radiation warnings on the other side a more effective deterrent than any barbed wire could be.

I couldn't see anyone around on the other side. Both factions were staying indoors, a temporary ceasefire held together only by the weather. The Romans would have taken a storm like this as a warning from the gods, but the Elders only paid attention to signs and wonders when they told them what they wanted to hear.

I cut the fence and slipped inside. I found a quiet spot, changed out of the radiation suit and hid it behind a generator. I wasn't going back that way, if I was going back at all. I was more worried about what kind of questions were going to be asked after my reappearance. It would be a toss-up whether they thought I was a walking miracle or a traitor.

I saw my first people outside the compound entrance. Joshua's bodyguards, Glass's soldiers, kept watch no matter what the weather. I skulked outside until I saw Sarah coming out alone, face shielded from the wind. I shadowed her footsteps until we were out of sight of the guards. She had the unconcerned gait of a child, afraid of nothing in this world, or confident an adult would be there to save her. When I grabbed her she gave no cry of surprise or fear, even before she saw who it was.

'Gershom,' Sarah said, but she didn't look that surprised to see me. She gave me a big hug, but when I saw her face again something was troubling its brow. 'I thought you were dead.'

'I got lucky. It's a long story and we don't have time for me to explain. Your life, and Joshua's, is in danger.'

She was bemused by the idea.

'Why would anyone want to hurt us?'

I had to take a deep breath before I could answer that question the way I needed to.

'The military considers you a threat to civil order. Do you understand what that means?' I said when Sarah didn't react. 'Sooner or later they'll make a deal with the feds out there. Once that happens they'll round you up and kill anyone who resists.'

'Our friends would never allow that.'

'Are you sure they're your friends?' I said. 'Last time I checked the police were pointing guns at you too. This comes from the Pentagon, Sarah. Nobody can stand in its way, even if they wanted to.'

'How do you know all this?' I could see the suspicion that had begun in her brow spreading to the rest of her face. 'Are you working with them?'

'I'm just a messenger. There are members of the Pentagon who want to avoid a bloodbath.'

I put my hands on her shoulders, resisted the urge to shake her until she started listening.

'I need to find General Glass.'

It took her a second to figure out who I was talking about. She thought of him as Joshua's surrogate father, maybe her own as well. The idea was too perverse to keep in my head for long.

'He's with Joshua.'

Sarah took my hand and led me towards the compound. As we approached the guards, the chance that she was about to turn me in loomed in my mind, but we passed by with barely a nod from her. She was still queen of this place.

'Joshua is praying and fasting in his tent,' Sarah said. 'He must be pure and focused when the miracle comes.'

'What miracle?'

Sarah didn't say anything, just opened the flap and stepped aside to let me pass. The inside was hidden by a screen that hadn't been there before. I parted it and looked inside. There was no sign of Joshua, but I did see four armed Sons of David inside, right around the time I felt the barrel of a gun in my side. I hadn't felt a weapon when she'd hugged me, but I hadn't thought I needed to look for one. It was my usual luck that now was the time that Sarah decided to start exercising her Second Amendment rights.

'I'm sorry, Gershom,' she said in my ear, and frog-marched me inside.

When the Sons saw Sarah, me and the gun, they snapped to attention and raised their sub-machine guns. The motion was so spasmodic I was afraid one of them was going to plug me by mistake. The interior of the tent was the same as before, the curtain to the media room pinned back. On the bank of monitors next to the recording equipment was a single landmark from a dozen separate angles: the Dome of the Rock.

'You've signed your own death warrants,' I said to them.

Sarah replied by turning the world black.

I awoke in the dark shackled to a chair. Again. For a moment I thought I was in IF. My body began to struggle no matter what my brain said, pulling on the cuffs, as strong as they'd been before, only cutting my arms and nearly falling over for all my trouble. After a few moments the darkness faded from my mind and I could breathe.

I wasn't in IF, but I wasn't in Joshua's tent either. The room was small and lit by a single overhead lamp. Behind me were metal racks containing drums of soap and disinfectant beside boxes of what looked like toilet paper. I was in a supply cupboard, and it could only be in the Houston Memorial building.

My spasm of resistance had attracted someone on the other side of the frosted-glass door. I could see lights but heard no voices. The door was opened by a Son of David I recognized: the kid who had shot that boy outside Denver while Bloom, and I, were rounding up penitents for the revival. Darby, that was his name. He grinned, but it was an impersonal smirk made of equal portions of entitlement and sadism. I doubt he even remembered me or the boy he might have killed.

After him came Sarah. She smiled at me as girls did at sick animals, if they were cute enough.

'How do you feel?'

'Fine, other than the headache. I wouldn't have thought you could swing a gun like that.'

'Necessity is an excellent teacher. Do you know why you're here, Gershom?'

'You think I'm a traitor.'

'You are disloyal, but not because of what you said.'

Sarah held up my bottle of medication. She must have felt it in my jacket pocket when she'd hugged me. The sight of it reminded my body that I was behind in the schedule. Nausea began to tickle the bottom of my stomach. The other symptoms wouldn't be far behind.

'What does my medication have to do with this?'

'Your poison, you mean. Joshua chased away the demon that

312

afflicted you. You don't need these narcotics any more. You'd know that if you had faith in him.'

'He can't cure the sick, Sarah,' I said. 'What did he do to me on stage?' I hadn't had the chance to think about it with everything that had happened. I'd felt something, even if it wasn't what Joshua said it was. Had it been drugs, or did he give me a shock? It had to have been some kind of magic trick.

'Joshua tried to set you free,' Sarah said. Maybe she wasn't in on the joke. 'He's done it before, for those whose faith is strong enough. This room will be your crucible, Gershom. You will feel the fires of Hell, but you will emerge from here a new, whole man.'

There was the catch. I wondered how many others like me had come to Joshua when they had no doctor and no hope. I wondered how many had died after Joshua had 'healed' them, and they stopped taking their medication.

'I need to see Joshua, Sarah.'

'He is busy, preparing for the great revival that will heal this nation.'

'I wasn't lying. The military is coming.'

'Let them.' She was untroubled, serene. 'No Christian soldier will raise his hand against the prophet of the Lord's return.

'It's not too late for you,' Sarah said, laying a hand on my shoulder in a gesture that she imagined was comforting. 'Forgiveness is within the reach of all God's children. You saved my life, Gershom. Now let me help you save your own.'

'By keeping me here?'

'It would be cruel of me to let you back into the world while you still struggle with a demon. Through fasting and prayer, and with the aid of the Holy Ghost, I know you can triumph over the false idol of medicine.'

When I'd first met Sarah, she struck me as far too smart to

believe in what she was saying. It made more sense to see her as a teenage girl who had built herself a role as a queen, and would say or do anything to maintain that position. Looking into her eyes, still full of that troubling serenity closer to death than peace, I knew now that I'd seen what I'd wanted to. I'd made the mistake of being rational about something that was anything but.

'Don't you have any brothers or sisters, Sarah? What about your parents? There must be someone out there who loves you.'

'All my brothers and sisters are right here, Gershom. The only thing out there is despair.'

'And what about all the other brothers and sisters who died?' I said. 'They turned a damn minigun on them under Glass' orders.'

'The Elders killed them, not him,' she said. 'He's one of us, he'd never hurt his family. I mourn for those we lost, but I know they died free. I will see them again.'

She smiled at me, still with great kindness, and I knew she meant every word.

'I'll leave you in the care of my brothers now,' Sarah said. 'Joshua needs me by his side. You are a good man, Gershom. I know you will conquer this demon. I have faith in you.' She closed the door, and with it any possibility that this would end well.

Hours passed. There were no windows in the storage room, but I caught sight of the fading day when they escorted me to the toilet. The memorial was actually a church, or at least laid out like one. It was mostly bare, with the tall, swooping ceiling of a cathedral. In its centre was the recovered statue of Sam Houston, encased in leaded glass to keep the legacy of the bombing inside. Behind it was a tall, plain cross, positioned so that the light from the glass ceiling would cast a shadow that swept across the whole room as the day progressed. There was a lectern for school talks and the occasional photo-op. Brother Isaiah had led ceremonies of remembrance every year from that lectern, usually brought outside because the crowds that he'd attracted couldn't fit within. The memorial was perhaps the only beautiful and restrained thing ever made by the Elders, if you didn't count the gift shop on the other side of the chapel.

Every inch of the chapel's walls was covered with names in tiny gothic letters. They were the victims of Houston, those burned and shredded by the blast, more who had died from the inside out in improvised wards, others who would never be found. It reminded me of the memorial in Grand Central, and all its brethren in other stations and bus stops all over the country. So many names, and so few faces.

I did the convict two-step down the hall and across the chapel, waiting, hoping the Sons guarding me would make a mistake. Darby was in front, his buddy in the rear. They kept their distance, neither giving me the chance to grab them or the guns they were carrying. The Sons of David didn't talk to me, which was probably the only thing that had gone right since I arrived at the camp.

They let me into the disabled stall but didn't remove the shackles, leaving it to me not to piss on the chains that bound my legs. Lucky for them I'd had a lot of practice.

# THIRTY-THREE

I woke up to the sound of the door opening. I was surprised I'd fallen asleep. I covered my head with my cuffed hands, but felt no new bruises. A new smell hit me during my self-examination: a burning cigar. I didn't have to raise my head to know who had arrived.

'I knew they'd try to liquidate the boy eventually,' Glass said, and took a drag on his cigar. 'I didn't think they'd send you. I suppose I should have put two and two together when the Mossad attacked that safe house, but I've been distracted with more important things.'

Glass must have meant Galilee Farm, where Iris had been held. He'd used the term 'safe house' without any apparent irony.

'You're a good choice: angry, murderous, far more capable than your mental history would suggest. You've got lone gunman written all over you. Who sent you, Jefferson?'

I said nothing but he nodded to himself anyway. Glass had never needed anyone to confirm his opinions.

'I suppose you're wondering why you're still alive.'

'Gimme a minute,' I said. 'I just woke up.'

Glass looked like hell. Up close the legacy of being shot in the face was even worse than on television. He'd lost most of his hair to surgery, not time. What was left had turned bone white and stood at attention, as if waiting for something. What surprised me most was the general air of weariness I could feel around him. In the longest days of Tehran, when the task force had run on nothing but adrenaline and fear, he had powered us with his infernal energy.

'Do you hear that?' Glass said.

The wind had picked up even more while I was asleep. This windowless room couldn't escape the sound.

'There's going to be a hell of a storm.'

'You kept me alive to talk about the weather?'

'The truth is I have some time to kill. My men are capable and loyal, but they've never been able to offer much in the way of conversation.'

Glass put on his reading glasses, opened the file in his hand and began to skim through it. Occasionally he chuckled to himself.

'I've been reading your greatest hits,' he said, and began to read out loud: 'At the end of services at New Life Evangelical Church, Roy St James was killed by a single shot to the head with a high-powered rifle at long range. No weapon has been recovered, and the Providence Sheriff's department has no suspects.'

He flipped through a few more pages.

'Gambi was shot execution-style after what appears to be a chase by his killer. The body of a small child was discovered in a search of his destroyed trailer, the body burned beyond recognition. Autopsy revealed a gunshot to the chest as the most likely cause of death.'

Glass stopped and looked over his reading glasses at me. He

was waiting for an angry denial, tears, threats, any kind of reaction at all. I didn't give him the satisfaction.

'I always knew you had potential, but this,' Glass said, tapping the file against his palm. 'I never thought you had it in you.'

'You've made a habit of underestimating me.'

'Have I?' Glass considered it. 'I don't recall thinking about you enough for that to be possible.'

'That's why Cassandra is enjoying herself badmouthing the Elders all over Europe, rather than being under your care.'

'Are you gloating? You have changed.'

The door opened. Two Sons pushed a TV on wheels into the storeroom. Another followed after with a chair for Glass. They delivered their furniture and left, careful not to look at Glass directly.

'What are we watching?'

Glass ignored me, pulled the chair near and sat down. This show was his, and I wasn't allowed to skip ahead.

'You know what your problem is, Strange? You lack discipline,' he said, before I had the chance to give his rhetorical question the answer it deserved. 'If you had stayed with me, you would have had a career; hell, a calling, maybe. You would have had the firm hand and the medical care you needed. You could have been a great Fisherman.'

'We can't all aspire to the heights of Peter Stonebridge.'

'You think you've done better than him?'

'I'm still alive. I doubt he can say the same thing.'

A hint of a smile, particularly difficult to see on Glass's wasteland of a face, was as far as he'd be drawn.

'It's been ten years since you left the army, a little more. You move to New York City, you make something of a living sniffing other people's laundry. Hand to mouth, day after day. All that potential, and you end up a private eye.' There was contempt in his voice, an inevitable inflection whenever he mentioned something in the civilian world. There was disappointment too, the timbre of a father looking over the wasted life of his son.

'You tell me, Strange, what have you got to show for all those years?'

'I survived.'

Glass sat back in his chair, worked on his cigar.

'And that's enough for you?'

'Do you really think I regret not being with you in the Holy Land, when you killed so many civilians the Israelis kicked you out? Or working for Fisher Partners when your incompetent employees let slip to the whole world the great terror you had committed for the Elders? What makes you think I would want to share in all your failures?'

Glass's eyes sparkled from the recesses of his misshapen face.

'You're trying to anger me.'

'Well, maybe I'm sick of your employees chaining me up.'

He stood up and turned on the television. Glass scowled at the snow that appeared, and began to look at the connections on the back.

'I'm still trying to figure out what you think you're going to accomplish here,' I said. 'This gig isn't your style; it's amateur hour all the way. You've got a couple of thousand kids who can make trouble, but that's all they can do. Do you really think you can extort a comeback just from that?'

He said nothing, still checking connections.

'I bet your real plan has something to do with that contractor Bloom burned to the ground.'

Glass came out from behind the TV, wary. I had his attention now.

'It won't work, whatever you're planning.'

'We'll see about that.'

The TV changed from snow to the same picture I'd seen on Joshua's monitors: an aerial shot of the Dome of the Rock in Jerusalem. It looked like a live feed, which meant they expected something to happen there soon. I began to get a very bad feeling, even worse than the others I already had on the go.

They were going to attack the Dome of the Rock: take it over, blow it up, something like that. It was the only thing I could think of, and it fitted Glass's MO. Bloom's attack on that Janus Intelligence office had to be linked somehow. Maybe they were trying to blind the Pentagon so they wouldn't see what was coming.

'Have you ever read the Book of Revelation?' Glass said.

'Lately I haven't had much of a choice.'

'"And the third angel sounded, and there fell a great star from heaven, burning as it were a lamp, and it fell upon the third part of the rivers, and upon the fountains of waters; And the name of the star is called Wormwood."'

Wormwood. That was the name Bloom had used for an operation when I overheard him during the revival. The rest of what he said came back to me: 'I'll contact you when phase three is complete, but you'll probably hear about it on the news first.' They'd shared a laugh over that. Blowing up that Janus office would have got the attention of some people in Washington besides Jefferson. That attack must have been phase three.

What was phase four? An attack of some kind on the Dome of the Rock was the only thing that made sense, but I didn't see how Glass could pull it off. An armed assault against the Temple Mount would come up against both American and Israeli troops. As crazy as Gideon had said the Settlers had become, I couldn't see them agreeing to this plan. Their first priority was holding on to as much of the occupied territories as they could.

320

It also wasn't that miraculous, even by Joshua's degraded standards. Armed men shooting things up had become all too commonplace. Glass may have been a maniac, but these kinds of operational difficulties were what he excelled at.

An idea occurred to me. For the first time I was glad that I was tied to this chair, because otherwise I might have fallen out of it.

'Look at those gears spin in your head,' Glass said. 'You always were a quick study.'

'And there fell a great star from heaven.' A duff Chinese satellite had re-entered the atmosphere without proper control a few years ago. It landed on a house in Belgium, of all places, levelled the building and killed everyone inside.

'You can't be serious.'

'And why not?'

'Physics, that's why,' I said. 'If you throw a satellite at the Dome, it'll burn up in the atmosphere before it touches the mosque. At best you'll break a few windows.'

'That would probably happen with a communication satellite,' Glass said. 'We've been launching military satellites hardened against attacks for years. Add in a little creative telemetry, and I've been assured that the result will be like a small nuclear weapon without the inconvenient radiation.'

'It'll never work.'

'Then you and your new CO have nothing to worry about.'

'Until someone finds out you threw United States' military property at the third holiest site in Islam.'

Glass thought he was covering all his bases. He wanted outrage, fury and death, and figured the plot's existence would give it to him regardless of whether it succeeded. He wasn't planning on using the Sons of David as a bargaining chip; they'd been nothing more than a smokescreen all along.

'So you set the whole Middle East on fire, and you figure

**321**

regardless of who comes out on top, the Elders or the Pentagon, they'll come crawling back to you.'

'They have before. The Elders thought they didn't need me after they turned chicken-shit about the Holy Land. They came back as soon as they got scared enough. I tried to warn you, Strange, society doesn't have much love for people like us. We frighten them, but they'll start calling us heroes as soon as they're more frightened of someone else.'

I wondered why Glass was telling me all this. For some reason it reminded me of that conversation with Mr Lim in Thorpe's shack, what seemed an eternity ago. Lim was a professional killer tired of being in the background, cleaning up the messes of others. I think he wanted someone to appreciate his work, and the same went for Glass now. I wondered what it was about psychopaths that made them desperate to be understood.

'You couldn't just retire? You have everything, why didn't you just warm the seats on a few boards and live off the interest like every other corrupt asshole in this country?'

Glass found the question more absurd than what he had planned.

'What was I supposed to do, die on some golf course? I'd left too many things undone.'

I got the feeling at this point that Glass would have liked to have looked out a window, maybe on the crowds that he'd helped to draw. The only audience here was me and the toilet roll, and neither of us had much choice about attending.

'The country was still insecure, defied, laughed at. I've given my life to the safety of this nation; I wasn't going to leave it in its time of need.'

I shook my head in disbelief. I just couldn't believe it had come to this.

'I've heard how big a deal you are for years,' I said. 'I think even Jefferson is afraid of you. I always was. Now I'm beginning to think I can see the emperor's balls flapping in the wind. All that power and influence, and the best comeback you could manage was a twelve-year-old boy with delusions of grandeur.'

'I wouldn't have to do this if they hadn't screwed up everything the first time!'

Glass turned his back and muttered something, to himself or the toilet supplies. For a moment he was just another cranky old man complaining about the state of things. I barely noticed, as I was too intent on figuring out what the hell he'd just said.

'What first time?' I said the words slowly, enunciated each one. It was the only way I could get the sentence out without screaming it.

'The destruction of Tehran was a victory. We finally showed the whole world that we weren't going to lie down and take it any longer. And what did President Adamson do with that victory? He used it as an excuse to leave, to retreat. I gave him what he asked for, and he wasted it.'

Glass was still talking to himself. They were bitter words, like he had personally been let down by the President. First Adamson, then the Elders had disappointed him. Glass never failed. It was others who failed him.

'What did we do?' I said. The dreams I'd been having of that last day in Tehran hadn't given me any insight. I thought again of those last moments, Lieutenant Blake calmly telling Glass that they'd been ambushed, most of the team dead, their position untenable. Glass had responded with questions about the robot they'd brought along, that loud walking metal box meant to contain whatever radioactive materials we'd expected to find. Glass had called it the package. I didn't know why at the time, the robot was empty. I thought it was its codename. The

**323**

package, Glass had asked Blake as his men died around him, where is the package?

'We bombed Tehran, didn't we?' I said. 'Adamson wanted a way out, peace with honour. You gave him the smoking gun you'd always told him you'd find.'

'Now you listen to me,' Glass said through his teeth as he came close. He grabbed the chair and stared right into my eyes, until the smoke from his cigar made them water and I could no longer see. 'There was no bomb. Do you think I'm insane? I never would have allowed something like that to happen with so many of our people in the city. You think what you want about me, Strange, but you know I'd never endanger my own men.'

'There are American troops stationed on the Temple Mount,' I said. 'Last time I checked, you were planning to drop a satellite on their heads.'

'It was radioactive material, nothing more. You may not have believed Stonebridge, but I did. The isotopes were just insurance. The stalemate we were in was killing Americans every day we let it drag on.'

'You think I don't remember that?' It's why I'd listened to Glass in the first place.

'If we found radioactive material, the Europeans would have to come out on our side. We might even have been able to convince the Russians and Chinese to stop selling weapons to the Iranians. I was trying to save lives.'

'You were trying to make yourself indispensable, just like you are now. Are you really going to tell me that the Iranians, after years of war, just happened to choose the same day you were going to plant evidence to set off some kind of city-sized suicide bomb? I may be half out of my mind right now, but even I can't believe in that kind of coincidence.'

'Believe what you want, it's the truth.'

324

'It's the truth you want to believe,' I said. 'Otherwise you'd have to admit that you killed hundreds of your own.'

Instead of replying to what I'd said, Glass knocked on the door. One of the Sons of David guarding outside opened it.

'I think it's appropriate that you're here now,' he said to me, one foot already out the door. 'You were there when it began, and now you'll see the end.'

The door closed. The room was dark except for the picture of the Dome of the Rock, glowing from the TV.

# THIRTY-FOUR

## National Houston Memorial, Texas

My symptoms measured the passage of time. There was no window, no light. It had been hours since I'd spoken with Glass, maybe a whole day. I know I hadn't fallen asleep; my joints were burning too hot, my stomach twisted in too many knots to allow it.

The Sons of David guarding me came inside and closed the door behind them. The last to enter was Darby. The way the other two looked at him, it was clear he was still the leader. He had the same unkempt brown hair, the same self-satisfied grin of a budding sadist.

He was wearing my hat.

They circled around me, wary, curious. It looked like I would be today's entertainment.

'Sarah said he's ill,' one of the others said. He was taller than Darby but scrawny, big frightened eyes that couldn't look at me directly. He'd been horrified when Darby shot that other boy, though he'd done his best not to show it.

'The general says he's a traitor,' Darby said.

'He doesn't look so good,' said the other one. 'We're supposed to leave him alone.'

'We're supposed to leave him alone,' Darby said back in a mincing voice. He grabbed my chin and lifted it to his face.

'The general won't let him live much longer. It doesn't mean we can't have a little fun with him first. You do it,' he said to the other boy.

He didn't move.

'Come on, Bobby, what are you, some kind of fag?'

The third stood against the shelves watching them. He was a chunky boy with short hair who seemed to have nothing to say for himself.

Bobby, who must have been the tall boy, disappeared behind me. The other two stayed in front. I tried to turn to see what he was about to do, but Darby held my chin in place.

I heard the sound of friction between metal and leather as Bobby drew his sidearm. He pulled back the slide. The click behind my right ear was the safety coming off.

'Put it against the back of his head,' Darby said.

Bobby did as he was told. Darby was enjoying himself. I wondered how many animals he'd tortured to death as a child.

'Load it.'

'I just did.'

I wasn't showing the appropriate level of fear. Darby looked disappointed, until his eyes lit up with the thought of another game.

'Choke him.'

I couldn't see Bobby's face, but I could tell by the look on Darby's that the boy wasn't too into the idea.

'We aren't supposed to kill him.'

'It's just practice.'

The third Son stayed in his place by the shelves, watching but saying nothing.

'Come on, chicken-shit, do that hold they taught us.'

Bobby didn't move. Darby let go of my chin and stepped back. The sneer he'd been wearing was joined by anger; Bobby's refusal to do as he was told was challenging the little bully's authority.

'Do it.'

I heard Bobby holster his pistol. There was some fumbling behind me before one of his arms encircled my neck. Bobby put the other hand against the back of my head. He'd put my head into the crook of his elbow, rather than putting his forearm against my neck as he should have. When Bobby began to apply pressure, it didn't work very well.

'Harder,' Darby said.

Bobby was leaning over me, standing as close behind as he could. My hands were cuffed, but the chain that bound them had about a foot of slack. I could have fought Bobby's arms, but in the position I was in it wouldn't have done any good. The hold was inexperienced and slow. It would cut off my breath eventually, but not fast enough for the enraged Darby.

'Do it right, you faggot.'

I was tired. Weak. When the pain in my joints receded I could feel the tingling in my nerves. My legs felt like they belonged to someone else, and I wasn't sure they'd take orders from me. I didn't have much time.

I had one more thing left to do.

Darby opened his mouth to yell at Bobby again. Before the words came out, he saw my eyes come into focus, saw what was in them. He saw, but there was nothing he could do.

I reached behind and grabbed Bobby's gun out of the holster. Darby saw the gun draw level with his heart and fire. The shock of the sound made Bobby stand up and pull back on my neck at the same time. I could feel my weight make him lose his balance. The third boy was going for his own pistol. I had just enough time as Bobby and I fell backward to get off a shot where I last remembered the third boy standing.

I was looking at the storage room's ceiling. Grey concrete. I heard the third boy, or his body, slide to the ground and stop moving.

I was on top of Bobby. He was still in a position to choke me, but wasn't trying to improve his technique now that I had his gun upside-down to his head. All he did was breathe hard in my ear.

'Okay,' I said. 'Bobby, is it? You and I are going to stand up together, slowly. At no point will this gun leave your head. Follow my lead, it'll be just like dancing.'

'I'm not supposed to dance,' he said, but followed my lead anyway.

We stood up together. It seemed to take about an hour. The third Son was slumped against the shelves he'd been propping up while his friends tortured me. My wild shot had gone through his chest and into one of the soap containers, pink gel oozing slowly down the shelf towards the boy's corpse.

I turned around to bring Bobby into view, keeping the gun against his temple at all times.

'Uncuff me.'

'I don't have a key.'

'Then get it.'

Bobby searched Darby's belt until he found a set of handcuff keys. He undid the leg irons first at my suggestion, then gave me the key so I could unlock my hands and keep the gun level.

'Are you going to kill me?'

I kicked the irons in his direction as an answer. He fastened them around his legs, and then I cuffed his hands.

When he was secure I went over to Darby's body. He'd lifted my forty-five and made it his sidearm. I guess stealing my hat wasn't enough of an insult. I took both, putting the kid's gun in my waistband in case I needed it.

'Where is Joshua?'

'He's still in the memorial, I think. We've been standing by the door.'

'Someone will find you in a few hours, probably the army. Don't make any sudden moves with them and you might survive this.'

'Sir?' Bobby said, when I got the door open. 'The boy that Darby' – he snuck a look at the corpse – 'the boy that Darby shot. What happened to him?'

'I don't know, kid,' I said, and closed the door.

The hallway I stepped into was familiar from my bathroom breaks. Behind me it dead-ended in water fountains. On the right it led to a left turn and then darkness.

'Tell me again,' Joshua said, from somewhere in the chapel.

'We don't have the time, and you know the scripture better than I do.'

'Please?' Joshua said, in a tone familiar to parents everywhere.

Glass's laugh would have been indulgent, if his face hadn't been so broken. Instead it came out more as a gurgle. I dragged myself down the hall towards the voices, leaning on the wall with one hand for support.

'Just the end, then: "And God shall wipe away all tears from their eyes; and there shall be no more death, neither sorrow, nor crying, neither shall there be any more pain: for the former things are passed away."'

'Does that mean I'll see my mother and father again?'

'Of course it does,' Glass said. 'You'll see both of them. Your father is whole now that you freed him from that demon. He sits at Jesus's side in heaven, and that's because of you.'

Glass sat at a folding table set up between the aisles of pews.

There was a bank of monitors behind it showing the crowds that had gathered outside the memorial. The commemoration services had always used the memorial as a backdrop but Joshua had set up his stage to the side of the building. The only thing behind it was a giant video screen and the empty desert. Joshua didn't want anything to distract from his miracle.

Two guards stood by the monitors. They looked like Seventeen men. Any sounds of gunfire that had escaped the storage room had been drowned out by the huge crowds just outside. That was where most of their attention was. They shifted their feet with boredom and looked out the windows on the opposite side of the building.

Joshua stood beside Glass. Instead of the Lil' Dictator costume he'd sported at his revival, he wore the white raiment of the pure and chosen.

'And the rest?' Glass prompted.

'"But the fearful, and unbelieving, and the abominable, and murderers, and whoremongers, and sorcerers, and idolaters, and all liars, shall have their part in the lake which burneth with fire and brimstone: which is the second death."'

Joshua's eyes were shining by the end, a conclusion to a much-loved story.

'They'll all pay, won't they?'

'Every single one,' Glass said, and ruffled his blond curls.

I waited until both guards were looking out the window, then came around the corner. The second guard had enough time to turn when I shot the first, but not enough to raise his weapon. Joshua stared at me, then at the guards, surprised more than afraid. It wasn't the first time he'd seen a bloody corpse. The general wasn't surprised at all.

'Son,' Glass said, 'you really have to stop trying to impress me.'

The sun was still in the sky, but it was hidden by the darkest clouds I'd ever seen. The great windows of the chapel showed a horizon half glowing red and half deep black, the night chasing the remains of the day into the ground. I could see lightning in the clouds, and though we were far enough away that the rain hadn't reached us yet, I could still feel the thunder rolling through me.

'Gershom?' Joshua said.

'He's here to kill you,' Glass said. I kept the gun on him while I tried to reason with the boy.

'Listen to me, Joshua. The only miracle that will happen today is the crime against humanity that this man has engineered. All your work has been a front for him, nothing more.

'You have no idea what you've done, how much damage you've caused. Some day you'll answer for it. If it was up to me that reckoning might have been today, but someone important has forgiven you. If you ever meet her, you'll know what a real Christian looks like. Neither God nor general compels you to be here, Joshua. Your fate is your own.'

The last part horrified Joshua more than the talk of killing him. He'd been running from free will ever since it had killed his father. I recognized the feeling. Joshua ran to the side door that led to the crowd and the stage. I followed him with my eyes and made the mistake of wondering what I'd done.

Out of the corner of my eye I saw Glass reach for his weapon. I had time to duck behind a pew before he fired. Then the old son of a bitch ran into the gift shop.

The shop was part of an extension that had gone up since I'd last been here. The architect had put it off a corridor so it wasn't visible from the chapel, out of a lingering sense of decency, or the fear it would to spoil the camera angles during televised services. The side door that Joshua had fled through was in there, but I doubted that was what Glass was after. He might fall back to a better position, but Glass never ran.

It was dark inside, the storm twilight outside providing the only illumination. I peeked around the corner, saw the outlines of clothes racks, bookshelves and a counter at the back. In my condition the old bastard was probably faster than I was. If I chose the wrong place to look for cover, he'd plug me and this would all have been for nothing.

'Did you spare the boy because you couldn't kill him, or just to prove me wrong about you?'

Glass was in there somewhere, but I couldn't place his voice.

'Maybe I'm just tired of your kind of justice.'

'Mine? I see. Do you—'

I made my move, knowing how much Glass liked to hear himself talk. I came in tight and low to the wall, legging it for the nearest coat rack. The general broke off mid-sentence – something that usually only happened when a bomb went off nearby – and put holes in the wall behind me. I fired back at the muzzle flashes, succeeding only in shredding a T-shirt emblazoned with 'Remember Houston!' above a picture of the monument.

The windows on the right wall looked out on to what should have been empty desert. Today it was filled with thousands of people, a haphazard tent city set up in front of Joshua's stage. Ranks of Sons of David stood in front in their white sheets. The crowd reminded me of the sprawling refugee camps that had appeared after thousands of Iranians fled our invasion. They ended up in places like this in Iraq and Jordan, were still there for all I knew. The people outside may have thought of themselves as refugees from a fallen world, but from here it looked more like a Woodstock of the deranged.

'What do you think will happen when Jefferson and his

bosses take over?' Glass said. 'He works for the fools and cowards who got the country into this mess in the first place.'

'If I have to choose between a psychopath and a coward, I'll take the latter.'

I fired at a shadow. The bullet went through a figment of my imagination and shattered a snow globe of Houston in a display case on the wall.

'You can't stop the tide of history, Strange.'

'Why don't you stand up, I'll make you a piece of history right now.'

Glass answered with a round that hit the cash register. He and I were both moving among the clothes racks, trying to outmanoeuvre the other.

'There's still time to end this. You'll never be able to control what you're about to unleash.'

'We spent decades coddling regimes in the name of stability, while they gave our money to terrorists. I've had enough of watching my country get attacked, dragged down and humiliated by that fucking part of the world. I will remake the region in one stroke, and solve the Middle East problem once and for all. What makes you think I want to control it, Strange? This is my legacy.'

I came out from behind a rack and there he was, standing in the aisle with his gun raised.

'Look at them out there, Sergeant. Look at all those people who have come to a desert so a boy can tell them fairy tales. Do you really think you can save them from themselves?'

'I can save them from you.'

We both fired. Neither moved. Glass was done running, and so was I.

I fell to my knees. Glass had slumped against one of the clothes racks, still upright and alive. I'd shot him three times. He'd hit me twice.

I guess that meant I won.

A strange serenity had taken over Glass's face. For some reason the scars didn't seem as awful any more.

'I'm tired, Strange,' he said. 'I gave my life to this country and it barely noticed.'

'It's over now. Stop the attack.'

He tried to laugh, but his lungs were filling with blood.

'You'll never live to see it,' I said.

'It's still my legacy. There will always be people like me, Strange, because there will always be people like you. As the good book says: "I am Alpha and Omega, the beginning and the ending."'

Blood from his lungs stopped up his mouth, bled out of his lips. Those cold, baleful eyes, never resting, always hungry, fell on me and were still at last. I let my gun fall from my hand. I didn't need it any more.

'Sir, we're ready to go. Awaiting final authorization.'

It was Bloom's voice, on the radio in Glass's dead hand. I crawled over and took it.

'Bloom.'

'Strange,' Bloom said. 'Glass told me about you.'

'Abort, I repeat, abort the attack.'

'I have orders.'

'Glass is dead.'

A long silence.

'Listen to me, Bloom. If you stop now, you and your team will have a head start. If you go through with this, then there's no rock on the earth big enough to hide you. Enough people have died already. You owe Glass nothing. Please, I'm begging you, abort.'

Another long silence. I hoped I'd get his answer before I bled out.

'Okay, Strange. Okay.'

The radio went dead.

'My brothers and sisters, we have spent long years wandering this desert,' Joshua said over the loudspeaker outside. God knows how he'd gotten to the stage so fast. His speech began without introduction or preamble, but he held the tone and music of his words against his fear. The screen made Joshua's face two storeys tall, each of the tears in his eyes larger than him. They weren't tears of fear or pain. He was smiling down on his thousands of followers with a benevolent resignation I'd only seen in the faces of the condemned.

The screen switched back to a view of the Dome of the Rock. In the night sky above it I saw a bright flash, and then several smaller ones. I hoped Bloom had meant what he'd said, and that was the satellite burning up in the atmosphere.

'These ten long years, we have drunk bitter waters and gnashed our teeth,' Joshua said, his face gigantic again. I wondered if he understood what he'd just seen, if Glass had even told him what was going to happen. I was sure the general had promised his child prophet a little more than a light show. It sounded like the kid had been smart enough to put it together, judging by the renewed, desperate fervour in his voice.

'We have prayed as the fornicators plied their trade and the idolators worshipped the golden calf. We have been patient and forbearing, as our Lord commanded us. The time for patience is at an end.'

In the desert behind him, the dark sky seemed to be falling. A finger of night reached down to touch the horizon, slamming into the ground and kicking up dust.

'I promised you a miracle,' Joshua said. His giant face disappeared from the screen as the camera followed his hand to the tornado in the distance. 'The whirlwind has come for me, as it came for the prophet Elijah. I am not afraid. I wear the white raiment; my name is already in the Book of Life. The Lord said, "he that loseth his life for my sake shall find it." Brothers and sisters, I go to the whirlwind, to confess your name before our Father and His angels.'

Joshua left the stage. He was a tiny figure in the distance, but the camera followed. The ranks of raiment-clad Sons of David in front of the stage were in chaos. They had no idea what their child leader was doing. The crowd of thousands was silent. Sarah was there, holding his hand, by his side as always. The wind from the storm threw their raiment back, swept it up into pale wings. She turned to look at her younger charge, and the camera showed a happy and contented face, untroubled by fear. Someone had opened the gate for them. Joshua walked into a radioactive wasteland I had just left, towards the spinning cloud of night in the distance. One by one, other Sons of David began to follow.

I got the side door open and fell into the dust outside. I rose, stumbled a little while, fell to my knees. The cavalry would be here soon, Jefferson assuming I was dead or had failed as soon as Joshua took the stage. I wondered how he was going to deal with the feds and the police, wondered but didn't really care, not any more. I might have failed him, but not Iris.

I hadn't let myself believe in much. This time I could believe Iris was here with me, when I'd failed so many times in IF and on the road. This time, the whirlwind was her fingers in my hair, her head on my shoulder, my hands on that incredible ass. She had found me. If Joshua, Glass, and Isaiah, if every last one of them could believe in fairy tales, then so could I.

I could, but I refused. I wanted to imagine Iris safe, happy, and a thousand fucking miles away from here. I wanted to imagine her finally having the boring, happy life I could never

**337**

have given her. That was where she belonged. As for me, here, if I was going to die, it would happen with my eyes clear and open.

I'd had a funny idea in IF, during one of those endless, sleepless nights. It made such perfect sense it had stuck with me. I'd died on that building in Tehran. I'd been too stubborn to admit it for the last ten years because I'd left something undone. If there was a God up there, whatever the name, I had only one prayer. I'd done enough, maybe too much, but if not it would have to do. Let me go, that was all I was asking for. Let me go.

I watched Joshua and his followers. They were a thin line of white on the desert sand, ants on the way to nemesis. I wanted to yell, to tell them to stop, but I had no more breath. I looked down at my hands. They were full of dust.

# BACKGROUND READING

Boyer, Paul, *When Time Shall Be No More: Prophecy Belief in Modern American Culture*, Belknap Harvard, 1992

Brichto, Sidney, *Moses: Man of God*, Sinclair-Stevenson, 2009

Gourevitch, Philip, and Morris, Errol, *Standard Operating Procedure*, Picador, 2008

Gray, John, *Black Mass*, Penguin, 2008

Hoffer, Eric, *The True Believer*, Harper Perennial, 2009

MacFarquhar, Roderick, and Schoenhals, Michael, *Mao's Last Revolution*, Belknap Harvard, 2008

Mayer, Jane, *The Dark Side*, Doubleday, 2008

Stafford Smith, Clive, *Bad Men*, Phoenix, 2008

Taibbi, Matt, *The Great Derangement*, Spiegel & Grau, 2009

# ACKNOWLEDGEMENTS

First, thanks must go to Rob Dinsdale and Kate Parkin, my agent and editor respectively. They've been taking a metaphorical bullet for the reading public ever since they had to sort through my first draft.

Besides being the reason I am alive, my mother is also responsible for the theological education I have employed in this book. The website biblegateway.com was the source of scripture cited in the novel. The fighting in this book is inspired by the teachings of Sifu Andrew Sofos and Sifu Mark Green.

And, of course, Alice.